RICHIE TANKERSLEY CUSICK

THE UNSEEN

IT BEGINS • REST IN PEACE

speak
An Imprint of Penguin Group (USA) Inc.

THE UNSEEN

THE UNSEEN

PART ONE: IT BEGINS

To Audrey, Suzie, B.J., Lynn, Michele, Victoria, and the whole special gang—for your fun, your faith and your friendship. I love you all.

SPEAK
Published by the Penguin Group
Penguin Group (USA) Inc., 345 Hudson Street, New York, New York 10014, U.S.A.
Penguin Group (Canada), 90 Eglinton Avenue East, Suite 700, Toronto, Ontario, Canada M4P 2Y3
(a division of Pearson Penguin Canada Inc.)
Penguin Books Ltd, 80 Strand, London WC2R 0RL, England
Penguin Ireland, 25 St Stephen's Green, Dublin 2, Ireland (a division of Penguin Books Ltd)
Penguin Group (Australia), 250 Camberwell Road, Camberwell, Victoria 3124, Australia
(a division of Pearson Australia Group Pty Ltd)
Penguin Books India Pvt Ltd, 11 Community Centre, Panchsheel Park, New Delhi - 110 017, India
Penguin Group (NZ), 67 Apollo Drive, Rosedale, Auckland 0632, New Zealand
(a division of Pearson New Zealand Ltd)
Penguin Books (South Africa) (Pty) Ltd, 24 Sturdee Avenue, Rosebank, Johannesburg 2196, South Africa

Registered Offices: Penguin Books Ltd, 80 Strand, London WC2R 0RL, England

First published in the UK by Scholastic Ltd, 2003
First published in the United States of America by Speak, an imprint of Penguin Group (USA) Inc., 2005
This omnibus edition published by Speak, an imprint of Penguin Group (USA) Inc., 2011

1 3 5 7 9 10 8 6 4 2

LIBRARY OF CONGRESS CATALOGING-IN-PUBLICATION DATA
Cusick, Richie Tankersley.
It begins / Richie Tankersley Cusick.
p. cm.—(The unseen ; pt. 1)
First published in the UK by Scholastic Ltd., 2003.
Summary: After a horrifying encounter in a graveyard, Lucy cannot get over feeling
that she is being watched, but is unwilling to trust the one person who might be able to help her.
ISBN 0-14-240463-2 (pbk.)
[1. Supernatural—Fiction. 2. Psychic ability—Fiction. 3. Grief—Fiction.
4. Orphans—Fiction. 5. Family problems—Fiction.] I. Title.
PZ7.C9646Itab 2005 [Fic]—dc22 2005043446

Speak ISBN 978-0-14-242146-8

Set in Perpetua Regular and Nosfer Regular

Printed in the United States of America

Prologue

She had deceived him!

He realized now with a terrible certainty that she'd deceived him from the beginning—planned this whole thing from the very start.

And she knew everything about him—*everything!*—what he was and what he'd done and all he was capable of doing . . .

She'd sought him out and gained his trust, for one purpose and one purpose only.

To see him destroyed.

After he'd been so careful . . . so cunning all these years . . . concealing the very nature of his soul . . . the ageless secrets of his kind . . .

And he'd trusted her. Taken her. Loved her more than he'd ever loved anyone.

Tears clouded his vision.

As though he were seeing the future through a dark red haze, a veil of blood.

He glanced down at his hands.

His strong, gentle fingers, wielding the power of life and death.

He hadn't even realized he was gripping the dagger, the dagger of his ancestors, nor did he remember even drawing it from its sheath.

He was gripping the blade so tightly that a stream of his own blood seeped from his fist. He watched it, strangely mesmerized, as it dripped onto the cold stone floor and pooled around his feet.

He hadn't thought he could feel such pain.

Not from the knife, for he had borne far worse injuries than this in his lifetime, had suffered the ravages of a thousand tortures. But those scars had faded quickly, like shadows swallowed by night, and the few that remained were points of honor to him now, sacred testimonies to his very survival.

No, this pain was different.

This pain burned from deep within, filling him with rage and a craving for revenge.

A craving so intense, he could almost taste it.

1

She should never have come here.

Not into this deep, dark place, not in this miserable weather . . . and *especially* not at night.

"A graveyard," Lucy murmured. "What was I thinking?"

But that was just it—she *hadn't* been thinking, she hadn't had *time* to think, she'd only felt that sudden surge of fear through her veins, and then she'd started running.

Someone was following her.

Not at first, not when she'd first left the house and started walking, but blocks afterward, six or seven maybe, when the storm had suddenly broken and she'd cut through an alley behind a church and tried to find a shortcut home.

No, not home! The words exploded inside her head, angry and defensive. *Aunt Irene's house isn't home, it won't* ever *be home. I don't have a home anymore.*

The rain was cold. Even with her jacket Lucy felt chilled, and she hunched her shoulders against the downpour, pulled her hood close around her face. She hadn't even realized where she was going; there was no sign posted, no gate to mark the boundaries of this cemetery, just an unexpected gap through the trees. She'd heard the footsteps and she'd panicked, she'd bolted instinctively into the first cover of darkness she could find.

But this was a terrible darkness.

Almost as dark as her own pain.

She crouched down between two headstones, straining her ears through the night. It had taken her several minutes to become aware of those footsteps back there on the sidewalk, and at first she'd thought she was imagining them. She'd thought it was only the rain plopping down, big soft drops, faint at first, but then louder and faster, sharper and clearer. Until suddenly they seemed to be echoing. Until suddenly they seemed to have some awful purpose, and she realized they were coming closer.

She'd stopped beneath a streetlamp, and the footsteps had stopped, too. She'd forced herself to look back, back along the pavement, across the shadowy lawns and thick, tangled hedges, but there hadn't been anyone behind her.

No one she could see, anyway.

But *someone* was there.

Someone . . .

She was sure of it.

And that's when she'd run . . .

"I'm afraid you'll find Pine Ridge very different from what you're used to." How many times had Irene told her that, just in the one agonizing week Lucy had been here? "We're right on the lake, of course, and the university's here, so there's plenty to do. And we're only a half-hour drive to the city. But our neighborhood is quiet . . . rather exclusive, actually. Peaceful and private, just the way residents like it. Not at all like that old apartment of yours in the middle of downtown."

But Lucy had loved her old apartment, the tiny, third-floor walk-up that she and her mother had filled with all their favorite things. And the sorrow she'd felt at leaving it only grew worse with each passing day.

She'd been too depressed on their ride from the airport that day to notice much about Pine Ridge; she had only the vaguest recollections of Aunt Irene pointing things out to her as they'd ridden through town. The college campus with its weathered brick buildings and stately oaks. The renovated historical district with its town square and gazebo; its bars, coffee shops and open-air cafés; its bookstores and art galleries and booths selling local crafts. They'd passed farms and fields to get here, and she'd caught occasional glimpses of the lake through dense, shadowy forests. And there'd been frost sheening the hillsides, and she remembered thinking that she'd never seen so many trees, so many vibrant autumn colors . . .

"And it's safe here in Pine Ridge," her aunt had assured her. "Unpleasant things don't happen."

You're wrong, Aunt Irene . . .

Lucy pressed a hand to her temple. That all-too-familiar pain was starting again, throbbing behind her eyes, stabbing through her head, that agony of unshed tears, of inconsolable sorrow . . .

You're wrong, because unpleasant things do *happen*—anywhere—horrible, bad things—*and just when you think they couldn't possibly ever happen to* you—

"Oh, Mom," Lucy whispered. "Why'd you have to die?"

For a split second reality threatened to crush her. Closing her eyes, she bent forward and clamped her knees tight against her chest. She willed herself to take deep, even breaths, but the smell of stagnant earth and rotting leaves sent a deep shiver of nausea through her.

Don't think about that now, you can't think about that now, Mom's gone and you have to get out of here!

Very slowly she lifted her head. Maybe the footsteps had followed her in here—maybe someone was waiting close by, hiding in the shadows, waiting for her to make the slightest move. Or maybe someone was coming closer and closer this very second, searching methodically behind every tombstone, and she'd never hear the footsteps now, not on the soggy ground, not with the sound of the rain, not until it was too late—

Come on, move! Run!

But where? Where could she go? She wasn't even sure where she was, much less which direction to run in.

"*Unpleasant things don't happen . . .*"

Lucy's heart hammered in her chest. She clung desperately to her aunt's words; she ordered herself to *believe* them. Maybe she really *had* imagined those footsteps back there. Maybe it *had* just been the rain and she'd panicked for nothing. After all, she hadn't really been herself since Mom's funeral. As mechanical as a robot and just as hollow inside, moving in slow motion through an endless gray fog of days and nights, confused by the long, empty lapses in her memory. But shock did that to a person, Aunt Irene had informed her, in that cool, detached tone Lucy was beginning to get used to—*shock and grief and the unbearable pain of losing someone you love . . .*

I can do this . . . I have *to do this . . .*

Lucy got to her feet. Steadying herself against one of the headstones, she pushed her long wet hair back from her face, then turned slowly, blue eyes squinting hard into the gloom. High above her the limbs of a giant elm flailed wildly in the wind, sending down a soggy shower of leaves. The sky gushed like a waterfall. As the moon flickered briefly through churning clouds, she saw nothing but graves in every direction.

Just dead people, Lucy.

And dead people can't hurt you.

The storm clouds shifted, swallowing the moonlight once more. Swearing softly, Lucy ducked her head and ran.

She didn't have a clue where she was going. She'd never had any real talent for directions, and now she ran blindly, stumbling across uneven ground, weaving between headstones, falling over half-buried markers on forgotten graves. She wondered if Aunt Irene or Angela would be missing her about now—or if they even realized she was gone.

"Or care," Lucy muttered to herself.

The truth was, she'd hardly seen Angela since their initial—and totally awkward—

introduction. Angela—with her perfectly flowing waves of jet-black hair and tall, willowy model's figure—had been slumped in the doorway of her walk-in closet, smoking a cigarette and surveying her extensive wardrobe with a petulant frown.

"Angela, for heaven's sake!" Irene had promptly shut off the CD player that was blasting rock music through the room. "This is your cousin Lucy!"

Angela's eyes had barely even glanced in Lucy's direction—huge, dark eyes ringed with even darker layers of mascara. "So?"

It hadn't been said in a rude way, exactly—more apathetic if anything—but Lucy had felt hurt all the same.

"And get rid of that disgusting cigarette," Irene had ordered, shoving an ashtray toward her daughter. "You know how I feel about smoke in the house. And would it kill you to be civil just once? On Lucy's first night here? After all, you two are the same age; you probably have a lot in common."

Angela hadn't flinched. "You're kidding, right?"

"Fine, then. Very fine, Angela. From now on, I don't care *how* the two of you handle it—you girls will have to work things out between yourselves."

A careless shrug. "Whatever."

"Honestly, Angela, you never think about anyone but yourself," Irene had persisted.

Angela had reached over then . . . mashed out her cigarette in the ashtray her mom was still holding. She'd raised her arms above her head, stood on tiptoes, and stretched like a long, lean cat.

And then she'd walked very slowly, very deliberately, out of the room . . .

"Of course they won't care," Lucy muttered again.

She hadn't told either of them she was leaving earlier—she doubted if they'd have understood her desperate need to escape the house where she still felt so lonely and unwelcome. All Lucy had thought about was getting away, and so the darkness of empty streets had felt comforting to her then. But now she felt stupid for being so scared, for getting so lost. She should have gone back the way she'd come; she shouldn't have listened to her overactive imagination.

"Damnit!"

Without warning she stubbed her toe and pitched forward, landing facedown in the mud. For a second she lay there, too surprised to move, then slowly, carefully, she reached forward to push herself up.

Her hands met only air.

Gasping, she lifted her head and stared in horror. Even in this downpour, she could see the deep, rectangular hole yawning below her, and she realized it was an open grave. She was sprawled on the very edge of it, and as she clawed frantically for something to hold on to, she felt the ground melting away beneath her fingers.

With one last effort, she twisted sideways, just as a huge chunk of earth dissolved and slid to the bottom of the chasm.

And that's when she heard the cry.

Soft at first . . . like the low moan of wind through branches . . . or the whimper of a frightened animal . . . faint and muffled . . . drowned by the rush of the rain.

An abandoned cat, maybe? A stray dog? Some poor outcast just as lost as she was, wandering alone out here in the dark? Lucy's heart broke at the thought of it.

"Here, baby!" Stumbling to her feet, she cupped her hands around her mouth and tried to shout over the tremor in her voice. "Come to me! Don't be afraid!"

A rumble of thunder snaked its way through the cemetery.

As Lucy paused to listen, she felt a sudden chill up her spine.

Yes . . . there was the sound again.

Coming from the empty grave.

2

As if trapped in a nightmare, Lucy forced herself to peer down into the gaping hole. She was sure she hadn't imagined the sound this time, certain now that it wasn't an animal.

The voice was all too frighteningly human.

"*Please!*" it was begging her. "*Please . . .*"

Pressing both hands to her mouth, Lucy tried not to scream. For she could see now that the grave wasn't empty at all, that there was something lying at the very bottom, camouflaged by layers of mudslide and rising rainwater.

As a sliver of lightning split the clouds, she saw the girl's head strain upward, lips gasping for air. And then the girl's arm, lifting slowly . . . reaching out to her . . .

"*Please . . . is someone there . . .*"

Lucy stood paralyzed. She watched in horror as the girl's head fell back again into the mire, as water closed over the anguished face.

"Oh my God!"

She didn't remember jumping in. From some hazy part of her brain came vague sensations of sliding, of falling, of being buried alive, as the earth crumbled in around her and the ground sucked her down. She lunged for the body beneath the water. She tried to brace herself, but her feet kept slipping in the mud. Dropping to her knees, she managed to raise the girl's head and cradle it in her arms.

"Help!" she screamed. "*Somebody help us!*"

Was the girl dead? Lucy couldn't tell, but the body was limp and heavy and motionless now, the eyes and lips closed. She could hardly see anything in this darkness—only brief flashes of the livid face as lightning flickered over the girl's delicate features. Ghostly white cheeks. Dark swollen bruises. A scarf wound tight around her neck—

"Somebody! *Somebody help us!*"

Yet even as she shouted, Lucy knew no one would hear her. Not through this wind and rain, not in this place of the dead. With numb fingers, she worked feverishly at the scarf, but the wet material was knotted and wouldn't budge. In desperation, she smoothed the girl's matted hair and leaned closer to comfort her.

"Hang on, okay? I'm going to get you out of here, but I have to leave—just for a little while—and get help. I'll be back as quick as I—"

Something clamped onto her wrist.

As Lucy's words choked off, she could see the thin, pale hand clinging to her own . . . the muddy fingers lacing slowly between her own fingertips . . .

They began to squeeze.

"Oh, God," Lucy whimpered, "stop . . ."

Pain shot through the palm of her hand.

Pain like she'd never felt before.

Waves like fire, burning, scalding through every nerve and muscle, throbbing the length of her fingers, pulsing upward through her hand, her wrist, along her arm, piercing her heart and her head. Pain so intense she couldn't even scream. Her body began to shake uncontrollably. Her strength drained in a dizzying rush. Through a blur of strange blue light she saw the girl's head turn toward her . . . saw the scarf slip easily from the fragile neck. She saw the jagged gash across the girl's throat . . . the raw, stringy flesh . . . the glimmer of bone . . .

Lucy pitched forward. The girl's body was soft beneath her, cushioning her fall, and from some great distance she heard her own voice crying out at last, though she understood somchow that this was only in her mind.

"Who did this to you? What's happening?"

Listen, the girl whispered. Had her lips moved? Had she spoken aloud? Lucy didn't think so, yet she could *hear* this girl, could hear her just as clearly as two best friends sharing secrets.

Dazed and weak, she managed to lift herself onto one elbow. The girl was staring at her now, wide eyes boring into hers with an intensity both chilling and compelling. Lucy was helpless to look away.

Tell no one, the girl said, and her lips did *not* move, and Lucy could only gaze into those huge dark eyes and listen to the silence. *Do you understand? Promise me you understand . . .*

Lucy felt herself nod. Tears ran down her cheeks and streamed with the rain over the girl's cold skin. The hand holding hers slid away; the dark eyes shifted from her face, to something far beyond her, something Lucy couldn't see.

If you want to live, the girl murmured, *you mustn't tell anyone . . . not anyone . . . what you've seen here tonight.*

"Don't die," Lucy begged. "Please don't die—"

Promise me.

"Yes . . . yes . . . I promise."

The girl's eyelids slowly closed.

But for one split second, Lucy could have sworn that she smiled.

3

She didn't remember climbing out of the grave.

She didn't remember running or even finding her way out of the cemetery—but suddenly there were lights in the distance and muffled voices and the wild pounding of her own heartbeat in her ears.

Lucy stopped, gasping for breath.

She realized she was standing on a low rise, with a sidewalk about thirty yards below her. She could see streetlights glowing fuzzy through the rain, and beyond that, the watery reflections of headlights from passing cars.

Oh God, what should I do?

She couldn't stop shaking. She couldn't get warm, couldn't think. Her knees felt like rubber, and it was all she could do to force herself the rest of the way down the hill.

Maybe it didn't really happen. Maybe I fell into a hole back there and knocked myself out and started hallucinating.

She wanted to believe that. Wanted to believe that with every fiber of her being, because to accept what she'd just seen in the cemetery was too horrifying to deal with. Nothing seemed real anymore, not the rain beating down on her or even the nice solid feel of the pavement as she finally reached the curb and peered to the opposite side of the street. There was a gas station on the corner, lights on but pumps deserted, and the voices she'd heard were actually coming from loudspeakers playing country music.

Again Lucy stopped. She glanced behind her into the darkness, into the hidden secrets of the graveyard, and her mind whirled in an agony of indecision.

I promised. I promised her.

And yes, it *had* been real, and there was a girl, a girl maybe her own age lying dead, and no matter how sacred a promise, Lucy knew she couldn't just leave her there all alone in the rain . . .

"*If you want to live . . . you won't tell anyone.*"

The girl's words echoed back to her, chilling her to the bone. Maybe it wasn't really a warning, she argued to herself, maybe it didn't mean anything at all. She knew people often said strange things when they were dying, when they were out of their heads from pain and confusion and that final slipping-away from the world. *Like Mom was at the end. Like Mom was—*

"No," Lucy whispered to herself. "Not now."

She took a deep breath and shut her eyes, but she couldn't shut out the image of those *other* eyes, those pleading, desperate eyes gazing up at her from the girl's bloodless face. Without even realizing it, she flexed her hand inside her jacket pocket. There was a vague sensation of pain, but she was too preoccupied to give it attention. As she stared over at the gas station, she suddenly noticed a drive-by telephone at one end of the parking area, and she knew what she had to do.

Keeping her head down, Lucy hurried across the street. Someone was working under the hood of a car inside the garage, but the lot was still deserted and the phone was far enough away that she didn't think she'd be noticed. She grabbed up the receiver and punched in 911, telling herself she wasn't *really* breaking her promise. It was only a compromise.

"911. What is your emergency?"

Lucy froze.

"*You won't tell anyone . . .*"

"911. What is your emergency, please?"

"*Promise me . . .*"

"Hello? Please state your emergency."

"Yes," Lucy whispered. "Yes . . . I—"

Without warning a horn blared behind her. Lucy slammed down the receiver and whirled around as a red Corvette screeched to a stop about three feet away. Then one of the windows slid down.

"You picked a hell of a night to run away," Angela greeted her blandly.

Lucy shook her head. Despite the fact that it was Angela, she felt an immense sense of relief. "I'm not running away."

"Oh."

She was sure her cousin sounded disappointed. The thought actually occurred to her to just turn and leave, but then she saw Angela nod toward the passenger door.

"So get in, already. Don't you know enough to come in out of the rain?"

With a last glance at the phone, Lucy hurried around the car and climbed into the front seat. *What am I going to do now?* Anxiously she wiped one sleeve over her wet face, then held out both hands to the heater.

"Look at this mess." Angela rolled her eyes. "You're dripping all over everything."

"Sorry." Scooting back, Lucy angled herself into the corner. She clamped her arms tightly around her chest, but the shivering wouldn't stop. "Do you have a towel or something?"

"No, I haven't got a towel. God, look at my floor."

"I got lost," was all Lucy could think of to say.

Angela grumbled something under her breath. She plucked a lighted cigarette from the ashtray, took a long drag, then blew a thin stream of smoke out through her nose.

"Irene's freaking out," she said at last.

"I'm sorry. I just wanted to take a walk, but then I got all turned around in the storm. I didn't mean to worry anybody—"

"Oh, she's not *worried* about you," Angela

seemed mildly amused. "She's freaking out 'cause you've made her late for a meeting."

Lucy bit hard on her bottom lip. She could feel a lump burning in her throat, anger and tears mixed bitterly together, but she was determined not to cry.

"Well," she managed to whisper. "Of course she would be."

"You should've known better."

"What?"

Angela rolled her eyes. "If you think wandering off like this is gonna get you *any* attention or sympathy from Irene, then forget it. You don't know her."

But I want to, Lucy thought miserably, *and I want her to know me, too . . .*

Right after she'd moved here, Lucy had made a habit of studying her aunt's face whenever Irene wasn't watching, longing for just a glimpse of the mother she'd lost. As if somehow her mother's spirit would be reflected in Irene's eyes or in her clothes or in the way she did things—living proof to Lucy that her mom was still with her.

But there'd been no similarities—no similarities whatsoever between the two women—and as the days passed, Lucy only felt more and more abandoned. No matter that Aunt Irene was her only living relative; Irene and Mom were as different as night and day.

Mom had been so . . . well . . . so *alive*. Fun and free-spirited, spontaneous and creative, with the wildest imagination and the most contagious laugh and the most stubborn determination when her mind was made up about something. Lucy had always admired her mother's disregard for rules and routines; there'd always been new things to try and new adventures to share on the spur of the moment. And she'd always loved hearing how much alike the two of them looked—the same blue-gray eyes and long, thick lashes, the same silky blond hair.

Mom had been a source of pride to her. A role model, an ideal she'd always aspired to. She'd never known her father, but Mom had been the best of *both* parents, not to mention her very best friend. Her whole world, really.

But now there was Aunt Irene.

Just Irene, who didn't seem anything like the sister she'd completely shut out of her life. Irene, who barely spoke to Lucy—barely even *looked* at her if she could help it. Who always acted tense and watchful and guarded, as though she expected something bad or dangerous to sneak up on her at any second. Irene and her high-profile job at the university . . . Irene and her endless very important meetings.

"She's self-absorbed," Mom had always told Lucy in those rare moments she ever mentioned Irene's name. "She's always been self-absorbed; she's never thought about anyone but herself. The only thing that makes her happy is getting her own way."

Lucy had never understood the estrangement between her mother and her aunt; Mom had always refused to talk about it. All she knew was that the women hadn't spoken for years, but when Mom was dying, trapped in the last throes of cancer, she'd requested—finally—that Irene be told.

And Irene had come.

To Lucy's shock, Irene had come and stayed—she'd doled out medications, stocked the refrigerator with takeout food, obsessively cleaned and tidied, and remained aloof while Lucy kept constant vigil in Mom's bedroom. And then something had happened one night. Something behind the closed door of Mom's room, something between Mom and Irene alone, something never discussed with Lucy. All Lucy knew was that Mom had suddenly seemed calm and strangely resolved, and the next morning, while Lucy sat beside her holding both her hands, Mom had slipped peacefully away.

Lucy didn't remember much after that.

Over the next few days the funeral had been arranged; over the next few weeks the apartment had been cleared out and rerented, her things had been systematically discarded, packed, or put into storage—all by Aunt Irene, she supposed, for she'd been too numb with grief even to function. And then Irene had brought her here.

"We're your family now, Lucy," Irene had announced in her cool, businesslike way. "This is your home."

And *some home*, Lucy had thought in awe,

laying eyes on the house for the very first time. Compared to the size and comfortable shabbiness of her old apartment, this new place seemed like a mansion, with its white brick walls and tall front columns, its circular driveway, its swimming pool in back. Yet surrounded as it was by thick woods, and only a short walk to the lake, Lucy would have sworn they were in the middle of a vast, lonely wilderness if Irene hadn't assured her that town was only a few blocks away.

Lucy had decided immediately that her life—and her happiness—were over . . .

"Looking for you is *not* how I planned to spend my evening."

With a jolt, Lucy came back to herself. She had no idea how long she'd been buried in her thoughts or how long Angela had been talking. She glanced at her cousin, but those dark-ringed eyes were focused on the rhythmic movement of the windshield wipers.

"I talked her out of calling the police, you know," Angela added.

"The police?" Lucy's tone was grim. "I

thought nothing unpleasant ever happened in Pine Ridge."

"Who told you that?"

"Your mother," Lucy mumbled, wishing they could just leave. She didn't want to sit here any more, here where she could see the cemetery right across the street. She didn't want to sit here knowing what she knew, and she didn't want to remember anything that had happened tonight because she was cold and hungry and exhausted, and if her 911 call *had* been traced, then she *especially* didn't want to be here when the police showed up.

But Angela took another long puff and glanced at Lucy with a tight smile. "How funny."

"What?"

"Nothing unpleasant ever happening here. And Irene—of *all* people—saying so."

Lucy frowned. "What do you—" she began, but Angela cut her off, gesturing vaguely toward the parking lot.

"So what were you doing just now? Trying to call somebody?"

Lucy stole a quick look at the phone box outside the car. How long did someone have to stay on the line for a call to be traced? How long did it take the police to find someone in Pine Ridge?

"Yes." Her mind was racing; the smoke was making her feel claustrophobic. "I was trying to call your house, but . . . but I couldn't remember the number."

"Well, I don't know where you were walking," Angela said matter-of-factly, "but you look like a zombie."

Lucy cringed. She thought of the girl in the grave. A sick taste of guilt welled up inside her, and she swallowed hard, forcing it down. "Can we please go?"

"Oh, great. You're not gonna get sick in my car, are you?"

"I hope not."

To Lucy's relief, Angela instantly buzzed down the driver's window and flicked her half-smoked cigarette out into the rain. Then she rolled the window up again, sat back, and turned up the heater full blast.

"Thanks," Lucy said. "I appreciate it."

"I didn't do it for you. I did it for my car."

Of course you did. What was I thinking? Lucy

tensed, listening. Was that a siren she'd just heard in the distance? Or only a muted sound from the radio? *Please . . . please . . . let's just leave . . .*

"Look, let's get this straight. If you came here expecting money, Irene's not gonna change her will. You're not gonna get one bit of the inheritance." Angela's voice was stony. "Just so you know."

Lucy faced her in surprise. "I didn't come here for your money. I didn't come here for anything, Angela. I didn't even *want* to come here—it wasn't *my* idea. Your mother *made* me come here." She hesitated, then said, "Just so *you* know."

"She's not my mother," Angela muttered.

"What?"

"I said, she's not my mother. She's my stepmother." Reaching over, Angela readjusted the heater again, then leaned back with an exasperated sigh. "My father married her when I was ten. And then he died two years later, and I was *stuck* with her. We've *never* gotten along, Irene and me—we've *always* hated each other. And I'm *leaving* here just as soon as—"

Abruptly Angela broke off. She reached for a

fresh cigarette, and Lucy could see how she trembled with anger.

"As soon as I turn eighteen," Angela finished defiantly. She held a lighter to the tip of her cigarette, the tiny spark glowing orange in the dark. "As soon as I'm eighteen, I'm taking off for New Orleans," she murmured again. "That's when I inherit my money, and I can do what I want. Till then I'm a goddamn hostage."

Lucy gave a distracted nod. *No . . . no . . . it's not a siren. It's going away now, in another direction . . .*

Taking a deep breath, she tried to focus once more on the girl beside her.

"I didn't know anything about you," Lucy admitted, unsure what else to say. "Not about you *or* Irene. My mom barely mentioned Irene the whole time I was growing up. I'm really sorry."

Angela's eyes widened, almost mockingly. "Sorry? Don't be sorry for me. Don't *ever* be sorry for me—I can take care of myself just fine."

"Angela, I didn't mean—"

"Just forget it. Who the hell do you think you are?"

I don't know anymore, Lucy thought miserably. *I used to know, but everything's different now . . .* I'm *different now . . .*

She was beginning to feel sick again. She wanted to leave, wanted Angela to stop talking and start driving. She could feel the girl's eyes upon her, and she could still see the eyes of that dead girl, and there was too *much* death, death in her past, and death tonight, she was drowning in it, drowning in all this death, and *if we don't leave right this minute I'm going to totally lose it and start screaming—*

"God, what'd you touch?" Angela asked suddenly.

"Touch?" A chill crawled up Lucy's spine, though she managed to keep her voice steady. "What do you mean?"

And Angela was leaning closer now, staring harder, her eyes like big black hollows in the shadows of the car.

"There," Angela told her. "There on your hand."

Startled, Lucy looked down.

She stared at the narrow black welts on the back of her right hand and between her fingers, at the misshapen black stain on the skin of her palm. In one more quicksilver flash, she saw the girl in the open grave, remembered the girl's hand closing around her own . . .

"I . . . I don't know," she heard herself whisper. "When I fell, maybe. That's what happened . . . I tripped . . . and I must have bruised myself when I fell."

For an endless moment there was silence.

"That's no bruise," Angela said at last.

She pulled the Corvette back onto the street and peeled away, but Lucy scarcely noticed.

Because the thing on her hand really *didn't* look like a bruise.

It looked like a burn.

Like something had burned itself right into her skin.

4

He'd come back one last time.

Just to make sure she was dead.

Some killers didn't like to come back, he realized, for fear of being seen, being connected in some way, being caught—these dangers, of course, were of no concern to him.

But after he'd done what he had to do, he couldn't get her out of his mind. He'd stood at his window watching the rain, replaying her voice over and over again in his head—her pleas for mercy, her screams of pain. And suddenly he'd begun to grow restless. Restless in a way he couldn't understand, a strange uneasiness in his veins that made him pace in the dark and jump at small sounds and warily watch the shadows.

And so he'd come back.

One last time.

She was just as he'd left her, naturally, and this soothed him a little. He'd stood over the crumbling grave and he'd stared down at her, and he'd stood for such a long, long time, waiting to see if she'd speak, if she'd move, if her eyes would open, if she'd look at him in the old familiar way he'd so loved being looked at.

But she didn't move.

And she didn't say his name.

The water and the mud were over her face, from the walls of the grave caving in, and if he hadn't put her there himself, he'd never have known she was there at all, he'd have thought she was just a pathetic mound of soggy earth at the bottom of the yawning hole.

He really was so amazingly clever.

The old graveyard. A violent storm. No one in Pine Ridge would even consider venturing into this place tonight.

So he'd thrown his arms wide to the rain, and his hair had blown wild in the wind, and he'd sucked in the darkness, until it filled him and sated him and consumed him and—

And then that restlessness again.

That vague, creeping uneasiness, gnawing in the pit of his soul.

He'd actually felt a moment of doubt.

And so he'd lowered himself into her grave.

He'd knelt down beside her and wiped the mud from her face, and he'd studied her in death, all the while wondering about her final moments of life.

She would have lingered awhile. Been aware of the warm blood pumping from her throat, leaking out between the torn chunks of her flesh, spurting with every heartbeat, then growing weaker . . . weaker . . . until it became merely a thin trickle, melting into the soggy earth.

The thought made him smile.

She was no threat to him now.

She was dead, and he was free.

And so he'd leaned over, oh so gently, and he'd put his mouth upon hers . . . cold lips together . . .

And then he'd kissed her.

One last time.

5

God, it was freezing in here.

It must be me, Lucy thought, as she slid lower in the claw-footed tub, closing her eyes, trying to relax beneath the bubbles. The bathroom was large and luxurious just like the rest of the house, but even with central heating, and even with the water as hot as she could stand it, she couldn't seem to get warm.

What am I going to do?

She could smell takeout pizza wafting up from the kitchen, and her stomach gave a queasy lurch. She could hear the muffled sound of the TV downstairs, and Angela's rock music blaring from the next room. And though Aunt Irene was now en route to yet another very important meeting, Lucy could still picture that formidable frown waiting for them when she and Angela had gotten home. Lucy had been relieved when Irene ordered her straight upstairs and into a hot bath. She hadn't felt like explaining any more details about her evening.

So what am I going to do?

She felt drained and bone-tired. Like her whole body had gone comatose and her brain had fizzled out. The cemetery . . . the girl . . . the warning . . . everything seemed like a distant dream now, or something she'd seen in a horror movie. An out-of-body experience that had happened to someone else's body . . .

"Hey!" Angela banged on the door. "Don't use up all the hot water!"

It was almost too much effort to answer. Groaning, Lucy roused herself and called back, "I'm not."

"And don't go to sleep and die in my bathtub."

"I wouldn't dream of it."

"Dinner's ready."

"I'm not hungry."

"Don't you like pizza?"

"Not three nights in a row."

Gently she massaged her forehead. She could imagine Angela leaning against the other side of the door, filing her fingernails and admiring the shape of her hands. No wonder her cousin looked practically anorexic, she thought—there hadn't been a single healthy or home-cooked meal in this kitchen since Lucy had been here.

The music abruptly shut off.

"If you die in there, you'll bloat and be all wrinkled," Angela informed her.

Lucy sighed. She listened to Angela's footsteps fading down the stairs, then she closed her eyes and drifted lower into the water.

I have to do something.

I have to tell somebody.

She couldn't call from here, that was certain. She didn't have a cell phone, and it would be too risky trying to call the police from a phone inside the house—too easy to be traced.

But besides that, something else was bothering her.

And even though she'd forced herself not to think about the obvious truth of the matter, she couldn't avoid it any longer. It had been lurking there in the farthest reaches of her mind, a mocking shadow keeping just beyond consciousness, ever since she'd made her gruesome discovery.

But now she had to face it.

Someone killed that poor girl.

Someone had *murdered* that girl, and not mercifully.

The death wound hadn't been clean or swift; someone had hacked at her throat, leaving her alone and helpless and frightened, leaving her to bleed to death in the rain.

Which meant the murderer was still out there.

And if I tell, he might find out.

And if he finds out it was me, then he'll kill me, *too.*

Trembling, Lucy readjusted the loose coils of hair she'd pinned on top of her head. She wrung out her washcloth, molded it to her face, and eased farther down into the water, resting her head against the back of the tub.

Could he have seen me? Could he have followed me?

Again she thought back, trying to convince herself she was safe: it had been so dark, storming so hard, she'd had the hood of her jacket pulled down around her face. And if the murderer really *had* been close by, wouldn't he have stopped her *then*? Done whatever he had to do to keep her from leaving?

No, something told Lucy that she and the girl had been the only ones out there in the cemetery. At least for those brief, terrifying moments.

Still . . .

A gust of wind rattled the bathroom window. Lucy jerked the washcloth from her face and sat up straight, her heart pounding.

At least you were with her at the end . . . at least she wasn't alone . . .

As the overhead light flickered, Lucy grabbed for her towel on the rack. Holding her breath, she waited. Within several minutes the lights slowly regained brightness, so she dried off quickly, pulled on her nightgown, and hurried through the connecting door into her bedroom.

Not my bedroom, she reminded herself grimly. *My prison.*

For the first two days after she'd come here, she'd simply stayed in bed, sleeping and crying, then sleeping again, missing her mother so much that her soul felt raw. The containers of takeout food that Irene regularly left on her dresser went virtually untouched. She hated the stark white walls and carpeting. She hated the sleek white furniture that looked like something straight out of a decorating magazine. She'd been so depressed, she hadn't even bothered to put out any of her favorite personal things. What she'd brought with her was still packed in boxes and suitcases, stored upstairs in the attic, all of them painful reminders of her happy life that had died.

"I'm sure you'll love your room, Lucy," Irene had assured her on the plane ride here. But Lucy had hated it at first sight, hated everything about it, including the sheer-curtained sliding doors that opened side by side out onto a little wrought-iron balcony, making her feel both exposed and accessible. She even hated the giant mulberry tree that grew beside it, the one that scraped and clawed at the railing and eaves and made it sound as though someone were trying to break in and kill her every single night.

God, Mom, what were you thinking, sending me here?

Sighing, Lucy shut off the overhead light and left just the lamp burning on the nightstand by her bed. She could hear Angela slamming cupboard doors in the kitchen and then tromping back up the staircase.

Lucy gritted her teeth and counted to five.

Angela's CD player blasted through the upstairs, vibrating the floors, rattling the windowpanes. Ten ear-shattering seconds of rage and defiance—Lucy knew it was ten, for she'd clocked it many times—before the volume cut off and silence reigned again, everywhere but in Angela's headphones.

It's a miracle she hasn't gone deaf by now, Lucy thought glumly. Rubbing her ears, she walked over and stood in front of the sliding doors.

Her room was at the back of the house, separated from Angela's by their adjoining bathroom, and at the opposite end of the hallway from Aunt Irene. From here she could look down onto the manicured lawn; the brick patio and terraced wooden deck; the glassed-in hot tub; the swimming pool, covered now for the winter; the landscaped flower beds and mulched pathways and discreetly camouflaged woodpile, all coated with a thin layer of frost. At the rear of the lawn stood a low stone wall with a gate, and beyond that, a narrow pathway led through dense woods to a private stretch of lake. Despite the heavy rain, a pale gray fog had begun to ooze through the trees. Lucy watched it, strangely fascinated, as it wound its way toward the house, smooth and silent as a snake. There was no moonlight. Only an occasional burst of lightning managed to rip the storm clouds and illuminate the landscape below.

Shivering, Lucy started to turn away.

And then she saw something.

What is *that?*

Frowning, she leaned closer, squinting hard through the glass.

Had she imagined it? That very slight movement just beyond the wall? As though one shadow had separated itself from all the others . . . as though it were hovering there, like a wisp of pale smoke, just on the other side of the gate . . .

Come on, Lucy, get a grip.

Of *course* there were shadows out there—*millions* of shadows out there—and of *course* things were moving. *Fog and wind and rain and*—

"Some animal," Lucy whispered. *A deer,*

probably. She'd spotted an occasional deer in the yard since she'd been here. Irene hated them, said they caused major damage to her expensive shrubs; she'd forbidden Angela to leave out food of any kind.

"Just a deer," Lucy told herself again, more firmly this time.

And yet . . .

Frowning, she pressed closer to the doors, lamplight soft behind her. "*Peaceful and private*" —isn't that what Irene had said about this neighborhood? Yet Lucy could feel a vague sense of unease prickling up her spine. As though something far more ominous than a deer was out there in the woods . . . watching her.

Don't be ridiculous . . . it's because of what happened tonight . . . you're only imagining things.

She thought of the girl. Of her own promise. She wondered again what she should do. She didn't want to stand here looking out anymore, but she couldn't seem to turn away from the dark.

Her breath quickened. She could feel her heart fluttering in her chest. Only moments ago she'd been freezing, but now a peculiar warmth was spreading through her, hot liquid in her veins. Her favorite nightgown, much too thin for these unforeseen autumn nights, now seemed unusually constricting. She opened the first three buttons down the front and leaned forward, resting her forehead against the glass.

Something moved on the corner of her balcony.

Gasping, Lucy's head came up, and she peered anxiously out into the night. *Just the tree . . . that stupid tree hitting the railing . . . nothing more!* But even as she tried to reason with herself, she was already tugging at the doors, sliding them open to the wind.

Rain swept savagely into the room. With a cry, Lucy grabbed both doors and after a brief struggle, managed to lock them in place. Then she backed away and sat on the edge of her bed, soaking wet.

What on earth were you thinking?

She was cold again—cold to the bone—and besides that, she felt unbelievably stupid.

"And paranoid," she reminded herself glumly. "Don't forget paranoid."

As her mind flashed back to the cemetery, she tried to block it out. No wonder she was seeing watchers in the woods now, and lurkers on the balcony, and danger in every shadow. And thank God Angela was buried in her headphones right now, completely oblivious to the rest of the world—Lucy wasn't up for any more confrontations or excuses.

Leaving her gown in the bathroom to dry, Lucy toweled off and changed into a warm pair of sweats. Then she shut off the lamp and tried to cocoon herself deep inside her blankets.

She lay there, wide-eyed, too exhausted to sleep.

She lay there feeling numb, and each time a vision of the dead girl floated into her mind, she tried to think of other things. *Home before. Mom before. My perfect and wonderful life before.* She'd had friends . . . she'd been popular . . . she'd had fun, and she'd had ambitions. What were her friends doing now, she wondered sadly. She'd withdrawn from them more and more during Mom's illness, and since she'd come here to live, she'd scarcely thought about them at all—hadn't written, hadn't even called. She'd promised a few of them to keep in touch, to send them her address—why hadn't she?

Because I hate it here so much. Because I'm so miserable, and I don't want them to know how horrible my life is now . . .

Her thoughts swirled and faded. The storm continued to rage outside her windows, and after a very long time she finally drifted off.

She wasn't sure what woke her.

It was a feeling rather than a sound.

A slow, cold chilling at the back of her neck . . . a vague sense that she wasn't quite alone.

Lucy struggled to open her eyes. She was lying on her side facing the sliding glass doors, and as lightning flashed beyond the rain-streaked panes, the room went in and out of shadow.

"Lucy," a voice said softly.

Raising herself on one elbow, Lucy stared. She could see the curtains blowing in, billowing like lacy feathers, though she knew it was *impossible*, that she'd already shut those doors, already bolted them tight against the wind—

"Lucy . . ."

Her eyes widened in alarm. A sob caught in her throat.

"Mom?"

She tried to struggle up in bed, strained her eyes to see. And yes, the curtains *were* moving, fanning out like delicate wings, only there was something *else* there, too—a hazy figure silhouetted against the glass—she could *see* it now, though it was flimsy and formless, as sheer as those fine gauzy curtains . . .

"*Mom!*" Tears streamed down Lucy's cheeks. "Mom, is that you?"

"Listen to me, sweetheart."

And it *was* her mother's voice, but so sad, so *sad. Why does she sound like that, so terribly sad and hopeless* . . .

"Mom—"

"Be careful, Lucy," the voice whispered, and it was already fading, scarcely more than a breath. "You're going to a place where I can't help you . . ."

"What do you mean, Mom? No, *wait*! Don't leave! *Please* don't leave me!"

Lucy flung out her arms, reaching . . . reaching . . .

But the mournful shadow was gone now . . .

And the curtains hung pale and soft and deathly still.

6

A knock.

Two loud knocks, and then another, firm and persistent, hammering their way into her warm, cozy dream.

"Go away," Lucy mumbled.

She was decorating the Christmas tree in their apartment. Mom was baking gingerbread men for all her fourth-grade students, and they were both singing carols at the top of their lungs, and Mrs. Manetti from downstairs was bringing up homemade soup later for all of them to share . . .

"Wake up, Lucy. You'll be late."

"Go away," Lucy said again, only this time the dream faded down a dark tunnel, and her eyes opened to hazy light and someone standing in the open doorway to the hall.

"We've already discussed this," Irene said firmly. "I said I'd give you one week to settle in. Today you're going to school."

"Today?" She was wide awake now, the announcement finally sinking in, along with a feeling of panic. "But it's Friday—why can't I wait till next week?"

"Because one day will be difficult enough to get through. And you'll have the entire weekend to recover before you start fresh on Monday."

"But it's too soon! I'm not ready!"

"You can ride with Angela, so hurry up."

Irene didn't wait for a response, and this time Lucy didn't give one. She lay there with her face buried in the pillow, too stunned to move. Her eyes felt swollen, as though she'd been crying . . . her whole body felt achy and stiff. She wondered if maybe she was catching the flu, yet there was a vague sense of uneasiness nagging far back in her mind.

No, not the flu. Something else . . .

Something dark and suffocating . . . something gnawing at the distant edges of her mind . . . something bad that she couldn't quite place . . .

Something horrible. But what?

Groaning softly, she turned onto her side. Her right hand was aching, as though she might have wrenched it in her sleep, so she propped herself on one elbow and leaned over to examine her palm.

Memory slammed her full force.

As every horror of last night came back to her in shocking, grisly detail, Lucy let out a cry and felt the room spin around her. How could she have forgotten—even for a moment! *The girl—the grave—my promise—*

She'd hoped so much to be wrong. That somehow she'd only imagined it in her mind, that it had only been a nightmare, that she'd wake up this morning and realize the whole thing had never happened!

But it *had* happened.

And now, as Lucy stared down at her hand, she could see the evidence all too clearly, the truth etched deeply into her skin.

It was a strange marking.

Not at all as it had looked last night, for the ugly welts and discolorations had practically faded away. Now there was only the smallest reminder—the pale, puckered flesh of a tiny scar—stamped into the exact center of her right palm. It looked like a sliver of something. Like a sliver of moon. *That's it . . . a crescent moon.* So perfectly formed, it seemed neither random nor accidental. As if some miniature branding iron had been used to sear a pattern into her flesh.

No. No, that's crazy.

Grabbing the blanket, Lucy rubbed it vigorously against her palm. These were crazy thoughts she was having, thoughts that didn't make sense, because this scar on her hand was just that—a *scar*—a *wound*—nothing more. She'd tried to help, and in their struggle the poor girl had scratched her, and eventually this little scar would fade, too . . .

But how did it heal so fast?

Lucy let go of the blanket. Despite the fact that she'd been rubbing so hard, her scar wasn't even red. She stared at it in disbelief, remembering how gruesome her hand had looked last night, remembering the excruciating pain she'd felt when the girl had grabbed her in the cemetery.

What's happening to me? Am I having some kind of nervous breakdown?

"Lucy!"

Angela's voice shocked her back to attention. The door from the bathroom flew open, and Lucy saw her cousin scowling at her from the threshold.

"What am I, your private chauffeur?" Angela's miniskirt barely covered her crotch. Her designer sweater looked as if she'd spray-painted it over her chest. She looked like an expensive hooker. "You're not even up yet, and I am *so* not waiting for you."

"Yes," Lucy nodded, throwing off the covers. "Yes, I'm hurrying."

The door slammed shut. As Lucy sat up in bed, she tried to ignore the sick feeling in the pit of her stomach. When had she eaten last—sometime yesterday? So much had happened since then . . . so much confusion in her head. She couldn't think straight. She couldn't think at all.

She closed her eyes, then opened them. Her gaze traveled slowly around the room. She could see the windows . . . the sliding doors . . . the slow dawn of an autumn morning struggling to break through.

Mom . . . I saw Mom . . .

Lucy's heart caught in her chest. *Yes . . . Mom was here . . . she said something to me . . .*

Her mind tried frantically to remember. She could almost hear the tone of her mother's voice . . . could almost see her mother's face . . . but the words she'd spoken were completely gone.

Frustrated, Lucy got up. She padded barefoot to the sliding doors and squinted down at the carpet, as if she expected to see a footprint or a distinctive clue, some confirmation of her mother's visit. She ran a tentative hand down the length of the curtains, and her eyes misted with tears.

Of course she wasn't really here. It was just a dream. She wasn't here, and she wasn't a ghost either, because ghosts don't exist . . .

Lucy opened the curtains and peered out. A watery sun was spreading across the backyard, and she could see Angela recklessly scooping seeds into all the bird feeders. The rain had stopped, but beneath a cold November sky lay the widespread destruction from last night's storm—piles of wet leaves, splintered tree branches, strewn garbage, uprooted plants, even a few wood shingles and a broken shutter—and as Lucy's gaze shifted to the stone wall in back, she saw that the gate was standing open.

Her heart clenched in her chest. She forced herself to take a deep breath.

It doesn't mean anything. It was just the storm.

"Just the storm," Lucy repeated to herself. Of *course* nobody would have been out there watching her window in the middle of a storm—she'd just been feeling overly paranoid last night. As fierce as the wind had been, it was a miracle the gate was even still there at all.

She let the curtains fall back into place.

"*Lucy!*" Irene shouted.

"Coming!" Lucy shouted back.

She hurried to the bathroom, but couldn't resist checking the clothes hamper first. There were her clothes, right where she'd tossed them last night, totally covered in mud. *What did you expect—isn't that scar proof enough for you? Are you still hoping last night didn't happen?* She picked up her toothbrush, squeezed toothpaste across the bristles. *Think, Lucy, think!* Why was it so hard to focus this morning? Why couldn't she brush her teeth without trembling? *Maybe I can sneak out of school and find another pay phone . . . maybe I can pretend I have an emergency and borrow someone's cell phone—cell phones can't be traced, can they?*

Lucy frowned at herself in the bathroom mirror.

I'll have to go back to the cemetery on my own. I'll have to go back there and find her. It's the only thing I can do.

Yet she knew in her heart it was pointless. She was certain the girl was dead—*had* been dead now, for nearly twelve hours. Not only that, but she'd been lost last night, panicky and disoriented—she didn't have a *clue* where the cemetery was. *And even if you* do *manage to find the cemetery, even if you* do *manage to find the grave—what then?*

What if the killer had come back, what if the killer were *there*? What if he really *did* recognize her from last night—she'd be as good as dead.

Sighing, Lucy leaned closer to her reflection. She had dark bruises under her eyes, and her normally tan complexion was pale. She'd never worn much makeup—Mom had always insisted that Lucy had a natural sort of beauty—but today she added a touch of blush and lipstick. Just for color, she told herself. *Just for confidence, you mean.*

"Angela's right," she sighed. "I *do* look like a zombie."

She didn't even know what outfit to put on—what did kids in Pine Ridge wear, anyway? She wasn't prepared for the chilly autumn weather here, and she'd never needed warm clothes at home—no matter what she picked out this morning, she was sure to look stupid. She made a face at the mirror and tied her hair back in a ponytail. Then she went to her room, took jeans and a pale blue sweater from her dresser drawer, and pulled on thick socks and sneakers.

"Lucy! Angela is waiting!"

"I'm coming!"

God, this was going to be an awful day. As if everything else weren't bad enough already, just thinking of going into a new school, and being introduced and having everyone stare at her, made her feel sicker than ever.

She could hear the TV as she came downstairs. Pausing on the bottom step, Lucy listened nervously to a brief review of the local news. Nothing about a murder. No body discovered anywhere. Not knowing whether to feel relieved or not, she started into the kitchen when the sound of voices stopped her just outside the door.

"You can't do this to me!" Angela cried angrily. "It's not fair!"

Then Aunt Irene, cold and utterly calm. "I told you if you got one more speeding ticket, you'd be grounded. You had plenty of warning."

"But the Festival's this weekend!"

"Keep your voice down. You're acting so high-strung—are you coming down with something?"

"Yes. Dreams. I'm coming down with dreams, Irene. Weird, sexy ones, all night long. Send me to the hospital."

"Angela, will you please be mature this morning? Must we go through this—"

"Every single day?" Angela finished. "I *have* to go to the Festival. *Everyone's* going! I *have* to be there!"

"You should have thought of that before. And you should have known better than to think I wouldn't find out about this latest ticket."

"Oh, right, I forgot. Your personal friends on the police force. Or was it the judge this time?"

"This discussion is over. You can use your car to drive to and from school, but nowhere else. There will be no social events of any kind until I say so."

"It's not even about me, is it?" Despite Angela's sarcasm, Lucy could hear the threat of tears. "It's just about you looking bad in front of your important friends—"

"That's quite enough, Angela."

"If it was Lucy, you wouldn't ground *her*."

"If it was *Lucy*, I wouldn't be *having* these problems."

"Right." Angela's tone was suddenly as cold as her mother's. "Right, I forgot. 'Cause Lucy's so goddamn perfect."

Lucy pressed a hand to her mouth. She heard the kitchen door fly open.

"Angela, come back here," Irene ordered. "You have to take Lucy to school."

"*You* take her," Angela threw back. "It was *your* idea to bring her here—*you* take her!"

The door slammed shut with a bang. As tears sprang to her eyes, Lucy flattened herself against the wall and fought down her own wave of anger. *Thanks a lot, Irene. Do you think you can get Angela to hate me just a little bit more?*

"Lucy!" Irene fairly shrieked.

Quickly Lucy went back to the stairs, then came noisily down the hall again, as though she'd just arrived.

"Yes, here I am. Sorry."

"Get in the car. We're already late."

"I thought you said Angela—"

"I forgot she had some errands to run before school. I'll be taking you. Where's your jacket?"

"I . . . it got so wet last night, I—"

"Here. Take this jacket of Angela's. She'll never miss it."

"But—"

"Just put it on, Lucy. I can promise you she will *never* wear it, simply because *I* gave it to her. And Angela would rather *die* than be seen in *anything* I pick out for her. I'm sure it will fit you nicely."

"If you say so."

Irene was silent for the whole drive. It wasn't until they pulled up in front of the high school that she finally graced Lucy with a comment.

"I know classes have already started this morning, but as you know, I've spoken with Principal Howser several times. He's assured me that everything's been taken care of, so all you need to do is go straight to his office. He'll be expecting you."

"Thanks. I'll be fine."

"I'm sure you will be. Have a nice day, Lucy."

As her aunt drove off, Lucy stood there on the pavement and made a quick assessment of the school: two-story buildings of ivy-covered brick; stone benches placed strategically around the wide, sweeping campus; a covered courtyard with tables and chairs; an outdoor stage; rows of bleachers and an athletic field in the distance. Lots of trees, lots of windows, lots of cars in the parking spaces, *lots of students to face* . . .

Taking a deep breath, Lucy took one hesitant step toward the gate. Then she stopped.

You don't have to do this now. You can wait and go Monday. You can tell Irene you got sick and had to go home, and it's not really a lie, and it's not like one more day will make that much difference . . .

Lucy turned slowly, her eyes scanning the sidewalk and street beyond. A quiet, residential area; nothing but houses as far as she could see. But she'd noticed a post office and a grocery store on their drive here—someone was sure to know where the cemetery was.

She glanced over her shoulder at Pine Ridge High.

Then she ducked her head and hurried away from the school.

7

It didn't take long to find what she wanted.

But then, standing beneath the weathered sign of PINE RIDGE CEMETERY, she realized it didn't look anything like she remembered.

There hadn't been gates where she'd come in before; there hadn't been a fence or a sign. *Maybe this isn't the right cemetery, maybe Pine Ridge has more than one.* But the old man she'd asked outside the post office hadn't even hesitated—he'd pointed her straight in this direction. The old part and the new part, he'd explained to her, with the empty old church still standing guard at one end. *You were disoriented last night, you were terrified, of course nothing's going to look the same today.*

Lucy glanced up and down the narrow, deserted street. Directly across from her was an empty lot; a block away, the street suddenly ended, giving way to an overgrown field and a rickety, boarded-up house set far back beneath some trees. There was no traffic here. Not a single pedestrian in sight.

Well, what are you waiting for? Just go in and get it over with.

Lucy began walking. She hadn't expected the place to be so big—much bigger than it looked from the sidewalk—with row upon row of perfectly aligned headstones and carefully placed markers. The grass was spongy, littered with remnants of last night's storm. Plastic flowers lay everywhere, along with shredded plants and broken vases, toppled wreaths and even some soggy toys.

As Lucy walked farther, she began to notice a distinct difference in her surroundings. How the ground seemed to be actually sinking, rainwater standing in shallow pools . . . how the trees seemed to be pressing closer, weaving their branches more tightly overhead. And *yes*, she thought suddenly, fear and hope beating together, fluttering in her chest—*yes, this all seems familiar* . . .

Back here, so far from the cemetery's entrance, these graves had been forgotten. Patches of dead weeds pushed against tombstones; piles of dead leaves obliterated names. It was colder here, and piercingly damp. Locks hung rusted from mausoleum doors, heavily shrouded in spiderwebs. Stone angels and sleeping children, once meant to be comforting, now gazed back at Lucy with hollow eyes and moldy faces, their tender smiles rotted away. As though weary of their burden, many headstones had slipped quietly beneath the ivy; others were crumbled to dust.

Lucy stopped beside an unmarked grave and lowered her face into her hands.

What am I doing here, Mom? Can you even believe this?

Suddenly she was furious with herself. She must have been insane to come here, wandering around alone in this isolated place instead of being in school! *Did you really think you'd find her—some dead girl in an open grave?* There were *hundreds* of burial plots in here—*thousands*, probably!—how long could she possibly keep searching? Not to mention how enraged Irene would be when she found out Lucy had skipped school.

"Bad idea," Lucy whispered to herself. "*Very bad idea.*"

Forget good intentions—she'd leave this place now and find a pay phone. Promise or no promise, she'd make an anonymous call to the police, and then she'd get back to the house. She'd go straight to bed, and when Irene came home, she'd swear she really *had* been sick all day, but next Monday she'd be—*miraculously!*—recovered and more than ready to begin her new life.

Resolved, Lucy raised her head. She hunched her shoulders against the cold, dank breeze and turned back the way she'd come.

She was scarcely aware of his shadow.

There were so many of them, really, surrounding her in deep, dark pools . . . soft and black like liquid, oozing between the graves, seeping beneath the low-sweeping branches of the trees . . .

And later she would wonder how he got there—appearing without a word or a sound—just suddenly *there*, his tall shadow figure blocking her path, one arm extended in front of her to prevent her escape.

She saw him gazing down at her—eyes without light, face without features—or was it her own fear distorting his image, blurring everything into an indistinct mask? She wanted to run, but she was frozen in place; she heard his voice, but it seemed like some strange, faraway echo.

"She's not here," he said. "The one you're looking for."

Lucy could barely choke out a whisper. "What? What are you talking about?"

And the angels were watching—all around her, Lucy could see their blank, empty stares . . . their dead, decaying eyes . . .

The stranger was above her now.

Leaning over . . . reaching out . . . a sharp black silhouette against pale, pale light.

"She's not here," the stranger said again. "He's taken her away."

8

Someone had ahold of her shoulders.

As Lucy fell back a step, she realized that strong hands were trying to steady her, to keep her facing forward. She willed herself to scream, but all that came out was a frightened whimper.

"Take it easy," a voice said. "Just breathe."

Breathe? Struck by a fresh wave of panic, Lucy began to struggle. The hands holding her immediately tightened their grip, and before she realized what was happening, she felt herself being pulled tight against her captor's chest.

"Stop it! I'm not going to hurt you."

Lucy stopped. With her arms pinned securely to her sides, she looked up to see a pair of dark eyes gazing back at her with calm, cool intensity. In a split-second appraisal, she guessed him to be a little over six feet tall, with a strong, lean build, probably about her own age, possibly a year or two older. High cheekbones accentuated the angles of his face; a faint shadow of beard ran along his chin and jawline and upper lip. His hair was thick and as black as his eyes, falling in loose, tousled waves to his shoulders. And he held himself very straight—though not so much a formal posture, she sensed, as a wary and watchful one.

Lucy realized she was staring. As fear and confusion coursed through her, her mind scrambled for some self-defense tactic, but the rest of her still felt too stunned to cooperate.

"I'm not going to hurt you," he said again. "I just want to talk."

He released her so unexpectedly that she nearly fell over. Recovering herself as best she could, Lucy watched as he took three steps back, then he raised his hands into the air where she could see them.

"You ran away," he stated. His eyes narrowed slightly, yet the piercing stare never wavered, even when Lucy began to back up.

"What do you mean?" she demanded. "I don't know what you're talking about. Who are you?"

Her heart was racing like a trip-hammer, her thoughts spinning in all directions. *He knows about the girl—how could he know? The only way he could possibly know anything is if he was* here*—if he was the one who—*

"You tried to help her, but it was too late. And if you tell anyone—anyone at all—you could die." His tone was so even, so matter of fact—which somehow made it all the more frightening.

Lucy's voice rose. "You don't know *anything*! You don't know—"

"And they wouldn't believe you anyway—"

"*Who are you?*"

"I'm Byron. I want to help you."

"I don't know you! And I don't need your help! Why are you doing this? Why are you saying these things?"

"Because they're true."

Slowly he lowered his arms. He slid his hands into the pockets of his jacket, and he turned his eyes to the ground, and when he spoke, Lucy could hear the cold contempt in his voice.

"It's not your fault, you know. You couldn't have saved her. Nobody could."

Tears blurred Lucy's vision. Wheeling around, she was finally able to run.

This is insane! This can't be happening!

She realized she was crying, crying so hard she couldn't see, and her chest was hurting, and her lungs were aching from the cold. She slid on wet leaves and sank ankle-deep in mud. Every breath she took was a knife blade between her ribs.

God, why had she ever come here this morning? How could she be so stupid, what could she possibly have been thinking?

And now, on top of everything else, here was some psycho lurking in the graveyard, acting like he *knew* her, acting like he knew about what had *happened* here last night—*some psycho who* must *be the murderer, who else could he be?—he saw me and he knows who I am and now it's a game—cat and mouse—he's taunting me and now he's going to kill me, too—*

"You're in danger," the voice warned.

Lucy screamed. She hadn't heard him following, hadn't seen him coming, but now her back was flat against a tree, and he was *standing* there, just inches away, gazing at her with those dark, dark eyes.

"People know I'm here!" she babbled. "They'll be looking for me—they'll be worried if—"

"I told you, you don't have to be afraid of me. I'm a friend."

"Leave me alone! I don't have any friends!"

"But you need one. Someone you love is gone now . . . you need one."

Lucy gaped at him. A wave of nausea rose up from her stomach, lodged in the middle of her throat. *I'm going to be sick . . . Oh God, I'm—*

"Sorry about your mother," he whispered.

As Lucy drew an incredulous breath, all feelings of nausea vanished. She simply stood there with her mouth open, staring at him in utter disbelief.

"Someone told you." At last her words choked out, tight with fury. "Someone *had* to tell you! My aunt or—or—my cousin—or someone at school—"

"No one had to tell me. I see it in your eyes."

She was vaguely aware of a rushing in her

head—a churning mixture of shock and rage and despair—and the tears that wouldn't stop, still pouring down her cheeks. For a moment she couldn't think, didn't even realize that she'd moved toward him, or that her hands had clenched into fists or that she'd shoved them hard against his chest.

"You really expect me to *believe* that?" she cried.

She saw him shake his head. Saw his hands close firmly over her fists, though he made no move to push her away.

"Some things take time to believe in," he said solemnly. "And right now . . . we don't have a lot of time."

As Lucy stared at him in bewilderment, he eased her hands from the front of his jacket. Then, still holding her wrists, he leaned down toward her, his voice low and urgent.

"Something happened here last night. Something important."

Yes, she thought desperately, *a murder. A cold-blooded murder and—*

"I think something touched you."

"You don't know anything," Lucy whispered.

But *"What'd you touch?"* *Angela had asked . . . and the dying girl's hand, squeezing so hard . . . the pain, the horrible pain, the excruciating pain . . . and "That's no bruise," Angela had said . . . That's no bruise . . .*

"I think something was . . . passed on to you," Byron murmured.

Lucy's eyes widened. As she tried to pull free, Byron's grip tightened, forcing her closer. With one smooth movement, he turned both her hands palms-up and gazed down at the tiny, crescent-shaped scar.

"Let go!"

Jerking from his grasp, Lucy stumbled back out of reach. She could feel her right hand beginning to tingle—ice-hot needle pricks spreading out from the center, out to her fingertips—and she clamped it shut and thrust it deep into her pocket. She told herself it was just the cold, told herself Byron had just held her too tight, shut off her circulation, but her hand was stinging . . . feeling so strange . . . and it was starting to tremble, just like her knees were trembling, just like her voice was trembling . . .

"Stay away from me!" she burst out. "I don't know why you're here, and I don't have a *clue* what you're talking about, and I'm *not* afraid of you!"

For a long moment Byron stared at her. "It's not me you need to be afraid of," he said at last.

It took every ounce of courage to turn her back on him. Holding her head high, Lucy made her way determinedly back through the graves, and she told herself that she wouldn't look back.

But when she did, he was still standing there, and she couldn't help thinking how very much he resembled some dark angel, some ominous messenger in the midst of all that death . . .

"Be careful," he called to her then, his voice as heavy as the shadows around him. "Someone won't be glad you're here."

9

The whole morning had been a disaster.

A complete, miserable, and utter disaster.

Lucy stood in the doorway of the cafeteria, clutching her books to her chest. She let her eyes wander over the laughing, chattering mass of students, then turned and walked slowly down the hall. She hadn't planned on coming to school this morning after her visit to the graveyard; she'd wanted to find a way back to the house and hide there and try to make sense of things—until she suddenly remembered she didn't even have a key.

She hadn't tried to find a pay phone. "*You tried to help her . . . it was too late . . .*" She hadn't reported last night's murder. "*You can't tell anyone . . . you could die . . . they wouldn't believe you anyway . . .*" She'd been so frightened, so thoroughly shaken by her encounter with Byron, that she didn't even realize she'd retraced her steps back to school. She'd simply looked up and found herself standing outside Pine Ridge High, wondering how she'd gotten there.

Oh, God. What's happening to my life?

She'd stared at the school, and she'd weighed her options—*Could I spend the day hiding out in some coffee shop? The library? How about the bus depot?*—but she hadn't been able to come to a single decision.

He knew *things! Byron* knew *things about last night, he knew things about* me *he couldn't possibly know!*

She'd rested her head against the fence while the world passed in a blur. He was a total stranger, but he'd known about her mother. He was a total stranger, yet it was almost as if he'd been *waiting* for her there, as if he'd *expected* her to show up there this morning . . .

Maybe he really *was* the murderer, Lucy thought again. And maybe he really *had* been taunting her, playing with her, trying to see how much she really knew. *So why didn't he kill me? Why didn't he kill me right then, when he had the perfect chance?*

She hadn't been able to shut out his words: "*She's not here . . . the one you're looking for . . . he took her away . . .*"

His words . . . those frightening, fateful words playing over and over and over again, relentlessly through her brain—

"*We don't have a lot of time . . .*"

"*Be careful . . .*"

"*Someone won't be glad you're here.*"

She'd stood outside Pine Ridge High, afraid to go in, afraid to go anywhere, until a teacher hurrying into the building had spotted her and ushered her to Principal Howser's office. To Lucy's relief, the man had actually believed her story about being sick that morning. He'd welcomed her warmly and offered deep condolences for her loss; he'd praised her high grades from her former school, and he'd talked about how wonderful Aunt Irene was. He'd gone on and on about some Festival the school was having, and how he hoped she'd enjoy living in Pine Ridge. Then he'd handed her a schedule, assigned her a locker, given her a tour, and escorted her to class.

"Here we are, Lucy. I believe your cousin Angela has Miss Calloway this hour, too."

Wonderful. My morning's complete.

He'd interrupted a pop history quiz to introduce her, leaving her to stand like an idiot at the front of the room while Miss Calloway tried not to look annoyed and all the kids had stared. She'd felt flushed and panicky and embarrassed. Some of the kids were laughing, she'd noticed—some of the girls whispering to each other, some of the guys whistling loudly. And then she'd spotted Angela, sitting in the very back row, snickering loudest of all.

It wasn't till she'd run to the bathroom afterward that Lucy realized she had dead leaves stuck in her hair and mud spattered over her clothes. She'd stared at her sorry reflection in the mirror and felt so mortified, she'd actually considered hiding in there the rest of the day.

Wonderful, Lucy, just wonderful. Leave it to you to make a great first impression.

But at least the humiliation had distracted her.

At least it had kept her from dwelling on the cemetery . . . the murdered girl . . . *Byron* . . .

Thank God lunch was over now; she had only a few more hours to get through.

By the time Lucy found her next class, her head was pounding. Dull ribbons of pain crept down one side of her face and unfurled behind her eyes. She was achy and stiff, her shoes and socks were damp, and she still hadn't had anything to eat. Her mind was worn out from worrying; her brain had turned to mush. She didn't have a clue how she was going to make it through math. Like a robot, she slid into her assigned desk and saw Angela sitting right beside her. The dark raccoon eyes fixed on her accusingly.

"I've been thinking about that jacket of yours," Angela frowned, leaning toward her.

Lucy braced herself. "What about it?"

"It looks really familiar to me. In fact, I have one exactly like it."

"I know." Lucy kept her gaze lowered. "Irene said I could borrow it."

"And you didn't even *ask* me?"

"You were already gone. And she said you never wear it anyway, because she gave it to you."

"I can't *believe* this!" Angela pulled back as several kids squeezed between them, book bags swinging dangerously. "*Look* at it! It's totally *ruined*!"

Someone bumped Lucy's desk and murmured an apology. She glanced up to see the back of his faded jacket as he leaned over the desk in front of hers. Then Angela snapped her back to attention.

"Did you hear what I said?"

"I heard you," Lucy sighed. "I'll pay to have it cleaned, okay?"

"You'll pay to buy me another one, is what you mean. God, who do you think you are?"

To Lucy's relief, Mrs. Lowenthal called the class to order and instructed them to take out their books. Then, while the woman droned on and on about numbers that made no sense, Lucy tried to ignore the venomous looks Angela kept shooting at her from across the aisle. *Don't let her get to you . . . right now Angela's the least of your worries . . .*

"—announcements regarding the Fall Festival," Mrs. Lowenthal was saying. Fall Festival? When had they finished with math? When had they stopped working problems on the chalkboard? Lucy didn't know . . . hadn't been paying attention.

Something soft hit her foot. Glancing down, she saw what looked like a necklace lying there on the floor, but she had no idea where it had come from. Her eyes did a quick sweep of the class, but everyone was focused on the front of the room. Lucy scooted the necklace closer with the toe of her shoe, then picked it up to examine it.

It was a simple piece of jewelry—nothing expensive, elaborate, or even professional, she thought. Just a single strand of tiny beads, dark green glass, that looked rather childishly handmade. *Pretty, though, in a plain sort of way . . .*

"—want all of you there early if you're working a booth," Mrs. Lowenthal continued.

Lucy put her left hand to her forehead. Was it just her, or was the room getting hotter by the second?

"—big fund-raiser of the year, as you all know," Mrs. Lowenthal said.

It *was* getting hotter in here, Lucy was sure of it. She could feel drops of sweat along her hairline; she shifted uncomfortably in her chair.

"—those volunteers will meet this afternoon in the library—"

Maybe I'm coming down with something—getting a fever—God, I'm burning up—

"—be sure to check the schedule to see which shifts you're working—"

Lucy slid lower in her desk. Her head was way past throbbing now—it felt like it was going to burst. She wound the necklace around her wrist, twined it between her fingers; she could feel the tiny beads cutting into the tender flesh of her palm—

"—can use my car to transport some of the food—"

For a brief second the room shimmered around her. A tingling pain shot through her hand, and Lucy tried to brace herself against the desktop, tried to prop herself up, but her wrists were so limp, so useless . . .

What's happening?

She couldn't hold her head up anymore. She couldn't hear . . . couldn't see—yet at the same time she could see *everything*, *hear* everything, everything all at once, every single sense wide open—

What's . . . happening?

The classroom vanished. The warmth building steadily inside her now burst into scalding heat, searing through nerves and muscles, throbbing the length of her fingers and upward through her hand, along her arm, exploding inside her head.

I've felt this before—oh God—just like last night—

And then they came.

Lightning fast and just as merciless—images so vivid, so sharp, her body reeled with the force of them—

Hands—such powerful hands—eyes glowing through shadows—lips on her neck, her throat, and blood flowing, life flowing, "Could have been different . . . could have been perfect . . ."

Wind! Ah, the cold, sweet rush of it, taste of it, caress of it—night smells night sounds damp and cold! And fog so thick . . . woods so black . . . black and deep as—

"Death," Lucy murmured. "I'm not afraid to die . . ."

And "Lucy?" . . . someone saying her name, over and over again, "Lucy . . . Lucy . . ."

"Lucy?" Mrs. Lowenthal's voice, anxious and loud. "Lucy, are you all right?"

Lucy's eyes flew open.

She was slumped on her desk, both arms pillowing her head. She was clutching something in her right hand, and her whole arm felt numb and prickly, as if she'd been shot full of novocaine.

"Lucy?" Mrs. Lowenthal said again.

Very slowly Lucy lifted her head. She could see that the classroom was there again, along with the faces of the students, all of them staring, and Angela smirking beside her, and Mrs. Lowenthal leaning over her with a worried frown.

"You're so pale, Lucy, are you ill? Do you need to be excused?"

Lucy tried to answer, but couldn't. Instead she opened her fingers and stared down at the necklace in her hand.

"I'll have someone take you to the nurse," Mrs. Lowenthal decided. "Angela can help you. Here, Angela, let me write you a pass."

But Lucy wasn't paying attention anymore to Mrs. Lowenthal or Angela or the curious stares of her classmates.

As the guy in front of her turned around, she saw that he'd taken off his jacket. She saw the thick black hair falling soft to his shoulders, and the calm gaze of his midnight eyes. And then she saw him reach back and slide the necklace from her hand.

"Thanks," Byron said quietly. "I must have dropped this."

10

She knew she was going to be sick.

As Byron faced forward again, Lucy got to her feet and rushed up the aisle to the door. Then, ignoring an alarmed Mrs. Lowenthal, she hurried down the hall in search of a bathroom.

She finally found one near the stairs, barely making it inside before dry heaves took over. She left the stall door open and fell to her knees, sweat pouring down her face, her insides like jelly. She dreaded Mrs. Lowenthal coming to check on her—or even worse, sending Angela.

"This might help," a voice said softly.

Lucy was too weak to lift her head. She felt a cold, wet paper towel on the back of her neck . . . a gentle hand smoothing her hair back from each side of her face.

She heaved again, but there was nothing in her stomach but pain.

"Thank you," she managed to whisper.

"No need," the voice whispered back to her. "The first time's always the worst."

Lucy lifted her head.

Turning around, she stared out at the bare floor, at the row of sinks and the dingy mirror stretching over them, reflecting nothing.

"Hello?" she called shakily. "Who's there?"

Her voice echoed back to her from the bathroom walls. With trembling fingers, she took the paper towel from the back of her neck and got slowly to her feet. One by one, she moved down the row of stalls and opened each door, but they were all empty.

"*The first time's always the worst . . .*"

Without warning a group of girls came giggling in from the hallway. Was one of them the kind-hearted stranger? But none of the girls even glanced her way, so Lucy ran fresh water onto the paper towel and blotted it over her face. Mrs. Lowenthal was right—she *was* pale—*frighteningly* pale. *Think, Lucy, think! Try and calm down . . . try to put things in perspective . . .*

Perspective? How could she possibly be calm or rational about all the things that had happened to her in the last twenty-four hours? She was way past confusion now—way beyond frightened. Something had taken hold of her back there in the classroom—something had *consumed* her back there in the classroom—something she didn't understand and certainly hadn't been able to control. Something had crept over her and through her, transporting her to another place and time—she'd *seen* things, *felt* things—*horrible* things, intense and painful and terrifyingly real, and yet . . .

And yet there'd been no *complete* picture, Lucy realized. Nothing like a carefully posed photograph or neatly framed painting or smooth sequence of movie scenes running logically through her mind.

No, this had been different.

Just flashes of things, glimpses of things, puzzle pieces spilled helter-skelter from a box. Things without order, things that made no sense, though she felt they *should make sense*, and *did* make sense somehow, if only she could put them together . . .

Frowning, she stared down at her hand. The strange crescent scar stood out sharply against her palm, and there was a faint, lingering ache along her fingertips.

The necklace.

Lucy shut her eyes . . . opened them again . . . drew a slow intake of breath.

There was darkness . . . and death . . . and it started when I picked up that necklace . . .

The bathroom door swung shut. As Lucy turned in surprise, she realized that all the girls had left, and that Angela was now standing beside her.

"I've been looking all over for you." Angela gave an exasperated sigh. "What the hell happened back there?"

Lucy couldn't answer. She watched dully as her cousin leaned toward the mirror and primped at her hair.

"Well?" Angela demanded.

"I . . . felt like I was going to pass out," Lucy murmured.

"I've never seen anyone shake like that before they passed out," Angela said, casting Lucy a critical glance. "God, you look even worse now than you did last night. Whatever you've got, you better not be contagious."

"Who's the guy in class?" Lucy asked tersely.

"*What* are you talking about?"

"The dark-haired guy sitting in front of me."

"Byron?"

Lucy nodded, tight-lipped.

"Well, what about him?" Tilting her head, Angela gave her hair one more fluff. "Oh, please. Don't tell me you're *interested*."

Lucy merely shrugged.

"Right. Another smitten female falls under the spell of the mysterious Byron Wetherly," Angela announced. Then her lips curled in a dry smile. "Well, yeah, he's gorgeous. *And* sexy. *And* so very, *very* cool. But . . . you know . . . every girl in school is after him."

She paused a moment, as if considering a matter of great importance. Then she lifted one eyebrow, amused.

"Frankly, Lucy, I wouldn't bet on your chances."

Ignoring the remark, Lucy pulled a fresh paper towel from the dispenser. "What do you mean, mysterious? Why is he mysterious?"

"Well, who knows *anything* about him, really? He keeps pretty much to himself."

"Maybe he's shy."

"He doesn't talk much. But with a face and body like that . . . why would he need to?"

"I see." Lucy played along. "The quiet, secretive type. *That's* what makes him mysterious."

"Not just that. His family, too."

"So his *family's* mysterious."

"They're poor." Tilting her head sideways, Angela studied her profile in the glass. "And extremely weird. I mean, the word is that Byron must be adopted or something—he's the only normal one in the whole bunch. He lives with his grandmother—well, takes *care* of his grandmother; she's an invalid. His mother's been locked up for years."

Lucy looked startled. "Locked up?"

"As in *loony bin*? As in *institution*?" Angela pointed to the side of her head and made wide circles with her finger. "As in *psychopathic maniac*?"

"Yes, Angela, I get it. What's wrong with her?"

"She murdered her kids."

"Come on . . . you're not serious."

"Burned down the house with them in it. Oh, for God's sake, it happened years ago. I'm not sure anyone around here even remembers the woman *personally*—it's just something everyone knows about." Angela paused, thought for a second, then once again faced the mirror. "You know. Like a campfire story. Or one of those urban legends."

"But what about Byron?" Lucy asked.

"Well, *obviously* he got out, didn't he? Him and his crazy sister. Are you finished in here?"

Lucy nodded. She ran some water over the towel, squeezed it out, then pressed it against her cheeks, stalling for a little more time.

"So . . . is the mom in prison?" she asked.

Angela rolled her eyes. "No, just in a straightjacket for the rest of her life. Poor Byron. I mean, can you even imagine? Everyone knowing your mother's a cold-blooded killer? And, like *that's* not bad enough, that sister of his was turning out just as bad—it was only a matter of time before *she* got carted off to the funny farm. Lucky for everybody, she ended up leaving town before anything really horrible happened."

"I guess that *was* lucky," Lucy agreed quietly. "So tell me about the sister."

"She *saw* things." Another dramatic sigh. "Well . . . at least that's what she wanted people to believe. She *saw* things."

"You mean . . . like hallucinations?"

"Call them whatever you want—*she* called them *visions*."

Lucy's heart caught in her chest. She was feeling colder by the second. "What kinds of visions?"

"How would *I* know? *I* never saw her have one." Angela sounded impatient. "Telling-the-future-and-talking-to-the-dead kinds of visions, I guess. I mean, the girl was *way* creepy."

"So she never had a vision in school?" Lucy's voice was scarcely a whisper.

"She didn't go to school. She didn't go anywhere, really. I mean, nobody ever saw her."

"Then if nobody ever saw her . . . how do you know she even existed?"

Angela gave a sniff of disdain. "Well . . . nobody *normal* ever saw her. Nobody *I* know ever saw her. But there were stories, you know?" Leaning closer to her reflection, she rubbed at a tiny smudge of lipstick on her tooth. "Sometimes people would drive past the Wetherly place at night, and they'd see her watching from an upstairs window with bars on it. And sometimes, people just going down that road at night would hear screams coming from inside the house. That's why they never let her out. She was totally dangerous."

Despite her uneasiness, Lucy frowned. "Sounds like old wives' tales to me."

"Whatever. But she ran away last year, so that was a big relief to everybody. *Especially* to Byron, I imagine. I mean, God, how humiliating—so *not* cool for his social life. Now there's only him and his grandmother." She paused, her brow creasing in thought. "Good thing he's so gorgeous—he certainly doesn't have good breeding going for him."

"Then how can you really know him?" Lucy asked tightly. "How can you be so sure he's *not* like his mother? *Or* his sister?" *How can you be sure he doesn't stalk unsuspecting victims, or murder girls in cemeteries, or see into a person's mind . . .*

"Well . . ." Angela's look was blank. "That's just silly."

"*Why* is it silly? You said he keeps to himself . . . that no one really knows him—"

"God, what is this whole *obsessing* thing?"

"What about his life away from school? What about his private thoughts? What about his feelings?"

Angela made no effort to hide her amusement. "His feelings? Oh, I'd like to feel him, all right—in places *besides* my fantasies. Just like every other female around here."

She stepped back from the mirror. She ran a slow gaze over Lucy, then shook her head in mock disappointment.

"Poor Lucy . . . take my advice, okay? Forget about Byron. As a matter of fact, forget about *anybody*. You look like you've been run over by a bus. And you just had some kind of weird fit—not to mention nearly throwing up—in the middle of class. I mean, it's so *embarrassing*. Everyone already thinks you're a freak, and it's only your first day."

It took all Lucy's effort to compose herself. She wadded up her paper towel, tossed it into the trash, and carefully smoothed the front of her sweater. "You know what? I'm actually feeling much better. In fact, I don't think I even need to see the nurse now."

"Then why'd I waste my time trying to find you?"

Biting back a reply, Lucy followed Angela back to class. Byron didn't even glance at her as she slid into her seat, didn't seem to feel her eyes boring into him as she tried to ignore the stares and whispers around her. He was out of his chair as soon as the bell rang, and though Lucy hurried to catch up with him, he'd already disappeared into the crowded hallway by the time she reached the door.

She didn't see him again the rest of the afternoon, neither in class nor on campus. As though he'd vanished from her life just as quickly as he'd appeared.

By the time the final bell rang, Lucy was never so glad to have a day end—it took every last effort just to drag herself to her locker. Everywhere she turned, there was talk about the big weekend ahead, exciting plans for the Fall Festival, but all *she* planned on doing was locking herself in her room and staying in bed. She was just rechecking her homework assignments when Angela showed up, greeting her with a sullen frown.

"Hurry up," Angela complained. "I have better things to do than stand around and wait for you all day."

"You just got here. You've been waiting for—what? Two whole seconds?"

"Do you want a ride or not?"

Lucy slammed her locker door. Lowering her head, she did a quick assessment of her books, oblivious to the kids shoving past her till she felt a quick, light pressure on her arm.

"What?" Startled, she looked up. Angela was standing several feet away, watching her with growing impatience.

"What?" Angela echoed.

"Did you just touch me?" Yet even as she asked, Lucy knew it hadn't been Angela. Somehow, in that precise moment, she *knew* it was the girl who'd come to her aid in the bathroom. *That's impossible . . . how could I know that?*

"What are you talking about?" Angela frowned.

Immediately Lucy stood on tiptoes, anxiously

scanning the corridor. It was packed with students eager to start the weekend, but none of them seemed to be paying any attention to her.

This is just crazy.

"Someone touched my arm," Lucy insisted. Puzzled, she turned to Angela, who was now making an exaggerated show of checking her watch.

"You *think*?" Angela threw back at her. "I mean, there're only about a *million* people around here bumping into each other."

"No, but . . ."

"But what?"

"This was different. It wasn't an accident. She . . ."

"She, who? She, *what*?"

She wanted me to know. The realization came to Lucy with warm, calm clarity. *She did it on purpose because she wanted me to know she was here, that she was* real, *that I* didn't *imagine her—*

"You're not gonna have another fit, are you?" Angela was regarding her warily. "Because if you are, I'm leaving."

"No," Lucy murmured, taking one last

puzzled look around. "No . . . I'm ready."

"Then let's go."

For once, Lucy didn't mind Angela's music blaring—in fact, she hardly even noticed it at all. While her cousin sang loudly off-key all the way home, Lucy leaned her head against the window and tried to sort out all the troubling events of the day. *Explanations? None. Logic? None. Worry factor? Definitely rising. And Byron . . .*

She could still see those dark, dark eyes searching hers . . . hear the edge in that low, deep voice . . . feel those strong hands on her shoulders. It was his ominous warning that had finally convinced her *not* to report the dead girl . . . at least not yet. She'd been frightened of him, still *was* frightened of him—only now that fear was tempered with an almost fascinated curiosity. He had answers—she was sure of it—but answers to things she *wasn't* sure she wanted to pursue. As the car pulled into the driveway, Lucy wished she could ask her cousin more about Byron—but she didn't dare. Her life was complicated enough already without having Angela any more involved.

The house was empty when they went in. As

Lucy shut herself in her room, she thought she heard Angela scrolling through the messages on the answering machine . . . thought there might be one from Irene, though she couldn't make it out. She stood for a moment with her back against the door, eyes closed, weary relief flooding through her body.

And then her eyes opened with a start.

What's that smell?

A very faint fragrance . . . and pleasantly sweet . . . yet nothing she recognized, nothing she could recall ever having smelled before . . .

Frowning, Lucy dropped her stuff on the desk and walked to the sliding glass doors. She opened them all the way, letting in crisp fall air, then she stepped out onto the balcony and stared off across the lengthening shadows over the lawn.

The woods still looked menacing, even in the last few hours of daylight. A slight breeze was blowing, and as Lucy gazed into the trees' shifting patterns of darkness and fading autumn colors, a shiver crept slowly up her spine.

That feeling again . . .

That feeling of being watched . . .

"Bad habit," Lucy muttered. "Get over it, for crying out loud."

Irritated with herself, she turned back into the room.

She took a few steps, then stopped abruptly by the bed.

That's strange . . .

Despite the fresh air blowing in, she could still smell that aroma . . . delicate . . . sweet . . . and . . . *something else* . . .

Lucy tilted her head. Breathed deeply and long.

The fragrance flowed down easy . . . soft and smooth as wine . . . velvet in her veins . . .

Intoxicating.

Yes . . . that's it. Intoxicating.

Light-headed, Lucy reached out a hand toward her bed. She sat down unsteadily, then lay back and closed her eyes.

The scent floated from the covers.

Like an exotic perfume, it rose up around her, enveloped her from every side—sheets, blankets, pillows, comforter—even her nightclothes, which she'd carelessly tossed across the headboard that morning in her hurry to dress. It seeped into the pores of her skin, and brushed softly across her eyelids, and tingled along the fingertips of her right hand . . .

And that's when Lucy realized.

That's when it hit her full force that someone had been in here today.

In her room . . .

And in her bed.

11

"Lucy! What the hell are you doing?"

Lucy could hear Angela shouting at her from the bathroom doorway, but she didn't care. She didn't care, and she didn't stop—she kept right on stripping the linens from her bed.

"Lucy! Did you hear me? You know we have a cleaning lady who does that!"

"I don't care about the cleaning lady—I don't want to *wait* for the cleaning lady. I want these off now. I want them washed. I want clean sheets. I want a new bedspread. I want—"

"Have you totally lost your mind?" Angela yelled. "Florence was here *today*! Everything already *is* clean!"

Lucy froze. She stood there like a statue, then very slowly turned around.

"Today?" she murmured. "You mean . . . the cleaning lady—"

"Florence, yes, our cleaning lady. She always comes on Fridays—"

"That's not true. My room's different. Someone was in my room."

"You've hardly come *out* of your room since the first day you got here," Angela reminded her sharply. "Irene told Florence not to go in there till you felt better. So today she cleaned it."

No . . . that's not right.

Lucy stared at her cousin with a puzzled frown. Of course it made perfect sense . . . of course it must be true . . .

"There's . . . a smell," she finished lamely.

Angela came farther into the room and sniffed.

"Well, *yeah*—probably air freshener. Or furniture polish. Or stuff she puts in the carpet. Florence always sprays *everything* around here. *Especially* when we've been sick or something."

No! That's not right!

"You are so weird." Angela glowered at her. "Didn't anybody ever use air freshener where you came from?"

Lucy didn't answer. She sank down on to the foot of the bed and gazed in bewilderment at the sheets and blankets piled around her on the floor.

"Put on something warm," Angela said then. "We're going to the Festival."

"What?" Lucy looked up just in time to see her cousin disappear into the bathroom. "We're doing . . . what?"

"Going to the Festival!" Angela's voice hollered back to her. "It's Friday night—I can't stand to be here one more second!"

"But you're not supposed—" Lucy began, then stopped. Not a good idea to let Angela know she'd eavesdropped this morning, that she'd heard Irene grounding the girl. But not a good idea either, aiding and abetting a criminal . . .

Your choice. Get out or stay in this creepy room.

She heard the shower running, so she went over and shut the door. Then she crossed her arms over her chest and leaned back against the wall, studying her bed as though it were some unwelcome alien dropped in her midst.

I don't believe you, Angela. Why don't I believe you?

Lucy was beginning to think Angela might be right—that maybe she truly *was* losing her mind. Some sweet-smelling air spray had sent her into a complete tailspin—she'd jumped to the most ridiculous conclusion. Someone in her room? Well, of *course* someone had been in her room—*Florence* had been in her room, simply doing her job!

And yet . . .

Lucy chewed mercilessly on a fingernail. Something inside her—*deep* inside her—still felt uneasy . . . uneasy and unconvinced. *Why?* She'd always been so sensible, so logical, always prided herself on her levelheadedness. But that was before the cemetery, she reminded herself now. Before the girl in the grave . . . before all the *other* crazy things that had happened to her, *before I started jumping at every shadow and letting my imagination spin entirely out of control—*

"Florence," Lucy said firmly to herself. "Florence, Florence, Florence. Florence the cleaning lady."

But, *no*, her mind answered her, without the slightest hesitation . . . *No, not Florence* . . .

Someone else.

"Lucy!"

Startled, Lucy looked up to see Angela glaring at her from the doorway again.

"Irene has a very important meeting tonight that'll last till at least eleven. If we leave now, we can beat her home."

Lucy couldn't resist. "And why would we want to do that?"

"I've been having some car trouble." Angela didn't miss a beat. "I promised her I wouldn't be out on those dirt roads after dark. Just, you know, in case something should happen."

"I see."

"So if we're back early, she won't have to know about it. I mean, I wouldn't want her to worry."

Lucy shook her head. "Of course not."

"So come on!"

The door slammed between them, and Lucy gazed at it for a few seconds, wrestling with her conscience. It *would* be better than staying here in this room right now. And since she wasn't supposed to know Angela was grounded, *she* certainly wouldn't be the one in trouble if Irene discovered they'd gone out. Besides, Lucy reasoned, doing this for Angela might help make a truce between them.

It was just the Fall Festival, after all.

And what could possibly happen to them at a Festival?

12

He'd been fascinated when he'd first seen her—that beautiful girl at the window.

He hadn't been able to turn away, gazing at her through the trees, through the rain—he hadn't expected anyone to be there, hadn't even realized there was a house at the edge of the woods. Once his work was done at the graveyard, he'd needed a safer, darker sanctuary, and so instinct had driven him deep into the moonless shelter of the forest.

He often prowled after he'd killed.

City streets . . . neighborhoods . . . country roads . . . any convenient place to work off those lingering effects of restlessness and release.

He hunted unhindered. Undetected. *Unseen . . .*

It amused him to stand over people while

they slept . . . people who didn't know he was there, people unaware that their lives were in his power. With one quick decision he could determine if they awakened tomorrow, or if they languished for hours or days on end, or if their hearts stopped suddenly, midbeat, without the slightest warning.

Just as *his* heart had had no warning when he saw her there at the window.

He'd watched her curiously, the light glowing pale behind her, the outline of her soft, sweet curves beneath the flimsy fabric of her nightdress. At one point he thought she might have seen him, too, for she was peering at the woods, at the low stone wall . . . but he was always much quicker than a glance. He'd been a shadow for a while, and then a wisp of fog. He'd watched her unbuttoning her gown, the delicate swell of her breasts as she'd leaned forward against the glass, and then he'd been outside on her balcony as she'd slid open the doors and gotten drenched from the rain. He'd reached out and touched her cheek, but she hadn't known; he could have gone inside with her, but he'd waited.

He didn't need an invitation—not from her,

not from anyone—he went where he pleased, when he pleased.

How he pleased.

But her sorrow had stopped him.

Like a fragile aura, it surrounded her and flowed from her—he could feel the palpable grief, the vulnerability and despair, and though it would have been so easy, so pleasurable, to take her then, he'd decided against it.

He'd taken the other girl instead.

The other girl had left her window open just the tiniest crack, and he'd slipped through the screen, slipped right inside on the cold, wet breeze, and he'd stayed till nearly dawn. Even in slumber she'd reeked of anger and rebellion, and he'd found this exciting, this wild, defiant nature so very much like his own.

She'd thought she was dreaming, of course.

When he'd pulled down her covers without the slightest disturbance . . . when he'd caressed her naked body with his eyes, his hands, his mind . . .

Her thighs had parted, her back had arched, such a delicious nightmare, inviting him to join her.

He usually came as a dream.

At least the first time.

A dream that lingered long past waking . . . like a deep, slow burning that could not be satisfied.

And when he'd finally left her, languid and sated with his memory, he'd waited in the woods behind the house.

He'd waited for the sun to come up and the house to be empty, and then he'd willed himself onto that balcony and let himself in through the sliding glass doors.

Her name was Lucy, he discovered.

Lucy . . .

He'd found it stamped on an airline ticket that she'd tossed on her dresser; he'd seen it written on a luggage tag still attached to a suitcase full of clothes.

Lucy. Lucy Dennison.

He hadn't expected an interruption. He'd paused and listened, mildly annoyed, as the back door unlocked, as the kitchen cupboards banged open and shut, as the cleaning lady made her slow, labored journey up the stairs and down the hall.

But still, he'd had time to walk around Lucy's room.

To touch Lucy's things.

And, in those last few seconds before taking his leave, to lie down . . . smiling . . . in Lucy's bed.

13

"Why don't *you* drive?" Angela insisted as she opened the garage door.

Lucy paused beside the little red Corvette, her eyes wide with feigned innocence. *Good one, Angela—now you can honestly say you didn't drive your car anywhere except back and forth to school.* "Me? Oh, no, I'd rather *you* did. I mean, if you've been having trouble with it—"

"The thing is," Angela said quickly, "is that I'm sort of getting a headache."

"Oh. Well then, maybe we'd better stay home."

"I can't. I mean, I shouldn't. I mean, I promised my friends—you know, I'm supposed to be working one of the booths tonight at the fair, so I have to at least show up and help."

Was she telling the truth? Lucy doubted it, but told herself it didn't matter anyway. What was more important right now was just getting out of the house and getting along with her cousin.

"So what exactly is this Fall Festival?" she asked, as Angela guided her through the neighborhood and toward the opposite end of town.

Angela slumped down in her seat and sounded bored. "It's the school's biggest fund-raiser, and they have it every year."

"That's it?"

"It's like a fair, okay?" The girl gave an exasperated sigh. "They do it every year. Anyone can participate, so the school rents space to set up booths and then we get to keep whatever money we make. Lots of people come in from other towns, and there's, like, this little carnival, and they have food and stupid crafts for sale, and dumb games and prizes and stuff."

Lucy was only half listening, driving with one hand, using the other to fiddle with the radio. "Sounds fascinating. So where do you work?"

"Hey, that's my favorite station!" Angela complained. "What do you think you're doing?"

"I just wanted to catch the news. Just for one second, okay?"

"*One*."

"Thanks. Now . . . *where* do you work?"

"Pin the nose on the scarecrow."

"Really?" The announcer was highlighting the day's local headlines. Fall Festival . . . daycare facility closing . . . fender bender on the old highway. . . "You make scarecrows?" No mention of dead bodies, no girls in open graves, no murders in Pine Ridge. *I couldn't have imagined it* all, *could I? Did I imagine Byron, too? And the necklace in class . . . and the girl in the bathroom . . . and the scar on my hand—*

"Watch out!" Angela yelped. "What is *wrong* with you?"

Startled, Lucy swung the car back to her own side of the road. "Sorry."

"Well, it might help if you stopped looking at your hand and kept both of them on the steering wheel, for God's sake."

"Sorry." Lucy's brain struggled to reengage. "What were you saying about scarecrows?"

"I *said*, of course I don't make scarecrows. It's a *game*. You blindfold people and spin them around, and then they have to stick this ridiculous nose on the scarecrow."

"Like pin the tail on the donkey?"

"Exactly. And if you get the nose in the right place, you win a prize. Except we use velcro, not pins."

"What kind of prize?"

Angela sighed. "A scarecrow doll, what do you think?"

"Well . . . it sounds kind of fun."

"Yeah, if you have no *life*. Turn here."

Lucy did as she was told. They followed a narrow strip of blacktop for about ten minutes, then turned off again onto an even narrower dirt road, this one winding off through thickly wooded countryside for several more miles.

"That's it up there," Angela finally announced.

To Lucy's relief she saw the fairgrounds up ahead, a noisy carnival bright with lights and busy with activity. Across the road and a good walk away stretched a large unlit field where kids with flashlights directed traffic and motioned them to their parking spot.

"Okay," Angela said, unstrapping her seat belt.

"Why don't we just meet back here about ten-thirty?"

Lucy looked doubtful. "You're sure that's enough time to . . . to not worry Irene?" she remembered to say. "I mean, how can you know for sure how long her meeting will be?"

"Trust me. It's a stupid disciplinary committee, and they never end before eleven. Night's the only time they can get everyone together without having *other* very important meetings to go to."

"What kind of discipline?" Lucy couldn't help asking.

"A bunch of stupid frat guys. They're always such jerks, and they're always in some kind of trouble. I mean, you'd think they'd learn by now that it's *not* cool to get drunk and act like total idiots in the cemetery."

Lucy's hand froze on the door handle. "What . . . about the cemetery?"

"Some guys went into the cemetery last night and got drunk and were messing around. And I guess somebody saw them and complained."

It was all Lucy could do to keep her voice casual. "What were they doing, do you know?"

"The usual stuff, probably. Breaking things . . . stealing things . . . spray-painting the headstones . . . just your usual damage to private property. Oh—and I always love this one—making out with their girlfriends on the graves."

"So . . ." Lucy could barely choke out the words, "it was just a . . . a joke?"

"Well, *they* thought it was. But they're gonna get suspended and their fraternity will get put on probation." Angela thought a minute, then gave a wry smile. "That's the part Irene really likes. The punishment part."

But Lucy wasn't listening anymore. As she got the door open and climbed out, her mind was spinning with rage and disbelief. *A joke! Kids drunk and playing pranks!* No wonder there hadn't been any news coverage . . . no murder investigations . . . no reports of missing girls . . . And all the agony she'd suffered . . . the terror . . . the guilt and regret and horror and—

"Are you coming?" Angela was waving at her from the other side of the car. "The Festival's *this* way. God, I can't believe they made us park way out here in all this mud!"

Yet that still didn't explain her encounter with Byron that morning, Lucy reminded herself, following Angela through the field. Still didn't explain the things he'd said . . . the things he'd known . . .

Unless he was part of the joke, too. Unless he was there last night with those other guys, and he guessed I might come back this morning, and he wanted to scare me into not saying anything . . .

"*If you tell anyone . . . you could die . . . they wouldn't believe you anyway . . .*"

"Did you hear me?" Angela snapped.

"What? Sorry—what?" *Still doesn't explain Byron . . . still doesn't explain a lot of things—*

"I *said*, let's just meet back here at the car. Are you *listening* to me?"

"Yes," Lucy murmured. "I'm listening. Ten-thirty. Here at the car."

She felt betrayed. Mortified and furious at being the butt of such a cruel, twisted joke. How those guys must be laughing at her right now—if, in fact, they even remembered the sick charade they'd carried out last night.

"Okay," Angela said. "See you later."

They parted at the main gate, but Lucy

stood on the sidelines for a moment, taking everything in. It was after six now, and the Fall Festival was in full swing. Angela was right about one thing, she noted—it seemed the whole town had turned out for the event—the whole town and a whole lot more. The place was packed with people in the mood for fun. Lines were already long at the concession stands, and the air throbbed with loud music and the wild rumble of rides, the carousel calliope, and barkers hawking games of various skills and staminas. Lucy could smell food from every direction—hot dogs, doughnuts, cotton candy, barbecue. For the first time in hours she actually realized how hungry she was; she'd barely eaten anything since yesterday.

She bought a greasy hamburger and a watered-down Coke and ate while she walked. It had been years since she'd been to anything like a carnival, and it brought back happy memories of her childhood, of her and Mom off together on their special adventures. Despite the tasteless food and poignant memories, she actually began to feel better. And despite the pain and embarrassment of her entire day, she felt herself almost smile.

She tossed her trash into a bin and kept walking, squeezing her way in and out through the crowds. The night was chilly, the breeze sharp but not unbearable in her flannel shirt and oversized parka. She was glad she'd opted to leave her purse at home tonight—with her money and ID tucked tightly into the pocket of her jeans, she felt a lot safer. *Safer . . . that's funny.* For some reason, the irony of that nearly brought another smile to her face.

She paused at a booth selling candy apples. She bought one and bit through the hard, sticky sweetness, and then she headed back into the crowd.

The slow, shivery prickle at the back of her neck had nothing to do with the cold.

Lucy stopped, and three people ran into her from behind. She felt a sharp burst of pain as her upper lip split between the candy apple and her two front teeth.

Mumbling apologies, she worked her way over to a booth and stood with her back to the wall. She could feel the blood swelling from the cut, and she wiped it carelessly with the back of her hand. Her eyes roamed anxiously over the teeming mobs of people.

Someone's following me. I feel it.

Just like last night . . . when she'd run from those footsteps . . . when she'd run from one nightmare, straight into another . . .

She didn't see anything suspicious, of course—in that solid mass of faces, how *would* she? And after all that had happened in the last two days, Lucy wasn't even sure how much she could trust her own instincts anymore.

She dabbed at the blood on her lip.

She took another survey of the crowd.

You're imagining things. Enough's enough. Pull yourself together, for crying out loud.

She was almost past the carousel when she saw him.

He was moving quickly, shoving his way toward her through the mob, and as she recognized his face, Lucy instantly turned and headed the opposite way.

"Lucy!" she heard him yell, but she didn't answer, didn't even acknowledge him, just kept walking.

"Lucy! Wait! We've got to talk!"

She thought she could outrun him, but Byron caught up with her easily, grabbing her arm and forcing her around. Dropping her apple, Lucy twisted furiously from his grasp.

"Haven't you done enough already?" she exploded.

The look he gave her was grim, his voice low and urgent. "Come on, we can't talk here—"

"You've had your fun, okay? Now leave me alone!"

"Fun? What *fun*? What is this—?"

"Those frat guys playing jokes at the cemetery—and you were there, too—that's how you knew I'd come back! Well, are you proud of yourself?"

"I don't have a clue what you're talking about, but please, just listen to me—"

"I've listened to you enough. Now I'm going."

With one smooth movement, Byron caught her shoulders and steered her over to a booth. Then, pinning her flat against the wall, he leaned down over her, his black eyes narrowed.

"There are things you need to understand."

"No, *you* need to understand!" Lucy tried to break free, but he only held her tighter. "If you don't leave me alone right now, I'm going to scream as loud as I can and have you arrested!"

"Look, I know you're scared—you have every right to be. What happened last night was horrible, and you have no reason in the world to trust me. But you *have* to. You *have* to meet me tomorrow—"

"I'm not meeting you anywhere—"

"—the old church—nine o'clock—"

She opened her mouth to scream. She felt his fingers dig into her shoulders as he gave her a firm, quick shake.

"You saw something today," he said. His lips moved soft against her ear; his voice dropped to a whisper. "When you touched the necklace, you saw something happen. *You* know it . . . and so do I."

This time when she struggled, he let her go. Lucy bolted into the crowd, frantically shoving her way through, not caring where she ran, only desperate to get away.

She looked back once and thought she saw him following.

Instinctively she veered from the midway, cut behind the Ferris wheel, and raced down a narrow path between two busy picnic shelters. It took her a minute to realize she'd lost him. Another minute to catch her breath and get her bearings. She bent over, hands on knees, and took deep gulps of air, waiting for her heartbeat to return to normal.

Then slowly she lifted her head.

That smell . . .

Frowning, Lucy glanced at her surroundings. It was darker back here, and though several groups of people had congregated nearby to socialize, the booths had thinned out, giving way to weeds and trash Dumpsters and a tall wire fence. *Great. I must be at the back of the fairgrounds.*

The night seemed colder. Without the insulation of the crowds, Lucy felt the sting of the wind and tugged her parka tight around her. Even the air felt different, she realized—softer and heavier and mysterious somehow, ripe with the scent of woods and fields and deep lake waters . . .

And that other smell . . .

She could feel her heart quickening again in her chest. Her throat constricting. The blood chilling in her veins . . .

That other, familiar smell . . .

That sweet, lingering smell that had filled her room and her bed.

14

She had to follow it.

Despite the sick fear coursing through her, Lucy knew she had no other choice.

She had to follow it, and she had to find it.

But where?

It didn't seem to be coming from one particular spot, or even from one specific direction, but rather permeated the air around her like a fine, invisible mist. Very deliberately this time, Lucy breathed it in . . . sweet like before . . . delicate like before . . . only this time stirring something deep within her, as though long-dulled senses were struggling to awake.

Several girls walked by and gave her strange looks. Didn't they smell it, Lucy wondered? *How can they not smell it?* Such an unusual fragrance . . . tantalizing . . . weaving its way through the festival, separate and distinct among the millions of other aromas hanging in the thick night air . . .

She didn't go back the way she'd come. Instead she passed bumper cars and a petting zoo, and then she began walking faster, making her way behind a barn where an auctioneer competed with enthusiastic bingo players. She could smell fried chicken and fried pies, popcorn and cotton candy, and still, *still*, that heavenly fragrance, wafting just out of reach . . .

She turned a corner and walked faster. Past country singers on makeshift stages. Games of darts. Tables of homemade pickles and jams. The smell was getting stronger now—she could feel that it was close. As she broke into a run, she suddenly spotted a big orange tent ahead of her, with a huge display of scarecrows around it.

Scarecrows . . .

She could see the whimsical sign over the entrance—PIN THE NOSE ON THE SCARECROW—and the boisterous line of kids waiting to take their turns. *Isn't this where Angela's supposed to be working?*

Mumbling apologies, Lucy pushed her way to the front. It didn't make sense, but the fragrance actually seemed *stronger* here, more tangible than any other place she'd been so far, almost as though she could reach out and touch it and hold it in her hand. If only she could find Angela, she was sure her cousin would confirm it—how could *anyone* forget that curious aroma once they'd breathed it in?

"Hey, get to the end of the line!" A solemn-faced girl stopped her at the door, holding up one hand while trying to blindfold two squirming kids with the other. "Aren't you a little old for this game?"

Lucy hurriedly identified herself. "Sorry, I'm Angela's cousin—Angela Foster? Do you know where she is?"

"I thought you looked familiar—you were in some of my classes today." The girl nodded, though her expression didn't change. "Angela's having a smoke."

"I really need to find her."

"Go around back. I just saw her talking to some guy out there a second ago."

What a surprise. "Thanks."

Lucy didn't waste any time. As she slipped around the side of the tent, she saw that it backed up to a fence, with just a narrow grassy space between. Thick woods pressed so closely from the other side that some of the trees hung over, their branches practically sweeping the ground. In spite of the festivities going on in front, it felt weirdly isolated here, shadowy and claustrophobic.

"Angela?"

Turning the corner, Lucy stopped. The light was dim at best . . . yet she thought she saw the glimmer of a cigarette at the opposite end of the tent.

"Angela? It's me . . . Lucy."

Without warning, something soft slid over her forehead . . . covered her eyes. With a startled cry, Lucy reached up and felt something like cloth—felt it being tied snugly at the back of her head—and realized it was a blindfold.

"Angela, cut it out! This isn't funny!"

"Did you come to play?" the voice whispered.

Lucy stiffened. She could *feel* someone now, a body standing close behind her, someone tall, someone strong, pressed lightly against her back.

Someone who *wasn't* Angela.

"This isn't funny," she managed to choke out. *Kids playing pranks! Friends of Angela maybe—or just a case of mistaken identity*—that's it*! They think I'm someone* else*—they must think I'm* Angela—

"I'm not Angela," she said, more forcefully this time. "You've got the wrong girl."

"On the contrary . . ." the voice murmured, "I've got *exactly* the girl I want."

Her body turned to ice. Her mind fought for calm. There were people only yards away, yet she was alone. She could scream, but she doubted anyone would hear her over the noise of the fair. Should she scream anyway? Try to run? She could feel his body, the lean, firm length of it, touching hers, yet not forcefully, *not threateningly*, she realized with slow surprise.

He wasn't even holding her.

He was only holding the blindfold at the back of her head, and as Lucy's heart hammered wildly in her chest, she tried to keep her voice even.

"I think you've made a mistake," she said. "I'm not from here, and I don't know anyone. I'm just trying to find my cousin."

"But you haven't. It seems you've found *me* instead."

Again her mind raced. Had she heard that voice before? Did she recognize it—*anything* about it? He was talking so softly, as though his lips barely moved . . . a low whisper from deep in his throat . . . warm and resonant . . . thick and smooth as . . . *what*?

Lucy's breath caught.

His hand slid leisurely down the back of her neck . . . lingered upon her left shoulder. Every instinct told her to break away—to tear off the blindfold and run—yet her body felt strangely paralyzed.

"Where's Angela?" she demanded. Her voice had begun to quiver, and she knew he could hear it, though she tried to disguise it with anger. "They said she was out here with someone—you must have seen her!"

Something brushed gently across her mouth.

"You're bleeding," he murmured.

She'd forgotten the cut on her upper lip, but

now she felt it swell . . . felt the tender skin split open. A warm drop of blood seeped out and began to trickle down.

Lips closed over hers.

A kiss so tender that time faded and stopped . . . so passionate, it sucked her breath away.

Lucy's senses reeled. Searing heat swept through her—pain and pleasure throbbing through her veins. With a helpless moan, she leaned into him and realized with a shock the kiss had ended.

At last she ripped the blindfold from her eyes.

The scent that had lured her here hung heavy in the night, though its fragile sweetness now held a trace of something more . . . something musky and faintly metallic . . .

Trembling violently, Lucy stared into the shadows.

But she was alone.

And she was cold.

15

It can't be ten-thirty.

As Lucy paused outside the scarecrow tent, she shook her wrist, tapped her watch, then held it to her ear and listened. Yes, it seemed to be working fine . . .

But there's no way it can be ten-thirty already!

"It's ten-thirty," the serious-faced girl said again. She was still trying to blindfold kids and maintain order at the same time, and as she frowned at Lucy, she added, "Did you have an accident or something?"

"Accident?" Lucy echoed. "No—what do you mean?"

"You're white as a sheet. And your lip's all swollen."

Lucy put a hand to her mouth and immediately winced. The skin on her lip felt pulpy and tender; she could feel a thin crust of dried blood.

"Are you sure Angela's not here?" she asked weakly.

"I told you, she left at ten-thirty. She said she had to meet her cousin—you—at the car."

"Right. Thanks anyway."

Her knees had turned to rubber. She wasn't sure she could walk three feet, much less the entire distance back to the parking lot. Her insides wouldn't stop shaking; she felt strangely disoriented. She'd stepped right into a dangerous situation with her eyes wide open, and she'd simply stayed in the middle of it, simply allowed the rest to happen. *What in God's name is wrong with me?*

She was probably lucky to be alive. The stranger—whoever he was—could have done a hundred horrible things to her—*and what did I do? I stood there and let him—I let him* . . .

Shame and confusion flushed through her. She could still feel his hand on her neck . . . on her shoulder . . . his body touching hers. And his kiss. That unexpected moment, senses reeling, his low whispery voice, intimate somehow, almost as though he knew her . . .

Her memory groped back—searching, searching. Trying to recall someone—*anyone*—he might have been. The guys from the cemetery last night? Had they followed her here, intent on more jokes? It seemed highly unlikely, given the disciplinary meeting tonight. Some guy at school she didn't know? *Byron?* Byron had a low, deep voice, but Byron had seemed agitated when she'd seen him earlier, he'd been tense and upset, and why follow her and frighten her when he'd already asked her to meet him secretly tomorrow?

And what about the smell?

Just thinking of that brought a fresh wave of panic. Because there *was* no explanation for it . . . none she could possibly think of . . . none that made any sort of sense. Before, she'd been almost willing to consider the air-freshener theory, but now . . .

As Lucy wandered out of the exit gates, she wished she had someone to leave with. The Festival was still in full swing, and only a handful of people were straggling toward the parking lot. Within minutes they'd located their cars, leaving her to walk the rest of the way alone.

The lights grew dim behind her. The noise began to fade. Out here in the field it was eerily quiet.

Now where exactly did we park?

Lucy stopped, cursing herself for her horrible sense of direction. It had gotten her in *major* trouble last night; she wasn't about to let it happen again. She glanced around, trying to find some sort of landmark, but all she could see was row after row of cars.

Why hadn't she thought of that earlier? Picked out a checkpoint to help her find her way back?

Frustrated, Lucy went on, trying to dodge puddles and sinkholes in the dark. Maybe Angela was in the car waiting for her—hadn't that girl at the tent said she'd already left?

"Angela!" Lucy called. "Angela! Are you out here?"

No answer. Just her own voice drifting back to her on the chilly breeze.

Lucy tried to walk faster. Why hadn't anyone thought to put temporary lighting out here? Why hadn't she thought to bring a flashlight?

Why hadn't she and Angela agreed to meet somewhere *inside* the Festival where it was bright and crowded and safe? *God, it's really, really spooky out here . . .*

She dug her hands in her pockets and felt the keyless entry to Angela's car. *Of course!*

Pulling it out, Lucy immediately hit a button. She could hear the blip of a horn in the distance, and she thought she saw the faraway flicker of headlights. *Well, at least I'm headed in the right direction.*

With the help of the mechanism, she finally spotted the Corvette, still about ten rows away, right on the end near the woods. The ground was even soggier out here, forcing her to walk close to the treeline. As she tramped her way through the weeds, she suddenly lifted her head to listen . . .

What was that?

She was sure she'd heard a sound just then . . . a faint scuffling off through those trees to her right. As though some animal were moving invisibly through the darkness . . .

A deer. Just like last night when I thought I saw something, just a deer in the woods. That's all it is.

Lucy stopped.

The noise stopped, too.

Very slowly she turned her head, eyes probing the bare, shifting branches of the trees . . . the deep, black underbelly of the forest . . .

Or maybe it's a bear—bears live close to lakes, don't they? Or a wolf? Or—

She broke into a run.

Because suddenly she didn't want to think what else it could be, this invisible presence keeping pace alongside her, skulking through the dark where she couldn't see.

It was last night's horror all over again.

With a burst of speed Lucy veered off between the cars, away from the woods, punching the entry over and over again, so the horn of the Corvette kept blasting and the headlights kept flashing on and off—on and off—

God—oh God—help me—

But it was *behind* her now—she could hear it thudding over the ground, *gaining* on her—coming closer—*closer—*

"Damnit, Lucy!" Angela yelled. "Wait up!"

With a cry, Lucy whirled around, just as her cousin closed the distance between them.

"Angela, you idiot! You scared the life out of me!"

"*I* did?" Braking to a stop, Angela tried to catch her breath. "*You're* the one running away— I thought something was *after* you!"

"Well, *I* thought something was, too!" Lucy exploded. "Were you in the woods just now?"

"What would I be doing in the woods?"

"I *heard* something in the woods."

"Oh, for God's sake—there's, like, about a *million* things you could've heard in the woods!" Angela gestured angrily toward the trees. "And where the hell have you been? I waited and waited by the car, but you never came. And *you* have the damn keys!"

Lucy thought quickly. There was no way she was going to mention what had happened back there at the tent. Not now . . . not ever.

"Sorry—I guess I lost track of time."

"I guess you did. Come on, let's get outta here."

Nodding, Lucy followed her to the car and got in, but not without a last anxious look at the woods. *Had* something really been there, following her? During the last few days, she'd lost so much faith in her instincts, she didn't know *what* to believe anymore.

She locked the doors and windows, but even after leaving the parking lot, Lucy still couldn't relax. The narrow, winding road was even harder to maneuver now that full night had fallen, and it took all her concentration to miss the endless potholes. Even Angela seemed edgier than usual, Lucy observed, watching the girl light up one cigarette after another, then mash them out half-smoked.

"Are you okay?" Lucy finally asked her.

Angela pointed to the clock on the dashboard. "I just want to get home before Irene does, that's all. Thank God she's going out of town tomorrow night, so I can have some peace. Lucy—hurry!"

"I'm hurrying."

"Well, hurry faster."

Glancing at her, Lucy sighed. "With all these stupid holes around here, if I hurry any faster, we're likely to bounce right off and—"

"*Look out!*"

As Lucy's eyes shot back to the road, she saw a quick streak of darkness in front of them. Jerking the wheel, she swerved the car sharply to the right, then slammed on the brakes as they slid dangerously along the shoulder. Angela gaped at her in alarm.

"Did you see that?"

"I saw *something*. But what was it?"

The Corvette had stopped now, and the two of them peered nervously out into the darkness. There was nothing on the road. Nothing moving in the beam of the headlights, nothing stirring at the sides of the car.

"We didn't hit anything, did we?" Angela finally asked.

"I don't think so. I didn't feel any sort of impact, did you?"

Angela shook her head. "It looked big. I mean, I only saw it for a second, but it was *big*."

"A deer, maybe?"

"No. It didn't seem like a deer. And it was so *fast*—just there and gone. I mean, what could move so fast that you can't even see it?"

"I don't know," Lucy answered uneasily. She

made a quick check in the rearview mirror. "Are you okay?"

"Yeah. I just hope my car is."

For my sake, I hope so, too. But the minute Lucy hit the accelerator, she heard the furious spinning of the tires. "Oh, great," she muttered.

"Oh, great, *what*?

"We're stuck."

"Stuck?" Angela seemed incredulous. "How can we be stuck?"

"Because there's about a foot of mud out there, and we drove right into it."

"No, *you* drove right into it." Shifting around, Angela unlocked her door. "If you've scratched anything out—"

"Stop," Lucy said. "Don't open it."

As Angela turned toward her in bewilderment, Lucy reached out slowly . . . put a hand on her arm.

"Lock your door," she whispered. "Now."

Even in the dim interior, she saw Angela go pale. She waited for the click of the lock, then leaned slowly toward the windshield.

"What is it?" Angela asked tightly.

"I saw something."

"Are you sure? Where?"

Lucy pointed. The car had skidded at a forty-five-degree angle, its headlights slicing off through the trees at the side of the road. As Lucy watched the illuminated pocket of woods, she felt a chill creep up her spine.

"Something's out there, Angela. It's watching us . . . don't you feel it?"

The girl's eyes widened slowly. Then she gave a forced laugh. "Come on, Lucy, you don't really expect me to fall for that, do you?"

But Lucy's tone was dead serious. "Do you have your phone with you?"

"Well, sure, but—"

"Call 911."

"Stop it. This isn't funny, and I don't believe you anyway."

"Well, you better believe me, because I'm telling you, there's something out there. And . . ."

As Lucy's sentence trailed off, Angela threw a quick, wary glance out her window. "Look. You're just shook up because of what happened. But I'm telling you, that thing was moving *fast*! Whatever it was, it's long gone by now—"

"Give me your phone," Lucy said tersely.

Before Angela could stop her, she grabbed the girl's purse and started rummaging through it, but Angela quickly snatched it back.

"What are you doing?" Angela snapped at her. "That's mine!"

"Your phone, Angela—your phone!" Lucy's voice was louder now, thin with rising panic. "Hurry up! Call 911! *Do* it, Angela, call for help!"

But she could see now that it was finally sinking in, Angela's eyes the size of saucers, her hands digging through her purse, tossing things out, searching for her cell phone. "This is sick, Lucy, do you hear me? This is *sick*!"

"It's coming closer! Make the call!"

Lucy's heart was racing. She could *feel* something out there—something furtive—something evil—a sense of danger so intense that every nerve vibrated with terror. It was standing just out of sight, standing just beyond the trees, one with the woods, one with the darkness, and it was waiting to strike . . . waiting to see what they would do . . .

"Oh, God," Lucy whispered, "Oh my God—"

"What is it!" Angela shouted, thoroughly frightened now. She dumped her purse upside down, the contents spilling everywhere, shaking it back and forth, helplessly close to tears. "I can't find it! I can't find my phone!"

"It's too late!" Lucy cried.

Something hit the side of the car. As both girls screamed, the Corvette rocked from the impact, and there was a frantic clawing at Angela's door.

"Get down!" Lucy yelled, even as she grabbed the girl and forced her to the floor.

"*What is it?*" Angela shrieked. "I can't see anything!"

Once more something lunged at the side. As the car swayed and slid, they heard a scratching at the door handle, as though something were trying to wrench it open. Terrified, Angela huddled beneath the dashboard, while Lucy whirled around just in time to see a dark shape dart behind the car. *Oh, God, it's coming to my side!* She leaned on the horn, the harsh sound splitting through the night, and then she gunned the motor.

The tires spun in the muck. Without even

thinking, Lucy shifted forward, then back, forward, then back—*tires whining, horn blasting, Angela screaming*—

The car lurched free.

Without warning, it popped from the mud and skidded sideways onto the road. Clutching the wheel for dear life, Lucy floored the accelerator, not stopping, not even slowing down till they'd reached the main highway once again.

"Stop it, Angela," she said then, quietly. "We're safe now."

"Safe?" The girl was practically hysterical. "*Safe?* How do you know we're safe? What *was* that thing?"

Lucy shook her head and said nothing.

"Then how do you know it didn't follow us? How do you know it's not sitting up there on the roof right now? Or—or—riding back there in the trunk?"

"Because it's not." Lucy's lips pressed into a tight line. "It's not. I just know."

As they paused at a stop sign, she shifted in her seat and took a long, deliberate look through every single window.

How do *I know*? she wondered. *How do I really know?*

There were houses around them now, and quiet, tree-lined streets.

And the peaceful silence of neighborhoods settled in for the night.

But Angela was crying.

And Lucy's heart was still beating wildly in her chest.

How did I know that thing was out there to begin with?

16

It was a miracle they got home before Irene.

The girls pulled into the garage with just minutes to spare, leaving no time to examine the car or discuss what had happened back there on that dark country road. Not that Angela would have wanted to anyway, Lucy figured—which was perfectly fine with her. Trying to rationalize it to herself was hard enough.

She stood in the shower, trembling beneath the hard spray of the water. Still badly shaken from the attack on the car . . . still badly frightened from her encounter with the stranger behind the tent. *Only frightened?* Again she berated herself for being so careless, for putting herself in such a dangerous situation . . . yet at the same time she could still hear that low, whispery voice . . . feel the gentle urgency of that kiss . . .

How could cold, stark fear be so alluring at the same time? She was furious with herself for even considering such a notion. *What's wrong with me?*

She turned the water as hot as she could stand it, washing her hair, her face, her lips, every inch of her body, as though she might be able to wash away every memory, every horror, every single event that had touched her in the last two days. All she wanted to do was crawl into bed and have a peaceful night of dreamless, uninterrupted sleep. So it surprised her when she heard a soft knock on her bedroom door about an hour later and saw Angela peek in.

"We need to talk," Angela said.

Lucy nodded and motioned her inside. She'd been sitting up, too, unable to relax; now she scooted over so Angela could plop down beside her. The girl's dark raccoon eyes had been wiped off for the night, her long hair braided down her back. She was wearing a polka-dot flannel nightshirt and looked almost normal.

"I can't stop thinking about what happened," Angela blurted out. Her expression seemed strained and almost embarrassed. Her hands twisted nervously in her lap. "What do you think that was? I mean . . . really?"

"I don't know. I've been thinking about it, too . . . and I honestly don't know."

"Well, it must have been a wolf," Angela announced flatly.

"Are there wolves around here?"

"Well . . . usually farther north, but sometimes they leave their territory, right? I mean, like if they're hungry, or certain areas get too populated, I've heard of animals doing that."

Lucy wanted to believe her. "It's possible, I guess."

"But . . . it could have been a bear, too, maybe," Angela mused. "I was thinking maybe it was wounded. When an animal's wounded, it makes them kind of crazy, and then they attack things they wouldn't normally attack, right? I mean, haven't you heard that?"

Lucy nodded. "It makes sense."

"So if something was hurt . . . and hungry . . . and smelled us in the car . . ."

Angela paused, her eyes almost pleading. "It *could've* happened that way. Right?"

"Sure. Sure it could."

"Great." Angela let out a huge sigh of relief. "And it's probably not a good idea to tell anyone else about it, do you think? Just so we don't cause a panic or something. And especially Irene. Because of her worrying, I mean."

"Absolutely. Our secret."

Another relieved sigh. Angela stretched her willowy limbs, then hopped off the bed.

"Great. Good night, then."

"Good night."

Mildly amazed, Lucy watched her go. How did Angela do it, she wondered? How could she make something go away so easily—or not even exist at all—just by refusing to accept it?

But isn't that what you're doing?

"No," Lucy mumbled to herself. "That's different."

Is it?

And in that very instant, razor-sharp images began strobing through her mind—images of Byron at the cemetery, Byron at the Festival, Byron trying to talk to her, to warn her about something: "I want to help you . . . some things take time to believe in . . . we don't have a lot of time . . . something happened . . . something important . . . touched you . . . was passed on to you . . . you need to understand . . ." As Lucy pressed her hands to her head, it was as if she could suddenly *feel* all those crazy puzzle pieces tumbling through her mind . . . falling into place . . . beginning to make a frightening kind of sense.

Could it possibly be true? Could there *honestly* be a connection between Byron's warnings and the bizarre events that had begun to darken her life?

"*. . . no reason in the world to trust me . . . have to meet me tomorrow . . .*"

"You're right," Lucy mumbled again. "I don't have the slightest reason to trust you."

"Did you say something?" Angela asked.

Lucy jumped and stared at the door. Angela was back again, propped in the threshold, smoking a cigarette and frowning at her.

"I didn't say anything," Lucy muttered.

Her cousin shrugged. "You'll need to get my car washed in the morning."

"*I* will?"

"Well . . . *yeah*. Irene didn't see it tonight 'cause someone picked her up and she didn't go in the garage. But tomorrow she'll probably be using her car—and if she sees the shape *my* car's in, she's bound to know we were out tonight."

"But what about the damage? How are you going to explain all those scratches?"

"Vandalism *happens* in the school parking lot, Lucy." Angela gazed down at the floor, her expression bland. "It happens all the time. So just take it to the car wash, okay?"

"And who was your servant this time last year?"

Angela rolled her eyes. "Very funny. Just do it?"

"No, I won't do it. If she sees your dirty car, too bad." Grumpily, Lucy stacked up her pillows and fell back on top of them. "And you can *stop* giving me all these excuses about Irene worrying—I heard you two this morning, and I know you're grounded."

Angela stared. A flush went over her face, though from anger or embarrassment, Lucy couldn't tell. She hesitated a moment, as if trying to decide what to do. Then with a sound of exasperation, she tossed her cigarette into the toilet, walked back to the bed, and flounced down on the edge.

"If you knew, then why'd you take me tonight?" she demanded.

"Because I thought it would help things between us. I wanted us to be friends."

"That's stupid. How could we ever be friends?"

"My point exactly. Which is why I'm not going to get your car washed tomorrow."

"If Irene finds out I left tonight, she'll cancel my credit cards!"

Lucy shrugged. She reached over and flipped off the lamp. Angela flipped it back on.

"Fine!" Angela pouted. "Look, if I tell you something *really* important and *really* secret about someone I met tonight, *then* will you wash my car?"

Lucy stared at her. Really *important*? Really *secret*? What could be more important than being stalked, than girls in graves, than hungry predators on lonely roads? What could be more secret than strangers with blindfolds, and painful visions, and disembodied voices in bathrooms?

She'd had enough. She switched off the light.

Angela switched it back on.

"Okay," Angela sighed. "I'll be your friend. Are you satisfied?"

"Angela, you don't know the meaning of the word."

The girl looked blank. "*Friend*? Or *satisfied*?"

"Neither one. Now get out of here and let me go to sleep."

This time when she reached for the lamp, Angela grabbed her arm. "I'll tell her *you* took my car. I'll tell her *you* stole my keys, and I didn't know anything about it. And if you deny it, I'll tell her you're lying . . . that you . . . that you . . . sneaked out to meet somebody!"

Lucy gave a humorless laugh. "Yeah, that's a good one, Angela, I'm sure she'll believe *that*. And while you're at it, be sure to tell her about the wild orgy I had out there behind the tents."

It slipped out before she even thought.

She saw Angela's eyes go wide, her face go red, saw her cheeks flinch as she drew in her breath.

"You bitch," she muttered. "You were *spying* on me!"

"What? Angela, no—I wasn't!"

Shocked at her cousin's reaction, Lucy tried to take her arm, but Angela was already halfway across the room.

"I was joking!" Lucy insisted. "I was joking about *myself*—I don't even know what you're talking about!"

"The hell you don't," Angela said furiously. "How long did you stand there watching, anyway? And it *wasn't* an orgy!"

"I wasn't watching anything! I was just making fun of myself!"

She saw Angela turn toward her then, a range of emotions flickering over the girl's face—indecision, guilt, embarrassment and the horrible realization that she'd just given herself away.

"Well . . . well . . . me, too!" she announced, with a forced little laugh. "*I* was just joking, too. I just wanted to see what you'd say."

Lucy stared at her as though she'd lost her mind. "Okay," she offered tentatively. "So we're even, right?"

"Right." The laugh again, almost brittle. "Okay, then. Great jokes. Good night."

"Good night." Lucy paused, then, "Angela?"

"What?"
"How late does Irene sleep on Saturdays?"
"Till around ten. Why?"
"I'll get your car washed. But I want to leave early, just in case she gets up."
"Like, how early?
"Like, before nine."

17

It was no problem slipping out of the house the next morning.

Everyone else was still asleep, and since Angela had already given her the keys and explicit directions to the car wash, Lucy was away in no time at all.

The car wash hadn't opened yet. Checking her watch, she saw that it was only eight-thirty, so she made a quick run through a fast-food drive-through, then sat in the parking lot, trying to digest both her food and her thoughts.

This is really stupid. Byron probably won't even be there. And if I do *go, and it really* is *another joke, I'll never be able to show my face anywhere in Pine Ridge again.*

But obviously he'd gotten there before her.

As Lucy drove slowly past the church, she noticed an old Jeep pulled alongside the curb in front, but not a soul to be seen. *Strange that Byron would park here in plain sight*, she found herself thinking. Especially since he'd made this meeting sound so secret and so mysterious . . .

Still, this *was* an abandoned church, and it *was* in an abandoned area—*not like there's going to be anyone around here watching us or wondering what we're up to*. Besides, seeing his Jeep out here in the open made her feel a whole lot safer.

Lucy parked, then made her way slowly up the crumbled walkway. The church had looked so spooky that night of the storm, and here in the daylight, it didn't look a whole lot better. Like the original section of the cemetery stretching off behind it, tall weeds had taken over, and shadows lurked beneath the gnarled branches of giant old trees. The steps to the door were rotted. The belltower didn't look at all sturdy. Several stained-glass windows were broken, and dead ivy crept over the walls.

It was very still. No breeze this morning, and frostily cold. Lucy's breath hung in the air as she glanced nervously back at her car. She'd parked close for a quick getaway. She told herself to go inside, then stopped with her hand on the door. *You're doing it again—walking right into an isolated, unknown place—have you completely lost your mind?*

When girls in *movies* did this, they always got killed, she reminded herself. But this wasn't a movie, this was real life—*my life!*—and she needed answers, and right now it seemed that Byron was her *only* chance at getting those answers.

She saw then that one of the large wooden doors was slightly open. That there were muddy footprints on the steps, leading inside.

Very slowly Lucy inched open the door. "Hello? Is anyone here?"

The silence was unnerving. Again she glanced back over her shoulder, but nothing moved within those calm, black shadows.

"Byron?" she called softly. "Hello?"

Lucy strained her ears through the quiet. Had the door creaked then, just ever so slightly? As though someone might be pushing it from the other side?

Instinctively she released it and stepped back. "Hello?"

Why wasn't he watching for her, why wasn't he out here waiting to see if she showed up? It had been *his* idea, after all—if he'd wanted her here so badly, why wasn't he coming out to meet her?

But it was very cold, she reasoned, and it made perfect sense that he'd probably go inside to wait. And these doors, made of such thick solid oak, surely muffled any sounds from outside. *Don't be so paranoid . . . Angela knows him . . . apparently all the girls at school are in love with him . . . it's not like he's some total creep that nobody's ever heard of . . .*

Still, Lucy suddenly wished she'd told somebody where she was headed this morning. Just in case.

Okay . . . here goes.

She took a deep breath and yanked hard at the door. As it moved on rusty hinges, a low groan echoed back through the vast interior of the church.

She smelled dampness and old stone. Cold, stale air, long unbreathed, long undisturbed.

Shivering, Lucy stood there a moment, her eyes trying to adjust to the gloom. As the door swung shut with a dull thud, she moved farther into the vestibule.

"Byron?"

The church was still sadly, hauntingly beautiful. In the muted stained-glass light, Lucy could see saints gazing down at her from niches along the walls, their painted faces filled with loving concern. Wooden pews stood empty, sifted with dust, and high in the rafters of the arched ceiling, doves fluttered gently as she passed beneath them. Lucy walked slowly up the center aisle. She could see the main altar ahead of her, draped with a dingy white cloth, decorated with arrangements of long-dead flowers.

Despite the eerieness of the place, Lucy felt strangely fascinated. She stopped before the altar, trailing her fingers over the musty cloth, over faded droplets of candle wax, over brittle chrysanthemum petals. Even her heart seemed to echo in here; she could hear the faint beat of her pulse.

God, it's so cold . . .

Blowing on her hands, Lucy turned in a slow circle and glanced uneasily at her surroundings. Was it her imagination, or had the temperature dropped about ten degrees just since she'd walked through the door? *You* are *imagining things.* Yet as she blew once more on her hands, she could see her breath forming, a soft vapory cloud right in front of her face.

"Byron?"

Her own voice whispered back to her from the shadows.

The doves stirred restlessly with a muffled beating of wings.

"Come on, Byron, if you have something to say, you'd better say it—*now*!"

This is stupid. He's not here, and he's obviously not going to show up, and all you're doing is creeping yourself out.

With growing anxiety, Lucy gnawed on a fingernail. *Not again . . .* not again*! What did you expect, anyway? Haven't you learned your lesson by now?*

But she'd wanted this time to be different—she'd wanted so *much* to believe that Byron could help her. She'd wanted to *prove* to herself once and for all that it wasn't just her, that there were reasons and answers and explanations for the things that were happening, that she *wasn't* just making up dreams in her mind—

Something's here.

Lucy gasped as a sliver of dread snaked its way up her back and lodged at the base of her neck.

Something's here!

Instantly her eyes swept over the walls and ceiling, the massive wooden cross above the altar, the partially shattered glass of the crucifixion behind it, the confessionals in the darkened aisles along the side . . .

The confessionals . . .

A soft sound slithered through the church. A sound like . . . *what*? A sigh of wind? A flurry of feathers? Or . . .

Breathing.

Lucy's body stiffened, every nerve electrified. *No, it can't be . . . there's no one here . . . no one . . . no one . . .*

Yet she could feel herself moving across the cold stone floor, moving steadily toward the confessionals, almost as though something were *drawing* her forward, some force against her will.

She tried to stop, but she couldn't. Tried to resist, but the pull seemed only to grow stronger.

She stopped outside one of the doors.

Byron?

She tried to whisper, but the words stuck soundlessly in her throat. She could see the door cracked open, barely an inch, but she couldn't see what was inside. And yes—*yes!*—there was the sound again . . . like the faintest breath, the most feeble attempt at a sigh.

Steeling herself, Lucy jerked open the door.

The space was cramped and narrow, murky with shadows, and as she stepped tentatively across the threshold, she could see the small priest's window to the left, the bit of screen and gauzy curtain concealing it from the other side, the kneeler beneath it on the floor.

The compartment stank of mildew; it was covered thickly in dust.

No sins had been confessed here for a long, long time.

See? Nothing. Just your imagination.

Almost weak with relief, Lucy turned to walk out.

And saw the door slowly creak shut.

Startled, she stared at it a moment, then gave it a push. The door didn't move. She pushed harder, then leaned into it with her shoulder. It wouldn't so much as budge.

That's strange . . . She couldn't remember seeing a latch on the outside of the door, and it hadn't stuck when she'd yanked it open. Trying not to panic, Lucy tried it again, harder this time, then harder still, but the door refused to give. Dust swirled into the air, choking her, irritating her eyes. She yelled and pounded on the walls. The space seemed to be growing smaller, the dust thicker, the high walls closing in—*Oh God—let me out of here!*

The thought briefly shot through her mind that no one would find her, maybe not for days and days, maybe not ever—she'd simply die here in the dark, in this tiny dark space, trapped in an upright coffin.

"Byron!" Lucy screamed. There was a *car* parked outside, for God's sake, *somebody* must be around! "Please! Please, somebody, I'm stuck in here—*let me out*!"

"Have you come to seek God's forgiveness, my child?" the voice murmured.

Lucy went cold. Her fists froze upon the door, her mouth gaped in a silent scream.

Her eyes turned fearfully to the wall . . .

She could see the priest's window, only now it was open. The curtain had been pulled back, and beyond the small screen was the dim outline of a face.

A face . . . yet somehow . . . and even more terrifyingly . . . *not* a face.

"Who are you?" Lucy choked out. Her back was against the door now, her knees so shaky she could hardly stand. It took every ounce of willpower to focus on that window and the featureless profile beyond. "*Who are you?*"

"Your salvation."

And she *knew* the voice, and he seemed to be all around her now, in the air, in the dust, in the echo of her heartbeat, in the thoughts inside her head, in the ice flowing through her veins . . .

"You were at the Festival," she realized. "Behind the tent, you were the one—"

"Meant to save you," he whispered. "No more sorrow . . . no more pain. Reprieve from the lifetime of loneliness that awaits you. Redemption from yourself."

"Please—"

"I know how lost you've been without your mother."

Tears filled Lucy's eyes . . . trickled slowly down her cheeks. "Why? Why are you doing this?"

"It's no longer a matter of why. It's a matter of when. Of how."

"I don't understand. I don't know you . . . I haven't done anything to you. Why won't you just leave me alone?"

"But you *have* done something to me. We have a connection, you and I." The voice sounded mildly amused. "So let me ask you again . . . have you come to seek God's forgiveness?"

"Forgiveness for what?" she cried desperately.

"For the places your heart will take you . . . where your soul cannot go."

Without warning the door came open.

As Lucy stumbled out into the aisle, she grabbed the door of the priest's compartment and flung it open.

But the darkness inside was empty.

And the dust not even disturbed.

18

Lucy stood there, unable to move.

Like a distant observer, she watched herself staring into the confessional, felt her slow-motion shock and disbelief—yet at the same time, felt oddly detached from reality. As she wheeled around to run, a tall figure suddenly materialized from the shadows behind her, sending her back with a scream.

"Hey, sorry!" he laughed. "Didn't mean to scare you! Guess I should've yelled or something, right?"

Before she could even react, the young man stepped closer, right into a narrow beam of light angling down from an overhead window. He had a friendly, boyish, dirt-streaked face and an equally friendly smile. Mid-twenties, probably—broad, solid shoulders . . . slender build . . . thighs and arms leanly muscled beneath skintight jeans and the pushed-up sleeves of a grimy sweatshirt. His eyes were deep blue, fringed with long dark lashes. His thick brown hair, though dusted with cobwebs, still showed a few golden streaks of fading summer sun. He was slightly out of breath and carrying a large cardboard box, which he immediately wrestled down to the floor.

Lucy gazed at him with open—and hostile—suspicion.

The young man merely grinned. "Is there something I can help you with?"

Lucy's gaze hardened. The stranger seemed oblivious.

"Matt," he said, reaching toward her. "Oh, wait. Sorry." He swiped his hand across the back of his jeans, then offered it again. "Matt. Well . . . *Father* Matt, actually. Well . . . Father *Matthew*, really. But you can call me Matt."

Lucy was dumbfounded. "You're . . . a *priest?*"

"Hmmm . . ." He glanced around in mock concern. "Should I apologize?" And then, as she continued to stare at him, he added, “Hey, it’s okay. I’m out of uniform. And you are—?”

Lucy said nothing. Matt gave a solemn nod.

“Speechless,” he said.

“Lucy,” she finally whispered.

“Nice to meet you, Lucy. But I hope you weren’t planning on confessing anything today, because as you can see, we’re slightly out of service at the moment. Have been, actually, for years.”

Lucy’s eyes narrowed. Was this guy for real? Was he telling the truth? She tried to concentrate on his voice . . . what would that voice sound like, low and deep and whispering?

“Listen, are you okay?” Matt’s smile seemed genuinely concerned. “Would you like to sit down?”

“Where were you just now?” Lucy murmured.

She saw his smile falter, but only for a second. “Sorry?”

“Just now. Where were you?” Her voice was trembling from aftershock; she fought to keep it steady. She watched his glance flicker toward the confessionals . . . the altar . . . the empty pews behind him.

"Just now?" This time he gestured vaguely with one arm. "Going through some closets in back. Sorry, I didn't know you were here—otherwise I'd have been a lot more hospitable."

"You didn't hear me yelling?"

"Yelling?" Matt frowned. Then, as though a thought had just occurred to him, he pulled some headphones from the box and dangled them in front of her. "I've been lost in Mozart. Just pulled these off when I saw you standing here. What were you yelling about?"

"I was . . ." Lucy's mind raced. "I was yelling . . . to see . . . if anyone was here."

Matt's smile widened. "Well, now you know."

He must be telling the truth . . . he wouldn't have had time to run from the confessional and grab that big box from somewhere and come back without me seeing him or hearing him or—

"Is it my face?" Matt asked, deadpan. "Or are you having a religious experience?"

Lucy snapped back to attention. "What?"

"You're staring at me like I have horns growing out of my head or something."

Flustered, Lucy looked away. "Are you alone here?"

"Alone?"

"Is there someone else here with you?"

Matt's eyes made a quick survey of the church. "Not that I know of. Why?"

"Nothing . . . I . . . I just thought I heard something, that's all."

"Now you're making *me* nervous," he teased, though once more his eyes swept the room. "It was probably just me rummaging around back there. There's a major echo in this old place, and—"

"No. No, it . . . it wasn't like that. It was a voice."

"A voice? Well, what did it sound like?"

Lucy shook her head. He *seemed* sincere, but how could she know for sure? And if he really *was* who he said he was, then how could she explain something so totally unbelievable? For an instant she dug deep into her memory, trying to recall the exact sound, the exact tone of that voice in the confessional . . . that voice at the fair. It *could* be Matt's voice disguised . . . just like it could be *anybody's* voice disguised.

Or maybe it wasn't disguised at all . . .

Lucy wrapped her arms about herself, suppressing a shudder. "I must have imagined it. I thought I heard someone."

This time Matt turned and took a good hard look toward the entrance. "Well, I didn't lock the door behind me this morning. So I guess it's possible someone could've sneaked in. Kind of like you did."

This seemed to amuse him, especially when a slow flush crept over Lucy's cheeks. Quickly she stammered out an explanation.

"I was . . . *supposed* to be meeting someone."

"Ah. A clandestine rendezvous. How intriguing."

Flushing hotter, she mumbled, "It's not what you think."

"No? And how do you know what I think?" Matt's eyes sparkled with humor, and he ran one hand back through his hair. "Maybe it was this friend of yours you heard. Maybe he really did show up, but he thought you weren't here."

And maybe I was a total fool for believing what Byron said and for coming here to meet him. "I don't think so."

"Well, maybe it was burglars," Matt said practically. "And when they realized there wasn't anything to steal, they got disappointed and left."

Lucy was ready to change the subject. "What happened to this place, anyway?"

"Don't you know?"

"I'm not from here. I just came a few weeks ago, to live with my aunt."

"I see." Matt leaned back against the wall, crossing his long legs, folding his arms casually across his chest. For a second Lucy thought he was going to ask her some personal questions, but instead he said, "All I know is that a bigger, fancier church was built in the center of town, and that's when this place became . . . shall we say . . . a sort of ecclesiastical warehouse."

"So you must remember when this place was really beautiful."

Matt shook his head. "Actually, no—I'm not from Pine Ridge either. And in *theory*, I'm only supposed to be here temporarily."

"In theory?"

"Well, that's what Monsignor's telling Father

Paul at the moment. That I'm only here till he gets back on his feet."

"Who's Father Paul?"

"The priest at the *real* church," Matt explained. "He's *old*—no, let me rephrase that—he's *ancient*. And very set in his ways. He's been refusing to take on an assistant for years, but I guess you could say he finally got a dose of Divine Intervention."

"How's that?"

Matt chuckled. "He fell down a flight of stairs." Then, at Lucy's look of alarm, "No, no, he's *fine*—but now that he's got a broken leg, it's forced him to slow down and listen to reason."

"And how does he feel about *you* being here?"

Again Matt laughed. "Let's put it this way. Since he's been here for about a hundred years and has a very particular way of doing things, I *obviously* am a complete and total moron. And just trying to wade through his particular way of doing things is probably going to take me the rest of my natural life."

Pausing, he gave Lucy a helpless look

"*If* he doesn't kill me before then. Like right now, I'm supposed to be looking for some statues he *swears* are stored down here in one of the cellars. But I can't seem to find the right doors—*or* the right keys."

He looked so distressed that Lucy couldn't help smiling. But as she caught a sudden movement from the corner of her eye, she gasped and spun toward it.

"Hey, easy," Matt soothed her, "it's just one of the cats."

"Cats?"

"Yeah, there're a bunch of them in here—the cleaning lady's always bringing them in. Just call it environment-friendly rodent control."

As Lucy nodded uncertainly, he frowned and lifted a hand to her forehead.

"You know, Lucy, maybe it's just this bad light, but you sure don't look like you feel very well. Why don't you sit down, and I'll get you some water."

His touch was firm, but gentle. His fingertips skimmed lightly over her skin and carefully brushed a strand of hair from her eyes. With no warning, Lucy felt a strange, slow warmth pulse softly at her temples . . . flow like liquid to the back of her brain . . .

Flowing . . . flowing . . . blood *flowing . . . a dark red pool of blood on . . . on . . . a floor and something—something*—sharp!—cutting!—*pain and blood and anger—*

"You hurt yourself," Lucy said. She stepped back and saw a look of dismay on Matt's face. "You hurt yourself, and it was very painful, and you bled for a long time."

The throbbing in her head was gone now, but her body felt shaky and drained. She watched as Matt frowned at her, as he lowered his hand. As he stared at the long, narrow cut on his palm and cautiously flexed his fingers.

"Well, yeah, but it's okay now," he assured her. "I mean, it happened a few days ago . . . it's not infected or anything, if that's what you're worried about."

Lucy took another step back, her emotions whirling. *He thinks I saw it*, she realized, *only I* didn't *see it, not the way he thinks—not with my eyes, but somewhere inside my head—and not* exactly *what happened—just those flashes again—flashes and feelings and colors and—*

"—broken glass," Matt was saying, as she tried to quiet her mind, focus in, act normally. "From one of those windows . . . it sliced right through me. It hurt like hell."

"I'm . . . I'm sorry." Flustered, Lucy pointed to the front of the church. "I'm feeling better now. I need to go."

But she could tell Matt wasn't convinced, even as she began walking away from him.

"What about your friend?" he asked her. "Is he supposed to pick you up?"

Lucy shook her head.

"Well, how are you getting home?"

"I have a car."

Look," Matt said kindly, "I'd be more than happy to drive you. Someone can come back later for your car."

"No. I'm fine, really. But thanks."

She was almost outside when he stopped her. She heard him call her name, and she turned to see him running after her, waving something in his hand.

"Lucy," he said again, catching up with her at the door. "I think you must've dropped this."

Lucy stared down at the thing he was holding.

And felt her eyes widen in alarm.

"I don't know anything about it," she said quickly. *Too quickly?* Because she could see the way he was looking at her now, that quizzical expression on his face, as though he *knew* she was lying, as though he *knew* and was waiting for her to confess . . .

She backed away, trying to put distance between them. "Sorry. It's not mine."

"Oh, that's too bad." Matt shrugged. "I found it on the floor near the altar. I just assumed it must be yours."

He gazed down at the necklace he was holding.

A single strand of tiny green beads.

"No," Lucy said again breathlessly, "no, it's not mine."

"Well, I guess I'll just leave it, then. Just in case whoever lost it comes back."

"Yeah. Maybe."

She hurried down the walkway, and she didn't once look back.

But if she had, she would have seen him still standing there . . . watching . . .

Watching her . . . even as he slipped the necklace casually into his pocket.

19

Lucy couldn't get into the car fast enough.

She locked the doors and fumbled the key into the ignition, turning it, pumping the accelerator, but the engine only coughed uselessly.

"Damn!"

Leaning forward, she rested her head on the steering wheel and alternately struggled to catch her breath and not give in to tears.

So Byron *had* been at the church. He *must* have been; otherwise, how would the necklace have ended up there? Yet she couldn't imagine him leaving it behind. Even from her brief encounters with Byron, it was obvious the necklace was important to him, that it tied in somehow to that girl in the cemetery. And Lucy had definitely experienced something when she'd handled it yesterday—and Byron had definitely known.

What if something's happened to him?

A million thoughts ran through her mind. Could he have left it as a message to her? A warning? Or could it even have been some sort of trap? But a trap for what?

Like so many other things these last few days, it didn't make any sense to her, didn't fit into any concept of logic or reality.

Lucy groaned and lifted her head. As she reached out again for the key, she suddenly saw a movement in the rearview mirror. With a shocked cry, she spun around just as Byron clamped a hand down on her shoulder.

"Ssh . . . it's just me," he said tightly. "Look, I really need your help."

Furiously, Lucy flung his hand away, then fixed him with a glare.

"What the *hell* do you think you're doing!" she shouted. "You nearly gave me a heart attack!"

"Then lock your doors next time." He frowned back at her. "Are you listening to me? The necklace is gone."

"*What?*"

Byron's jaw stiffened. "It was gone when I got home last night."

"After the Festival?"

At Byron's nod, Lucy gave him a puzzled look. "But I just saw it."

"What do you mean you just saw it?"

"In there. Matt has it."

"Who?"

"Matt . . . uh . . . Father Matt," Lucy stammered.

"Who's that?"

"The priest. The new priest at the church."

"*What* new priest?"

Lucy bristled. "How should I know? Father Paul's new assistant—he's here helping out because Father Paul broke his leg."

"So that's who was in there," Byron muttered. "Well, did you get it from him?"

"No, I didn't get it from him. It's not my necklace. Why would I get it from him?"

Facing forward again, she redirected her glare to his reflection. She saw him rub a hand across his forehead; she saw the visible strain upon his face.

"Are you sure it was the same necklace?" He sounded almost accusing. "That just doesn't make sense."

"He said he found it on the floor."

"But that's impossible, I didn't even *have* it when I was in the church."

Lucy couldn't keep the sarcasm from her voice. "And speaking of that—why exactly *weren't* you in there? If you were supposed to be *meeting* me?"

"Because I heard someone come in. Because I didn't know who it was, and I wasn't sure it was safe."

"Well, you were right. It *wasn't* safe. But, hey, it wasn't *you* being scared to death, so why were you even worried about it?"

"What do you mean?" His glance was sharp. "What happened?"

"I don't *know* what happened!" Lucy could hear herself getting louder, could hear the edge of hysteria in her voice, but couldn't seem to stop herself. "I don't know why I even *came* here today! I don't know why I'm even *speaking* to you! Get out of my car!"

"Drive," he said.

"*What?*"

"Just drive. I'll tell you where."

"No, I'll tell *you* where! *No*where! I'm not moving one inch till you get out of this car."

"I'm not getting out until we talk." She felt his hand on her shoulder again. His voice softened, tired. "Please. You have to listen to me. You're the only one I can talk to."

Lucy lowered her head. She chewed anxiously on her thumbnail, then shot him another look in the mirror.

"I can't go. The car won't start."

Byron stared at her a long moment. Then a faint smile played at the corners of his mouth.

"You flooded the engine, that's all. Try it again."

This time when she tried to start it, the car sprang to life. Grumbling under her breath, Lucy headed off down the street.

"So what happened in the church?" Byron asked again. He'd scooted closer to her now, leaning in between the bucket seats, and Lucy could feel the faint pressure of his arm against hers.

"If I tell you," she answered wryly, "you won't believe me."

"I doubt that. Turn here."

"Where are we going?"

"Someplace private."

Lucy cast him a sidelong glance. "I can't believe I'm doing this. Why should I even trust you?"

"Because you have to trust somebody. Because I'm guessing your life's suddenly been turned upside down."

Lucy tried to keep her expression blank, tried to ignore her shiver of apprehension. "I'm not sure that's an answer."

"Okay. Then for the same reason I have to trust you," Byron replied flatly. "We're the only ones who know about the cemetery. The only ones who know that something happened."

Lucy gave a terse nod. "So you're telling me that what I saw *wasn't* the fraternity prank I heard about. That what I saw was—"

"Real. Yes."

"So that girl . . ."

"Was murdered."

"But . . . by *who*?"

"That's why we have to get the necklace back. So you can tell us."

"So *I* can tell us? Tell us *what*?"

"Who killed her."

"Oh, now, wait a minute—"

"Hey, watch the road," Byron warned, as the car veered sharply into the wrong lane. "I'll tell you everything when we get to where we're going. Even the stuff you won't want to hear."

Lucy gripped harder on the steering wheel. "And how do I know *you* didn't kill her?"

She hadn't known she was going to say it; the words burst out before she could stop them. She felt his steady gaze upon her, and her heartbeat quickened in her chest.

"Just drive," he said tersely.

Yet with a start, Lucy realized how very sad he sounded.

Following his directions, she drove several miles outside of town, then turned off onto an isolated road that followed the curve of the lake. After another half hour, they finally pulled up to a cabin nestled among tall green pines, with a breathtaking view of the water.

"This is so beautiful," Lucy murmured. "Is it yours?"

"No. Somebody's summer home."

"Somebody's?"

"It's locked up now for the winter, but I have the key."

"And how did you manage that?"

Byron turned and glanced out the back windshield. With a twinge of uneasiness, Lucy wondered if he was afraid they'd been followed.

"Just park the car," he told her. "Over there behind those trees."

It wasn't until they were inside—door securely locked and bolted—that Byron seemed to relax a little. The cabin was very cold, and as Lucy stood rubbing her hands together, Byron went into the adjoining room, returned with a quilt, then motioned her into a rocking chair beside the fireplace.

Lucy sat. "Will you please just tell me what's going on?"

"Do you promise to believe me?"

"Probably not."

She thought a reluctant smile might have tugged at his mouth. He tossed her the quilt, then waited while she snuggled beneath it.

This is insane, Lucy thought. *This is completely insane. With everything else that's happened to me, I can't believe I'm sitting here in a cabin in the woods with some stranger who's asking me to trust him. If he murders me right now in this rocking chair, then I guess I deserve it.*

As Byron leaned down over her, her breath caught in her throat. His stare held her for an endless moment and then he slowly straightened.

"You still don't trust me. I see it in your eyes."

Lucy didn't miss a beat. "I don't believe you can see anything in my eyes. When I first saw you in the cemetery, you knew my mother had died, that I was alone. But you go to school with Angela—anyone could have known that."

"You're right. Anyone could've known, because Angela told everyone you were coming. Except . . ."

"Except what?"

Byron stepped closer. "Except I didn't know what you looked like. I'd never seen any pictures of you . . . never heard any descriptions. And I didn't know when you came to the cemetery that morning, that you were Angela's cousin."

Again that tiny shiver of apprehension; again Lucy tried to ignore it. "So . . . what are you trying to prove? That you have some sort of supernatural power? That you can know things about people just by staring at them?"

She wanted to laugh, to make light of it, but she suddenly realized that Byron had taken her hand, her right hand, that he was lifting it toward him and placing it over his heart.

"What do you feel?" he murmured.

And without warning, a whole range of emotions surged through her—*warmth . . . gentleness . . . fear . . . pain . . . sorrow*—all in a split-second rush that made her numb, that made her dizzy—*anger . . . loss . . . love*—

With a cry, Lucy jerked her hand from his grasp and cradled it against her chest, staring at him with wide, shocked eyes.

"You've been given a gift," Byron said solemnly. "And your life will never be the same."

20

"Do you think this is easy for me either? Having to say all these things to you—somebody I just met? And knowing how crazy it all sounds? And knowing—*understanding*, even—that the last thing in the world *you* want to do is *believe* me?"

Byron stopped . . . shook his head. There was bitterness in his tone.

"And why *would* you believe me? I mean, why would anyone believe *any* of this?"

Lucy couldn't do anything but stare. She watched as he crossed to the other side of the room, as he began pacing, slowly, back and forth between the fireplace and the door.

"That night at the cemetery," Byron's voice was low. "Try to think, Lucy. Try to remember."

But still Lucy sat there, paralyzed.

"Remember when I told you that something had been *passed on*?" Byron asked her.

At last she managed a nod.

"This gift you have . . . I think it was passed on to you from the girl who died. I suspected it . . . but I wasn't really positive till you picked up the necklace in class yesterday."

As if from a distance, Lucy heard herself ask, "I don't understand. Not about any gift . . . not about the necklace—"

"It was *her* necklace. She never took it off. So I know the only possible reason she did was to leave a clue behind. To try and tell me who killed her. To tell *you* who killed her."

"No. No . . . wait a minute. This is too much, this is—"

"True." Byron paused and shot her a level glance. "It's *true*, and no matter how much you want to forget about it, you *can't*. You have a responsibility now. You have—"

"A responsibility to who?" Lucy's voice went shrill with anger. "I don't have any responsibility to *anybody*—not to *you*—not to—"

"She had powers," Byron insisted. "She had powers nobody understood—and most people didn't believe in. And she used them for good, and she used them to help others when she could. But at the same time, she suffered for them her whole life. And now—now she's given them to you."

Lucy's lips parted soundlessly. For a second, Byron seemed to recede into some black void, then reappear again at the side of her chair.

"She could sense things," he said urgently. "See things that had already happened—sometimes even things that *hadn't* happened yet. By touching. Do you understand?"

Lucy shook her head. She wished he would stop talking, would leave, would just go away, but he knelt on the floor in front of her, where she couldn't ignore him.

"It didn't happen every single time—that's not the way it worked. But when it *did* happen, it was very powerful. She could never anticipate when the visions might come—sometimes they came from a person, sometimes from an object, just some little thing you'd never even think about."

Again Lucy shook her head. "So these visions she'd have . . . what were they, exactly?"

He stared at a spot beyond her, deep in thought, choosing his words carefully. "When she tried to describe it to me, she always said there weren't complete pictures. More like . . . like quick images or feelings. Sometimes colors or smells or sounds. She said it was like all her five senses had been peeled open, and raw, and they just kept absorbing all these impulses, with nothing to protect them."

His focus shifted back to her. Lucy saw his face through a fine mist and realized that tears had filled her eyes.

"Oh my God," she whispered. "Yes . . . it *is* like that . . ."

"You mean . . . like when you held the necklace?"

Without answering, she began to rock . . . a slow, gentle rhythm of self-comfort.

"Why'd you go there that night?" Byron asked quietly.

Lucy shut her eyes . . . tried to will the pain away.

"Please tell me, Lucy."

And so she did . . . recounting every moment from the time she'd left the house till Angela picked her up and took her back to Irene's. She told him everything, still feeling as though this were all some strange, distorted nightmare . . . still wishing she'd wake up, safe and warm in her mother's home. Still wondering why she was taking a chance with this mysterious young man she didn't know . . . why she was here trusting him and believing him, and in some painful way, feeling so grateful for his company . . .

And when she'd finally told her story, she realized that he'd taken her hand . . . spread her fingers wide apart . . . was gazing down at the tiny crescent scar upon her palm.

"She had a scar just like this," he said, not meeting Lucy's eyes. "In the same spot . . . on the same hand."

"It hurt," Lucy acknowledged numbly. "When she grabbed me . . . the pain I felt was unbearable—not like anything I'd ever felt before."

Nodding slightly, Byron placed her hand on the arm of the rocking chair. "I was supposed to meet her that night. She'd been away, and I hadn't seen her in nearly a year. Then I got this message from her—just out of the blue. Something important, she said. She told me to come alone, she'd be waiting at the old church. I could tell from her note that she was really scared. Only . . . she never showed up."

"So . . . I just happened to be walking past there at the same time?"

"I think the person following you that night was me."

Byron rocked back on his heels, his expression thoughtful. "I'd just gotten to the church when I saw you running away. And it was storming so bad, I couldn't really see anything. For a minute I thought it might be her, so I went after you—but then you turned under the streetlight. And when I realized it wasn't her, I went back."

"And that's when I ran into the cemetery. Because I thought you were stalking me."

"I should have known it was something bad." Byron's eyes were as hard as his voice. "When she didn't show up on time, I should have left right away—I should have looked for her then. But I just kept thinking maybe it was the storm, she was having trouble getting there, but that she'd *be* there, just five more minutes, she'd *be* there . . ."

He paused. Drew a sharp breath.

"I don't think I wanted to believe it. Even when I got in my van and started driving around, looking for her. I didn't want to believe something had happened to her. And that's when I saw you again."

"Me?"

"You were coming out of the cemetery, and you ran across the street to use the phone. And you looked terrified."

Lucy's heart gave a sickening lurch. How easily those feelings of terror returned, just from talking, just from remembering. She watched as Byron stood up and walked to the window. He propped his hands upon the sill and leaned forward, his shoulders stiff with tension.

"I knew," he mumbled. "I mean, there you were, scared and muddy and soaking wet—and suddenly I just *knew*. I knew it had something to do with her."

For several long moments there was quiet between them. Only the patient creak of the rocking chair upon the wooden floor. The muted songs of birds outside the windows. Until at last Byron spoke again.

"I tried to get over to you . . . to see if you needed help. But by the time I got the van turned around, you were gone. So I went back to the cemetery. And I looked for her." Byron's head lowered. "I never found her."

Lucy stopped rocking. She stared at his back with a puzzled frown. "But when I saw you the next morning—the things you said—how could you have known those things if you never found her? If you weren't actually there?"

"Because she told me."

"She . . ." Lucy sat straight in her chair. The quilt slid down to her waist, and she impatiently pushed it aside. "What do you mean, she told you—what are you saying?"

"In a dream that night. She told me in a dream."

He turned around to face her. As Lucy held his steady gaze, she slowly shook her head.

"You know something, Byron . . . you're asking me to believe a *lot*."

"Haven't you ever had a dream so real, you knew it was *more* than a dream?"

"Yes, but . . ." Lucy's voice trailed off. Until that moment she'd almost forgotten her *own* dream of two nights ago . . . her mother at the window, sounding so sad . . .

"But what?" Byron persisted.

"I did have one like that," Lucy murmured. "That night, after I got home from the cemetery. My mother came back to me. It was like . . . like she was trying to warn me about something."

"What'd she say?"

Lucy's voice faltered. "She said . . . that I was going to a place where . . . where she couldn't help me."

Byron gave an almost imperceptible nod. His eyes shone even darker.

"So your mother shows up with a warning. On the very night a dying girl touches you and leaves this scar on your hand. Doesn't that seem a little more than coincidence?"

"Oh God . . ."

"When I finally went to sleep that night," Byron said tightly, "I dreamed she was in a grave. I saw the storm. I saw her covered in blood . . . and I saw her reaching out."

"But . . . you didn't see who killed her?"

"No. She was talking to me . . . she wanted me to know that she was gone. And that she hadn't been alone when she died. She told me I should go to the cemetery the next morning and wait for someone. And then she said, 'Help her . . . now *you* must help the one who helped *me*.'"

Lucy didn't know how to respond. As Byron fell silent, his sorrow seemed to fill the room, yet at the same time she sensed his own defenses struggling to pull it back.

"So . . . what you're saying," she stammered, "is that *I* have these . . . these powers now. And *I'm* going to start having visions . . . and . . . and *feeling* things I don't want to feel just because I *touch* something?"

But when Byron didn't answer, Lucy's tone grew almost pleading. "Are you absolutely sure? Are you positive it was her? I mean . . . maybe she didn't even show up that night. Maybe she was never here in town. Maybe it was just some girl you didn't know, who just happened to be in the wrong place at the wrong time—"

"Lucy, stop," he said tightly.

"But it could have been, right? I mean, it *could* have been a mistake and maybe she's still alive somewhere, maybe she—"

"She's not alive."

"Then where's her body? Where's the grave? If she's really dead, you would have *found* her—you would have found *something*—"

"Lucy, stop!" His voice struck out at her, cold and final. "There are just some things you *know*, because every part of you feels it, because you have a bond with somebody that's special and unique. And she and I had that kind of bond. So . . . no. *No.* It wasn't a mistake."

He raked a hand back through his hair. His face twisted in pain.

"She's dead, Lucy. She's dead."

Lucy's heart ached at the sight of him. "You really loved her, didn't you?" she whispered.

A muscle clenched in his jaw. He turned stiffly back to the window. "Yes."

"So . . . she was your girlfriend?"

"No. Katherine was my sister."

21

"Your sister?" Lucy echoed. "The one who—"

She broke off, flustered, as he shot her a cold glance over his shoulder.

"Was crazy?" he finished sarcastically.

"I was going to say . . . the one who went away."

"Well, you *have* been in Pine Ridge awhile. Time enough to have heard all the gruesome stories about my family, I'm sure."

"I'm sorry." Lucy's cheeks reddened. "I haven't heard that much."

"It doesn't matter. Actually, it's not so bad, being part of the local folklore. People tend to leave you alone."

"Is that what you want? To be left alone?"

He leaned back against the wall, folding his arms across his chest, fixing her with another intense stare. "I guess that depends on who it is."

Lucy dropped her eyes. She heard him move to the fireplace and sit down upon the hearth.

"Are you sure you want to hear the rest of it?" he asked pointedly.

"Can it get any worse?" She gave him a wan smile, and he almost—but not quite—returned it.

"These . . . powers . . . forces . . . psychic abilities . . . whatever you want to call them," he began tentatively, "they run in our family. At least that's what my grandmother says. When I was little, I thought she was magic. Sometimes she could tell us things before they actually happened."

"What kinds of things?"

"Well . . . like when a certain neighbor was going to knock on our door—and then they would. Or who'd be on the other end of the phone before she even picked it up. Just simple things like that. She could tell you where to find things you'd lost . . . or that a storm was coming when there wasn't a cloud in the sky. And I never thought it was strange. It was normal to me."

Intrigued, Lucy leaned forward. "So *all* of you had psychic talents?"

"It was always so obvious with Katherine. From the time we were little, she was already having visions and seeing things nobody else could see. It was just a part of who she was. But mine was different. I was older the first time it happened. Probably around ten or so. And a woman—someone I'd never met before—had come to see my grandmother, and I remember she was so sad."

He hesitated, as though reluctant to venture too far into the past.

"I remember she was sitting at our kitchen table, waiting for Gran to come downstairs. And I sat down across from her, and suddenly she just *looked* at me. Looked me full in the face, and her eyes were so big and so desperately unhappy."

Byron's voice lowered. A poignant blend of sorrow and awe.

"I stared right back at her. Right back into her eyes. Deep, deep into that terrible sadness. And I said, 'I'm sorry about your little girl; I'm sorry she drowned.' And I remember she tried to smile at me, but she *couldn't* smile—all she could do was cry—and I felt so bad for her."

Again he paused. Then he met Lucy's gaze with a level one of his own.

"There was no way I could have known about her *or* her daughter; she didn't even live around there. Gran told me later that I'd had a glimpse of her soul."

"Eyes," Lucy murmured. "Eyes are supposed to be windows to the soul."

"Some people say so," he agreed. "I couldn't explain it then, and I don't even try anymore. But if that's true—about windows to the soul—then the daughter she'd lost was the most important feeling in her soul that day. And I had a glimpse of it."

"Is it like"—Lucy struggled for words—"looking beyond pain? Or seeing something that's even deeper than grief?"

His shoulders moved in a shrug. "It's nothing like Katherine could do—nothing that clear or sharp. No smells or sounds or things like that. It's like . . . looking through a veil. There's fog . . . mist . . . no definite features or details. Yet somehow I'm able to pull something out of it."

"Like . . . through a curtain . . . or a screen?"

"Sort of, yeah. Lucy? What is it?"

But as the memory of the confessional flashed through her mind, Lucy hurriedly shook her head. *Not now. Not yet. This isn't the right time . . .*

"Nothing," she assured him. "Tell me more about Katherine. About this gift of hers."

"A gift sometimes. But also a curse."

The edge was back in his voice, and Lucy felt a prickle of apprehension as he continued with the explanation.

"As she got older, she didn't want to use it anymore, because it scared her too much. She'd get nervous and embarrassed because she never knew when the visions would hit her—how strong they'd be, or how frightening—and most people didn't understand. Most people didn't even *try* to. All they knew was that she was different, and that sometimes she acted strange. And so some people laughed at her, and some made fun of her. And others were just plain scared."

Byron pressed both hands to his forehead . . . gently massaged his temples.

"But of course, she *couldn't* just not use it

anymore—that was impossible. It's not like a switch she could just turn on and off whenever she wanted. It was *part* of her; part of who she was. So it got to where she wouldn't even leave the house. Gran and I were the only ones she trusted; home was the only place she felt safe."

Lucy frowned, taking everything in. "But if that's true," she asked carefully, "then why did she end up leaving?"

She saw him tense . . . saw the briefest flicker of indecision over his face. She sat up straighter in her chair as her voice grew suspicious.

"There's something else," she accused him. "Something you're not telling me."

Byron stood up from the hearth. He pulled her from the rocking chair, then turned and strode purposefully to the door.

"Come with me," he said. "And I'll tell you the rest of the story."

22

It was a relief to get out.

Despite the coziness of the cabin, Lucy was beginning to feel claustrophobic. As if every new revelation of Byron's cast a dark, uneasy shadow over her heart and her mind.

The crisp, cold air felt wonderful. As they walked together toward the lake, the pungent fragrance of pines swirled through her head, almost making her forget, almost sweeping the doubts and fears away.

"It's so beautiful out here," Lucy murmured. She followed him to the shore, to the wooden dock stretching out over the water. A boat was tied at the end, bobbing peacefully upon the barely rippled surface, and with one smooth movement, Byron helped her down into the bow and slipped the rope free.

Here I go again, Lucy thought ruefully, watching the dock glide farther and farther from view—*getting myself into another dangerous situation*. And yet, out here in this pristine wilderness, surrounded by such stillness, watching Byron rhythmically work the oars, she felt a sense of peace that she hadn't felt for days.

"Don't ruin it," she said suddenly, and felt her cheeks flush as Byron gave her a curious look.

"What?"

"The mood. The minute."

He cocked his head . . . lifted an eyebrow. A playful wind tugged at his hair, streaming it back from his face. "I'll just keep rowing, then."

"So much has happened," she tried to explain, her words tumbling out in a rush. "*Too* much—too much to comprehend and understand and try to believe. And from what you're telling me—and maybe from what you're *going* to be telling me—things might be getting worse."

He didn't answer, but still, she could see the seriousness in his eyes.

"So just give me this one minute, okay? To breathe? And be away from everything that's bad? And see the world in a way that makes some sense to me."

Lucy's voice caught. She turned from him abruptly and fixed her gaze on the distant shoreline . . . on the woods and the hills and the endless blue sky above. For a long time there was only the sound of the oars dipping water . . . the music of the birds . . . the soft sigh of pine-rich breezes. Lucy shut her eyes and pretended wishes came true, and she wished this could last forever.

But wishes never come true. At least not mine. At least not the good ones.

As she felt the boat jar, her eyes came open. A second later the dinghy was scraping up onto a narrow stretch of beach, and Byron was out of the boat, anchoring it securely between a small shelter of trees.

"Grab those blankets under your seat," he said, reaching for her hand. "We'll go this way—I think you'll like the scenery."

"What is this? Some kind of island?"

"No, just another side of the lake. We could have driven—there's a road off that way about half a mile—but I think the boat ride's much nicer."

"How do you know about these places?" Lucy asked, as he pulled her up a steep rise and on to a stretch of level ground.

"I grew up here, remember? And I take care of a lot of these cabins off-season. And in the summer I do some maintenance work."

"What kind of maintenance work?"

"Handyman stuff, mostly."

"So that's how you had that key."

"I have all the keys."

Taking the blankets, he led her along the beach for another five minutes, then suddenly veered off again toward the shore. After maneuvering several more rocky slopes, Lucy found herself in a small, wooded cove with a breathtaking view of the lake.

"You're right, it is beautiful," she said appreciatively, gazing out across the shimmering expanse of water.

"And private." Byron shook out a blanket and spread it over the ground. "Sit down . . . wrap this other one around you. It's pretty cold out here."

Lucy did so. She watched as he sat beside her, his eyes narrowed intently on the opposite horizon. She hugged her legs to her chest and rested her chin on her knees.

"Do you believe in evil?" Byron asked.

Lucy turned to him in surprise. Somehow, surrounded by all this peaceful beauty, his question seemed almost laughable . . . and far more than ominous.

"Evil?"

"An evil that can transcend time and space? An evil so obsessive that you can't escape it, no matter how hard you try?"

Her brow creased in a frown. She drew back from him and stared harder. "You're really serious."

"You told me you thought you were being stalked the other night, when you ran from the church. Do you remember how you felt?"

"Of course I remember. I was terrified."

"Well, that's how Katherine felt all the time . . . like she was being stalked by someone. Except she couldn't outrun him. And she couldn't hide. Because he was in her visions and in her dreams."

"Byron—*what* are you talking about?"

But he wouldn't look at her, just kept staring

out across the water, at the play of light and shadow off the woods across the lake.

"They started about three years ago," he said gravely. "When she was sixteen. And they weren't like the other visions she'd had her whole life. These were like the worst kind of nightmares. Nightmares she couldn't wake up from. Nightmares she couldn't escape. Things more horrible than you could ever imagine."

With an unconscious gesture, Lucy pulled the blanket closer around her. The breeze off the beach had nothing to do with the sudden chill in her veins.

"She said it was like looking at the world through the essence of evil . . . as though *she* were inside his head, thinking out through his thoughts and seeing things through his eyes."

"Sort of"—Lucy was struggling to understand— "like a camera taking pictures?"

"Yes, capturing every gory detail as it happens."

Despite the blanket, Lucy felt even colder. "Did she tell you what these things were?"

"Never. Only that they were inhuman. So violent and hideous, she couldn't bear them anymore. Never knowing when they'd come . . . or how long they'd last. And worst of all, never being able to stop them. Just having to stand by and watch, over and over again."

"So where were these visions coming from?"

"From the mind of a monster. From someone sick and twisted, who enjoyed causing pain and watching his victims suffer."

"My God . . . so you think . . . you think this person was *real*?"

Byron's expression turned grim. "Katherine did. And she was convinced he'd keep right on killing and brutalizing people, and that he'd never get caught. Because *she* was the only one who knew about him."

"And she didn't have any idea who he was?"

"None. She never saw his face. Because she was always seeing things from *his* perspective."

Lucy could feel goose bumps along her arms. Could feel a cold, stealthy uneasiness gnawing at the back of her mind. Determinedly she tried to force it away, tried to concentrate on what Byron was saying.

"—a connection," he continued. "But why? We never knew."

"You mean, a connection between their minds? Between their thoughts? Like the bond *you* had with Katherine?"

Byron's face went rigid. "How can you even compare the two? That's—"

"No, I'm sorry, that's not what I meant," she said quickly. "I'm just trying to understand this. So Katherine could see these . . . these *atrocities* this guy was committing. *As* he was committing them?"

"Yes. *Forced* to watch him. But *helpless* to stop him."

"Then . . . was it someone she knew?"

"Impossible."

"Someone she met just one time, maybe? Someone with psychic abilities as exceptional as hers, who was somehow able to lock into her mind?"

"You mean . . . sort of like a psychic parasite?"

"Exactly."

"She hardly left the house. And this is a small community—people tend to know each other around here. I can't think of anybody who fits into an evil mode like this one. And believe me . . . I've tried."

"But you said she sensed things—*saw* things—by touching. So maybe she bumped into him in a crowd . . . I mean, he could have just been passing through town, or visiting somebody here. Maybe he dropped something . . . or . . . or accidentally left something of his behind. And Katherine just happened to pick it up."

Byron sounded weary. "I've thought of that, too. And I guess it *is* possible . . . except I think she'd only have felt a connection to it when it was in her hands. Just when she touched it. *Not* on and on for three years."

"But maybe she kept it. Maybe she found something, and took it home with her and didn't realize."

"She'd have realized, Lucy, believe me."

Lucy went silent. She watched as he leaned back on the ground, propping himself on his elbows. He stared far out at the opposite bank, and his gaze narrowed, hard as steel.

"Katherine was such a gentle person. Probably the only truly good person I've ever known in my life. And that's what made it so much worse. The way she suffered . . . her fear and her pain . . . There were times she really thought she was losing her mind. And sometimes I think . . ." His voice faltered . . . softened. "I think maybe . . . finally . . . in a way . . ."

A shadow seemed to cross his face. After a moment of uncertain silence, Lucy gently touched his shoulder.

"Wasn't there anyone she could talk to? Someone who could help her?"

"And who would that have been? How do you explain something like that—especially in a town like this? Hell, everybody here *already* thought she was crazy."

"But maybe someone who has experience in—"

"Ssh!" Jerking upright, Byron grabbed her shoulder. "Did you hear something?"

Lucy's heart took a dive to her stomach. As she slowly followed the direction of his gaze, she listened hard through the quiet.

Wind sighing through trees . . . water lapping gently at the shore . . . her own pulse pounding in her ears . . .

"What?" she mouthed silently. "What is it?"

But she could feel his grip relaxing now . . . his body easing back down beside her. His hand slid away from her arm, though his expression remained wary.

"What?" she asked aloud, but Byron only frowned and turned his attention back to the view.

"Nothing. Just jumpy, I guess."

Lucy glanced nervously over her shoulder. Strange . . . she hadn't really heard anything, yet she could feel a tiny sliver of dread at the back of her neck.

"It's okay," Byron reassured her again. "This is one of my secret places . . . and nobody's around here this time of year anyway."

Lucy wasn't entirely convinced. She picked up a broken twig and nervously began scratching circles in the dirt.

"What about your grandmother?" she asked then. "Does she know about Katherine?"

His mouth twisted in a rueful smile. "There's not much Gran doesn't know. But I haven't told her, if that's what you mean."

"So . . . do you think *she* believes Katherine's dead?"

Byron fixed her with a calm stare. "When Katherine left home a year ago—that was before

Gran had her stroke—Gran told me I'd never see Katherine alive again. I didn't want to believe that, of course. I should have known better. Maybe if I'd tried harder to stop Katherine from going . . . or maybe if I'd gone with her, maybe she'd still be alive now. That's why you have to listen to me—maybe we can stop it this time—before you get hurt—"

"Before *I* get hurt?" Lucy shrank back in dismay. "What do you mean—"

"Because maybe he hasn't realized it yet—"

"Byron—"

"—hasn't realized yet who you are—"

"Stop it! You're scaring me!"

"You *should* be scared, Lucy—you *need* to be scared! It might be the only thing that keeps you alive if—"

He broke off abruptly, his body tensing, his glance shooting once more toward the trees. As Lucy followed the direction of his focus, she felt that fine prickle of fear again, though now it was creeping down the length of her arms.

Very slowly Byron got to his feet. As Lucy started to follow, he shook his head at her and held a finger to his lips.

"No," he whispered. "Wait here."

"Where are you going?" Thoroughly alarmed now, Lucy watched him disappear into the woods. She stood there, heart pounding, listening to the faint rustle of branches as Byron moved away from her. But even that sound faded within minutes.

All that remained was silence.

Dangerous silence.

Should she call his name? Ignore what he'd told her and go after him? Lucy didn't know what to do. With the lake on one side and the woods on all others, this spot that had seemed so idyllic just five minutes before, now seemed more like a . . .

Trap.

That's it. I'm going.

Lucy started toward the trees, toward the exact spot where Byron had gone in. Surely he couldn't be that far ahead of her—it should be easy to catch up. But what if she got lost? She'd be of no use to him then, and someone had to be able to go for help.

She wished she had a weapon. Quickly her eyes scanned the shore, coming to rest on a large branch dangling over the water. With some effort, she managed to wrestle it loose; she could use it as a club if she had to.

"*Lucy!*"

Lucy froze. She hadn't imagined it, had she? That voice calling through the trees . . .

"Byron?" she yelled back.

It had sounded so faint, that call—distant and muffled. *Oh God, maybe he really* is *hurt.* Why had he just gone off like that, anyway—what a stupid thing to do!

Lucy squinted off through the shifting shadows of the forest. Cupping her hands around her mouth, she shouted as loud as she could. "By-ron!"

No answer.

I didn't *imagine it—I'm* sure *I didn't imagine it!*

Yet at the same time the hairs lifted at the back of her neck, and her nerves went taut as wires. *Just like I didn't imagine that voice in the confessional, that voice behind the tent at the fair . . .*

She wished now that she'd told Byron about that voice—*why* hadn't she told Byron about it?

"*Byron!*" she called frantically. "Byron, where *are* you?"

The wind blew a long cold breeze in off the lake.

It wrapped around her like a damp caress.

"Lucy!" the voice seemed to echo, ghostly through the hills. "Please, Lucy! I need you!"

"Oh, God . . . oh God . . ." She knew then that something *must* have happened to him—something bad—something terrible—and it was all she could do to hold her panic in check.

"I'm coming!" Lucy shouted.

And ran headlong into the woods.

23

"Byron! Where are you?"

But she hadn't heard him call in several minutes now, and she knew she'd be hopelessly lost if she went much farther.

Frightened and frustrated, Lucy stopped and yelled one more time. "Byron! *Please!* Answer me!"

Even the breeze seemed to have stopped. Even the trees seemed to hold their breath around her.

Maybe he'd been injured so badly that he'd lost consciousness by now. Mauled by some animal. Lying broken at the bottom of some ravine. Slowly and steadily bleeding to death. *Oh God, what should I do?* If she ended up lost in these dark woods, it wouldn't do *either* of them any good.

Instinctively, Lucy turned and raced back to the beach. Had there been a radio in the boat? A cell phone? She didn't remember seeing any, but she hadn't been paying much attention. As she broke through the trees, she suddenly halted in her tracks and stared in shock at the lake.

A small boat was floating some distance from the shore.

An empty boat.

Our boat?

"*No!*"

Lucy couldn't believe it. A thousand menacing scenarios rushed through her head, muddling into a numbing darkness. Fearfully she spun around and peered off into the forest.

"*Byron!*"

Her shout echoed back to her, mocking.

She had to think . . . think what to do. Try to find help—but where? She didn't have a clue where to go—and what if Bryon roused again and called for her? Still, he was familiar with this place . . . perhaps even now he was on his way to safety . . .

The road!

Lucy suddenly remembered—hadn't Byron mentioned a road when they'd first gotten out of the boat? A road about half a mile from here?

Praying she could find her way back to the cove, Lucy tried to retrace the route they'd taken earlier. She'd noticed a pathway, a narrow trail leading back from the beach and angling off through the woods. As she finally reached the place where they'd originally docked, Lucy could see the path clearly, and she took it without hesitation.

The trail wound mostly uphill, and though she'd been chilly when she first started out she soon grew sweaty and out of breath. She was thankful she'd worn her sneakers. More than once she was forced to scale fallen logs and sharp boulders that blocked the rugged terrain.

She wasn't sure when she began to be aware of the quiet. It seemed to slip up on her gradually, like shadows stalking through underbrush. As she stopped to listen, Lucy realized that the birds had stopped singing, that there wasn't a breath of wind.

The forest filled with an eerie silence.

Just like it felt back there when I was looking for Byron . . .

Her heart fluttered beneath her jacket. She forced herself to keep walking, to keep her thoughts carefully focused on the emergency at hand. Find help. Find Byron. She couldn't let herself think of anything beyond that. She just hoped he wasn't hurt—

"*Maybe we can stop it this time—before you get hurt—*"

Lucy's eyes widened as his words sprang unexpectedly into her mind. *No. No. I won't think about that; I refuse to think about that . . .*

"*Because maybe he hasn't realized it yet—hasn't realized yet who you are—*"

And Byron had started to tell her something, something important, had been trying to warn her about something, when the sound had come, when he'd looked so startled and so wary, when he'd gone into the woods and never come out again . . .

"*You* should *be scared, Lucy—you* need *to be scared! It might be the only thing that keeps you alive if—*"

Lucy broke into a run.

And the silence was so loud, so dangerous, threatening her from every side, silence like shadows, silence like stalkers . . .

No—no—it's just my imagination—

Silence like evil . . .

No!

Silence like death—

Her feet slid off into nothingness; her body hurtled down through an endless black void . . .

She didn't even have time to scream.

Just fell farther and farther . . . down and down . . . into the silence . . .

And finally lay still.

24

She was so beautiful.

Beautiful in this brief spell of sleep . . . lost in her dreamless drifting . . .

Is this what peace looks like? he wondered.

The way *she'd* looked that night at her window, and the way she'd looked at the Festival . . . her face tilted, smiling, bathed in the glow of the lights, just so . . .

And now . . . as she lay here on her back, unconscious from falling, sprawled before him in innocent slumber . . .

He could do anything he wanted to her at this very moment, anything he pleased, for she'd be helpless and completely unaware . . .

But time enough for that later.

Right now all he wanted to do was look at her.

At her hair spread around her head like a halo, her lashes soft against her cheeks. Her fingers curled in upon her palms, like flower petals unopened, and her arms wide in an empty embrace, half buried beneath the leaves that had cushioned her fall.

She was still wearing red.

He loved her even more when she wore red.

It seared into his soul, this brand-new image, like the pink of that very first night . . . like the blue of the Festival . . . and oh, how he'd loved the deep bloodred of her panic and terror at the church just this morning . . .

He'd carried those sights of her, those smells of her, deep in his heart through every single hour since then.

Like a seductive dream, both sleeping and waking.

It was sheer luck that he'd tasted her, as well . . .

He'd picked up the apple she'd dropped at the fair, and she'd never suspected, never stopped to look back, never even realized he was near. And ah, how it tasted just the way he'd imagined . . . the blood from her lip still fresh on the fruit . . . so luscious, so sweet, with its red candy coating.

He'd savored the juice of it inside his mouth, and then he'd lured her to a dark, hidden place.

She'd caught his scent, and she'd come to him . . .

He *loved* how she loved the scent of him.

The way he *always* smelled after he killed.

For blood, as he'd come to learn through the years, was a very personal thing.

It mingled with one's own essence . . . and tempted . . . like expensive cologne or perfume.

She'd followed him there, and she'd found him there, and when he'd sucked the blood from her lip, her heart had beat wildly, as frantically as his own . . .

And after that—*especially* after that—he vowed that *nothing* would stop him from having her.

Only . . . not now.

Not now.

Now he would simply watch and admire . . .

For this was the sweetest torment of all.

The ache of her loneliness . . . the pain of her grief . . .

He *fed* off emotions such as these, they *called* to him like shining beacons in pitch-black rooms.

They made him dizzy with longing, and they made him want to possess her totally.

Soon, he told himself. *Soon* . . .

He had to be patient with this one.

Not arouse suspicion . . . gain her trust. That was how these things were done . . . slow and methodical . . . and he was nothing if not methodical.

It was a fine art he'd perfected through these many years—that when he desired something, he'd do *anything* to get it.

Say anything . . . *be* anything . . . no matter how deceitful, no matter how ruthless.

It was his nature.

And he could wait for however long it took.

No need to hurry, he reminded himself.

No need whatsoever to rush.

After all . . . he had eternity on his side.

25

"*Lu-cy . . .*"

"Mom?" Lucy mumbled.

She always sounded like that when she'd locked herself out of the apartment, standing down on the street corner, yelling up at Lucy's bedroom window . . .

"*Lu-cy . . .*"

It was ridiculous; she was always telling Mom how ridiculous it was, a grown woman forgetting her keys all the time, leaving them at work or at the grocery store or on the kitchen table: *I mean, one of these days I'm not going to be here, I won't* be *here to let you in, and* then *what are you going to do?*

"*Lucy!*"

"Hang on, I'm coming . . . I'm . . ."

Cobwebs drifted through her mind, but they

were getting thinner now, almost transparent, and there was light coming through . . .

"Coming . . ." she murmured.

Lucy sat up so quickly that the world spun around her and the cobwebs burst like bubbles.

She didn't realize at first what had happened.

Not until she shook herself out of the leaves and squinted up at the walls of the ravine and saw a shadowy blur of trees and sky high above her.

I was running just a minute ago . . . how'd I get down here?

She ached all over. Her clothes were twisted around her, and she was covered with dirt. *This is starting to feel normal*, she thought disgustedly, stretching out her arms and then her legs. At least nothing seemed to be broken or sprained. *So far, so good . . .*

Byron!

It all came back to her then—why she was out here in the middle of the woods, what must have happened. She should have been paying attention, watched where she was going—now what was she going to do? If Byron were still out there somewhere, wounded or even dying, she'd never get help back to him in time. Gazing up at the steep incline, she wasn't even sure she could help *herself*.

"Damnit," Lucy muttered, fighting down panic. "*Damnit!*" Her body winced with pain as she tried to stand up. She hobbled over to one side of the gorge, then suddenly noticed the outline of a head hanging over the ledge above her.

"Lucy!" Even from down here, she could hear Byron's sigh of relief. "Are you okay?"

"Am I okay?" her voice shot back to him, dangerously close to tears. "Do I *look* okay? My *God*, Byron—where have you *been*?"

"What are you doing down there?"

"Trying to save you!"

He leaned out farther over the edge. Lucy heard the sarcasm in his voice. "And a fine job you're doing, too."

"Get me out of here! You scared me to death!"

"I'll be right down."

Lucy sagged back against the wall of the escarpment, wiping furiously at her eyes. By the time Byron finally worked his way down beside her, her nerves were raw.

"I thought you were dead!" she exploded. "Where *were* you? Why didn't you answer me?"

Byron regarded her solemnly. "I could ask you the same question."

"What are you talking about? *I'm* not the one who was lost!"

"Then who have I been looking for? I heard you calling for help, but I couldn't find you anywhere."

"*I'm* not the one who called for help—*you're* the one who called for help! *You're* the one who disappeared!" Lucy was trembling now, with anger and relief. "You're the one who went off and *left* me! I called and called, and the boat floated away!"

Byron's eyes narrowed. "You mean, *you* didn't take the boat?"

"Why would I do that? It was out in the middle of the lake! Then I tried to find a road—so I could get someone to look for you! And then—"

"Lucy," he interrupted, taking her shoulders, giving her a gentle shake. "Lucy, listen to me, I'm telling you the truth. I heard your voice, but it was so deep in the woods—and you kept saying my name, calling for help. You sounded like you were crying, like you'd been hurt. But I looked and looked, and I couldn't find you. I've been searching for three hours!"

Lucy stared back at him, calmer now, but bewildered. "But . . . I heard *you*, too—and I thought *you* were hurt—"

"You heard *me*? When?"

"Right after you went into the woods! I was so scared and—" She broke off abruptly at the expression on his face. "What? What is it?"

"I didn't call you, Lucy. I *never* called you. I was . . ."

"*What?*"

"I was afraid for you." For a second he seemed almost angry. He clenched his jaw, and something dark flickered far back in his eyes. "I didn't want anyone to know you were here. So I didn't call you."

Lucy hadn't realized she was trembling again. Taking her arm, Byron sat her on the ground and knelt beside her.

"Then who did?" Lucy whispered. "Who did?"

Byron shook his head, his gaze lowered. Then

finally he said, "I was trying to tell you when I heard something in the woods."

"What's going on, Byron? I don't understand."

The lines of his face went hard. "The truth is, I brought you here to warn you."

"To . . . warn me? Why? About what?"

"Lucy, the night Katherine left home, she woke me up and told me she couldn't stand to see Gran and me hurting for her anymore. And that she was going to *go* wherever she had to, and *do* whatever she had to, to learn the truth about those evil visions. She swore that no matter what it took, she'd put them to rest, once and for all."

"So you think she actually tried to find that evil person who was connecting to her thoughts?"

"I think she *did* find him. And I think he killed her."

Lucy watched the carefully controlled rage in his expression . . . the muscle working tightly in his cheek.

"Katherine was wearing that green necklace when she went away. It was a present I'd given her years before, and she never took it off. But yesterday morning I found it in the cemetery, so I knew—*I knew then for certain*—that she was dead. She'd never have taken it off otherwise. Never."

"So you think it came off in the struggle?"

"I think she *took* it off *because* of the struggle. To leave a clue behind . . . and a warning."

He paused a second, chewing thoughtfully on his lower lip. Then he turned to Lucy with a grave frown.

"I think Katherine's murderer touched that necklace while she was fighting for her life. And I think she left it there on purpose *because* he'd touched it, and I think she passed her power on to you, so *someone* would know who killed her."

Lucy went pale. "So you're saying . . . that when I held the necklace, I was actually seeing her . . . her death?"

Without another word she jumped up and started pacing.

"Lucy!"

"No, I don't *want* this—I don't want any *part* of this—I didn't *ask* for this—I—"

"You don't have a choice." Byron was on his feet again, beside her in an instant. "You *are* part of it now, whether you like it or not. There's nothing you can do but accept it."

"And anyway, when I *did* hold the necklace, I didn't see anyone!" Lucy babbled, as though she hadn't heard a single word Bryon said. "I didn't see the face of any killer! I just felt wind and there were eyes and hands and blood and . . . and . . ."

He reached out for her and held her at arms length, forcing her to look at him. "I told you, sometimes it doesn't happen all at once. The next time you touch it, you might see something else, something more—"

"There won't *be* a next time! I'm *not* going to hold that necklace! I'm not going to touch *anything*!" Angrily, Lucy broke free from his grasp. "You don't even know if the guy in Katherine's visions and the guy who killed her are the same person! You don't even know for sure if the guy in her visions was real! I mean, maybe she truly was . . . was . . . sick, and she couldn't help it. I'm sorry, but it *is* possible—people can be sick—"

"Like my mother." Byron's tone was frosty. "I'm assuming that's who you mean?"

"I . . ." Lucy looked at him helplessly. Everything was wrong, everything was falling in on her, the *world* was falling in on her, and she was all alone, and she couldn't get away. "I didn't mean—"

"I want to show you something," Byron said.

Lucy watched him reach into his pocket and pull out a crumpled piece of paper, ragged and soiled around the edges, as though it had been folded and unfolded, read and reread many times.

"This is the last message I got from Katherine. She asks me to meet her at the church. She says she needs to talk to me about something important. And then she ends it with this."

He thrust it out to Lucy. Reluctantly she looked down at the note, where two words had been hastily scrawled at the bottom of the page.

HE LIVES

26

A feeling of numbness crept over her.

She handed the paper back.

"I'm going now, Byron. I'm going to climb out of here and find the road and go home. Even if I have to walk all the way back to town."

"Lucy—"

"No. Don't talk to me. I just want to go."

Somehow she made it up the embankment. As she reached the top, she was surprised to see cuts and scrapes all over her hands, and rips in the knees of her jeans. Dusting herself off as best she could, Lucy started walking. From somewhere behind her, she was vaguely aware that Byron was following. But it wasn't till he yelled after her that she stopped.

"But you can't ignore it, can you? Because things have been happening to you, haven't they? Other things besides the necklace? Things you can't explain? And they're scaring you, aren't they? They're scaring you to death!"

Lucy spun around, enraged. "Leave me alone! You don't know anything!"

"Then tell me! Why don't you tell me? I want to help!"

"How can you help?" Tears brimmed in her eyes and she fought to keep her voice steady. "You couldn't even help Katherine! You couldn't even keep her from dying, could you?"

She saw his face, the anger and grief in his tortured expression. "Don't you think I know that? Don't you think I've been tormented by that? Do you have any idea how horrible it was, watching her go through that? Watching somebody you love suffer like she did, with no explanations and no help?"

His voice quivered with rage. His dark eyes flashed with helpless frustration.

"And the same thing will happen to you. You'll try to warn people, but they won't believe you. You'll try to save people, but you'll fail. You'll see tragedies that you won't be able to prevent, and you'll feel every single human grief and suffering and sorrow like a knife thrust deep in your heart. I saw what it did to her. Day by day, and tragedy by tragedy, it wore her down, it poisoned her mind. I *know* in my heart she was happy to die in the end . . . she was *glad* to be free from that *gift* of hers."

Lucy stood there, unable to move, watching the anguish pour out of him. It was like watching a dam break in slow motion, and then, finally, wondering how it had ever held up for so long.

"Oh, God, Byron," Lucy whispered. "I'm so sorry."

She moved toward him at last. She reached out and gently touched his cheek, and for a brief moment, the walls remained down and unguarded.

"All right," she murmured. "I'll tell you everything."

With almost numb detachment, Lucy recounted every strange and frightening event of the past few days. They sat together on a low outcrop of rocks, facing each other while she admitted her doubts to him, questioned her reasoning and wild imagination, allowed for the possibility of coincidence.

Byron listened attentively . . . but it wasn't until she'd finished that he finally allowed himself to comment.

"You can't *really* believe you imagined all that." His tone was slightly incredulous. "You *can't* believe those are coincidences. And especially after what just happened now in the woods."

Lucy let out a weary sigh. "I don't know what I think anymore."

For an endless moment silence settled between them. Then Byron said quietly, "Katherine warned you not to tell anyone, didn't she? Because your life could be in danger."

"Yes." Reluctantly Lucy nodded. "So . . . why? Because she was afraid he'd kill me, too?"

"What did he say in the confessional? When you asked him who he was?"

She shuddered, merely thinking about it. "He told me he was my salvation."

Byron looked thoughtful. He ran his fingers slowly along his chin. "You said he wasn't there when you found Katherine. He may not even realize yet that she passed her powers on to you. In fact . . . he might not even know you were there at all."

"If that's true, then why is he suddenly so interested in me?"

"I'm not sure. But I think if we can figure out what his connection was to *Katherine*, that might help us figure out what his connection is to you."

Lucy's shoulders sagged. Lowering her head, she covered her face with her hands and groaned. "And what if we don't? What if we never do?"

"He could have been here today," Byron speculated, dodging her question. "Tricking us into getting separated. Untying the boat. Hoping you'd be alone . . ."

"So what you're telling me is, he could be anywhere. He could be anyone. Watching me. All the time."

"That's why we have to go back and get the necklace. I think we need to start there. It'll give us a clue to who killed Katherine. And why."

"I just hope it's still there at the church," Lucy said glumly.

"You said some priest had it?"

She nodded. "Matt. Father Matt."

"And what'd he do with it?"

"He just said he was going to put it back where he found it—by the altar. In case whoever dropped it came back for it. But if you want to talk to him, I think he's going to be there all day, going through storage closets and stuff."

Byron hesitated. "I don't think we should go back till he leaves."

"Why not? Why would he think anything about it?"

"You're the one who heard voices in the confessional. You tell me." Then, at Lucy's distressed look, he said quickly, "Look, I just think the less people who know about any of this, the better. Doesn't that make sense?"

"You're right," she agreed. "And by the way, how did you get into the church this morning, if Father Matt wasn't there yet?"

Bryon raised an eyebrow. "Gran used to be the cleaning lady at the church. I have a key."

"So you weren't lying. You *do* have all the keys. To just about everything."

She thought he almost smiled at that. He stood and pulled her to her feet.

"Do you really think the necklace is going to help me?" As Lucy gazed up into his face, her eyes were almost pleading.

Byron stared down at her, a faint frown creasing his brow. Then, with wary tenderness, he lifted his hand and lightly touched her cheek.

"Only if we find it before the killer does."

27

Luckily, they didn't have far to walk.

As they finally came out on the other side of the woods, Byron recognized the driver of a passing pickup truck and flagged him down for a ride.

"Well, Byron, what brings you up today?" The old man greeted Byron with a grin.

"Just checking some cabins, Ray." Byron introduced Lucy, then added, "Do you think you could help me out? I borrowed Mac's boat, and it came untied back there at the cove. I don't have time to look for it 'cause I need to get Lucy back to town."

Ray gave them a wink. "Don't you worry. I'll tow it back, and nobody'll ever know it was gone."

"Thanks, I appreciate it."

As they neared the cabin where Lucy had

left the car, Byron casually asked if anyone had noticed any suspicious activity around the area.

"Haven't seen anything like that," Ray said anxiously. "Why? Something wrong?"

Byron's answer was casual and calculated. "Just wondering. It looks like someone might have tried to break into the Millers' place."

"Well, I'll sure keep a lookout," Ray promised. "If I see any strangers, I'll be sure and report them right away."

Squeezed tightly together in the front seat, Lucy gave Byron a grateful smile. When Ray let them out at the cabin, they waited till he was out of sight, then locked up and headed back into town.

"How about I pick you up around seven?" Byron asked her. "The church should be locked up again by then."

"I think we should meet somewhere," Lucy suggested instead. "Angela's way too nosy, and Irene's been in a horrible mood. I'd rather not borrow more trouble."

Byron agreed. "What about the Festival, then?"

"Well . . . I'm pretty sure Angela will want to go back. But she's supposed to be grounded, so I'll have to see if we can sneak out again."

"Can you lose her once you get there?"

"No problem. The less she has to be with me, the more she likes it. Besides, I think she's been hanging out with some guy there she doesn't want her mom to know about."

"Perfect. I'll meet you at the carousel."

After letting Byron out at his house, Lucy went on to the car wash. She hadn't realized how exhausted she was, but now, with the turbulent morning behind her, she could feel all her emotions letting down at last. She drove through the car wash, relishing the blasts of water and churning brushes all around her, feeling in some strange way almost as cleansed as the Corvette.

It gave her time to collect her thoughts. Angela would demand an explanation when she got back; that much she could count on. She told herself she had to act normally, think clearly, come up with some logical excuses for being so late. She remembered the few times Irene had suggested that Lucy go shopping for new clothes, mentioning stores where she could use Irene's accounts.

Yes. Good cover. Glancing down at her stained jeans and jacket, Lucy thought how funny that was. On a whim, she stopped at the same fast-food restaurant she'd stopped at that morning, and slipped into the women's restroom. Using bunches of paper towels, she did her best at a hasty cleanup, then ran a comb through her hair. *Fine. That'll work.*

Driving home, her thoughts kept wandering, even though she tried to keep them in check. Thinking too much was dangerous to her now, she decided—the slightest little thing might send her over the edge. How could a day start off so innocently, then turn so deadly? How could your life change completely in a matter of seconds? And how could she and Katherine—a girl she'd never met and would never even know—become so tragically intertwined?

So much for fate, Lucy thought wearily.

How strange it was, the way events wove themselves together, pulling innocent people into the middle of darkness, into the middle of bad surprises. If only she hadn't gone for a walk the other night, none of this would have happened. *If only Mom hadn't died, I wouldn't be here in the first place. If only . . . if only . . .*

No use going there, she told herself sternly. There was nothing she could do about any of it till tonight. *Except drive yourself crazy with worrying.*

She heard the battle before she was even halfway in the back door. Irene and Angela in the kitchen, voices raised at fever pitch. Angela's furious tears, and Irene's unyielding authority.

"You were *seen* there last night, Angela!" Irene was livid. "I *told* you you were grounded, and you *deliberately* disobeyed me!"

"It wasn't my fault!" Angela whined.

"Did you actually think it wouldn't get back to me?" Irene countered. "In this town where I know so many people? I can't trust you for a minute, can I? But I *told* you what would happen, and now you have to accept the consequences. No car. Period. Not to school, not anywhere. And your credit cards—as of right now—are canceled."

"You can't do that!"

"I just did."

"I'm not giving them to you!"

"Angela, it doesn't matter. I have all the numbers right here in my briefcase, and it's as good as done. Now go upstairs."

"Daddy would *never* have treated me this way!"

"Well, he's not here. And if he *had* treated you a little more this way, you wouldn't be so selfish and self-indulgent."

"I'll run away!"

"Oh, Angela, don't be ridiculous. You couldn't survive for one night without all the comforts of home. Just once I'd like to be able to walk out this door and leave this house without having to go through all these theatrics."

"I swear I will! I'll run away where you'll never find me—"

"It was my fault," Lucy announced.

Irene and Angela both turned in surprise. Lucy took a deep breath and came boldly into the room.

"It was my fault," she said again. She could see Irene's mask of a face, her look of perpetual disapproval.

"Lucy?" Irene raised one suspicious eyebrow.

"I wanted to go to the Festival last night, and I didn't know how to get there." Lucy squared her shoulders. "And you know how horrible I am at directions. And Angela *told* me she was grounded, but . . . but I begged her."

Irene wasn't to be swayed. "That's no excuse. Angela should have known better."

"But it was my fault," Lucy insisted again. "Angela didn't even stay. She dropped me off there, and then she came back to pick me up later. And . . . I forgot where we were supposed to meet, so she had to come and look for me."

Irene gave an impassive nod. "I see."

Lucy glanced at Angela. Angela's expression was stubborn and defiant. Irene looked at one girl, and then at the other.

Finally she said, "Lucy, I also expect *you* to abide by house rules."

"I know." Lucy nodded contritely. "I'm sorry."

"Both of you go upstairs."

"What about my credit cards?" Angela demanded.

"I told you," Irene said. "Canceled."

With a cry of rage, Angela stomped up to her room. As Lucy stood by uncertainly, Irene gathered her overnight bag, briefcase, her purse and her coat.

"I've left the hotel number by the phone. I should be home early tomorrow afternoon."

Lucy nodded. As Irene passed through the door, she gave Lucy a frosty glare.

"That was very noble of you, Lucy. It's admirable of you to want to protect your cousin . . . but in the future, I won't tolerate lying. Even if you *are* trying to be noble."

Lucy made a hasty exit, bracing herself against the blast of Angela's music that shook her bedroom walls. After a while she heard Irene leaving and the music promptly shutting off.

She lay down across the bed and buried her face in her arms. She wanted to sleep. She wanted to sleep and sleep and just forget . . .

She drifted. She heard the kitchen door open and shut several times, Angela going up and down the stairs, but she was too tired to wonder about it. She wondered instead how she could rearrange the evening now, how she'd manage to get out of the house. Irene had not only issued orders, she'd confiscated Angela's car keys. It would be tricky now, getting back to the Festival.

She shouldn't have worried.

"Come on!" Angela announced several hours later, bursting through the door. Lucy nearly jumped out of her skin.

"What do you think you're doing?" she demanded.

"What do *you* think? Going to the Festival!"

"Angela, are you insane? After that major blowup with Irene?"

"Do I look like I care?"

"If someone saw you there *last* night, they're bound to see you again tonight! Irene's probably hired spies! She'll be furious!"

"Trust me . . ." Angela said mysteriously. "Irene will never know."

"Angela, what—"

"Don't ask questions. Just get in the car."

"But the keys—"

With a Cheshire cat grin, she dangled an extra set between her fingers. "Do I look that stupid to you?"

"Angela—"

"Do you wanna go or *not*?"

Lucy thought about how much trouble they'd be in. And then she thought about the necklace and all that was at stake.

And then she nodded and grabbed her jacket.

"Yes," she said. "I definitely want to go."

28

Despite Lucy's reluctance—and the fact that Irene had confiscated her license, as well—Angela insisted on driving. Lucy spent the whole ride slumped down in the seat, as though by making herself invisible, no police would dare to stop their car. Unfortunately, Angela wasn't in such a law-abiding mode—she couldn't wait to do every single reckless thing she could think of, now that Irene had left town.

"I have a bad feeling about tonight," Lucy said, but Angela just laughed.

"Trust me. I will *not* get grounded for this."

"Angela, you've lost your mind. You truly have."

"I will *not* get grounded or punished in any way, shape, or form, thank you very much."

"If you say so."

"Come on, Lucy—just have a little faith."

Lucy breathed a sigh of relief when they arrived at the Festival. As the two of them walked through the gates, she didn't even have to come up with an excuse. Angela flipped her a wave and headed straight into the crowd.

"Meet you same time same place," Lucy said.

Angela beamed at her. "Hey! Don't count on it!"

"Angela?" Lucy shouted, but the girl just ignored her. "Angela!"

What is she up to? Lucy didn't have time to worry about it, though. Byron was waiting for her, as promised, right by the carousel.

"Ready?" he asked.

"As I'll ever be."

Taking her arm, he steered her toward the exit. Lucy couldn't help noticing some of the looks they got on their way—girls eyeing them with a mixture of curiosity and blatant envy. When she was certain he wasn't looking, she stole a look up at Byron's face—the handsomely chiseled features set off by that guarded, mysterious stare. Now she found herself wondering if anyone else really understood that expression, the way she'd come to know it today. She doubted if he'd ever shown such vulnerability before; she doubted he'd ever be so willing again.

Still, seeing the wistful looks cast in their direction she couldn't help but get a warm feeling inside. She was only human, after all. *Nothing like calling attention to yourself, Lucy.* Her appearance with Byron Wetherly would be all over school by homeroom Monday morning.

The world lay shrouded in black. There were no stars tonight, only a bloodred moon, full and round. As they drove through town to the old church, Lucy watched it, fascinated, as it seemed to follow them through the pale tattered clouds.

"Full moon," Byron said, noting the focus of her stare. "No wonder things have been so strange around here."

Lucy suppressed a little shiver. "I've never seen the moon that color before—it's creepy."

He glanced at her sideways, but said nothing.

The church looked ominous as ever when they pulled up and parked. Byron cut the headlights, and they sat there a moment, listening to the muffled sounds of the night. The sky flowed like thick oil overhead . . . a light mist swirled through the graveyard.

"Nice horror movie," Byron commented dryly.

Lucy nodded. It was the only church she'd ever seen that made her feel so unsettled. And she didn't feel any *less* unsettled once they'd gone inside.

They stood side by side, their eyes readjusting to an almost stygian darkness. Byron took a flashlight from his jacket pocket and quietly flicked it on. They seemed to be alone. Their footfalls echoed hollowly as they walked up the aisle, and Lucy could hear the faint scurryings of mice darting beneath the pews. As they neared the altar, a fiendish howl suddenly rose up, disembodied, from the gloom. It echoed back from the damp stone walls . . . wafted through the shadows . . . shivered down along her spine.

Instinctively she grabbed for Byron's arm.

Then let out a nervous laugh.

"Cats," she mumbled. "Matt said they keep cats in here. For rodent control."

Even Byron seemed momentarily unnerved by the spectral howl. As a large black cat slipped around the end of the altar, he shone his flashlight on it, causing it to freeze instantly. It arched its back and hissed, then crouched down again and slunk away.

"Not very friendly," Byron murmured, putting one hand on her back, guiding her gently forward.

"Well, he sure didn't seem to like *you* much."

Byron ignored the remark. "Do you see it?" he asked her, squinting through the blackness.

Lucy, too, strained her eyes, running her hands over the dusty altar cloth. "No. But he said he'd leave it right here."

"Maybe he forgot."

Lucy sighed. "Then we'll never find it—he could have put it anywhere. He could have taken it with him, for that matter."

She turned to see Byron standing by the confessionals, and her heart gave a fearful twist.

"Is this where it happened?" he asked softly. "Where you saw . . . well . . . whoever he was you saw?"

Lucy nodded reluctantly. As if merely conjuring the memory might bring it back again in all its terror.

“He must have been in here already,” Byron mused. “Before you showed up. From where I was sitting, I would have seen him go in.”

“He could have come through some other way though. Matt mentioned some cellars. In these old places, there could be lots of entrances, right? Even secret ones.”

“Possibly.”

Byron’s voice echoed, empty and toneless. Even the shadows seemed to slither away from it, skulking along the walls and ceiling, worse than any cats. She watched uneasily as he opened one of the confessional doors. As he shone the light in and skimmed it over the dark, cramped space.

“And when you came out from here . . . it was just the priest,” he murmured.

Lucy wished they could talk about something else. “But it couldn’t have been him,” she said, almost defensively.

He lifted an eyebrow. “I didn’t say it was.”

He opened the priest’s compartment, following the same slow ritual with his flashlight. He opened the door on the opposite side.

All of them, empty.

"Byron," Lucy said suddenly, "let's go."

He turned to her in wary surprise. "What's wrong?"

"I . . . I don't know. I just . . ."

Her voice trailed away. She cast a nervous look around them, down the center aisle, the intersecting pews, the dirty linen altar cloth.

"Please," she whispered. Was it getting colder in here? Just like the time before . . . just like the last time when she'd heard the whisper . . . followed the voice . . . seen that malevolent shadow behind the screen . . .

"Byron . . ."

And she could see *him* looking now, too, trying to follow the direction of her eyes, trying to see what was wrong. And somehow she knew what would come next . . . she was *expecting* it—was *ready* for it—and yes, she realized with a shock, *longing* for it, as well, like the scent of a favorite flower or the warmth of a favorite memory that transported the spirit back to sweeter times . . .

Without another word she turned and ran for the doors.

"Lucy! Wait!"

She could hear Byron shouting at her, but she didn't stop. She put her hands against the doors and pushed, but they wouldn't open.

"Oh, God!"

She struggled against them, pushing, pushing, and she could see the crazy arc of the flashlight sweeping the ceiling, over the faces of the saints, the broken shards of agonies and ecstasies and long-forgotten prayers . . .

"Lucy—for God's sake—"

With one last effort, her body fell against them, and the doors burst wide and welcomed the night in.

Screaming, Lucy toppled right into a strong pair of arms.

And a very shocked expression.

Shielding himself from her flailing limbs, Matt tried to steady Lucy and keep his balance at the same time. The next thing she knew, Byron had ahold of her, both his arms around her, restraining her and pulling her back.

"Lucy—what is *wrong* with you?"

She stopped struggling. She stared at Matt, who was staring back at her—tousled hair, easy grin, only now the grimy jeans and sweatshirt had been replaced with black pants, black shirt, and a priest's collar.

"Lucy!" He gave a relieved laugh. "I didn't expect to see you in here! I thought I saw a light—thought maybe someone was breaking in."

She clamped her arms across her chest. Byron had released her now, but she could feel him, the warm, lean strength of him, pressed against her back.

"So," Matt was trying to peer around them into the darkness. "Is there something wrong? Is there—"

"Byron," Byron said quickly. "Byron Wetherly."

The two stared into each other's eyes. Held each other's gazes for an extended moment. Exchanged handshakes, firm and slow.

"Oh, Byron, hello. Matt."

"The new priest," Byron said.

"Well, more of a gofer right now."

Their hands unclasped and slid away.

"Well," Byron said politely. "Welcome to Pine Ridge."

"The necklace," Lucy blurted out. "Do you still have it?"

For a second Matt looked puzzled. Then his grin relaxed.

"Right! That green necklace I found this morning. What happened—did you suddenly remember it was yours?" At Lucy's wan smile, he moved his shoulders in an apologetic shrug. "But . . . I'm so sorry . . . somebody else already came by for it."

Lucy and Byron traded glances. "Who?"

"Well . . . I don't know, actually." Another gesture of apology. "I left it by the altar like I said I would. But I had to leave for a while, and the cleaning lady was here. She said someone came by to claim it."

"But you don't know who it was?" Lucy persisted.

"I sure don't, sorry."

"What about the cleaning lady? Would *she* know who it was?" Byron asked casually.

"Well . . . from what I understand, she knows just about everybody around here. Do you know Mrs. Dempsey?"

"Sure. Come on then, Lucy." Byron nudged her from behind. "We better go."

Nodding, Lucy looked back over her shoulder,

making one last survey of the church. No cold now . . . no fragrance. But her heart was still racing, and her blood still had that chill . . .

"Sorry we worried you," Byron mumbled, pushing past Matt onto the steps.

"I wasn't worried," Matt said.

Lucy glanced up into his face as she passed him. His smile was still warm, still teasing. He gave her a conspiratorial wink, and she quickly glanced away.

As they reached the sidewalk, Matt suddenly called them back.

"Hey, wait a minute—I *do* remember something she said." At Lucy's perplexed look, he added, "The cleaning lady. When the guy came for that necklace."

He was quiet a moment, thinking. Byron's fingers dug sharply into Lucy's shoulder blade.

"Right." Matt nodded. "A guy. That's what she said, a good-looking guy . . . he said he'd gotten it as a present."

"A present?" Lucy echoed. "For what?"

"Not what . . . *who*. For a girl." Matt chuckled. "He said it was a present for a girl he'd met at the Fall Festival."

Lucy froze. A sick taste of fear rose slowly into her throat.

"Did he . . . did he say what her name was?"

Matt cocked his head and thought again. "Just . . . oh, now I remember. Something about New Orleans."

Lucy spun and stared up at Byron.

"Oh my God," she choked. "Angela."

29

"Wait—slow down! You're not making any sense."

"Hurry! We've got to get back to the Festival!"

"Lucy, calm *down*! Will you please tell me what's going on—"

"I don't *know* what's going on, okay? Just drive! All I know is that Angela's in some kind of trouble."

"*How* do you know that? And start from the beginning."

Lucy leaned toward him in the front seat, her voice tense with anxiety. "Remember when I told you she was hanging out at the fair with some guy Irene didn't know about? *He* must be the guy who picked up the necklace."

"That's impossible. The necklace doesn't have anything to do with Angela." Byron's hands tightened on the steering wheel. "What *possible* connection could Katherine's stalker have with Angela?"

"I don't know—I don't *know*! But that's why we have to find her!"

"You don't even know if it *is* Angela this guy picked up the necklace for."

"He said New Orleans! And Angela wants to go to New Orleans!"

"So? Lots of people want to go to New Orleans. *I* wouldn't mind going to New Orleans—"

"Call it a hunch then. Just please hurry."

They reached the Festival again in record time. Leaving Byron to follow, Lucy went immediately for the scarecrow-game tent and shoved her way to the front of the line amid irate kids and their equally irate parents. At the entrance she recognized the same girl who'd been there last night, the one with the serious face.

"Where's Angela?" Lucy asked breathlessly.

"Huh! Wouldn't *we* like to know! She left just the two of us here tonight with twice as many brats!"

"But have you seen her?"

"Yeah, a little earlier, but—"

"Please—it's important!"

The girl shrugged. "She said she was going with some guy."

"Going? Going where?"

"I don't know. Getting a ride? Or going away? Or—"

"Was it the same guy she was with last night?"

This time the girl rolled her eyes. "How would I know that? They were pretty busy, if you know what I mean. It's not like I could really see his face."

"Can't you remember anything about him? Anything at all?"

"I think he might have been tall. Maybe dark hair . . . but you know, they were back in the shadows."

As Byron caught up with her, Lucy spun to face him. "We have to go after her."

"After her *where*? How can we go after her if we don't know where she went?"

Lucy looked so desperate that the solemn-faced girl sighed sympathetically, then called out to her coworker. "Did Angela say where she was going tonight?"

"You mean, with that guy?" the other girl called back.

"Yeah."

"Uh . . . something about New Orleans, I think."

"Did they say how? Driving? Flying?"

"Maybe driving. I heard something about a bus."

Again Lucy whirled to face Byron. "We've got to stop her."

As Byron attempted to calm her down, they heard the second girl speak up.

"Oh, hey, wait a minute? Are you Lucy?"

Lucy nodded. "Yes."

"Well, somebody left this for you."

"Was it Angela?"

The girl planted herself in the tent doorway, grabbing some rowdy children, trying to establish some semblance of order. "You know, I'm not really sure, okay? Just somebody left it for you. See? It's got your name on it."

The girl handed her a small manila envelope. Lucy's name was printed across the front, and with trembling fingers, she slid open the flimsy seal across the back.

"It's the necklace," she murmured, her eyes going wide. "I know it is . . . oh, Byron, I can't do this . . . I can't—"

Byron grabbed it away from her and ripped open the flap.

Out fell Angela's car keys.

30

He hadn't meant for it to come to this.

At least not with this one . . . and especially not this soon.

He always enjoyed playing with them awhile . . . luring them . . . teasing them . . . manipulating them with praises and with promises . . .

And this one had been so easy, so predictable.

But sometimes, he simply grew tired of them.

Sometimes, after a day or a week or a lifetime, he simply discovered they no longer fit into the well-ordered chaos of his world.

She'd been shocked, of course.

That instant of disbelief—that depth of betrayal in her eyes.

"But don't you remember what you told me?"

she'd pleaded, as he'd tasted the tears of her sorrow. "Don't you remember what you said?"

"Of course," he'd soothed her, "of course I do . . ."

"Don't you remember you promised?"

And he'd pressed her against his heart, and plunged the dagger through her throat, and twisted it with cold, calm ease.

And then he'd smiled.

"Of course I remember, Angela . . . but I lied."

31

Lucy stared in disbelief.

As she glanced over at Byron, she saw him hold the envelope upside down and give it a shake. If she hadn't been so stunned, it would have been comical.

"I thought . . ." she stammered, "I really thought—"

"Me, too. But are you sensing anything?"

Trying to break the tension, Lucy bounced the keyless entry in the palm of her hand. "Yeah. I've got a sense these are keys."

"Your psychic abilities are impressive," he deadpanned. He balled up the envelope and tossed it into a trash can, then gave her a curt nod. "Come on."

"Where are we going?" Lucy asked, hurrying to match his long stride.

"You heard her. Let's try the bus depot."

They were there in ten minutes. Not only was the place small, but the waiting room was practically empty. While Byron checked the schedules for southern destinations, Lucy questioned the clerks at the ticket counter. No one remembered Irene Foster's daughter buying a bus ticket today, but after thinking a moment, one of the clerks remembered a young couple bundled in coats and hats and sunglasses who'd taken a southbound express about an hour before.

"I think it's worth a try," Byron decided. "They don't have that much of a head start, and they'll be making stops along the way. It should be easy to catch them."

Lucy felt sick. Sick to her stomach and sick at heart. As she climbed up beside him into the van, she shot him a look of desperation.

"What if you're right?"

"How so?"

"What if this whole thing with the necklace has *nothing* to do with Angela? I mean . . . what if she's really and truly found the love of her life, and they're going off to live happily ever after, and we're going after them and being stupid?"

Byron put the key in the ignition. He stared thoughtfully at the dashboard.

"Then," he said carefully, "at least we know. Then we turn around and come back home. And they have their lives . . . and we have ours."

Lucy sighed. "I can't help it, though. I just still *feel* something—just *here*." She clamped her arms around her midsection and fixed him with a worried frown. "I just feel like something about this isn't right. It's just this awful *nagging* feeling, and it won't go away."

"You're probably feeling a lot of things right now," Byron reminded her. "You thought you had the necklace, and you'd psyched yourself up to face it."

"So did you," she said quietly.

He shrugged. "Emotional roller coaster."

"You're right. I don't know whether to be scared now, or relieved."

"How about a little of both? It's okay, you know, to feel both."

She tried to smile at him, but her emotions were at full pitch. As they sailed along the highway, she leaned against her door and stared out the window of the van. Everything's flowing tonight, she thought vaguely . . . *flowing road . . . flowing van . . . flowing curves . . . flowing hills . . .*

She could still see that strange red moon watching her through the clouds. The color of rust . . . the color of decay. A stain of old dried blood on the wrinkled flesh of the sky.

Shivering, Lucy hunched her shoulders and burrowed deeper into her jacket. It felt like it was getting colder, both outside and in. And the moon . . . that eerie red moon . . . actually seemed to be growing. Growing and glowing among the tops of the trees, like some forgotten Christmas ornament.

Lucy frowned and burrowed deeper. Why did full moons like that make her feel so weird? Make her think of creepy things like . . . like . . .

Prey . . .

"What?" She sat up straight and looked at Byron, who looked back at her suspiciously.

"What?" he echoed.

"Did you just say something?"

"Yeah, I said, just pray my brakes hold out."

"Oh my God, don't tell me that—your brakes?"

"Well . . . all these curves sure aren't helping my van."

"Thank you, Byron. That definitely eases my mind, your sharing that with me."

She saw that slow half smile working at one corner of his mouth. She realized that she really loved it when he smiled like that. She wished he'd do it more often.

"Stop staring at me," he said, and, grinning, she turned back to her window.

She closed her eyes. The hum of the motor, the rocking motion of the van on the road . . . she could feel herself drifting off. That pleasant state between sleep and attention, when everything seemed soft and warm and safe. She forced her eyes open and searched for taillights up ahead of them, but the road was so twisted, she couldn't see a thing. There wasn't even traffic out tonight, she suddenly realized. But she could see the slow, pale curls of fog beginning to creep in over the highway . . . blurring the yellow line . . . swallowing the road ahead of them.

That feeling again. Gnawing at the pit of her stomach.

"Byron," she said uneasily, "be careful."

He cast her a sidelong glance. "Always."

"No, I mean it. Please."

"Are you okay?"

"Yes . . . just . . . I don't know. Restless. Nervous."

"If you want, we can stop for some coffee the first place we see. It might be a good idea."

She gave a distracted nod. She gazed out into the darkness . . . out at that bloody moon. She wished it would go behind a cloud for the rest of the night . . . she wished it would just go away.

She sensed something beside them on the road.

Something she couldn't actually see, something just out of sight off the shoulder, something moving swiftly through the tall weeds, keeping pace with the van.

Strange . . .

Lucy looked over at the speedometer. Sixty. Yet she was sure—she was *certain*—that something was out there running, running even faster than the van could go, running even faster than the wind could go . . .

"Byron," she mumbled.

"What?"

She saw him turn toward her.

Saw his hand slide across the seat and reach for her.

She looked into his eyes . . . deep and black as midnight . . . and in that moment she could see in their depths all the truths and emotions that she'd felt that morning with her hand upon his heart.

A sob went through her.

Byron opened his mouth and started to say her name.

But he never got the chance.

As the dark shape came out of the fog, Byron hit the brakes, the tires screeching, the van skidding, sliding, going into a spin. As they whirled around and around, Lucy could see it there—the huge, black shape silhouetted against the fog, standing on all fours, statuelike in the middle of the road. Watching them . . . *watching them* . . .

She tried to reach for Byron—reached *desperately* for Byron—

But her head slammed the window, and the

van careened off the hill, and all she could think in those last few seconds was *he never got to say it . . .*

Byron never said my name.

32

So this is what it's like to die . . .

Lying there on her back in the grass, all alone in the darkness, she could sense the wet, runny mask of her face—tears? blood?—she couldn't be sure, couldn't be sure she even *had* a face, couldn't be sure about anything except that her body screamed in pain each time she tried to draw even the shallowest of breaths.

I can't move . . . help . . . somebody, help me . . .

With a ragged cry, Lucy tried to lift her head, tried to peer through the thick, endless night surrounding her. As in a dream, she could see the faraway sky blazing bright, lit by a giant fire—and along with those sickening smells of pain and fear and despair that threatened to choke her, now there was the gasoline . . . burning rubber . . . white-hot metal . . . and something else . . . something dear to her heart . . .

Byron!

That's Byron's van!

She'd been sitting in the front seat beside him, and she'd been staring at the moon. That bloodred moon hovering there behind the trees and glowing out through the dark, shredded fabric of the clouds. She'd been staring at the moon, and then she'd jolted with the first sharp swerve of the van. Confused and groggy, she'd heard Byron's shout, the piercing shriek of brakes and tires; she'd felt the road give way to air beneath them as they dove off the shoulder and off the crest of the hill, and out through the foggy night, plummeting down and down into nothingness . . .

Byron? Can you hear me?

She knew somehow that she hadn't spoken aloud, knew somehow that her thoughts had burst free of her pain, only to fall silent among the shadows. It was so dark out here. So dark, so frighteningly still, except for those flames leaping and glowing against the distant horizon . . .

Something ran in front us.

With a moan, Lucy struggled to shut out the pain, struggled to focus her hazy thoughts.

Byron tried to swerve, he tried to miss hitting it, but something ran in front of us . . .

She wished she could remember. She wished she could remember what it was that had caused the accident. But there was only the briefest glimmer of memory in that last fatal second, only the briefest image of something caught in headlights as the car veered and left the road.

What was *that?*

It seemed so familiar somehow . . .

But her thoughts were fading . . . fading . . . and she knew she was slipping away. In desperation she stared up at the trees overhead, great gnarled branches etched thickly against the black dome of the sky. And then she noticed that moon.

So full and round. So red like blood. Caught in a web of tangled limbs, oozing out through the clouds, wine stains on velvet.

Byron, I'm so scared! Please help me!

And that's when she heard it.

The soft rustling sound, like wind sighing through grass. Except that she couldn't *feel* any wind, not even the faintest of breezes, in this heavy night air.

The sound was close by.

Coming even closer . . .

Oh God!

Once more she tried to lift herself, to call out for help. But the rustlings were in her head now, in her thoughts and in her pain, like so many urgent whispers, whispers of great importance.

As Lucy's head turned helplessly to one side, she saw shadows all around her, shadows slinking along the ground and through the trees, slivers of black, and pale, pale gray, and sparks of amber light . . .

Terror exploded within her. Even through the paralyzing numbness of pain and shock, she sensed that these were animals, and she sensed why they were here. Instinct told her that she was surrounded, though one stood closer than the others. She could hear the slow, calm rhythm of its breathing as it watched her from a place she couldn't see.

Oh, God, don't let me die like this!

She thought of Byron. The vision burst inside her brain with such force that she choked and gagged and vomited blood in the grass. In that one instant of agonizing clarity she saw his midnight eyes, heard his calm, deep voice, telling her not to be afraid. Now she remembered how he'd turned to her in that last split second of his life, his eyes desperate with helplessness and disbelief as he'd reached for her hand. *Did he touch me*? The thought drifted through her mind, light as a feather. *Did we touch one last time?*

But the whispers were louder now, and the fire was brighter than ever, and she was so weak . . . so tired.

Please . . . please . . . just let me die fast . . .

Night swayed around her. As tears ran silently down her cheeks, something huge and dark leaned in over her, blocking her view of the sky.

She steeled herself for the end. Felt hot breath caressing her throat . . . smelled the faint, familiar scent of something sweet . . .

Byron . . . I'm so sorry. . .

"Byron has gone," the voice murmured. "Only I can save you now."

Who are you? What *are you?*

Down . . . down she sank into the endlessness of time.

And that voice . . . fading far into nothingness . . .

"Oh, Lucy . . . There's no name for what we are."

THE UNSEEN

PART TWO: REST IN PEACE

For Sandra, Barbara, Julie, Susan, Jenifer, Anna, Suzanne, Janice, Ellen, Peggy, Richard, Pete, and Bill—I could never make it through these writing days without you. Thanks with all my heart.

SPEAK
Published by the Penguin Group
Penguin Group (USA) Inc., 345 Hudson Street, New York, New York 10014, U.S.A.
Penguin Group (Canada), 90 Eglinton Avenue East, Suite 700, Toronto, Ontario, Canada M4P 2Y3
(a division of Pearson Penguin Canada Inc.)
Penguin Books Ltd, 80 Strand, London WC2R 0RL, England
Penguin Ireland, 25 St Stephen's Green, Dublin 2, Ireland (a division of Penguin Books Ltd)
Penguin Group (Australia), 250 Camberwell Road, Camberwell, Victoria 3124, Australia
(a division of Pearson Australia Group Pty Ltd)
Penguin Books India Pvt Ltd, 11 Community Centre, Panchsheel Park, New Delhi - 110 017, India
Penguin Group (NZ), 67 Apollo Drive, Rosedale, Auckland 0632, New Zealand
(a division of Pearson New Zealand Ltd)
Penguin Books (South Africa) (Pty) Ltd, 24 Sturdee Avenue,
Rosebank, Johannesburg 2196, South Africa

Registered Offices: Penguin Books Ltd, 80 Strand, London WC2R 0RL, England

First published in the UK by Scholastic Ltd, 2004
First published in the United States of America by Speak, an imprint of Penguin Group (USA) Inc., 2005
This omnibus edition published by Speak, an imprint of Penguin Group (USA) Inc., 2011

1 3 5 7 9 10 8 6 4 2

LIBRARY OF CONGRESS CATALOGING-IN-PUBLICATION DATA
Cusick, Richie Tankersley.
Rest in peace / Richie Tankersley Cusick.
p. cm.—(The unseen ; pt. 2)
First published in the UK by Scholastic Ltd., 2004.
Summary: Having survived the accident that killed her friend Byron, Lucy tries to cope
with her new powers and attempts to figure out who—or what—is stalking her.
ISBN 0-14-240464-0 (pbk.)
[1. Extrasensory perception—Fiction. 2. Horror stories—Fiction.] I. Title.
PZ7.C9646Res 2005 [Fic]—dc22 2005047435

Speak ISBN 978-0-14-242146-8

Set in Perpetua Regular and Nosfer Regular

Printed in the United States of America

Prologue

He stood and he watched her.

Watched the frantic rolling of her eyes beneath her closed, bruised eyelids . . . the terrified heaving of her breasts beneath the torn, mangled material of her blouse. From time to time a whimper escaped her lips . . . or a gasp . . . or even a whispered plea for help, as she dreamed her terrible dream. And sometimes her hands would thrash against the darkness, clawing at shadows and bloodstained bandages, as she relived, over and over again, those last tragic moments of her waking nightmare . . .

He knew this dream well.

Knew every scene—every gory, meticulous detail—for he had been with her the night it began, and he had been with her every night since, feeling it replay endlessly, torturously, through her sleep . . .

So this is what it's like to die . . .

Lying there on her back in the grass, all alone in the darkness, Lucy could sense the wet, runny mask of her face. Tears? Blood? She couldn't be sure, couldn't be sure she even had *a face, couldn't be sure about anything except that her body screamed in pain each time she tried to draw even the shallowest of breaths.*

I can't move . . . Help . . . Somebody, help me . . .

With a ragged cry, Lucy tried to lift her head, tried to peer through the thick, endless night surrounding her. As in a dream, she could see the faraway sky blazing bright, lit by a giant fire—and along with those sickening smells of pain and fear and despair that threatened to choke her, now there was the gasoline . . . burning rubber . . . white-hot metal . . . and something else . . . something dear to her heart . . .

Byron!

That's Byron's van!

She'd been sitting in the front seat beside him, and she'd been staring at the moon. That blood red moon hovering there behind the trees and glowing out through the dark, shredded fabric of the clouds. She'd been staring at the moon, and then she'd jolted with the first sharp swerve of the van. Confused and groggy, she'd heard Byron's shout, the piercing shriek of brakes and tires, she'd felt the road give way to air beneath them as they dove off the shoulder and off the crest of the hill, and out through the foggy night, plummeting down and down into nothingness . . .

Byron? Can you hear me?

She knew somehow that she hadn't spoken aloud, knew somehow that her thoughts had burst free of her pain, only to fall silent among the shadows. It was so dark out here. So dark, so frighteningly still, except for those flames leaping and glowing against the distant horizon . . .

Something ran in front of us.

With a moan, Lucy struggled to shut out the pain, struggled to focus her hazy thoughts.

Byron tried to swerve, he tried to miss hitting it, but something ran in front of us . . .

She wished she could remember. She wished she could remember what it was that had caused the accident. But there was only the briefest glimmer of memory in that last fatal second, only the briefest image of something caught in the headlights as the car veered and left the road.

What was that?

It seemed so familiar somehow . . .

But her thoughts were fading . . . fading . . . and she knew she was slipping away. In desperation she stared up at the trees overhead, great gnarled branches etched thickly against the black dome of the sky. And then she noticed that moon.

So full and round. So red like blood. Caught in a web of tangled limbs, oozing out through the clouds, wine stains on velvet.

Byron, I'm so scared! Please help me!

And that's when she heard it.

The soft rustling sound, like wind sighing through grass. Except that she couldn't feel *any wind, not even the faintest of breezes, in this heavy night air.*

The sound was close by.

Coming even closer . . .

Oh God!

Once more she tried to lift herself, to call out for help. But the rustlings were in her head now, in her thoughts and in her pain, like so many urgent whispers, whispers of great importance.

As Lucy's head turned helplessly to one side, she saw

shadows all around her, shadows slinking along the ground and through the trees, slivers of black and pale pale gray, and sparks of amber light . . .

Terror exploded within her. Even through the paralyzing numbness of pain and shock, she sensed that these were animals, and she sensed why they were here. Instinct told her that she was surrounded, though one stood closer than the others. She could hear the slow, calm rhythm of its breathing as it watched her from a place she couldn't see.

Oh, God, don't let me die like this!

She thought of Byron. The vision burst inside her brain with such force that she choked and gagged and vomited blood in the grass. In that one instant of agonizing clarity she saw his midnight eyes, heard his calm, deep voice telling her not to be afraid. Now she remembered how he'd turned to her in that last split second of his life, his eyes desperate with helplessness and disbelief as he'd reached for her hand. Did he touch me? *The thought drifted through her mind, light as a feather.* Did we touch one last time?

But the whispers were louder now, and the fire was brighter than ever, and she was so weak . . . so tired.

Please . . . please . . . just let me die fast . . .

Night swayed around her. As tears ran silently

down her cheeks, something huge and dark leaned in over her, blocking her view of the sky.

She braced herself for the end. Felt hot breath caressing her throat . . . smelled the faint, familiar scent of something sweet . . .

Byron . . . I'm so sorry . . .

"Byron has gone," the voice murmured. "Only I can save you now."

Down, down, she sank . . . into the endlessness of time . . .

Who are you . . . ? What are you . . . ?

And that voice . . . fading far into nothingness. . .

"Oh, Lucy . . . there's no name for what we are . . ."

And so he stood, and he watched her.

How lovely she was . . . and how curious . . . so small and fragile, her pale skin nearly transparent, her expression as remote, as beautiful, as death.

But not quite.

Not quite dead yet.

Shock was just a stepping-stone. It would be so easy, he knew, to ease her across that tenuous threshold; just one swift, silent act on his part.

But there was something entrancing . . . mesmerizing . . . about the way she hovered there—just on the edge, between life and eternity—that was exciting to him.

There had been no time to take her before.

Before, as he dragged her to safety, and then as she lay there in the tall scorched grass, bruised and battered and drenched in blood, the others sweeping in silently around her, quivering with anticipation . . .

But "No," he had ordered them. "Stand away—this one is mine."

Damn those who had stopped to help!

And a firetruck, no less—a whole *convoy* of emergency vehicles, in fact—heading homeward from some tragedy, following a careful distance behind the van, yet still close enough to witness its fatal careen off the road, its hurtling descent down the rocky hillside, the bits and pieces of its broken shell raining like fireworks through the shattered night.

So many people! Sirens, lights, confusion!

The others of his kind had fled at once, but he alone had stayed.

He alone had stayed behind . . .

Hidden and silent . . .

Guarding his prize.

So there had been no time to take her then, in the panic, the chaos, of that hopeless rescue, the air stinking of futility and death even as he swept her away with him through the fog-shrouded woods, to this place of dark secrets and solitude. And every night afterward . . . including this late night . . . he had been here, watching over her, slinking through the terror of her dreams.

It was these dreams he feasted on in the meantime.

The loneliness, the heartache, the empty black holes of despair.

Hazy images of a mother who had died . . . a cozy home that was no more . . . and now this loss of someone new, this grievous, unexpected loss of Byron . . . such painful memories buried within her, buried deep, because to remember them would be far too much agony to endure.

"Cold . . . I'm so cold . . ."

He heard her whimper, a plea as faint as breath. And there was no hesitation as he leaned down over her, his lips drawn instinctively to that perfect, most sensitive spot.

Relief was instant and needle-sharp—teeth stabbing like fire, piercing hot through her skin, sinking deep through her flesh, clamping down and holding on, suspending her on boiling waves of panic and burning pleasure . . .

"*Lucy* . . ." His breath caressed her cheek, the delicate lids of her eyes, the tender flesh of her throat . . . "*No more cold . . . no more pain . . . no more loneliness . . .*"

Had she smiled? Ever so softly in her sleep?

He pondered this as he gazed upon her, as she stirred languidly in the aftermath of his kiss. Pondered this so intently that he failed to anticipate the slight, sudden movement of her hand as it groped through the shadows and brushed the side of his face, touching him with an innocence that caught him completely unaware.

He drew in his breath, every muscle tightening. His keen eyes narrowed, gleaming with annoyance and a hint of wonder. He had let his guard down—a weakness he could not afford—and yet for that one fleeting second, the gentle reward of her hand upon his cheek had been well worth his carelessness.

He drew back from her now, strangely unnerved, as her hand lowered once again to her side. As she lay weak and helpless, lost in the sorrow of her memories.

But little by little he would take those memories.

Devour them until the past, as she knew it, existed no more.

And then she would be filled with him . . . her mind, her body, her soul.

Like life's rich blood . . .

Filled with him and him alone.

1

Lucy's eyes flew open.

With a gasp of terror, she tried to scream, to fight her way free, but *free from what*, she wondered groggily, *I can't move, I can't see, something's holding me down . . .*

"Aunt Irene?"

She'd meant to call out, yet she couldn't hear her own voice. There was only silence, as still and deep as a grave, and the frantic pounding of her heartbeat.

"Aunt Irene, are you there?"

Slowly . . . hazily . . . her surroundings began shifting into focus. Lucy realized that she was lying on her back, and that the thing holding her down was a blanket—a blanket that should have been easy to push back, except that she didn't have the strength to kick it away. Beneath her the ground was cold and damp; beside her a candle flickered weakly, its melted stub drowning in a puddle of wax. As she gazed up at the curved ceiling, grotesque shadows leaped across in a macabre dance.

Where am I?

There were smells in here. Curious smells from every direction, smells she couldn't quite identify. Like the one lingering upon her blanket and in the tangled strands of her hair . . . an outdoors smell, wild and earthy, and not altogether unpleasant. It reminded her of frost and snowy moonlight, autumn wind and warm, wet fur . . .

A musky smell. A primitive smell.

Some sort of animal?

Moaning softly, Lucy struggled to sit up, totally unprepared for the wave of dizziness that pulled her down again. Her whole body reeled from the force of it; her nerves screamed in agony as pain ripped through every bone and muscle. Clutching her head with both hands, she felt a strip of wet, sticky cloth sagging low over her left eye.

"*Aunt Irene!*"

A spray of stars burst in her brain. It blurred behind her eyes, and memories began struggling to the surface of her mind, clawing their way through a sludge of fear and rising panic.

Byron! Oh, God, I remember . . . I remember everything. The accident . . . fire . . . and he didn't get out . . . Byron didn't get out—

"Can anyone hear me?" Lucy cried. "Please! Is anybody there?"

Oh my God, what's happening?

Trembling violently, she eased the blanket down from her shoulders. Her skin felt raw against the roughness of the fabric, raw and chilled and unusually sensitive. To her shock, she suddenly realized that all her clothes had been removed.

Lucy curled herself tightly beneath the blanket. *Please let this be a dream—please let me wake up!* Her mind was wild with terror, her heart pumped out of control. She couldn't breathe, couldn't stop shaking, couldn't stop the frantic spinning of her thoughts. Where was she, and how had she gotten here? How badly was she injured? How long had she been unconscious, and who had been here with her while she'd slept? She had to get away—*run* away—but from what? From whom? And where would she go? How could she possibly escape from one unknown to another?

And then a much more chilling thought crept in among all the others. Was someone here with her right now? Watching as she realized her hopeless predicament? Waiting for her to make a move? Cat and mouse, waiting to pounce?

Without warning, the ground gave a slow, deep shudder beneath her. As Lucy cried out in alarm, she felt another rumble of thunder resonating through the shadows; she heard the muffled, but unmistakable, downpouring of rain.

A storm. And it sounded close by.

Clenching her teeth against another onslaught of pain, Lucy reached out for the candle. She pried it from the glaze of dried wax, then held it at arm's length, moving it in a slow, deliberate arc.

She seemed to be in a cave. A small, denlike space with damp, water-stained walls and a low ceiling. About fifteen feet off to her left, the ceiling vanished completely into the pitch-blackness of a tunnel—while the same distance to her right, it sloped sharply upward before dead-ending.

No . . . not a dead end . . .

As Lucy's gaze followed the angle of the ceiling, she realized it led to an opening—a tiny opening scarcely big enough to squeeze through, an opening she hadn't recognized at first because it was covered up. But now she could see a hint of gray light around its edges, and a ragged hole near the bottom where part of the camouflage had blown away, and she realized that tree branches had been stacked up and wedged in from outside.

Someone had deliberately disguised the entrance to the cave.

To keep others out?

Or to keep me in?

A dank breeze snaked across the floor, threatening the candlelight and swathing Lucy in those strange and secret smells. But there was another odor she detected now—a much stronger odor than the one she'd noticed before. Something dead. Something spoiled.

Only bats, she tried to convince herself. Bats and rats and other creepy things that hid in dark places, shying away from the light. Or some wounded animal that had wandered in here once upon a time to die. Some poor creature, lost and trapped.

Trapped like me.

With sheer willpower, Lucy pulled herself to her knees. The feeble candlelight revealed several small puddles of water around her—black, shiny pools, shallow but thick. She could see dark splatters over the ground, and dark smears trailing back into the tunnel where her light couldn't reach.

She drew in her breath and closed her eyes. She opened them again and swallowed down a sick taste of fear.

Clutching the blanket, Lucy worked her way slowly to the nearest wall. It took several moments for her queasiness to pass, even longer to stand up. The gloom spun around her as she braced against the stone. She forced herself to take three halting steps.

There was no time to lose.

Moving toward the front of the cave, Lucy

spotted a pile of clothes lying directly in her path. She picked it up and ran her fingertips through the tangled shreds, relief giving way to disappointment. Her blouse—or rather, what was left of it—was completely useless. Her jacket was there, too—torn and stained, with one sleeve ripped away, but at least it was dry. Her jeans were missing. Also her socks. No shoes. No underwear.

Lucy eased her arms slowly, torturously, into her jacket. Then once again she wrapped the blanket around her shoulders and started walking.

Keep going. You can do it. One step at a time . . .

Her foot sank into something wet.

Wet and cold and slimy.

At once a stench rose into the air, the same foul odor she'd smelled before, except it was overpowering now, *suffocating* now. She jerked away, wiping her foot across the ground, and in the weakening candlelight saw one of the thick, black puddles she'd stepped in. She stumbled back, only to realize that the hem of her blanket had also trailed in the pool. Quickly she yanked it up again, losing her balance as her other foot slammed down on something small and furry.

She felt the sharp snap of tiny bones.

The gush of curdled liquid squishing between her toes.

Screaming, Lucy toppled over, landing hard on her stomach, fighting desperately not to pass out. As she lifted her head, she found herself staring into the dull, sightless eyes of a rabbit.

It had been dead for quite a while.

She could tell from the lolling posture of its neck, the jagged slash through its underbelly, the way it had been savagely gutted, leaving only a few strings of raw flesh and muscle and leftover entrails smeared across the bottom of her foot.

Lucy's mind went dark.

As her fingers dug into the ground, the whole world turned upside down, and her brain exploded in a kaleidoscope of panic:

Running—racing—right left zigzag path—paws thundering silently—shadow swift—scent of hopeless terror—screams—shrill screams—breath razor hot—sprays of red gurgling bubbling—

One last look at the sky . . . one last smell of the pines . . . sweet woodland home fading . . .

Lucy's eyes slowly opened. Shaking violently, she turned her head sideways and threw up.

The candle flared one last time.

As Lucy tried to reach it, to revive it for another second, the hot red wax dripped over her fingers, molding to her like a second skin.

As though her own hand was stained with the innocent blood of her vision.

2

It was madness, she knew.

Sheer madness to run, not knowing where she was or what lay outside the cave, not knowing where she could possibly go.

Sheer, utter madness.

Yet not nearly as crazy as staying here, Lucy reminded herself. Here in this place of death and darkness, not knowing when her captor might return. She knew now that those pools and splatters on the ground, those stains leading back into the tunnel, could be only one thing—and that much blood could never have come from one small rabbit.

What kind of person was she dealing with?

What kind of insanity?

Peeling the wax from her fingers, Lucy staggered to her feet and limped to the entrance of the cave. Her earlier suspicions had been right—someone had tried to cover it with brush and branches, but where some of the limbs had fallen away, she had a clear view of the world beyond.

Trees.

Trees as far as she could see. A leaden gray sky overhead. Ghostly gray mist . . . a solid downpour of cold gray rain. Lucy couldn't tell if it was dusk or early morning.

He could be out there right now. Hiding. Watching. Waiting to see if I'll try to escape. Waiting so he can catch me and bring me back again.

It was a chance she had to take.

Steeling herself, she began tearing at the barricade. The branches were heavy and cumbersome, most of them hopelessly entwined, and Lucy had to stop frequently to catch her breath, brace herself against the wall, will her dizziness away, and force herself not to cry out. The blanket slipped from her shoulders onto the wet ground. The few remaining buttons on her jacket were useless against the chill. Every simple movement was almost more than she could bear.

But at last she began to make headway. The opening grew larger; she could see more of the woods beyond. The rain fell harder, and as she stopped once more to catch her breath, she gathered the soggy blanket and shoved it through the opening. *Not much protection, but better than nothing*. She watched it land in a puddle on the other side, and then, gathering all the strength she could, Lucy squeezed through after it.

The ground was frozen. The wind was raw. Her whole body recoiled from the shock of the elements, and for several agonizing moments all she could do was lie there, sprawled in the mud where she'd fallen. Something slid down over her left eye, and she managed to pull it off. She remembered feeling a strip of cloth there earlier. Now she could see that it was a bandage, and that it was soaked with blood.

My blood? Oh God . . . how bad am I really hurt?

With cautious fingers she touched the swollen places on her forehead, the ragged edges of split skin, the crustiness in her hair. She choked down a fresh wave of horror and stumbled to her feet, then pulled the blanket around her and began to run.

She had no idea where she was going. She simply plunged into the woods, ignoring the dizziness in her head, the weakness in her knees. Her body felt like a stranger's body as she tried to drag it through the forest, tripping over the soggy blanket, crawling through the mud and underbrush, forcing herself up again. She could see her breath—short gasps of pain hanging frosty in the air—and her nose was running, and her tears seemed to freeze upon her cheeks. Her heart thudded in her ears, and every clumsy footstep seemed to echo around her, causing her to look back in terror, certain she was being followed.

Don't stop—run! Run faster, run harder! Run for your life!

But run *where*?

Lucy was completely lost. Like a liquid dream, minutes flowed into hours, and then into no time at all. The woods were endless. With so many twists and turns, she wondered if she might even be going in circles. It was definitely growing darker. She couldn't feel her feet anymore. As she glanced down to see if they were still at the end of her legs, she realized that the blanket had fallen off, though she didn't remember dropping it.

It doesn't matter! Keep running!

She tried to hold her jacket around her, but her arms had gone numb. Through the steady rush of rain, she was aware of trees like phantoms, and the dying brilliance of fallen leaves, thick cushions of pine needles, and the ups and downs of hills that went on and on.

She wanted to give up.

To collapse and simply lie there, to close her eyes and drift away.

Better to die out here than back in the cave. Better to die on her own terms than at the hands of some maniac.

She paused a moment, breath sharp in her ribs, trying to peer off through the dense maze of trees. Surely there was a house out here somewhere—a farm, a cabin? Surely there must be a pathway or a road? She thought about screaming for help, but decided against it. She doubted anyone could hear her above this rain, and if her captor had returned by now to find her missing, she couldn't take the chance of giving herself away.

Lucy turned slowly in all directions.

There must be a way out—there *had* to be a way out!

And then her body went rigid with fear.

A shadow?

Had she seen a shadow just now . . . off to the side of her . . . slipping through the woods?

Seconds crept by but she couldn't move, could scarcely even breathe. Of course she'd imagined it. The rain was playing tricks on her. It was just leaves swirling to the ground, branches swaying in the wind, some startled animal taking cover between the trees.

That's all it is, Lucy. That's all.

Rallying her courage, she forced herself to go on. Then stopped again, almost immediately.

She *hadn't* imagined it—she was sure this time!

A dark silhouette through the foggy rain, just a glimpse as it glided up the incline about twenty yards away, then vanished behind some rocks.

Lucy's heart ricocheted into her throat. A

bear? Yet it seemed too graceful, too fast to be a bear. And the vague, unsettling shape of it . . . something so dangerous . . .

So familiar . . .

The low stone wall behind Irene's house . . . the woods, the deserted road at the Fall Festival . . . the large, murky figure darting in front of Byron's van . . .

"Oh God," Lucy whispered. "Oh God, please help me!"

In sheer panic she began to run. Mindless now with terror, exhausted beyond reason, she stumbled deeper and deeper under cover of the forest, never even noticing the sudden glimmer of light just ahead of her. As Lucy plunged through the trees, the ground disappeared without warning.

There was a dreamlike sensation of falling, of floating, before she suddenly slammed back to reality and rolled down the side of the hill. The earth was soft where she landed, but her body screamed on impact. She lay there, too stunned to move, her breath completely jolted out of her. Against her icy cheeks, the flow of blood felt warm and almost comforting.

Cautiously, Lucy tried to lift her head. She was lying in tall dead weeds, and as she moaned softly and squinted through her pain, she imagined she could see a dirt road not five feet away.

Her head fell back again. She closed her eyes against the rain and tasted blood trickling into the corners of her mouth.

And then she heard a sound.

A sound like an engine, like a car.

Tears came to her eyes, and she pinched the skin on her arm, pinched it hard to make herself wake up, because she knew she couldn't bear one more nightmare, one more disappointment.

But the sound was still there.

And it was coming closer.

With her last ounce of strength, Lucy dragged herself onto the road. She tried to lift one arm, tried to give a feeble wave as the car bore down on her. She knew the driver probably couldn't see her through the rain, through the dusk, and as the headlights blinded her, she braced herself for the shock.

There was a loud squeal of brakes, a wet skid of tires.

And then a door opening . . . hands on her shoulders, turning her over, rearranging her jacket, smoothing back her hair.

Arms lifted her. Carried her without the slightest effort, then settled her gently onto the backseat.

And then, as she finally surrendered to blissful unconsciousness, Lucy heard soft words whispered through the dark.

"Remember to look both ways, Lucy. It's a dangerous road you're on."

3

“My meeting will probably run late tonight, Lucy. Will you be all right here alone?”

Startled, Lucy glanced up to see her aunt standing in the living room doorway. With one quick movement, Lucy managed to hide the piece of paper she’d been holding, slipping it underneath some magazines stacked beside her on the couch.

“I’ll be fine.” Lucy forced a smile, even though her heart gave a sickening clench. *Of course I’ll be fine, I’m used to it; even when you* are *here, I’m still alone*. But still, she couldn’t keep from asking, “Are you sure everything’s locked?”

“The house is completely secure, I’ve told you before. And I’ll set the alarm on my way out.”

But it didn't matter *how* many times Irene had told her, Lucy never felt entirely protected, never entirely safe. She merely *pretended* each time to be reassured by her aunt's promises, because she knew Irene would never believe her if she told the truth. Neither Irene nor anyone else would ever believe that something, or someone, was after Lucy. Sometimes Lucy wasn't even sure she believed it herself, yet the nagging dread was always there, like a shadow over her shoulder.

And anyway, Lucy told herself, *where else could I go?*

Her aunt turned to leave, hesitated, then faced her again. *Like a robot*, Lucy thought, *more cold and withdrawn than ever*. As though Angela's disappearance had added a final layer of distance to those steel barriers around Irene's heart. Lucy couldn't help wondering how differently things might have turned out if that relationship between stepmother and stepdaughter hadn't been so strained. But speculations were pointless, and now she watched curiously as her aunt's lips twisted into a tight semblance of a smile.

"Did Dr. Fielding mention your going back to school?" she asked, and Lucy nodded.

"Yes. On Monday."

"He feels it's best for you to get back into a normal routine. I agree with him."

Of course you do. Out of sight, out of mind.

"He called me this afternoon." Irene seemed to be struggling for conversation. "He says you're doing well. He says you're coming to terms." Another uncomfortable pause, and then she straightened. "You should eat. Fix yourself something in the microwave. There's pizza. Angela always . . ."

Abruptly her aunt walked away. Lucy waited for the sound of the back door to close, then jumped up and went systematically around the house, checking windows, double-checking that shades were drawn and curtains were closed, inspecting locks and deadbolts and the security system. Then, as satisfied as she could be that the house was impregnable, she sat down again and pulled out the paper she'd hidden.

Angela, Lucy thought miserably, *where are you?*

She stared down at the crumpled poster. A

poster of Angela, just like the ones she'd seen plastered all over town.

With a weary sigh, Lucy snuggled deep into the couch and leaned her head back against the cushions. No one had seen or heard from Angela since that Saturday night of the festival, the night of Lucy and Byron's accident, that strange and fatal night just over a week ago.

Things like this don't happen. How many times had Lucy told herself that in the days following the tragedies? *Things like this happen only in movies. Happen only to strangers. Things like this don't happen in real life, not to normal people.*

But I'm not normal anymore, she had to remind herself now for at least the hundredth time. Not since she'd wandered into the cemetery that night and found Katherine. No matter how much she tried to pretend, nothing would ever be the same again, and it had taken Byron to convince her of that.

Byron . . .

She'd cried buckets of tears, cried until she couldn't cry anymore. The guilt was more than she could bear—the doubts, the regrets, replaying those last moments of Byron's life.

Her heart and soul felt empty. So empty, in fact, that she often found herself wondering if maybe *she* had died, too, and that this strange half existence was but a lingering dream. Her salvation had become a cold sort of numbness, a distancing of herself from both memories and emotions. This was the only way she'd been able to survive.

The only way she would *ever* be able to survive.

Reaching over, Lucy lifted a mug of cocoa from the end table, then tested the foamy marshmallows with her tongue. The chocolate was sweet and hot, but did little to warm the chill inside her. As she took a cautious sip, her gaze returned to the small poster she'd placed in her lap.

MISSING: HAVE YOU SEEN ANGELA?

Looking back at her was a color-copy image of Angela's face, taken from her senior class photo. Those perfect cheekbones and flowing black hair, that model-perfect smile. *I wonder where that smile is now? I wonder if she even* can *smile?*

Lucy fought off the familiar waves of guilt and set her mug back on the table. Then she put the poster aside, drew both knees up to her chin, and wrapped her arms tight around them.

"Not your fault," Dr. Fielding would say if he could share her thoughts now. "Circumstances beyond your control," he'd remind her, and "You can't keep torturing yourself."

Good old Dr. Fielding. Aunt Irene's personal choice of prominent friends, who was supposed to be helping Lucy through the nightmares, helping her to readjust, helping her to come to terms with all that had happened.

Except Dr. Fielding didn't know the half of it.

And Lucy knew she could never tell him.

"It's only been a week, Lucy," the doctor had reminded her in their session just that afternoon. "These things take time. Often, quite a lot of time."

And Lucy had given her dutiful nod and tried to listen politely. Because how could Dr. Fielding even *begin* to have a clue as to what she was going through? How could she even *begin* to tell him everything that had happened to her since she'd first come to Pine Ridge?

"Like I explained to you in the hospital, you

might experience dizziness or light-headedness—possibly fainting spells. You may become disoriented or suffer memory lapses. There could be flashbacks pertaining to the accident, or you might even experience panic attacks."

"Great," Lucy had responded. "That certainly gives me something to look forward to."

But Dr. Fielding had smiled his kind smile and patted her on the shoulder. "These occurrences are all very common with a head injury, Lucy—nothing to be overly concerned about. The important thing is to accept the fact that even if they *do* happen, you really are okay. And you really *are* going to get better."

"But you still think I made everything up."

She'd watched his face, that carefully controlled doctor face, as he'd steepled his fingers beneath his chin and studied her from his leather chair.

"I think that trauma-induced memories are very tricky things," he'd answered, as she'd known he would.

"I'm not lying about what happened."

"I know you're not lying. I believe that *you* believe everything you've told me. And it's still amazing to *everyone* how you could have survived that accident, much less survived for three days afterward."

Lucy's hands had twisted in her lap. "I told you. I was in a cave. But I don't know how I got there."

"And those are three days and nights still unaccounted for," he'd sighed. "The police didn't even know you'd been with Byron until your aunt came home the next day and reported you and Angela missing. And even then, it took time to track down witnesses at the Festival who saw you and Byron leave together. After that, search parties combed that entire area around the accident site. Hundreds of people, even scent dogs, spread out for miles. No one discovered a cave. There wasn't a house or a trail or a single clue. But you must have found shelter somehow, somewhere. It's a total mystery. And nothing short of a miracle."

Lucy had heard it all before. She'd told the police everything she could remember about her ordeal—the muffled sounds and shadows, the pools of blood, the dead rabbit, how someone had tried to camouflage the entrance to the cave, and how she'd finally escaped in spite of it. She'd told the doctors, too, and Aunt Irene, and even the private investigator her aunt had hired to search for Angela. But she knew they didn't believe her. Like Dr. Fielding, they all thought she suffered from delusions, the results of her head injury, exposure, and shock.

"But someone found me and brought me to the hospital," she couldn't help reminding him. "And that was real."

Dr. Fielding had conceded with a smile. "Yes. That was definitely real. Three days after the accident, someone left you outside the door of the emergency room. No one saw this person come or go, and no one's been able to find out who it was. If they could, it might help enormously in solving your disappearance."

"I just wish I could thank him. I think of him every day, and I try so hard to remember something about him . . . *anything* about him."

"Maybe you're trying too hard."

"All I know is, he wasn't the one in the cave."

"And how can you be so sure?"

"I can't explain it, but I just know. His voice was different."

"Hallucinations can seem very, very real."

Hallucinations? Well, maybe she really *had* imagined it. Maybe she really *was* going insane.

"You remembered drifting in and out of consciousness," Dr. Fielding had said, going over his notes once more. "And the will to survive is an incredible thing. It gives us the endurance we might never have under normal circumstances."

"But what if I'm right? What if I'm right, and whoever I escaped from comes after me again?"

"You're catastrophizing, Lucy. Even if this person *were* real, how could you be any safer than you are right now, with all this attention being focused on you? No one would dare try to kidnap you twice."

Lucy had bitten her lip in frustration. Twisted her hands even tighter in her lap.

"So if I wasn't kidnapped, then what did I do after the wreck? Just wander around for miles and miles? Find shelter in some place that doesn't even exist?"

"There was no serious frostbite on your feet; the hypothermia you suffered was relatively mild. Not nearly severe enough to suggest your wandering outdoors for any extended length of time. Your other injuries were consistent with those from a car accident, or from falling down a hill, as you described—scrapes, bruises, mild concussion, those nasty gashes on your head. No broken bones, incredibly. And the rest of the examination showed no evidence whatsoever of any sexual molestation."

Lucy had turned her head away, and stared out the office window. *But someone took my clothes. And someone touched me. And something stung like fire, something I've never felt before . . .*

She still remembered the sensation. Remembered it all too clearly, though she hadn't been able to find any unusual marks on her skin; no tell-tale punctures, no secret scars, nothing intimate or the least bit intrusive. Yet a few times it had come back to her in the middle of the night, in writhing dreams, flushing her entire body with heat and a sense of perpetual emptiness.

Just remembering it in Dr. Fielding's office today had caused that strange, unsettling ache deep, deep within her. An untreatable ache that made her squirm restlessly in her chair.

"I'm very pleased with your test results," the

doctor had continued, not seeming to notice her sudden uneasiness. "Your stitches can come out in a week or two; your soreness, I'm afraid, will take a little longer. And I expect you to make even more progress in the days to come. But injuries take time to heal, you know." His gaze was one of genuine sympathy. "Not just the physical ones, but the emotional ones, as well."

The ache inside her had suddenly focused on her heart.

"You want me to talk about Byron," she said quietly.

"I understand his funeral is this weekend."

Lucy had swallowed tears, barely able to answer. "Tomorrow."

"Are you going to attend?"

But the tears had only thickened as she shook her head. "I can't. There's no way I can do it."

"Do you think it might help give you some sort of closure?"

"How can there ever be closure? I can't stop thinking about him. I can't stop thinking about his grandmother, and how she's going to manage now that he's gone."

"Do you know his grandmother?"

"I've only heard about her. I know she's sick and that Byron took care of her. And I feel so responsible, and I keep thinking how can I possibly help her—"

"Lucy," he'd said, cutting her off gently, "right now you're in no condition to take care of anyone. Right now you need to concentrate on yourself and—"

"Can we just not talk about it anymore?"

There'd been that uncomfortable silence between them then; that silence, Lucy knew, that always preceded some sort of lecture.

At last Dr. Fielding spoke. "I think there are certain things that each of us must work through in our own time, in our own way. Loss and grief are just two of those things. You know I'm always here to help you. Whenever you're ready."

For one split second she'd almost given in. He'd looked so wise, so sincere, that the need to unburden herself had almost been more than she could bear. *Since you're so interested in knowing, Doctor, it all started when I went into the cemetery, found a murdered girl, was touched with a supernatural power, met Byron, and then found myself having weird visions and being watched and followed by some dark shadowy thing . . .*

She'd actually leaned forward. She'd stared into Dr. Fielding's eyes, and her fingers had gripped the arms of her chair.

"When I'm ready," she'd finally answered.

She could tell he'd been disappointed. Yet he'd reached over and given her hand an encouraging squeeze. "With that said, I see no reason why you can't start back to school. I think a normal routine would be very beneficial at this juncture, offer some stability. People your own age . . . fun activities . . . anything to distract you from the terrible ordeal you've just experienced."

"Byron's dead. Angela's missing." These were the words she'd repeated so many, many times that she'd lost count. "It's all my fault."

And once more, Dr. Fielding had given his tireless response. "None of this is your fault, Lucy. None of this was *ever* your fault. Life has its own agenda; it never asks our permission or approval. You're alive, and you're safe. And, believe me . . . that's nothing to feel guilty about."

How simple he made it sound, Lucy thought

now, shifting positions, slumping down on the couch. Had it been only six days since Angela slipped away from the Fall Festival with her invisible boyfriend—generating search parties and volunteers, police investigations and nationwide alerts, false leads and dead-end tips? Lucy could still recall her cousin's behavior that Saturday night—rebellious and excited, mysterious and hopeful with thoughts of love. Now Angela was just another teenage runaway, just another statistic, like millions of other girls that vanished every year.

Except there was nothing typical about Angela's disappearance—Lucy was sure of it. And there was no one—no one at all—whom she could share her suspicions with.

Only Byron.

Byron whose funeral was tomorrow.

Guilt slammed into her with merciless force—the same guilt that battered her day after day, ripping her heart, wearing her down.

"*If you want to live,*" Katherine had told her, "*you mustn't tell anyone what you've seen here tonight.*"

The words of the murdered girl echoed

through Lucy's brain. Katherine had warned her that night, and Lucy had chosen to ignore it; Katherine had warned her and died, yet Lucy hadn't really believed.

My fault. I told Byron, I told Byron everything, and now he's dead.

How could she have been so stupid? So irresponsible? How could she have dismissed Katherine's warning so easily?

Because Byron already knew what was happening . . . because Byron already understood the danger . . . because Byron was strong and brave and determined to take a chance . . .

Lucy buried her face in her hands.

She would never escape the guilt. It would never stop tormenting her. And no amount of prayers or tears, no well-meant platitudes or rationalizations, could ever bring Byron back.

She'd felt so horribly alone before.

But that was nothing compared to now.

4

The whole world seemed to be weeping for Byron.

As if in keeping with Lucy's mood, the day dawned gray and bitterly cold. Mist hung thick in the air, and after several feeble attempts to break through, the sun sank despondently behind a mourning veil of clouds.

Lucy closed the sliding glass doors to the balcony. In spite of her warm room and layers of clothes, she dug through her closet and put on another sweatshirt. She hadn't been able to stop shivering since she'd woken up. She'd hardly been able to keep her thoughts straight.

"Are you certain you don't want to go to the funeral?"

Lucy spun around. She hadn't heard Irene in

the hall, and now, as her aunt peered at her from the threshold, Lucy's stomach went queasy. Irene was dressed in conservative black, and her face was completely expressionless.

"I understand he's being buried in the old cemetery, but you needn't go if you feel uncomfortable," the woman went on. "You don't even have to stay for the entire service. Apparently his grandmother requested a casket, but it won't be open, of course, and—"

She broke off, looking uncomfortable.

No open casket, no body, Lucy's guilt taunted her. *Just charred remains*.

"I'm going to be sick," Lucy whispered, and bolted for the bathroom. When she finally came out again, Irene had gone, and a morbid silence settled throughout the house.

For a long while Lucy sat on the edge of her bed. She stared at the clock on her bedside table and watched the slow, torturous passing of time. Less than an hour till Byron's final farewell. Her heartbeat kept time to the tick of the clock. Her chest was so tight, she could hardly breathe. On unsteady legs she went back into the bathroom and stood at the sink, running a cold, wet washcloth over her face.

She looked so pale. Empty and haunted. The way her reflection had looked when Mom died. As though this might be the way she was going to look from now on.

She ran one hand slowly through her long blond hair, wincing at the tiny stitches near her scalp and the ones high up on her forehead. No point using makeup, she decided—nothing could hide the dark smudges beneath her eyes or the hollow expression gazing back at her, and her face would be covered anyway. She wove her hair into a single braid and tucked it down the back of her shirt. Then, returning to her room, she opened the top dresser drawer and took out her jewelry box.

Sadly she gazed down into the jumbled contents. She sifted some tangled necklaces between her fingers, and she sorted through a clump of earrings and silver bracelets. And then she found what she was looking for.

A pin.

A tiny, gold, heart-shaped pin that her mother had given her on her thirteenth birthday.

It had always been special to her, something she'd loved and cherished.

And that's why she wanted Byron to have it now.

Tucking it into her pocket, Lucy hurried downstairs. She went straight to the coat closet in the front hall, where she pulled on an oversized jacket and a pair of thick raglan gloves. She wound a knitted scarf around her neck and up over her chin; she stuck a wool cap on her head and worked it down as far as it would go.

Lucy felt satisfied with her disguise. She wasn't exactly sure when she'd changed her mind about the funeral, but now that she had, she felt an urgency to get the whole thing over with. She was sure no one would recognize her, and especially at a distance. She didn't plan on staying long anyway, just long enough for everyone to leave the gravesite, so she could have one last moment with Byron.

Turning abruptly, she headed for the garage. Yesterday morning she'd found Angela's car key lying on her nightstand, along with a brand-new cell phone—emergencies only—and a note from Irene encouraging her to use the Corvette. It made her uncomfortable, remembering how Irene had confiscated that same key the night Angela disappeared. There was something about using Angela's car that stirred Lucy's guilt all over again—almost as though she were *betraying* her cousin—but the truth was, she needed a car, and Irene was seldom around to offer transportation.

So as she drove slowly through the wet streets, her thoughts were focused on how ironic fate could be. The fact that she was using Angela's precious car only because Angela was missing. And the fact that she was going to the cemetery, where so many things in life ended—but where so many things in her life had begun.

The place where she'd first met Byron.

And now, the place where she would tell him good-bye.

Lucy had no trouble finding the old church that adjoined the town's even older burial grounds. By the time she arrived, the solemn cortege had wound its way along a narrow dirt lane through the graveyard and come to a respectful stop behind the hearse. Parking her car around the block where it wouldn't be noticed, she ducked her head and slipped in the back way.

The funeral was not far. The low drone of a solitary voice told her the service had already begun. To her surprise, there was a stone mausoleum instead of a grave, and like several other structures she'd noticed throughout this neglected part of the cemetery, Byron's family crypt reminded her of a miniature house for the dead. Dreary and decayed, with roof and walls draped in withered ivy, each corner was guarded by a faceless angel cradling a skull beneath its wings. Two broken urns flanked the gated doorway; the wrought-iron gates were flaked with rust. And the name WETHERLY, carved above the entrance, was nearly invisible, worn smooth by the ceaseless passing of time.

Suppressing a shiver, Lucy spotted a small grove of elm trees a safe distance behind the gathering, and hid herself deep in its shadows.

The mist had turned to light rain. Rainlike tears, wept from cold, gray sorrow. She could see the large crowd of mourners huddled together, sharing umbrellas and hugs and grief. She could hear the echo of muffled sobs. Byron might have been a loner, Lucy realized, but there was something about losing one of its own that bonded a community. Students, teachers, neighbors, strangers, old and young alike, she guessed, but especially the young people of Pine Ridge. They watched with pale, stricken faces and tragic disbelief.

Lucy shut her eyes, clamped her arms tight around her chest. A desperate wail rose up inside her and exploded in her mind, and as her eyes opened once more, she braced herself against one of the trees, not trusting her legs to hold her. She thought of Byron's grandmother, so frail and all alone. Tears streamed down her cheeks. Through the dim blur of autumn she could see Byron's coffin banked with flowers; she could see the vague figure of a priest. Words of comfort were being spoken—stories related and memories recalled—and prayers that held no meaning drifted back to her on the sad sigh of the wind.

And then it was over.

With hushed finality, people walked slowly

past Byron's casket, some adding more flowers and special mementos, some reaching out with one last touch, before wandering back to their cars. The hearse, empty now of its burden, led the procession of mourners away.

Lucy stood still for a moment as bitter reality sank in. She could see several men in work coveralls lounging across the lane, talking and laughing among buckets and tools, acting as though this were just any other ordinary day. It suddenly occurred to her that theirs was the most final job of all—that of interring Byron's coffin inside his family tomb.

With an effort, Lucy roused herself from her sorrow. She'd wanted some time alone with Byron, a private good-bye—but now she'd have to hurry before the workmen came over. Swiping a gloved hand across her cheeks, she eased from her hiding place and started toward the casket.

The feeling came without warning.

That cold prickly feeling of being watched.

Lucy froze in midstride. As her heart quickened, she turned and peered off through the drizzle, seeing nothing but headstones and crosses and statues, faint blurs beyond the rain.

Get a grip—you're imagining things.

Of course that was it, Lucy told herself firmly. Just the culmination of stress and fear, and everything else she'd endured over the past week, playing tricks with her mind.

You're just upset—not thinking straight. Hurry and do what you have to do.

Burrowing deep in her jacket, Lucy slowly approached the mausoleum. The workmen in the distance had noticed her now; she could see them shifting restlessly, anxious to finish their job, but allowing her some time. She kept her back to them and pretended they weren't there. She bent low over the coffin and ran her hands along its surface, breathing in the warm scent of the flowers, letting her sobs come at last, quiet and soul-wrenching cries of despair.

"I'm sorry, Byron," she wept. "I'm so, so sorry . . ."

She truly hadn't thought she could cry any more. But at last, empty and exhausted, she straightened up, reached into her pocket, and withdrew the heart-shaped pin. For a long moment she stared at the bouquets and personal tributes heaped upon the casket, wondering what she should do. If she left the pin on the coffin, it could so easily slide off. Become lost. Get stolen or thrown away.

She felt her eyes shifting to the family crypt.

Maybe there was another place she could put it—a hidden place no one else would ever know about. An eternal secret between Byron and her.

Squaring her shoulders, Lucy pretended to leave. She walked briskly off through the cemetery, then doubled back through the trees. From behind the mausoleum she watched the workmen gathering up their tools and strolling leisurely across the lane. She was certain they hadn't seen her—if she hurried, she'd be gone again before they even reached the tomb.

She glanced around quickly, the pin clutched tight in her glove. Beside her on a corner pedestal knelt one of the four angels, holding a ghoulish skull beneath its wings. On impulse, Lucy reached over and tried to lift the statue, surprised when it moved slightly off center. With a little effort, she managed to tip it sideways, just high enough to slide the pin under its base. Then she lowered it, gazed at where the angel's face should have been, and whispered a silent prayer.

Goose bumps crawled over her skin.

With a gasp, Lucy whirled around, her eyes probing the mist and the shadows, her heart stuck in her throat.

She was sure she hadn't imagined it this time.

Someone was watching her.

And it's someone I know . . .

Frantically she pushed the thought from her mind. It wasn't possible. She knew hardly anyone in Pine Ridge, the funeral was over, the mourners had gone, and except for the workmen she was all alone.

And yet her blood felt cold in her veins.

Because for one brief second, she could have sworn she'd seen a figure in the distance, standing still and silent among the graves.

A human figure that vanished just as soon as she'd turned to look.

5

School was even worse than before.

Lucy knew she must look like something straight from a horror movie, with her cuts and bruises and stiff, jerky movements. As she went slowly from class to class, she fought off fatigue and depression and kept her eyes averted from the other students. Since Byron's funeral she'd slept little, and even the medication Dr. Fielding had prescribed hadn't prevented the nightmares and sudden awakenings, the chills and sweats and frantic heartbeats as her mind endlessly replayed the car accident, her ordeal at the cave, her unknown rescuer, the shadowy figure at the cemetery.

After she'd returned home on Saturday she'd made up her mind not to discuss any more fears with Dr. Fielding. She knew he meant well, but she also knew he'd never believe her. Confiding in Irene was out of the question. And still being an outsider at school, there was no one Lucy could trust. If there were problems to be fixed and mysteries to be solved, it was totally up to her. She was on her own.

So she'd resigned herself to school today as Irene and Dr. Fielding had insisted, but she'd avoided any contact with her classmates. Not hard to do, Lucy thought ruefully as she made her way through the halls, all too aware of the anger and hatred aimed in her direction. She could feel the open hostility like knives in her back.

Testaments to Byron were everywhere. From the black armbands students wore, to his photographs watching her from lockers, corridors, bulletin boards, the walls of every classroom. A shrine had been set up outside the library—notes and letters, signs and posters, flowers and stuffed animals, and personal gifts. In every one of his classes, his desk remained empty, adorned with flowers and presents.

Lucy felt sick to her stomach and sick at heart. She didn't know how she was ever going to survive the day.

But besides the tributes to Byron, there were reminders of Angela, too. MISSING posters in every building, lining the halls, tucked among teddy bears, bouquets, and cards in makeshift memorials. Across the entire campus, yellow ribbons fluttered from every tree. No matter where Lucy went, she couldn't escape the guilt or the sorrow. Even the teachers seemed strangely uneasy around her, and when Principal Howser called her to his office to express sympathy and inform her she'd be meeting with a grief counselor, he kept the talk brief, as though she might be bad luck and highly contagious. By study hall, she felt like a leper.

Eager to escape, Lucy dumped her purse and books in her locker and slipped out a side door. Despite the overnight drop in temperature and the warning of possible snow, she found a bench at the far end of campus near the athletic field and sat down with her back against the fence. Irene had bought her a new coat that was fleecy and warm, and new boots perfect for winter. Lucy huddled into a snug ball and wrapped her wool scarf high around her cheeks, thrusting her mittened hands deep in her pockets. She seriously doubted she'd freeze to death out here, but even *that* prospect was more appealing than going back in to endure those accusing faces.

She let her eyes do a slow sweep of the school yard. A few kids were straggling in and out of the gym; a maintenance man on a riding mower was clearing leaves from the lawn. Several students had decided to brave the cold and were sharing notes at one of the picnic tables in the courtyard. Lucy sighed and began to tick off a mental list in her head. Her favorite purse and everything in it had been destroyed in the crash, and though she'd gotten her student ID this morning, and—thanks to Irene (who had friends in high places)—her driver's license had been reissued in no time at all, there were still some items she needed to replace. Funny how you took those little things for granted, didn't even notice them, in fact, till they were gone. Like her pen with the fuzzy top and her lucky pink stone. Chewing gum and breath mints and chocolate-covered raisins. Her mini-mirror and matching comb, the little green notepad, a tiny vial of spray perfume. Her leather key ring, with the key to her old apartment still attached.

Lucy closed her eyes and swallowed a lump in her throat.

Her red wallet and her address book, and all the pictures of the friends she'd left behind. Symbolic, somehow, she thought bitterly. Her life was different now—her *world* was different now. There was nothing and no one she could ever go back to.

She swallowed harder as tears welled behind her eyelids. Maybe it was time to fix up that bedroom she hated so much, unpack her boxes stored up in the attic, make the room her own. Maybe she should try to get a job. Buy some new clothes like Irene had been encouraging her to do. Resign herself to reality.

Reality . . . right. Being a freak and being alone.

She was so intent on her misery that she didn't even notice someone had stopped beside the bench. As she heard the sound of twigs snapping, she opened her eyes and saw a pair of raggedy sneakers planted firmly on the ground in front of her.

Lucy stared up in surprise.

"You know," the girl said somberly, "death by freezing isn't quite as painless as you might think. Even though you probably don't care much about that fact right now."

There was something vaguely familiar about this person, something Lucy couldn't quite put her finger on. So instead she returned the comment with a frown.

"I'd like to be alone, if you don't mind."

"That's probably a bad idea." The soft-spoken girl gestured toward the bench. "How about if I join you for a while?"

It was obvious she wasn't going away. Lucy considered her options, frowned harder, then grudgingly scooted over. The girl promptly sat, her legs splayed out in front of her, both arms wrapped around a beat-up knapsack. Lucy continued to frown, then felt a small stir of recognition.

"I know you. You're the girl at the Festival—the one working with Angela."

"One and the same. I'm also in homeroom and three other classes with you, but I doubt that you've noticed."

"I . . . sorry. I guess I haven't."

"Well, it's hard to notice much of anything when you're staring at your desk all the time.

And anyway, when you saw me at the Festival, I was pretty rude."

Lucy recalled her clearly now. The girl at the entrance to Pin the Nose on the Scarecrow, the one with the serious face. "You look different."

"Because I no longer have a bunch of wild brats hanging all over me." The girl gave a mock shudder. "What was I thinking anyway, volunteering for that stupid game? I don't even like kids."

Lucy's resistance melted. She could feel a hesitant smile coming on.

"Dakota." The girl held out a small, wind-chapped hand. "Dakota Montana. I swear I'm not making it up."

This time Lucy did smile. And as the two shared a handshake, she managed a quick, head-to-toe appraisal of her new acquaintance.

The girl had been frazzled and distracted at the Fall Festival, surrounded by children and distorted by colored lights—but now Lucy could see the waist-length red hair; the large, solemn, pale blue eyes; the thick straight brows; the sprinkling of tiny freckles across the fair skin of her cheekbones. Her nose was delicate; her mouth too wide for her heart-shaped face. A good three inches shorter than Lucy, she was wearing faded overalls with ripped knees, a dingy sweater that might once have been white, and the most ridiculous scarf Lucy had ever seen—at least twenty feet of it—knitted in every color of the rainbow. It was wrapped not only several times around Dakota's neck, but also draped down her chest and back, hanging all the way to her sneakers—one pink and one green—both laced with orange ribbon. Despite the unique fashion statement, there was an almost ethereal quality about her, Lucy realized—like a woodland elf or a fairy queen from some fantasy bedtime story. And as she met Dakota's eyes, the girl gave a faint smile, a smile that hinted of wisdom and experience far too old for such a young face.

"They won't act like jerks forever, you know," Dakota said quietly. "It's just because of Byron."

Lucy was taken aback. Her mouth opened, then closed again, with no words of defense. Dakota shot her a glance of sympathy, leaned back, and tucked both hands beneath the bib of her overalls.

"Everyone knows you were with him in the accident," she went on matter-of-factly. "They don't care about knowing anything else."

Lucy could barely choke out the words. "They hate me because he died and I didn't."

"Well . . ." Dakota seemed to be thinking, rocking slowly back and forth in her seat. "It's more complicated than that. They hate you because the two of you got together. And Byron never got together with anyone."

"We . . . we were just friends, if that's what you mean."

"That's *not* what I mean. And it's none of my business anyway. It's just that Byron was here for so long—in this town, in this school—and no one really *knew* him. Then *you* come to school for one day, and he actually spends time with you. You make some sort of connection with him that no one's ever made."

Lucy said nothing, only stared miserably down at her feet. *If only you knew the truth . . . if only you knew the whole story . . .*

Dakota stopped rocking, her brow creased in a puzzled frown.

"Guilt's such a weird power," she mused. "It makes people do crazy things. Mean, hateful things sometimes. And right now everyone's closing ranks, trying to figure stuff out, trying to pretend they were all Byron's friends." She paused for a moment, her voice growing hard. "Now that he's gone, they're upset and they're missing him. The school's brought in grief counselors to help them deal with it. They've put Byron's pictures all over the place. I mean . . . I didn't know Byron very well either. But I think he'd *hate* all this, all this attention from a bunch of hypocrites."

For some strange reason, Lucy felt comforted by these words. She watched as Dakota started rocking again, as the girl plucked up one end of her knitted scarf and twirled it between her fingers.

"I think you're right," Lucy said at last. "I think he *would* hate it."

Once again, Dakota went still. For a long moment the two girls stared at each other. And then they both smiled.

"You *really* didn't want to freeze to death, did you?" Dakota asked, standing up, holding out both her hands.

Still smiling, Lucy shook her head. She let Dakota pull her off the bench, then fell into step beside her as they headed back across the grounds.

"Do you know Byron's grandmother?" Lucy asked, trying not to stumble over Dakota's trailing muffler.

"I know *about* her—but no, I've never met her. To tell you the truth, I don't really know anyone who's ever been to their house."

"I heard about his sister. The rumors, I mean."

"Well," Dakota shrugged philosophically, "what does *crazy* mean anyway? I saw her around town sometimes, she and Byron—but she's been gone for quite a while. She was beautiful . . . always seemed kind of shy. And you can't believe everything you hear—especially in *this* town."

"Well . . . actually I heard it from Angela."

"Even more reason not to believe it." Dakota stopped in her tracks and looked embarrassed.

"Sorry. I shouldn't have said that. I keep forgetting you're her cousin."

"Not really. More like her stepcousin."

"Well . . . still . . ."

"We weren't that close," Lucy admitted regretfully as they started walking again.

"Hmmm. Big surprise there."

"I mean . . . *aren't* that close," she corrected herself quickly, as if speaking of Angela in the past tense would guarantee a bad ending.

Dakota threw her a knowing look. "It's okay. You're not jinxing anything by being honest."

"It's just that . . ." Lucy's voice faltered, "it's bad enough that everyone blames me for Byron. But they blame me for Angela, too."

"Not all of them, Lucy. Maybe not even *most* of them, in fact. And how could you ever think that anyway?" But at the pained expression on Lucy's face, Dakota's tone softened even more. "Oh. So I guess you *don't* know."

"Know what?"

"That this isn't the first time Angela's disappeared."

Now it was Lucy who stopped. "Wait . . . I don't understand."

"I mean she's run away from home before. *Three* times, in fact—at least that I know of. And each time there's a big search and a big investigation because her mom has a lot of clout in this community. And each time her mom hires some private detective who ends up finding Angela and bringing her back home."

Lucy felt stunned, her thoughts whirling in confusion. So was *this* all there was to the mystery? Just another of Angela's normal escapes? Another routine act of rebellion—another cry for attention? A selfish game to cause worry and fear—*and the accident—and Byron's death—*

"No," Lucy whispered, not even realizing she'd spoken aloud. *No, this time there's more to it. The mysterious stranger at the Festival . . . and the green necklace . . . and stalking shapes and bloodred moons . . .*

Every instinct had told her so then, and every instinct told her so now. This time was different. Dangerous . . . and potentially deadly.

"Deadly," she whispered again.

"What?" Dakota leaned forward, but Lucy shook her head and took a step back.

"Nothing. I just . . . nothing."

"Look, I don't mean that something bad couldn't really happen to Angela," Dakota explained, resting her hands on Lucy's shoulders. "It only takes *one* time to be the *wrong* time. And people can never be too careful." She thought a moment, then added, "But when I saw Angela at the Festival that night, it wasn't like she was being carried off against her will. She didn't act the least bit scared or upset. When she left me the envelope to give you, she seemed happier than I've ever seen her."

"So you actually saw the guy who took her away?"

"I was too busy with the kids to really notice. I saw her go off with someone, but it was from the back, and they disappeared into the crowds. The only thing I could tell the police was that he was taller than her, and he had dark hair."

Lucy shivered, remembering the deep voice, the mysterious presence, that she herself had encountered behind the scarecrow tent. "Do you think it was the same guy Angela met the night before?"

"I have absolutely no idea. Angela would flirt with anybody. I'm not surprised she'd go off with a total stranger."

"That evening before we left the house, she actually dropped some hints about running away. But I didn't catch on. It didn't hit me till later."

Dakota nodded understandingly, her hands sliding from Lucy's shoulders. The two of them picked up their pace as the bell rang for class.

"I have to help out at the bookstore tonight," Dakota told her as they approached the side entrance. "My family's bookstore, actually—Candlewick Shop. It's kind of a dumpy little place in the old part of town—but you can drink coffee there and probably find every used book in the universe. So, if you feel like company later on, why don't you come over?" She dug into one of her pockets and pulled out a card. "Here's the store number; my home number's on the back. My dad doesn't believe in cell phones. He says they're just an expensive way to annoy the people around you, and he can do that for free. Anyway, if you need a ride, just call me, and I'll come get you."

"Thanks. I just might."

They jogged the last few feet to the building. Before Dakota could reach for the door, however, it burst open, and a giggling trio of cheerleaders pushed past them. As one of them jarred Lucy's arm, Lucy immediately froze.

The girl with her friends didn't notice. She hurried with the others toward the gym, but Dakota turned and stared at the stricken expression on Lucy's pale face.

"Lucy? What is it?"

Lucy didn't answer. As she gazed after the cheerleaders, Dakota followed the direction of her shocked stare.

"Lucy?"

"That girl . . ." Lucy's voice was scarcely a breath, and Dakota moved closer to hear.

"Lucy, what's wrong?"

Lucy pointed to the girl in the middle of the threesome. "That girl . . . there . . ."

"Who? The one with the really short hair? Wanda Carver?"

"She's going to die on Thursday."

6

For a second the world went dark.

It was as though a thick black cloud had settled in Lucy's line of vision, blotting out the entire rest of the world.

And then slowly, a glimmer came through. It parted the shadows in her brain and began to glow, sending light and sensation into her body once more. With a gasp, she blinked her eyes and saw Dakota peering anxiously back at her.

"What did you just say?" Dakota murmured.

Lucy gave herself a mental shake. Her head hurt, and her legs felt as though they might crumple at any second. "I . . . I said . . ."

Sweat dripped from her forehead, though her whole body was chilled. She stared back at Dakota with a blank frown.

"I said . . ." What *had* she said? *Something about a girl . . . something about dying* . . . Lucy put a trembling hand to her temple and pressed gently.

"You're white as a sheet," Dakota informed her. "Are you going to be sick? Do you need to see the nurse?"

Lucy managed a nod. She felt Dakota take her arm and steer her through the door, and as they walked together down the hall, she tried desperately to replay what had just happened outside. *Dakota and I were talking . . . someone bumped my arm . . . and then . . .*

And then . . . what?

A vision? Yet she didn't recall actually *seeing* anything in her mind, no flashes, no pictures, only a frightening sense of . . . *of what*?

"Falling," she whispered, and Dakota tightened her hold on Lucy's arm.

"You feel like you're going to fall?" the girl asked worriedly.

And Lucy nodded again, because she didn't know what else to do, or why *falling* had swept through her brain, or what she could possibly do to understand it or stop it or make it go away—*falling . . . a rush of breathless surprise . . . a slow-motion horror of no escape . . .*

"—lie down for a while?" a nurse was asking, and in total confusion Lucy stared up at her from the edge of a cot. She could see Dakota next to her, could see the girl's lips moving, forming soundless words that Lucy could somehow hear—*"Do you want me to stay with you?"*—but the nurse said no, that Lucy would be fine, that she had specific instructions from Lucy's doctor and that Dakota should go on to class.

"I'll see you later then." Dakota's voice was normal now, as real as the concern in her eyes. "I hope you feel better, Lucy."

Lucy didn't answer. She lay on the cot and gazed at the ceiling, her body numb, her mind vacant. As though the emotions she'd experienced only minutes ago had shorted out and entirely disconnected. *Something about falling . . . something bad . . . a girl is going to fall . . . going to die . . .*

"Are you feeling any better, Lucy?" The nurse was there again, her manner efficient but kind. "I tried to call your aunt, but she's out of her office at the moment."

"You don't need to bother her. Maybe I could just lie here a few more seconds?"

"Rest as long as you'd like. Dr. Fielding has already talked with us, so don't be afraid to stop in here anytime you need to. It's very important not to rush your recovery."

Lucy watched as a curtain was drawn around her cubicle. She closed her eyes and tried to relax, but the message in her head began to filter through at last, crystal clear and knife-sharp. *"She's going to die . . . She's going to die on Thursday."*

My God, where had that *come* from?

Dakota had given her such a strange look when it happened. *Did she hear what I said?* Lucy honestly couldn't be sure—but then again, she wasn't even sure now if she'd actually spoken the words out loud. *Maybe I didn't say anything . . . or maybe I said something different, something I don't even remember.*

"Memory lapses," she reminded herself, fighting for calm. "The doctor said I might have memory lapses. He said they were perfectly normal."

But *Byron* had said things to her, too—*proved*

things to her, too; warned her about feelings and powers and circumstances she'd be helpless to control.

So what if those powers were getting stronger? What if she was starting to turn into Katherine?

Oh, Byron, I'd give anything to talk to you now.

Exhausted, Lucy took a deep breath and slowly let it out. She could hear someone coughing in the next cot. She could hear the distant rumble of the marching band as they practiced on the athletic field. And then she heard a low exchange of voices just outside the curtain to her cubicle.

"Would it be possible to see her?" someone was asking in a hushed voice, definitely male. A familiar voice, too, Lucy thought. One she'd heard before and not so long ago.

"Of course," the nurse replied. "Principal Howser told me Lucy was scheduled to meet with you this afternoon."

Lucy gave an inward groan. *Oh, great. Just what I need right now. A stupid grief counselor.*

"She's right in here," the nurse directed.

"Thanks."

Lucy thought about feigning sleep. But at the last instant her curiosity got the better of her, and she opened her eyes just as the curtain drew back. She caught a glimpse of tousled brown hair . . . black clothes . . . a priest's collar . . .

"Welcome back, Lucy," Matt said. "It's so good to see you again."

7

He'd been disappointed that she wanted to leave.

Deeply disappointed, but not at all surprised.

He had known he couldn't keep her there forever, that eventually she would wake within the shadows, that awareness would begin to rouse her senses once again.

She would realize then that things were not as they should be in her world.

And then she would find strength she never knew she had.

And she would flee from him.

Believing that she truly had escaped.

Now, every time he thought of it, the irony made him smile.

Her wild, desperate flight through the woods—and how he'd always been just one step ahead of her, one step behind her, so close that he could smell her wild, delicious fear and the blood throbbing madly through her veins.

The blood that was partly his own . . .

The blood he had given her from his own lips . . .

She'd been practically dead by the time he got her to the cave.

Cold and motionless, yet still beautiful.

He had undressed her so carefully and tended her wounds. Licking her blood away . . . loving the taste of it.

At times she had moaned, moving instinctively beneath his mouth.

And he had stood there for hours in the dark, gazing down on her, his mind filled with an eternity of possibilities and desires.

Undiluted, his own blood would have killed her. So rich and pure and ageless, that the shock of it to her system would have been more than her mortality could bear.

So he had done the next best thing.

After all, he'd had no time for hunting—not for the prey he preferred and was accustomed to. So he had contented himself with smaller game instead—rabbits and squirrels and foxes—and after feeding on them, he had mixed their blood with his own and coaxed it between her pale, pale lips. And after a while, when her heart beat stronger, only then had he sunk his teeth into her flesh, forcing himself to hold back, injecting only warmth and bloody spittle straight into her artery. A place no one would think to look, and a place she would never suspect.

Not that it mattered anyway.

His mark would vanish within twenty-four hours, just as it had for hundreds of years.

Leaving his victim oblivious and unscathed.

So Lucy would not know, of course, that he had saved her life.

A life so sad and lonely, that it longed to be filled with his blood and his passion.

Yes, he had touched her.

Tasted her, but not *taken* her.

A noble—and most uncommon—sacrifice on his part.

A sacrifice that left him wanting her all the more . . .

He had seen The One who rescued her.

He had stood by and watched as Lucy was lifted from the road and placed inside the car and driven far away.

And he could have resolved it then and there, but it was neither the time nor the place for confrontation.

Not the moment for settling old scores.

So he had merely suffered the anger building inside him, the hatred boiling in his veins—reminding himself it was inevitable, that he should have expected it to happen.

Truth be told, it might make the Game more interesting, this vying for Lucy's surrender.

A surrender that must be willing and complete.

A surrender that must be gradual . . . so gradual that even Lucy herself would never see it coming.

For hers was a soul to be nurtured.

Hers was a soul to be understood.

And right now, more than anything else, hers was a soul that yearned to be loved.

Loved . . .

A rare and somewhat disturbing challenge, but not altogether impossible.

He had managed it before in his lifetime, and he was *nothing* if not a Master at deception.

So he would give Lucy what she most wanted. And appear as the faces she would trust. And be exactly what she *needed* him to be.

Soon, Lucy.

Soon I'll be the only one who matters in your life.

He ached with anticipation.

And he remembered fondly all the countless hearts he'd ever stolen, knowing *hers* would be the most precious one of all.

But for now he'd let her keep it . . .

At least for a while.

8

"Matt," Lucy murmured. "What are you doing here?"

"I was just going to ask you the same thing." The young priest eased down onto the side of her cot. "You didn't have to do this to get out of our counseling session, you know. You could've just asked."

Lucy ignored the mild attempt at a joke. "I didn't know it was going to be you."

"I've been here all week. A lot of kids have needed to talk, to work through their feelings. To just . . ."

His voiced trailed off. He leaned slightly forward, hands clasped between his knees.

"Lucy . . ."

"So am I supposed to call you Father Matthew

today?" Lucy interrupted, needing to change the subject.

"Whatever you like. Whatever makes you feel comfortable."

Comfortable? She recalled the few brief encounters she'd had with Matt before her accident—when she'd escaped in terror from the confessional . . . when he'd found the necklace that was missing from Byron's pocket . . . and when he'd given out the information that had sent her and Byron on their wild-goose chase after Angela. He looked like a symbol of death sitting here, Lucy thought now—dressed in his official black, with his face so grave and composed. Just another reminder of doom and loss, and things that made no sense.

"So." Matt's eyes locked gently with hers. "How are you? Really?"

As much as Lucy wanted to avoid this conversation, she couldn't look away. She noticed the pale streaks of sunlight through his hair . . . those long dark lashes . . . that boyishly handsome face . . . everything just as she remembered. Yet *something* in Matt had changed, she realized suddenly. Some secret inner sadness? Some profound hidden pain? Whatever it was, it had darkened the deep, deep blue of his eyes and tempered his smile.

For a moment it caught her off balance. As though in some strange way she should be comforting *him*. Then her defenses rallied once more.

"How am I *doing*?" she echoed mockingly. "I'm here. That's about it."

"That's a beginning."

In a gesture that seemed professionally instinctive, his hand covered her own. Yet as an unexpected warmth touched the cold places inside her, Lucy pulled free from him and quickly sat up.

"Is this where I get the lecture?" she challenged.

"And what lecture is that?"

"The one about Byron being in a better place, and how God had some very perfect reason for killing him? And how I should just accept it and go on with my life?"

"I don't know that lecture," Matt replied seriously. "And I think the issue here is that *you* still have a life."

"Right. Lucky me."

"I'm glad you were the one with Byron at the end, Lucy. I'm glad you were the last beautiful thing he saw in this world, and maybe *that* was God's plan. Byron was a wonderful person."

"How would you know?" Lucy couldn't keep the sarcasm from her tone. "You met him one time. You didn't know him."

"You're right, I didn't know him personally. But I've heard what his classmates say about him; I know he had friends he wasn't even aware of. I know he was close to his family, looked out for his older sister, took care of his grandmother. I know he shouldn't have died so young."

Lucy's eyes filled. She barely managed a nod.

"But there's something else I know." Matt stared down at the floor, his voice low and calm. "I know that as hard as it is to lose people we care about, sometimes it's even worse being the ones left behind."

Silence stretched between them. When Lucy finally spoke, her words were bitter.

"How about being the one everyone blames?"

"You know better than that."

"If I hadn't come to Pine Ridge, none of this would have happened."

"But *something* would've happened, Lucy. Things *always* happen. They would've just happened in different ways. That's called *life*."

Lucy hesitated. Her voice came out a broken whisper. "But I keep thinking about his grandmother. Who's going to take care of Byron's grandmother?"

"She has a nurse who comes through the week. And Mrs. Dempsey, who cleans at the church, is staying nights with her temporarily. Just till other arrangements can be made."

"What other arrangements?"

"Right now we're trying to find family members we can contact. Byron's sister—Katherine—moved away about a year ago, and no one seems to know where."

Lucy felt her heart skip a beat. Without even realizing it, she clenched her right hand, as though she could squeeze away the tiny half-moon scar. "There *must* be other relatives."

"Father Paul and I are working on it," Matt replied, but Lucy could tell he was discouraged.

"And what if you can't find anyone else?"

"Then I don't think we'll have a choice. She'll have to be moved to some sort of long-term care."

The ache in Lucy's heart grew worse. "Have you been to see her yet? Does she actually realize what's happened?"

She watched as Matt shifted positions. He leaned toward her slightly, his expression puzzled.

"The sheriff asked Father Paul and Mrs. Wetherly's doctor to be there with him when he told her about the accident. So Father Paul and I rode over with the sheriff that night, and the doctor drove up the same time we did."

While Lucy remained quiet, Matt cleared his throat and stared past her, frowning at a spot on the wall.

"It was so strange," he finally said. "I don't know what I was expecting, really. But when we all got there, the front door was unlocked and the porch light was on. And Mrs. Wetherly was propped up in bed, almost as if she'd been waiting for us. She didn't even look surprised. Just so sad . . . calm . . . resigned, almost."

A shiver went up Lucy's spine. Byron had told her how his grandmother *knew* things—how she'd even warned him that he'd never see Katherine alive again. *Did she see something the night of the accident, too? Did she know about me? Did she already know Byron was dead?*

"I have to get to class," Lucy said suddenly.

Matt stood as she swung her legs over the side of the cot. He watched her take several deep breaths, then he reached down for her elbows, drawing her slowly to her feet. As Lucy swayed a little, Matt's arms went around her, steadying her against his chest.

"Are you sure you feel like staying at school?" His smile was uncertain. "I'd be glad to take you home instead."

Flustered, but not exactly sure why, Lucy pulled herself from his grasp. "Of course I'll stay. I'm fine."

The thought of being alone again in Irene's house was unsettling. But staying here at school, even for two more hours, made Lucy feel even worse. Opening the curtain wider, she suddenly turned to face him.

"I drove Angela's car today."

"I'll bring it over later. I'm sure I can get Mrs. Dempsey to follow me."

"But will the office let me leave with you?"

"Hey," Matt deadpanned, more like his old self, "I'm on official business for the Big Guy—they wouldn't dare mess with me."

The temptation was just too great. After a quick stop at her locker while Matt got his things from the office and checked in with Principal Howser, Lucy joined him by the main entrance and followed him to the visitors' parking lot.

"My aunt lives on Lakeshore Drive," Lucy told him as they headed through town. "Do you know where that is?"

"I do. And I think you should be very impressed with how well I've learned my way around."

She knew he was trying to keep the mood light. She wished she could join in, wished she could rid herself of the terrible burden in her heart, but neither seemed possible to her now. So instead she stared out her window, so that he couldn't see her face when she finally spoke.

"Matt . . . I'm really sorry."

His voice was genuinely surprised. "For what?"

"For the things I said. How angry I got."

"You have every right to be angry."

"I know I'm feeling sorry for myself. I know how pathetic that is . . . how self-destructive. And I know I should be thankful that I'm . . ." Her thoughts stumbled over sudden bad memories. She closed her eyes and forced herself to finish. ". . . that I got through it okay."

She opened her eyes again and bit down on her lower lip. She waited for Matt to answer, but when he didn't, she turned in the seat to look at him.

"Aren't you going to ask me?" she burst out.

Matt kept his eyes on the road. "Ask you what?"

"What everyone's probably heard about—at least heard *rumors* about. Where I was—what happened to me—after Byron's car went off the road."

"I think this is your street," Matt replied.

He turned into the exclusive neighborhood, following Lucy's directions to the house. As he pulled into the driveway, he let out a soft whistle.

"Wow. I can see why your aunt's one of All Souls' most beloved benefactors."

"Nobody loves my aunt. And don't change the subject."

"You know, a lot of our parishioners live in this neighborhood. They don't attend mass either, but I'm pretty sure their tax deductions include very generous donations to the church."

Lucy stared at him. He tapped his fingers slowly on the steering wheel, then turned off the engine. His expression was thoughtful as he faced her.

"Yes, I've heard rumors, Lucy. *And* questions. *And* lots of theories and speculations. But until I hear it straight from you, I won't believe anything. And I'd never just *assume* that you'd choose to tell me anyway."

Before she could answer, Matt was out of the car. He tapped on her window, and she opened the passenger door.

"You have a key?" he asked, and Lucy nodded. "But you don't have to come with me."

"Oh yes, I do. I always walk ladies to their doors and make sure they're safe."

In spite of herself, Lucy almost smiled. "Is that a church rule?"

"No, it's my mom's rule," he corrected her,

helping her out. "Which is even *more* sacred than a church rule. And there's no absolution when you break a mom's rule, didn't you know that? Break a mom's rule, and you suffer damnation for all eternity."

"You can walk me to the front, then—it's shorter. But you don't have to check the house. Irene just got a new security system—she swears not even a fly could get in."

The two of them went up the walkway to the wide, columned porch. Matt waited patiently while she fumbled the key into the lock, got the door open, and disengaged the alarm.

"Are you sure you're going to be okay here?" he persisted, his gaze sweeping the entry hall behind her.

"I'm sure. My aunt will be coming home . . . sometime." Then as Matt frowned, Lucy quickly added, "And a friend might be picking me up later."

"I'm glad, Lucy. You need to get out and be with people. It's okay to have some fun, you know."

Despite his good intentions, Lucy felt that familiar stab of guilt. "And here's the key to . . .

to Angela's car. It's a red Corvette. On the far side of the student lot, near the Dumpsters."

"Don't worry. I'll take care of it."

"Thanks. I really appreciate this. And I really appreciate the ride home."

"Anytime. I don't just keep office hours at school and church, you know. I'm on call twenty-four / seven."

Lucy watched him walk to his car. She watched as he backed down the driveway, and she kept on watching, long after the black Jeep had disappeared.

The wind was growing restless. Just as the weatherman had predicted, a powdery snow was beginning to fall.

She wished she'd let Matt come inside with her.

Gripping the edge of the doorway, she fought down a sudden wild urge to call him back.

You're fine. You're strong. And you're absolutely safe.

But as Lucy shut the door and locked it, she couldn't help thinking that the house felt even colder than the raw November air.

9

She hadn't planned on falling asleep.

With thoughts to sort out and homework to catch up on, taking a nap was the last thing she could afford to do.

But she'd been exhausted after Matt dropped her off. Exhausted and completely drained. So once she'd changed clothes and lain down across the bed, she'd fallen asleep so fast, she didn't even remember closing her eyes.

But the nightmares told her.

The nightmares always told her.

Nightmares like this one, that trapped her in Byron's van and in hidden caves, abandoned in the darkness and surrounded by dangers too terrible to imagine. Something was holding her down, something was making her burn, and through it all, someone in the background kept sobbing, *"She's going to die on Thursday . . . on Thursday."*

A frightened cry woke her. As Lucy lay there, groggy and disoriented, she tried to figure out where the sound had come from, then decided she must have made it herself. Bad enough to suffer the nightmares . . . even worse when they encroached upon reality.

She wasn't even sure what reality *was* anymore.

Her mind drifted back to school. To the girl coming out of the building, to the image of someone falling. Was she meant to give Wanda Carver a warning? How could she possibly approach a complete stranger like that? Offer some dire prediction that might be nothing more than the result of a head injury?

Just thinking about the consequences made Lucy shudder. Popular cheerleader Wanda Carver would tell the entire school. As low as Lucy's status already was, this bit of gossip would annihilate it completely.

Feeling depressed and defeated, Lucy sat up in bed. Why even bother telling anyone *anything*? She'd *tried* to tell people about the cave. About her escape through the woods, about the unknown stranger who'd rescued her. She knew how much people doubted her; even worse, she'd started doubting herself. She knew she couldn't prove anything about her terrifying experience, but that didn't make it less real. As real as these stitches on her head, these bruises fading from her face, the cuts and scratches healing along her arms and legs.

As real as seeing things without warning . . . as real as knowing things I can't explain.

Somewhere along the way, the fragile boundaries between Real and Unreal had shifted. Somewhere along the way, the boundaries between Seen and Unseen had begun to unravel and disappear.

Frowning, Lucy reached over to the nightstand. *That's funny . . . I could have sworn that lamp was on.*

In fact, she distinctly remembered turning it on when she'd come in earlier, right before she'd changed clothes. And she'd been staring at the lampshade, too, right after she'd stretched out on the bed.

She jiggled the switch back and forth. But when no light came on, she swore under her breath and fiddled with the lightbulb. Still no luck.

She realized then that dusk had fallen. She could see snow outside the sliding glass doors, drifting onto the little balcony. The house was very quiet. A vast, empty quiet that told Lucy she was still alone. Nervously she got up, closed the curtains, and went out into the hall, rubbing her arms against the chill. The house felt even colder now than it had that afternoon.

The light in the hall didn't work either. As Lucy felt her way to the top of the stairs, she could see only darkness below. Irene had had automatic timers installed in every room—the whole first floor should be glowing with lamps by now.

Wonderful. The electricity must be off.

Lucy stood on the landing, trying to think. It wasn't the first time the house had lost power, but it usually happened only during storms. Maybe it was something simple, like a fuse in the circuit breaker. Maybe that's why the house felt so cold.

Cautiously she reached out to grip the bannister. She'd have to go down and check the fuse box. She'd have to go all the way down to the basement. Anger flared inside her, mixed with fear. Why did Irene always have to work so late? Why couldn't she stay home and care even a little bit about Lucy's feelings?

I need a flashlight. I need to find a flashlight before I do anything else.

Lucy forced her thoughts into a more positive direction. No need to panic. She'd reset the security system after Matt left; she was completely safe. Not even a fly could get in; isn't that what Irene had promised her? Everything was fine. Everything was normal. She'd fix the circuit breaker, and then she'd turn on every single light in the house.

Taking a deep breath, she turned and headed for her bedroom. There was a flashlight in her nightstand drawer, one Irene had insisted she keep there for emergencies. In fact, Irene had flashlights stored all over the house, if Lucy could only remember now where they were. She could always call 911 if she got really scared. *Quit being such a wimp—it's not like this is any big deal.*

Yet Lucy's heart was pounding as she groped her way back along the corridor. And this time, her hand just happened to touch the door of Angela's room.

It was like receiving a shock.

The wooden panel was so icy cold that Lucy gasped and jumped back, pressing her hand to her chest.

For a second all she could do was stand there in the dark. The chill in her fingers shot all the way up through her arm, all the way into her head. She was too stunned to move; it was too black to see. Yet her eyes stared straight ahead, straight at Angela's door.

Irene had kept it shut ever since Angela's disappearance.

As though Angela and everything about her must be sealed away from Irene's disapproval and the constant demands of Irene's busy life.

Holding her breath, Lucy reached out for the door.

And felt it move slowly inward.

Angela's window was open. Lucy could see it from where she stood on the threshold, though the room was thick with shadows. The curtains fluttered like restless ghosts, and snow had swirled in through the screen, lying still unmelted upon the carpet.

Oh my God . . . someone's broken in!

Yet through a surge of panic, Lucy could see that the screen hadn't been cut, the glass was still intact.

It didn't make sense. She couldn't imagine that Irene had come in here and opened that window. And Florence came to clean only on Fridays. But maybe Florence had done it—opened the window to air out Angela's room and then forgotten to close it again. *Yes, that's it*, Lucy told herself firmly. *That must be it—what else could it be?*

But as rationalizations swept through her mind, she began to be aware of something else. It came through to her slowly and faintly, and it took her several moments even to realize what it was.

A sound. A soft, muffled sound . . . like . . . ringing?

Lucy couldn't move. With mounting fear, she strained to listen, and her brain struggled to compute. *Yes . . . definitely a ringing sound . . .*

A telephone.

Goose bumps crept along her spine. Angela's telephone was ringing, and as Lucy turned reluctantly toward the sound, she heard Angela's answering machine kick on. "Hi," purred the sultry voice. "This is Angela. If you think you can handle me, leave a message."

Nobody spoke.

Lucy heard only silence on the other end of the line.

Terrible, frightening silence . . . as someone waited.

Wrong number, Lucy thought frantically—*everyone knows Angela's missing—no one who knows her would be doing this!*

Yet she felt herself walking toward the phone. Maneuvering through the darkness, as the silence on the answering machine stretched on and on and on . . .

In slow motion, Lucy picked up the receiver.

"Hello?" she whispered.

And the voice that answered turned her blood to ice.

"It's so dark here," Angela sobbed, "I can't get back!"

"*Angela!*" Lucy screamed.

She pressed the receiver hard against her ear, her voice rising in panic, her heart racing out of control.

"Angela! It's Lucy! Where are you? Are you okay?"

But there was nothing but static now.

"*Angela!*"

Frantically, Lucy began pushing buttons, but there was no voice, no dial tone, and after several more seconds, no noise at all.

"Hello?" she cried. "Hello? *Angela!* Angela, don't hang up—please talk to me!"

In desperation Lucy jerked the telephone from Angela's desk.

And that's when the truth finally hit her.

The cord was plugged into the wall.

But the electricity was still out.

10

It's a trick—it has to be some kind of trick!

Dropping everything, Lucy ran into the hallway and stumbled the last few feet to her room.

A cruel, sick joke! Kids from school tormenting me, because of Byron, because of Angela—

She locked her door and braced her back against it. Blood pounded in her ears, and her body jolted with every terrified heartbeat.

"Guilt's such a weird power . . . It makes people do crazy things . . . Mean, hateful things sometimes . . ."

Hadn't Dakota tried to warn her? Hadn't Dakota tried to warn her just today?

Lucy's head spun wildly. Maybe Dakota wasn't really who she seemed to be; maybe she wasn't a friend at all. Maybe her warning had all been part of this huge, sick joke she and her *real* friends had already been planning to spring on Lucy . . .

Calm down. Breathe. Think.

Lucy's palms pressed flat against the door. Her spine was rigid. Her vision blurred, then focused. Her eyes made a slow, thorough sweep of the shadows. The sliding glass doors were still shut; no invisible presence alerted her instincts to danger. Long minutes crept by. Finally she forced herself over to the nightstand and took the flashlight from the drawer.

The bright beam of light was a lifeline.

Still shaking, Lucy went into the bathroom and locked the connecting door to Angela's room. Then she sat down on the edge of her bed and gripped the flashlight to her chest.

Damn them! How could anyone be so mean, so heartless? Hadn't she been through enough? Would guilt and blame cling to her for the rest of her life?

Yet she couldn't figure out how they'd done it, how they'd managed to rig the whole scenario. Even with high-tech knowledge, wouldn't someone have had to get into the house to pull it off? Maybe they'd caused the power outage, too. But how had they managed to bypass such a sophisticated security system? It just didn't make any sense.

Unless . . .

Lucy's breath caught in her throat. She squeezed the flashlight tighter, so tight that her fingers ached.

No! No, what happened back there in Angela's room *couldn't* have had anything to do with psychic powers or gifts or curses. Her body hadn't signaled her like it so often had in the past. She hadn't seen visions; there hadn't been a feeling or impression or a warning too overwhelming to ignore. What had happened just now wasn't like anything she'd ever experienced. *So, no. No! It couldn't have been just me.*

Yet no matter how much she argued with herself, she couldn't quite shut out the whisper in her mind. The persistent little whisper that kept nagging her, trying to get through. *What if it's not a joke? What if it's real? What are you going to do?*

Moaning softly, Lucy lowered her head and cradled it in her arms. *No, no, there's a logical explanation, it's a horrible trick, and Florence just forgot and left the window open!* Because she couldn't bear to think otherwise. Because the sound of Angela's voice and the prospects of Angela's fate were just too chilling to imagine.

Imagine? Maybe I did *imagine it. Maybe I had a memory lapse or blacked out or hallucinated. One of those things that people with head injuries are supposed to do.*

Helplessness engulfed her. She couldn't call the police—they'd never believe her. She couldn't tell Irene—her aunt would put her straight into the hospital. So who? Dr. Fielding with his comfort-coated skepticism? All Lucy knew for sure was that she couldn't stay here a minute longer. She had to leave, and she had to leave *now*.

Leading with the flashlight, she hurried downstairs, yanked her coat from the closet, and stopped to check the battery backup on the security system.

And that's when she remembered she didn't have a car.

What time is it anyway?

She looked at her watch, surprised to see that

it was after seven. Surely Matt should have been here by now—surely he would have rung the doorbell when he dropped off the car.

Lucy pulled aside the front curtains and peered out at the driveway. The red Corvette was sitting there, parked about halfway down, covered with a thin layer of snow.

That's strange . . .

Grabbing her purse, she slammed the door behind her. But as she cut across the lawn and got closer to the car, she began to slow down.

The last thing in the world she wanted to do right now was drive that thing. Not after what had just happened upstairs. Not after what she'd just heard.

Lucy stopped. She stared at the Corvette and felt tiny prickles of apprehension creep along her spine. Maybe she should call a cab. She had no clue about taxi service here in Pine Ridge—*or* the drivers. And right now she didn't trust anybody. *Not anybody. Not even myself.*

She took her time going around the sports car, brushing off the feathery snow, shining her flashlight in all the windows. She told herself she was being silly; she told herself she was being safe. When she tried the handle, the door came open, unnerving her even more.

Why didn't Matt lock it? Why didn't he at least tell me he was here?

Climbing inside, she noticed the air was slightly warm, as though the heater had only recently been shut off. She closed the door and began hunting for the key.

Both visors were empty. Lucy ran her hands along the floor mats, then rummaged nervously through the glove box. She searched the backseat area but found nothing. Maybe it wasn't here at all. Maybe Matt had forgotten to leave it. Leaning her forehead on the steering wheel, she tried to stay calm. Snow was thickening on the windshield, and the car was getting cold.

On a whim, Lucy bent down and began groping beneath the seats. Far back under the driver's side, her fingers made contact with something soft and bulky, like thick cloth. It had been wedged in so tight, it took several minutes of intense pulling to finally work it free.

Lucy stared down at the bundle in her hands.

By the glow of her flashlight, she began to open the heavy folds of fabric. A blanket of some kind . . . a blanket that seemed familiar . . . covered with dead leaves and pine needles and stained with mud . . .

And with something wrapped inside it . . .

"No," Lucy whispered. "Oh God . . ."

Most of the jacket was burned away—just charred holes and black tatters—yet Lucy recognized it at once. Remembered the way it had looked on Byron the very first time she'd met him . . . and in that last split second before the crash.

She needed air. She couldn't breathe. The car was too small, too suffocating, and she clawed at the door, but it wouldn't open.

She didn't even notice the car key as it fell out of the blanket. Or when it landed on the floor at her feet.

She only saw the snowflakes turning to ashes as she slumped forward over the steering wheel.

11

"Lucy," the voice was saying. "I've got you, Lucy—you're safe."

Someone was holding her.

She could feel strong arms around her, and her head was tilted sideways, resting on somebody's chest.

"Let's get you inside," the voice murmured.

I know that voice.

"Lucy? Just relax . . . just lean against me."

Yes . . . yes . . . I know that voice, but I can't quite place it . . .

For a split second of panic, Lucy thought she might be back again, back in the places of her nightmares, back in the shadowy cave, the cold wet woods, the deserted road. But then, as her eyes began to open, she could see a world of pure white, and a door with a large brass knocker that looked vaguely familiar.

"Nobody's answering," the voice was telling her now. "Where the hell's your aunt?"

Lucy barely managed to shake her head.

"Then what's the code?" the voice asked. "Lucy, can you give me the code?"

The code . . .

Weakly, she squinted up into a face. A worried face, but calmly reassuring as well. His hair was sifted with snowflakes, and as a gust of wind hit the two of them, he drew Lucy closer into his warmth.

"Matt?" she whispered.

"Do you remember the security code, Lucy?" he asked her again. "I need to get you inside."

Her head was beginning to clear. She realized they were on the front porch, and that she was shivering from head to toe. With sudden clarity, images of the blanket and burned jacket burst into her mind, and she immediately began to struggle.

"Hey, calm down," Matt held her tighter. "I told you, everything's okay—"

"No, those things in the car!"

"What things?"

"In the car—the blanket, Byron's jacket— you must have seen them—"

"Lucy, I didn't see anything but you. What are you talking about?"

"He put them there! He must know where I live—how can he *know* that?"

"Ssh . . . Listen to me—"

"Why did you leave the car unlocked? Why didn't you make sure no one was following you? You must have led him straight here!"

"Stop it, Lucy, you're not making any sense." The shake he gave her was gentle, but firm. "Whatever this is about, we'll *discuss* it. I *promise*. But right now we need to go inside without setting off the alarm and looking like two half-wit burglars."

"But I *want* the police to come! They need to get fingerprints and DNA—"

"Lucy. Tell me the code."

The tone of his voice got through to her at last. It took her several minutes, but she was finally able to recite the correct numbers in their proper sequence. Then Matt turned the key, stepped into the house, and—following

Lucy's garbled directions—disarmed the system.

"Where's the couch?" Pausing at the foot of the stairs, he raised a quizzical eyebrow and looked for a place to set her down. "Couch, chair, or bed. Your choice."

But Lucy was babbling again. "The blanket? It was the one I took when I was trying to escape. The police will *have* to believe me now."

"Where would you be the most comfortable?"

"No, no, I can walk."

"Don't argue with me."

Seeing the determination on his face, Lucy pointed to a doorway. "The den's through there. But you've *got* to call the police, Matt. He had Byron's jacket, don't you understand? The same one Byron was wearing when we crashed! How could he have Byron's jacket? And I lost that blanket in the woods, so how did he find it? Why is he doing this to me?"

"Hush, Lucy." Carefully Matt lowered her to the couch, then began unbuttoning her coat. "Take this off and wrap up in something warm." He pulled the wool afghan from one end of the sofa and tucked it snugly around her. "I should probably take you to the emergency room. You're half frozen."

"Don't call a doctor—call the *police*! Haven't you heard a single word I've said?"

"What about tea? Do you like tea?"

Frustrated, Lucy grabbed his sleeve. "Listen to me. You've *got* to get that stuff from the car. I didn't have any evidence before, but now I do, and if he's out there right now watching us, the police might be able to catch him!"

"If *who's* out there watching us?" Matt demanded, easing himself from her grip. But as Lucy grew more agitated, he knelt down in front of her and took both her hands in his. "Yes, okay, I'll go out to the car. And if it's necessary, I promise I'll call the police. But first I'm going to fix you something hot to drink so we can get your blood flowing again."

"You're wasting time!"

"Time? Well, speaking of time, just how long were you lying out there unconscious in the car?"

"I don't know. What time is it now?"

Matt glanced at the clock on the fireplace

mantel, then double-checked his watch. "Your clock's wrong. Mine says about eight-thirty."

"That can't be right." Lucy stared at him in amazement. "I couldn't have been out there for nearly an hour."

"An hour? People have frozen to death in *half* that time!"

"It wasn't *that* cold. In fact, the car was still warm inside."

Now it was Matt's turn to look surprised. "That's impossible. I brought it over about five o'clock."

"But I'm sure it was . . ." Her voice trailed off as something began to dawn on her. "Matt, the electricity's on."

For the first time since they'd come in, she noticed the glare of the foyer light, the glow from surrounding lamps, the stuffy heat and muted hum of the furnace. Matt was staring at her as if she might clarify her remark with some earth-shattering revelation.

"It wasn't on before," she murmured.

"So that explains why your clock's wrong."

"Someone *shut* it off."

His expression grew more puzzled. "Shut your *clock* off?"

Before he could question her further, Lucy threw the afghan aside and stood up, only to feel Matt's hands on her shoulders, pushing her down again.

"Where do you think you're going?"

"To the car. I'm telling you, someone shut off the electricity in this house tonight. And someone deliberately put stuff in the car. And if you're not going to help me, then I'll do it myself."

"Okay, okay. Hold on." Sighing in defeat, Matt turned toward the hall. "I'll go."

"A blanket. And a jacket. They're both in the front seat."

"Right. But in the meantime, I want you to stay here and cover up again."

Lucy did as she was told. She sat huddled beneath the afghan, her mind spinning in a dozen different directions. Questions pounded at her brain. She could feel her body beginning to thaw, but fears and suspicions sent a different kind of chill to her heart.

She heard a door slam and looked up to see

Matt poised in the threshold. He was holding the car key in his hand.

The car key and nothing else.

"Where are they?" Lucy's voice rose hopefully. "You found them, didn't you? In the front, like I said?"

But when Matt didn't answer, the chill deepened inside her.

"No," Lucy whispered.

She saw him hesitate . . . saw the concern and sympathy in his eyes.

"Lucy—" he began, but she cut him off with an angry shout.

"*No!* Those things were *there*! I didn't imagine them—I'm *not* crazy!"

"Of course you're not crazy." Matt spread his hands in a conciliatory gesture. "I don't think that, Lucy. Nobody thinks that—"

"*Everybody* thinks that!"

"You're wrong. Please don't get upset. Just tell me what's going—"

"Maybe he did it at school! He could have broken in, right? In the student parking lot, when no one was looking? Can you tell if anybody broke in?"

"Who are you talking about? Nobody broke into your car at school—"

"How can you be sure? Did you check?"

"Lucy—"

"Then why did you just leave the car out there in the driveway where anyone could get in? Why didn't you come to the door and tell me you were here?"

"I *did* go to the door. I rang the bell over and over, but nobody answered. You said you might be with a friend tonight. I figured you'd gone out."

Was he telling the truth? Maybe the power outage had affected the doorbell. Had she been asleep?

"And I tried to call, too," Matt went on, "but nobody ever picked up. So I decided to drive by again, just to see if you'd gotten home." When Lucy didn't comment, he took a step toward her. "What's going on, Lucy? What's this all about?"

Lucy kept silent. She *wasn't* delusional! She could still see the scorched remains of Byron's jacket; she could still see the blanket with its crumbled, dead leaves. She'd *used* that blanket—she'd *touched* that jacket. No delusion could ever be that real!

"I'll get them myself," she muttered.

Before he could answer, she marched determinedly toward the hall. But halfway across the room, as a thought suddenly hit her, Lucy stopped and turned back to face him.

"Where was the key?" she asked.

Matt's frown was puzzled. "On the floor of the driver's seat."

"No," Lucy corrected. "I mean, where did you leave it when you brought the car over?"

He didn't even hesitate. "On the front porch. Under the mat."

12

It was strange, he thought, how a person's possessions could still retain such a part of them after death.

Like Angela's car, for instance.

It still smelled of her, even now. A smell so ripe and reckless, he could have found it anywhere in the world without any effort at all.

Expensive perfume . . . cigarette smoke . . . strawberry lip gloss and nail polish. Sex and desperation. Longing and sheer bad luck.

Smells that wafted so strong on the wind, even the snow couldn't dull them.

Sometimes he could still taste her eagerness.

But those memories were becoming more and more of an irritation to him. Taunting him when he yearned to be filled. Tormenting him when he ached to be satisfied.

Perhaps he shouldn't have been so hasty.

Perhaps he should have kept her longer . . . drawn out the deception more slowly . . . built the suspense to a more shocking and shattering climax.

At least . . . until Lucy was his.

His and his alone.

Ah, Lucy . . .

She was rarely out of his sight anymore . . . *never* out of his thoughts.

And she so innocently, so sweetly, unaware.

Believing him to be merely an errant breeze, blowing cold across her cheek.

Or the subtle stirring of a shadow coupling with her own.

Or the deep, impenetrable night gazing back at her beyond her sliding glass doors.

How could she know that *he* was the reason for her emptiness? The longing and restlessness she couldn't seem to absolve or understand?

So making use of Angela's car tonight had been gratifying to him in many ways.

Reminding Lucy of their special bond. Their past together that she so wished to forget . . .

their inevitable future she could not yet begin to imagine.

And dispelling those last lingering scents of Angela, once and for all. The car belonged to Lucy now, and it should *smell* like Lucy.

And there was no smell stronger than fear.

He preferred to think of it as a sort of exorcism.

One more move in his Game.

The Game Lucy would never win, no matter how many clues she might unravel, no matter how far ahead she believed herself to be.

The Game with Lucy as his prize.

But that wouldn't happen for a while yet.

Not when the mere *playing* of the Game was so much fun.

Especially when one played without rules.

13

"How could that key have ended up in the car if I didn't even know where it was?" Lucy's eyes were wide and fearful. "Doesn't that prove *anything* to you?"

"Lucy—"

"How did he find me, Matt? Why is he doing this?"

But before Matt could answer, Lucy pushed past him and ran outside.

"Lucy, wait!"

She was already halfway across the lawn. Even though she knew in her heart it was useless; even though she knew that when she looked inside the car, there would be no evidence whatsoever of her ordeal in the cave, not a single trace of Byron's untimely death.

Lucy yanked open the door. Her eyes made a

desperate sweep of the empty front seat, the empty floor. With a choked cry, she fell inside and started rummaging beneath the seats. Then she popped the latch and stumbled around to the trunk, lifting the cover, staring stupidly into one more empty space.

She should have known. Of course she should have.

"It's a trick," she mumbled. She wasn't even aware of Matt standing there now, reaching for her shoulder, trying to pull her away. "A trick," she kept mumbling. "A trick . . . a trick . . . how could anyone be so mean . . ."

"Come back to the house," Matt urged quietly. "Come back and get warm."

"But it couldn't be a trick, could it? No one else would know these things . . . no one else would have these things . . . so it must be real . . . somehow . . . it must be real—"

"Come on, Lucy. Please."

Lucy stepped back from the car. Through misty eyes she watched Matt close the trunk and slip out of his jacket. He threw it around her shoulders and led her back inside.

"Is the kitchen this way?" he asked her.

She wasn't even sure if she nodded. Every inch of her—body, mind, soul—had gone numb. She tried to think of Byron. Tried to remember all the things he'd told her, all the things he'd warned her about. Things about Katherine . . . powers and visions . . . the green necklace. Things about death and evil, and being stalked. Things about her life never being the same . . .

"I'm not crazy," Lucy whispered.

She realized they were in the kitchen now, that she was being pushed into a chair. Had the light been on in here before? She couldn't remember. Had the person who'd been in the car also been in the house tonight? Turning off the electricity, creeping through the halls? Leaving his mark on Angela's answering machine . . . watching Lucy while she slept?

"I'm . . . not . . . crazy."

But she felt like she was drowning. In a bottomless sea of darkness. Beneath crushing waves of despair. As though the entire world had gone black and swallowed her alive.

"Lucy," Matt said softly.

When had he crouched down beside her?

When had he eased his coat from her shoulders and draped it over the back of her chair? And when had he taken both her hands between his, rubbing them gently, trying to warm them? She could see his lips moving ever so slightly. Speaking silent words, with his head bowed and his hair windblown in long thick strands across his forehead.

"What do you do," Lucy murmured, "when nothing in your life makes sense anymore?"

Matt made a perfunctory sign of the cross. Then his eyes lifted calmly and settled on hers. "Why don't you tell me what's wrong."

"And I don't mean just *make sense*," Lucy went on, as if he hadn't spoken. "It's more than that. Things that can't be explained. Things that are so bizarre and so unbelievable, they actually *defy* reality. Except they *are* real. They *are* happening. And there you are. You're . . . you're just *trapped* there, in the middle of it. With no one who can understand. With no one who could possibly help."

Matt's gaze never wavered. "I'm not here to push you, Lucy. And the last thing I'd *ever* want to do is interfere where I'm not wanted. But I *would* like to help you. Whatever this is, you don't have to face it alone."

"You can't," Lucy whispered even lower than before.

"Why not?"

"You just can't help me."

"Then if *I* can't, I'll find someone who *can*. But you've got to tell me what's wrong."

I have powers, she longed to tell him. *And my world isn't like everyone else's, and nothing will ever be the same again, and I'm not even sure what's real anymore, I'm afraid I'm losing my mind.*

But instead she told him, "Even if I could . . . you wouldn't understand."

"Try me. You might be surprised."

"I don't want any more surprises tonight."

Matt hesitated, seemed to consider a moment, then slowly released her hands. "Where's the tea?" he asked.

"The thing is," Lucy went on, oblivious, "if I could only have taken those things to the police, maybe then they would have taken me seriously. But I can't tell them about it now. If I do, I'll look less credible than ever."

"Am I close?" Matt was rummaging his way

through every door and drawer in the kitchen. "Am I in the general vicinity? Can you at least give me a clue?"

"Sometimes, when things like this happen, then I start thinking maybe they're right. The police and the doctors and even my aunt . . . then I start thinking maybe I really *am* crazy."

"You're not crazy."

"How do you know?"

"Ah!" Matt sounded pleased with himself. "Orange spice tea. Smells good, too. Now, let's see . . . cups."

"But I know what I saw in the car. I didn't imagine what I saw."

"I'll just zap these in the microwave."

"It couldn't have been a flashback, could it? I mean . . . Dr. Fielding said things can come back to you when you've gone through a trauma."

"Done," Matt announced. "Sugar? Lemon? Cream?"

"Sugar and lemon."

"Ah, a woman after my own heart."

Another patient exploration, this time through canisters, the refrigerator, the silverware drawer. Finally Matt set her hot tea in front of her—

complete with spoon, sliced lemon, and sugar bowl—and took a seat directly across the table.

The silence went on for minutes. Lucy stared morosely at her steaming cup.

"If you can't tell me everything," Matt suggested at last, "then tell me what happened with the car tonight. At least just that."

After another lengthy pause, Lucy nodded. Slowly stirring her tea, she related the whole incident to him without once looking up. When she was finished, silence fell between them again.

"You don't believe me," she finally whispered.

Frowning slightly, Matt leaned toward her across the table. "I didn't say that. The thing is . . . why would someone have Byron's jacket? You said Byron was wearing it when you crashed, so it was obviously . . . destroyed."

Lucy winced at the thought, and his expression softened.

"And even if it hadn't been, I can't imagine anyone taking it from the scene of the accident. There were only emergency people there, right? Police, firemen, paramedics?"

Lucy gave a reluctant nod. She knew Matt

was right—it was next to impossible that Byron's jacket could have survived the fire in any way, shape, or form.

"And what about this blanket?" Matt persisted.

Lucy paused, frowning. She hadn't told Matt any details of her horrific ordeal; she'd kept her account to the barest minimum. For just an instant she actually considered confiding everything to him. But then, taking a deep breath, she opted to keep quiet. And tell a white lie.

"The heater was broken in Byron's van so he gave me a blanket to keep warm. When I woke up after the accident, I didn't know where I was, and I tried to find help. And then I lost the blanket when I was running."

"Oh. I see."

Lucy's heart fluttered. Matt's face was carefully composed, but she had an uneasy feeling that he hadn't believed a word of her story.

"So what was all that panic about earlier?" Matt asked her now. "You wanting the police to find fingerprints and DNA?"

Lucy hedged. "Is that what I said?"

He continued to watch her. Lucy quickly took a sip of her tea, relieved when he let the subject drop.

"So who knew about the blanket?" he asked instead.

"The police. The doctors. Irene, of course."

"Well, there you go," Matt said reasonably. "You've got to remember, Pine Ridge is a small town. From what I've been told—and am *definitely* starting to witness firsthand—*everyone* eventually ends up knowing everyone else's business."

Lounging back, he rested one foot on his opposite knee, and settled himself more comfortably in his chair. He didn't look at all like a priest tonight, Lucy noted, not in his faded jeans and flannel shirt and scuffed hiking boots. She waited while he placed both hands around his cup and stared down into the steam, his expression thoughtful.

"Dozens of people could've talked about that blanket—or overheard someone else talking about it."

Lucy pondered this. "So . . . what are you getting at?"

"Have you ever considered that someone's just trying to scare you?" Matt asked. "Deliberately upset you? Just plain mess around with your head?"

"Guilt's such a weird power . . . It makes people do crazy things . . . Mean, hateful things sometimes . . ."

Once again, Dakota's warning came back to her. As Lucy listened to Matt repeating the very same theory, she didn't know whether to laugh or cry.

"Kids at school?" she managed at last. "Is that what you mean?"

"Well . . . I just know how cruel kids can be. Especially at an overly emotional time like this."

Lucy wanted to believe him—wanted *so much* to believe him. It made perfect sense that anyone in town could have overheard specific details of her post-accident experience. And of course it was entirely possible—and probable—that some of those who blamed her for Byron's death could have staged something simply to frighten her.

"But why the car?" she asked. "And why tonight?"

Matt shrugged. "Convenience? Maybe they've

been waiting for a chance, and opportunity finally presented itself. Everybody knows Angela's car—and it was the only one in the parking lot this afternoon. Maybe they tried to break in then, but couldn't. Anyone could've followed me here. Watched where I put the key. Planted the blanket and jacket, then taken them out again after you went inside."

"But it *was* Byron's jacket. It *was* the same blanket."

"Lucy, you had a flashlight and that little dome light in the top of the car. There's no way you could've seen anything clearly. And you panicked. And I'm sure whoever did this was counting on exactly that."

Should she tell him about the telephone call, too? About the terrified voice—*Angela's voice*—that couldn't possibly have come through during the power outage? While Matt continued his speculations, Lucy debated what to do. She opened her mouth, then shut it again, and realized she was afraid. Afraid of the answer. Afraid she'd only imagined it. And even more afraid that she hadn't.

"Lucy?"

Matt's voice pulled her back again. Taking another sip of tea, Lucy tried to focus.

"Look," Matt was explaining, "I'm not saying that any of those kids really did anything. I'm just saying they *could* have. You're in a very fragile state right now, and the worst thing you could do is jump to conclusions."

Lucy squeezed more lemon into her cup. *No, I have to bring it up*, she decided. *I have to ask him*.

"Do you think—" she began, but Matt had stood up and pushed back his chair, the scraping sound on the hardwood floor drowning out her attempted question.

"When will your aunt be home?" he asked, rinsing out his cup in the sink.

"I don't know. She works a lot."

"So you're here by yourself most of the time?"

She nodded, though his back was still to her.

"Well, you may be by yourself, but you're never alone."

His reply startled her, caught her off guard. "What do you mean?"

Matt turned around, drying his hands on a dish towel. A faint smile touched his lips. "What do you think I mean? You always have the power with you."

Lucy's heart skipped a beat. *Power?* No one knew about her power—*only Katherine, only Byron—nobody else—how could Matt possibly—*

"His power's always with you," Matt said, tossing aside the dish towel, leaning against the counter, folding his arms casually across his chest.

"Oh." Lucy could hardly swallow. "You mean God."

Matt shrugged, still smiling that faint smile.

"To tell you the truth, I don't think God's been around for a while." The bitter words were out before she could stop them. She saw Matt raise an eyebrow, and she added quickly, "If God were here, He'd make things better, right? If God were here, He'd . . . He'd make things not hurt so much."

Matt lifted one hand, thoughtfully stroked his chin. "Yeah," he finally told her. "Hurting really sucks."

They stared at each other for several long moments. In spite of herself, Lucy almost smiled. "Did they teach you that at priest school?"

"Actually, I figured it out all on my own."

Grinning, Matt picked up his jacket and walked over. He reached out and playfully ruffled her hair.

"I've got church stuff to do, Lucy. But I don't feel right about leaving you just now."

"It's okay," she assured him. "I'm fine."

As Matt looked deep into her eyes, she could read the reluctance in his own. He seemed to be waging a fierce battle with his conscience.

"Go," Lucy insisted. "Irene's bound to be home before too much longer. And I'll lock up the minute you're out the door."

"Swear?"

"Swear."

But deep down Lucy wished he wouldn't go. She *wasn't* fine, and she was afraid to be alone after all that had happened tonight.

She told Matt good-bye at the door. She watched from the window as he got in his Jeep and drove away. Then, telling herself not to be such a coward, Lucy marched upstairs and went straight to Angela's bedroom.

Matt's right. I couldn't see clearly in the car.

She turned on all the lights. She closed the window and locked it.

Everything Matt said makes perfect sense.

She forced herself to take the telephone from the desk. She lifted the receiver and listened to the dial tone. She checked for messages, but there were none at all.

But I answered the phone, so of course the call wouldn't have recorded anyway.

Lucy replaced the receiver and stepped back.

The room was still cold, neat as a pin, everything organized and perfectly in place. *Not like Angela's room at all.*

And it struck Lucy then. How vacant it felt in here, despite all the furniture. How impersonal and abandoned.

Like an empty shell.

Or a body without a soul.

As if Angela would never come back to it again.

14

"She told you to take a cab home?" Dakota was clearly puzzled. "No one ever takes cabs in Pine Ridge, except for really old people. And we only have two cabs."

Wincing slightly, Lucy shifted her backpack to her other shoulder. "She said she couldn't leave work to pick me up. And I think she was upset that I asked her to drive me this morning. But the thing is, I've never driven in snow before."

"Two inches? Believe me, this is nothing—it's already starting to melt. You haven't even *begun* to see snow yet. Just wait a few weeks."

"Does it snow a lot here?"

"Not nearly as much as I'd like it to. And it's not that hard to drive in. They're pretty good about keeping the streets plowed, and I could help you practice. And till you feel more confident, you can just ride with me when it snows."

"That's really nice of you. Thanks."

Dakota watched closely as Lucy drank from the water fountain. "You still seem a little unsteady. Are you sure you should even be here today?"

"Doctor's orders." Lucy gave a wan smile. "And Irene's. Anyway, I'm behind enough in my classes as it is."

"If you don't mind coming to the bookstore, we could study together."

Before Lucy could answer, the first bell rang. There was an immediate chorus of voices yelling, locker doors slamming, and feet pounding up and down the nearby stairs.

"I meant to stop by last night." Lucy tried to speak over the commotion. "But I fell asleep. I guess I was more tired than I thought."

"Well, after what you've been through, who wouldn't be?"

The two of them started down the hall, shouldering bravely through a surge of fellow students. Lucy tried to convince herself that no one was pointing or staring at her today, but her senses told her otherwise.

"What exactly are people saying I've been through?" she asked Dakota cautiously.

Dakota shrugged. The knitted cap she was wearing this morning matched her long, trailing scarf and was at least three sizes too big for her head.

"That you were in an accident and then disappeared for three days. And that some good samaritan found you and left you at the emergency room, but you can't remember what happened in between."

"Well," Lucy gave a thin smile, "that about sums it up." She waited for Dakota to grill her for more details, but the girl merely pointed at a series of large colorful posters hanging along the corridor.

"I don't suppose you'd be interested in being on my team?" Dakota asked.

Lucy drew a blank. "What team?"

"The Holiday Treasure Hunt. It's a scavenger hunt, really. The whole senior class divides into teams, and we all compete for prizes. Very big tradition here at Pine Ridge High."

"And is this tradition as important as the Fall Festival?"

"Well, it depends on what you're into, doesn't it?" Dakota proceeded to wrap her muffler numerous times around her neck as Lucy followed her into homeroom. The two took their desks near the window, and Lucy turned her attention to the snowy landscape outside.

It had taken herculean effort to shut off her mind, to not rehash again and again the disturbing events of last night. Luckily, Irene had gotten home within twenty minutes of Matt's departure, but Lucy still hadn't been able to sleep. She'd tossed and turned for hours, trapped in answerless questions and startled at every sound. When she'd finally gotten up and seen herself in the mirror—ghost-white skin and tired hollow eyes—she'd actually found herself wondering if she'd been in another wreck.

Dakota had been tactful enough not to even mention Lucy's haggard appearance. She'd merely stopped by Lucy's locker to ask if she felt better this morning, making casual small talk, putting Lucy at ease, smiling that Mona Lisa smile of hers. At least that's how Lucy had begun to think of it—that slight, mysterious curve to Dakota's lips that hinted of secrets known but never shared. Now, as Mr. Parkin took attendance, Lucy turned and shifted her attention to the desk behind her. Dakota was wearing knee-patched overalls again, fuzzy socks with beat-up sandals, and a leather bombadier's jacket. Between the layers of scarf and the droopy hat, Lucy couldn't even see the girl's eyes.

Like most of the class, Lucy drifted through the morning announcements. Despite her best intentions, she could feel paranoia creeping in again, as her eyes darted around the room, as she wondered how many of her classmates might have conspired against her to set up last night's charade. Was it just her imagination or was everyone trying not to look at her? Were kids smirking at each other, trying not to laugh? And had Dakota been telling the truth about what people really knew? The girl seemed to have a handle on things here at Pine Ridge High—if there were any other rumors going around, Lucy sensed that Dakota would be honest about them.

The bell rang again, signaling first period. As everyone spilled out into the hallway, Dakota tugged on Lucy's sleeve.

"See there?" she mumbled.

Lucy saw. Matt was standing just outside the administration office, jotting in a notebook, and talking earnestly with a small cluster of female students.

Dakota tugged her arm again. "There hasn't been this much sexual excitement around here since Mr. Enright took over the chemistry lab."

"Are you talking about Matt? I mean . . . *Father* Matt?" she quickly corrected herself.

Dakota's tone was solemn. "I have to admit—he's very hot."

"He's also a priest."

"That doesn't mean he's dead."

Lucy opted for another look. Matt was all business again today—properly religious from head to toe. Yet those faint streaks of sunlight still showed in his hair, and his grin was still easy and warm, and his eyelashes still lay long and thick against the fading tan of his cheeks.

For the first time Lucy really noticed the vast number of girls in the hall, moving at a snail's pace despite the sound of the bell. It was obvious from their faces that holy vows of any kind were not uppermost in their thoughts at the moment.

"So are you trying to tell me he's your type?" Lucy couldn't help teasing.

"No. I'm just trying to tell you that's he's too hot to be a priest."

"As hot as Mr. Enright?"

"Hotter. Mr. Enright's gay."

As the girls continued to watch him, Matt suddenly glanced up, recognized Lucy, and waved. Immediately heads began to swivel in her direction. Embarrassed, Lucy took Dakota's arm and moved her rapidly down the hall.

"He's nice, though," Dakota observed. "And he looked kind of worried about you."

"I . . . he's just trying to help me through some stuff. You know . . . like he's trying to help everyone else."

"Well, I'm glad he took you home yesterday. You shouldn't have tried to drive by yourself."

Lucy felt a tiny ripple of uneasiness. "How'd you know he took me home?"

They'd reached their classroom by now. Dakota paused outside the door and began unwinding her scarf.

"Come on, this school can't be *that* different from your old one. You know how information gets around. And besides"—she leaned forward with a conspiratorial whisper—"you can't expect to keep something a secret when Father Matt announces it to the whole office."

"It's not a secret," Lucy insisted. But it *did* help explain all the weird looks she'd been getting this morning. And maybe it explained something else, as well . . .

The whole office . . . the whole school. Which means anyone *could have found out I was alone yesterday.* Anyone *could have planned to scare me,* anyone *could have put that stuff in the car. Just a cruel joke. Just a mean trick, like Matt said.*

But what about the call from Angela? Could someone have managed to sneak into the house? Tamper with the fuse box? Rig the telephone somehow? Imitate Angela's voice?

Please let it be that. Please let it all be just a trick.

"Ladies, you're not going to learn anything lounging out here in the hall. Except, perhaps, bad posture."

As the teacher's voice broke into her thoughts, Lucy jerked back to the present. Dakota was already halfway through the door, and Mr. Timms was motioning Lucy to follow.

"Sorry," Lucy mumbled. She slid quickly into her seat, trying to figure out what the biology assignment had been for today. She couldn't even remember now if there'd been homework last night, much less if she'd done it.

She watched as Mr. Timms began listing various body parts on the board. At the next table over, Dakota was digging through her knapsack, the brim of her baggy hat practically obscuring her eyes.

Lucy took out her notebook. She hadn't even begun to catch up on all the schoolwork she'd missed so far; she didn't have the slightest idea how she was ever going to manage it. Not with so many tests looming on the horizon, and definitely not in her current state of mind. Sighing deeply, she clicked her pen, opened her notebook, and flipped to the next blank page.

And that's when her heart stopped.

For an endless moment her heart stopped beating, and the blood chilled solid in her veins.

She could see the words scrawled there, in large messy letters.

In strokes that had dried to a dark reddish brown.

Words meant for her . . .

And for her alone.

VERY SOON, LUCY

15

"Please—isn't there *any* way I can get in to see him?"

Lucy stood in the office, shifting anxiously from one foot to the other. She watched as the secretary consulted a schedule. Lucy clutched her notebook tight against her chest.

The woman looked up with a regretful smile. "I'm sorry, but—"

"It's very important. *Please. Very* important."

"What I'm trying to tell you is that Father Matt's left for the day. But the other grief counselers are still here. Perhaps you'd like to speak with Father Paul? Or Dr. Kauffman?"

"No. No . . . I . . ." Lucy stood for a moment, unsure what to do. Her mind felt blank. The notebook felt heavy in her arms. "Thanks anyway," she mumbled.

"I can schedule you for tomorrow," the secretary offered, but Lucy was already out in the hall.

Maybe this was a bad idea after all, showing this to Matt. Because what could Matt do about it anyway? Calm her down again? Try to convince her it was just another spiteful joke? And maybe it was, Lucy argued with herself. Maybe it *was* just another vicious prank. If she freaked out about it, then whoever had done this awful thing would win—again.

But what if it's not?

And what does it mean?

Had she been right about her unknown captor following her back to Pine Ridge? Knowing where she lived? Taunting her with those things in Angela's car? He could have found her notebook in the house last night and written his message then. And if she *was* right, who was going to help her? Who was going to protect her? If the police and the doctors hadn't believed her before, they *certainly* weren't going to believe her now.

How she longed for someone—*anyone*—to believe her.

Her resolve to keep silent had weakened with last night's incident. Her determination to handle things on her own had become shaky. Matt had listened to her, stayed with her, offered halfway sensible explanations—and though she'd been thoroughly frustrated at the time, it had felt so wonderful to have the burden lifted and shared, if even for just an hour or so.

She wasn't sure how much longer she could go on like this. Recalling the real-life nightmares. Struggling to stay sane. Feeling so terrified.

Being so alone.

But if she broke down and confided in Matt, would *he* die, too? Like Katherine? Like Byron? And what could she tell Matt, really? What could she expect from him if she didn't even know what she was dealing with?

Oh, Byron, I'd give anything to have you back again.

More depressed than ever, Lucy stopped at her locker. There wasn't anything she could do about the notebook now. She'd have to deal with it later—decide in the meantime whether or not to show it to Matt. She was late for class as it was. The bell for second period had already rung, and the corridor was deserted. She threw her notebook inside and was fumbling with the combination lock, when she heard laughter and running on the stairs.

The cheerleaders were late for practice, Lucy supposed. The whole uniformed group of them, with pom-poms in hand, making a beeline for the door at the end of the hall. Lucy drew back as they passed, and her eyes immediately landed on the girl with the short-cropped hair.

Wanda Carver.

She's going to die on Thursday.

Lucy's heart pounded. She felt herself step forward. Lift her arm to wave. Open her mouth to speak.

On Thursday.

She stood and watched the cheerleaders head off toward the gym. Her hands were shaky as she rechecked the door of her locker, tested the lock just one more time to make certain it was secure.

What am I thinking? I must *be crazy.*

Trying hard to compose herself, Lucy walked

slowly to class. She got a lecture for being tardy and flunked a test she'd completely forgotten to study for.

She didn't know if she could survive school until the weekend.

And it was only Tuesday.

16

I'm going to show Matt the notebook.

Lucy sat in the kitchen, both elbows on the table, chin propped in her hands.

No, I'm not.

Yes, I am.

She'd struggled with the decision all day. She hadn't been able to concentrate on anything else. And when school was finally over, she'd half expected the notebook to be missing from her locker, just like the jacket and blanket from Angela's car.

But it was still there, right where she'd left it. She'd shoved it down in her backpack, wedged it in tight, as though by trapping it there, she could end all the torture once and for all.

It was after six now. Irene hadn't come home yet, and as Lucy hunted for a memo pad, she kept glancing over at her backpack by the door. She didn't want to touch that notebook again, at least not till Matt had seen it. She didn't even want it in her room. As soon as Matt read the ominous message, she planned on throwing the notebook away. She could always copy Dakota's notes later.

In fact, that's where she was going tonight—to the bookstore to study with Dakota . . .

"I can't believe your aunt leaves you alone so much," Dakota had told her that afternoon. She'd insisted on giving Lucy a ride home, and they'd been on their way to the parking lot. "Don't you two ever do anything together?"

Lucy's laugh had been humorless. "She hardly even talks to me. And since Angela's been gone, she's been more distant than ever. She keeps Angela's room closed up. And all she does is work."

"Aren't you scared to be there by yourself?"

"Sometimes." But then, as Dakota's eyes had searched hers, Lucy had given in. "Actually . . . most of the time."

"I'm sorry."

Lucy had tried to smile. "The weird thing is, I was never afraid before. We lived in the city, in a walk-up apartment, and there were lots of times I stayed alone. My mom was a teacher. Sometimes she had school things to do at night, or meetings kept her late. It just never bothered me."

"There's my truck," Dakota had said.

It was big and old and clunky and even more beat-up than Dakota's knapsack. It had probably been cherry-red once, beneath all the dents and rust and scratches. And there was an odd assortment stowed in the back—a toolbox without a lid, two fishing poles, a laundry basket full of books, a gasoline can, and a small wicker rocking chair tied down with rope.

When Lucy tugged on the passenger door, Dakota had given it a hard shove from inside.

"Tragedies change us, don't they?" The girl's look had been intense as Lucy settled beside her. "We're never the same people we were before."

How true, Lucy thought now, climbing into Angela's car. She mentally reviewed the directions Dakota had given her and headed into town.

As her friend had predicted, the snow had all but disappeared, leaving streets and sidewalks a wet, muddy mess. Lucy drove slowly, watching for landmarks and street signs on the way. She'd never actually visited Pine Corners—the old section of Pine Ridge—and though a lot of places were open tonight, they didn't appear very busy. The four-block area allowed only foot traffic; there were parking lots at each end and curb parking in nearby neighborhoods. After several trips around the perimeter, Lucy finally found a spot on one of the adjacent streets, then set off briskly to find the bookstore.

Souvenir shops . . . art galleries and local crafts stores . . . cafés and coffee shops and an all-night diner—Lucy passed row after row of charmingly restored buildings, keeping a lookout for the alley she was supposed to take. There were a lot of alleyways, in fact, each of them quaintly named and squeezed inconspicuously between shops, where Lucy could glimpse tiny courtyards and miniature gardens beyond. After making a turn onto Candlewick Lane, she finally found the bookstore. It looked older than the other buildings—narrow, two stories high, and not nearly as well kept—but the door and windows and droopy awnings sparkled with strands of tiny white fairy lights, giving the place an almost magical quality. A curious assortment of lawn furniture and statues filled the small enclosure—stone elves and birdbaths, gargoyles and angels, all adorned with the same twinkling decor. And hanging from a clothesline were thirteen wind chimes, clanging out the most discordant harmony she'd ever heard.

Opening the door, Lucy went in. The first thing that struck her was the smell. A warm, musty smell of worn bindings and brittle pages, old leather and aged wood, damp wool coats and wet shoes, dust, a hint of mildew, and the strong rich smell of coffee.

The second thing she noticed were the books. Books everywhere. Shelves of books, tables of books, books stacked in corners, piled carelessly on the floor. Overstuffed chairs holding books instead of people. Books on the front counter and the rolltop desk behind it, and books on the staircase at the back of the room.

"Welcome to the eighth wonder of the world," said a familiar voice.

Turning, Lucy saw Dakota standing beside her, balancing a stack of books in her arms.

"I've never seen anything quite like it," Lucy agreed.

"Yes. We work very hard to maintain our reputation for clutter. Oh—Lucy, this is my dad."

Lucy instantly saw the resemblance. Though very tall and lanky, with wire-rimmed glasses and an absentminded smile, Mr. Montana had the same red hair and blue eyes as his daughter. He welcomed her to the store, encouraged her to get some coffee, and made her promise to come back again. Then, as a telephone rang, he obligingly transferred Dakota's books, excused himself, and hurried away.

Dakota raised an eyebrow at Lucy. "He'll tell you the exact same things next time you come, so don't be offended. He never remembers anybody."

"I like him. He seems really sweet."

"He is, but he makes me crazy. Come on—I'll give you the grand tour."

Dumping her coat and backpack behind the counter, Lucy followed Dakota through the rest of the shop. There were two more equally cramped rooms downstairs, and Dakota kept up a running dialogue as the two of them tried to maneuver their way around browsing customers and through tightly packed aisles.

"We try to categorize everything," Dakota explained, pointing things out as they went. "Keep all the genres together, make things easy for customers to find. But we just don't have enough space."

Lucy could see what she meant. Shelves bowed beneath their heavy loads, and baseboards were lined with boxes overflowing their contents.

"We're already double-shelving, so the rows are two books deep. And people hardly ever put stuff back where it belongs. So lots of titles end up in the wrong places."

"How do you keep track of everything?" Lucy asked in amazement.

"We don't. If we ever tried to clean behind those shelves, I bet we'd find books that have been missing for years."

The second-floor rooms, though every bit as crammed with books, were far less occupied with people. The light seemed dimmer up here; the rooms more stale and cold. There wasn't space enough for even one chair.

"What's that?" Lucy asked, pointing to a door with a KEEP OUT sign.

"Oh, that goes to the attic. We have a little office up there, but mostly it's just more books."

"Impossible."

"My mom keeps talking about moving to a bigger place. A newer store." Tilting her head, Dakota straightened the lopsided sign. "My dad keeps holding out for character and atmosphere."

"Do they both work here?"

"My dad, full-time. He's a writer, so this is perfect for him when business is slow. My mom's an artist. In fact you probably passed her gallery on your way. It's about five doors down."

Lucy was impressed. "It must be great to have such a creative family."

"Not if you're the only one who's not creative."

"Come on, I don't believe that."

"It's true. My sister's an awesome photographer; my brother's in a rock band and writes his own music. I'm the middle sibling who got *completely* passed over when it came to talent."

"There must be something you like. Something you're passionate about."

Dakota nodded. One corner of her mouth tugged down, and her pale eyes narrowed in thought.

"There is something," she admitted.

"Well, tell me. What is it?"

"You'll think I'm strange." Dakota hesitated, then sighed. "But then, of course, I *am* a bit strange, so you would be right."

Lucy couldn't help smiling. "Just tell me."

"In here."

Abruptly the girl turned and led Lucy into the last of the upstairs rooms. This room was easily the smallest of them all, with an odd configuration of shelving much like a maze, reaching from floor to ceiling and completely obscuring the windows, with unexpected turns and dead ends, and no rhyme or reason whatsoever.

"This is my favorite place," Dakota said quietly. "This is my passion."

She leaned against the door frame as Lucy took a cautious step into the room. For several long minutes Lucy was silent, her eyes sweeping back and forth over the hundreds of titles around her.

"Do all these deal with the supernatural?" Lucy finally asked. A tiny chill crept through her, raising goose bumps on her arms.

"Some people call it supernatural. Some call it real."

"What do *you* call it?"

Dakota moved slowly into the room. Her expression was thoughtful as she ran one hand along a row of old books.

"Lucy, there are just so many things out there that can't be explained or understood—not by our limited human perceptions, anyway. But those things still exist. They still happen. People are still affected by them . . . destinies are still controlled by them."

"Is that what you believe, then—that our destinies are predetermined?"

"I believe in everything." A thin smile flitted over Dakota's face. "But the question is . . . what do *you* believe in?"

"I . . . I guess I never thought about it."

"Witches? Zombies? Ghosts?"

Lucy pretended to be studying some titles. Adamantly she shook her head. "I really don't know much about any of that stuff."

"But you must have wondered about *something* in your life, right? Hasn't anything ever happened to you that was just too bizarre for this world?"

Lucy's eyes shot to the girl's face. "Why would you say that?"

"Vampires? Werewolves? Spells and curses? Just because you can't see what's in front of you doesn't mean it's not there."

The chill spread to Lucy's heart. She was wearing warm clothes, but she was beginning to shiver.

"No," she heard herself say. "No, I guess nothing like that's ever happened to me."

"Oh, well." Dakota seemed totally comfortable

with Lucy's reaction. "I warned you, you'd think I'm strange."

"I don't. I don't think that."

"This is the problem I face with my particular passion, you see. It doesn't involve any sort of creative talent, and I happen to be the only one who believes in it."

Still stunned by Dakota's revelations, Lucy watched her leave the room. *Tell her. Tell her the truth. Maybe she'll believe you. Maybe she'll have some insights . . . maybe she'll know how to help.* But Lucy couldn't say a word. Instead she could only stand there, trapped in a curious web of longing and denial.

"Lucy, are you coming?" Dakota was poised in the doorway, watching her. "I guess we've put off studying long enough."

The two went back downstairs. Dakota cleared off a lumpy, well-worn couch by the front window while Lucy poured each of them a cup of strong coffee from the pot on the counter. Then the girls settled themselves at opposite ends of the sofa, with their notes and textbooks spread out between them.

Somewhere between lists of required book

reports and unsolvable math problems, Lucy's attention began to wander. From time to time, she caught herself glancing over at Mr. Montana scribbling at his desk, or at the big round wall clock creeping interminably toward nine, or at Dakota's head bent low over yet another school project. The shop was practically empty now. Through the half-fogged window, she had a clear view of the courtyard beyond.

"You're drifting," Dakota mumbled, without looking up. "Only two more pages, I promise. Pay attention."

"Sorry."

"Don't be. It's incredibly boring."

Amused, Lucy tried her hardest to focus on the subject at hand. Dakota kept up a monotonous translation of French verbs. The bookstore was quiet now, and despite her megadose of caffeine, Lucy could feel herself getting drowsy. Her eyelids were heavy. With a halfhearted effort, she forced them open again and stared sleepily out the window.

Night lay deep within the courtyard walls. Like diminutive candle flames, the fairy lights glimmered softly through the shadows. The shadows where someone stood watching.

His face was near the glass.

Staring in at her.

And he looked just as she remembered, just as he had the last time she'd seen him, except for the bloodless pallor of his skin and his blank, hollow eyes.

"Oh God . . ."

She felt herself trying to stand. Trying to rise from the couch, trying to hold herself up and lean forward on shaky, unsteady legs . . .

"Lucy?" Dakota broke off in the middle of a sentence, looking up at her with a quizzical frown. "Lucy, what is it?"

And Lucy's voice trembled out, no more than a whisper.

"It's Byron."

17

"*What?*"

The book fell from Dakota's hands. As she jumped off the couch and reached out for Lucy, her eyes shot straight to the window.

"*What! Where?*"

But Lucy didn't hear. She was frozen helplessly in place, unaware of anything now but a misty pane of glass and shimmering pinpricks of light and a blanket of nighttime shadows in the courtyard just outside . . .

The deserted courtyard outside.

"I—" From some dreamlike place, she felt Dakota trying to pull her down again. "Didn't you see him?"

"Lucy, there's nobody out there."

"No, there *is*. *Was!* I *saw* him!"

"Lucy?" Dakota tugged at her again. "Come

on, sit down. Let me get you some fresh coffee."

But Lucy brushed her aside and ran for the door. Ignoring a startled glance from Mr. Montana, she hurried out to make a hasty search of the courtyard. A raw breeze swept down the alley, stinging through her clothes. It snaked through the wind chimes and played a macabre melody.

"Byron?" Lucy called.

You're losing your mind; you know Byron's dead.

Yet she'd seen someone there.

She'd seen *Byron* there.

Lucy rushed from the courtyard and back out through the alley. She looked frantically in every direction, but the shops were all closed, as still and deserted as the sidewalks.

And then she saw him.

He was at least fifty feet ahead of her, head bowed, walking rapidly toward the corner. She could see his dark hair blowing wild across his shoulders, and the long, easy stride of his legs . . .

"Byron!"

Before she even realized it, she was following

him, racing along the pavement, oblivious to the cold.

He was turning the corner now.

For one split second Lucy saw him hesitate, as though he might look back at her. He seemed to be listening to the pounding of her footsteps. Then he lowered his head again and disappeared.

"Byron!"

Lucy ran faster.

As she came around the corner, she could see that Byron was moving faster, as well. His shoulders were hunched against the wind, his collar turned high around his neck. He cut across a parking lot, then headed for a gap between two buildings. It was all Lucy could do to keep up.

Her breathing was ragged; her chest burned from the cold. As she entered the narrow opening, she caught a shadowy glimpse of Byron at the other end of the alley. Once more he paused, but just for an instant, before stepping out into the dim light of a streetlamp beyond.

"*Byron! Wait!*"

Lucy burst from the passageway, her heart ready to explode.

And then she stood there, staring in disbelief.

The figure had vanished.

From end to end, as far as she could see, the area was completely deserted.

"No . . . no . . . it's impossible . . ."

She seemed to be in some sort of delivery zone. To her left stood a row of identical buildings, small loading docks, and Dumpsters, obviously back entrances to shops and restaurants. To her right was a fenced-in wooded area, which she guessed to be a park. The high spiked gates were chained with a padlock; there were benches and overgrown pathways inside.

Maybe he climbed the fence. Maybe he left through the park. Yet Lucy doubted he'd had enough time to cover that much distance before she'd come out of the alley.

My God, just listen to yourself.

She was talking about Byron as if he'd deliberately led her here. As if he'd deliberately eluded her.

She was talking about Byron as if he were still alive.

But I saw him. I saw *him!*

Lucy strained her ears through the darkness. The wind had gone still. It was so unnervingly quiet, she could hear the echo of her own heartbeat.

So quiet . . .

Too quiet.

Suddenly she wanted to get away from here. For the first time it dawned on her just how foolish she'd been to follow some shadowy figure into an isolated part of town. He wasn't Byron—of *course* he wasn't Byron! And now he could be anywhere—*close* to her—*watching* her. The one in the cave . . . the one in her nightmares . . . the one nobody ever believed existed . . .

Lucy turned and ran back.

Back through the alley, back to the sidewalk, where she saw Dakota standing on the corner and looking frantic, trying to figure out where Lucy had gone.

"Lucy! Thank God!"

There was relief in Dakota's voice. Relief and fear mixed together, as the girl ran up to her and caught her in a hug. "Are you okay?"

"I saw him, Dakota. I'm not crazy."

"No, but you're frozen. Come back inside."

"It was Byron."

"We'll talk about it."

Reluctantly, Lucy allowed Dakota to lead her to the bookshop, where Mr. Montana was waiting for them at the door. He handed each of the girls a refill of hot coffee, then tactfully retreated to his desk.

"Sit down." Dakota steered her firmly to the couch. "Drink this. And don't try to tell me anything till you stop shaking."

But Lucy was too upset to follow orders. "I'm sorry," she blurted out. "I . . . I know it sounds impossible—"

"No. It doesn't."

"I know it sounds *insane*, but I really think it was him."

"It doesn't sound insane."

"Well, of *course*, it sounds insane, Dakota. *Byron's dead!*"

Dakota sat beside her. She propped her elbows on her knees and wrapped both hands around her cup. She blew gently on her coffee. She stared thoughtfully at the floor. "If you believe it's real," she said at last, "then it's real."

Lucy's tone was bitter. "But haven't you heard? I hit my head in the accident. I have flashbacks and I forget things. I'm prone to delusions, and I make things up. Most of the time, I don't even know what I'm talking about."

"That's crap."

Surprised, Lucy watched as Dakota looked up, took a cautious sip of coffee, then turned to face her.

"You are not delusional," Dakota said calmly. "You are brave. And you are gifted. And I am certainly not the person who's going to think you're imagining things."

Lucy hadn't expected this. It was such a shock and such a relief that quick tears sprang to her eyes. For a long moment, she couldn't even speak.

"Weren't you listening to a single thing I said upstairs?" Dakota went on. "I told you, I believe in everything."

"But you told me you didn't see anyone out in the courtyard."

"I didn't. But that doesn't mean *you* didn't." Dakota blew on her coffee again. "Reality's in the eye of the beholder."

"But what if you don't *know* what's real anymore?"

Dakota's gaze was steady and serene. "*You know*, Lucy. You have an aura about you . . . a special kind of energy I've never felt before. Except from one other person."

Mystified, Lucy stared at her. Dakota reached out and squeezed Lucy's hand.

"Byron," Dakota said softly. "I felt it with Byron. He had a gift, and so do you. Only yours is much, much stronger. Maybe even stronger than you realize."

18

"Dakota . . . what are you saying?"

A hint of a smile crossed Dakota's face. She tucked her legs beneath her and settled back against the cushions.

"I remember the first time I saw Byron," Dakota explained. "He came into the bookstore, and the whole atmosphere changed."

"I don't understand."

"I told you . . . it's like this individual energy that every person gives off. I didn't know Byron then, but when he walked through that door, it was like a physical shift in the air. I knew there was something very different . . . very special . . . about him. But I never knew what."

Lucy gave a curt nod. She was fascinated by Dakota's observations and wanted to hear more.

"I'd heard stories about his sister, of course—being psychic, being a witch, being a fortune-teller. But people turn cruel when they don't understand someone. And Byron was really protective of her. So I didn't pay much attention to all the rumors."

Lucy felt tension building inside her. The temptation to blurt everything out, to reveal everything to Dakota was suddenly unbearable. Through sheer willpower, she forced her emotions down again, kept her face impassive, focused on Dakota's narrative.

"But with Byron," Dakota continued, "something was definitely there."

"But . . . you don't know what it was."

"No." Dakota took a sip of coffee. "But I think *you* do."

Lucy looked out the window. She could hear the scrape of Mr. Montana's chair, could hear him going through the shop turning off lights. She felt Dakota lean forward again on the couch.

"Lucy, trust your instincts," Dakota said urgently. "Don't let anyone tell you they're not true."

Without waiting for a reply, Dakota began gathering up their books and papers. It was almost as if nothing out of the ordinary had happened tonight, and Lucy sat for a few minutes longer, letting it all sink in.

"Dad and I are stopping for something to eat," Dakota finally said. "Why don't you come with us?"

"No, I really can't. But thanks."

"Are you going to be okay?"

Still avoiding eye contact, Lucy nodded. "I'm okay."

"Then we'll at least give you a ride to your car."

Lucy was glad for the escort. This old section of Pine Ridge reminded her of a ghost town now, and her car was the only one in the lot.

"Be careful going home," Dakota warned her. "There's a bunch of one-way streets around here, and it's easy to get turned around."

Lucy watched the Montanas drive off. She let the motor idle and waited for the heater to warm up. Her thoughts were clamoring for attention, but she couldn't sort them out. All she could concentrate on was the fact that

Dakota hadn't asked for any explanations, hadn't expected any confidences, hadn't questioned her sanity.

Dakota had believed her.

Hadn't she?

Lucy rested her cheek on the steering wheel. It had been so long since she'd felt validated by anyone that suspicions began creeping in. Maybe Dakota was just pretending. Maybe she was just some weirdo who enjoyed acting out supernatural fantasies. Maybe she was just trying to get close to Lucy so she could play another cruel trick on her.

Yet Lucy didn't think so.

"*Trust your instincts . . . don't let anyone tell you they're not true.*"

And Lucy's instincts were telling her now that Dakota believed her. That Dakota was a friend.

Sitting up straight, Lucy adjusted the heater and switched on her headlights. Then she pulled onto the street and started for home.

It didn't take her long to realize she was lost.

Landmarks started looking way too familiar, and after an endless series of frustrating turns, Lucy saw that she'd been going in a complete circle. *Come on, don't panic—after all, this is a small town . . .*

She tried to recall the exact sequence of street names Dakota had given her. But despite her best efforts, Lucy eventually found herself in a neighborhood of run-down houses and broken streetlights, with no clue as to how she'd gotten there.

Damn! Swearing under her breath, she looked for a place to turn around. The houses were spaced wide apart, the yards neglected and overgrown, with wide patches of shadows in between. As she started into a driveway, a dog suddenly lunged toward the car, barking furiously. Lucy jerked the wheel hard to the left. She felt the car swerve, then bump noisily over something piled along the curb. To her relief, she spotted a cul-de-sac at the end of the street and immediately stepped on the gas.

One house stood alone in the cul-de-sac. An old Victorian surrounded by tall trees and clipped hedges and a picket fence without a gate. Though it had definitely seen better days, it looked more well kept than the other houses on the block, and a porch light cast a welcoming glow over the leaded glass in the front door.

Lucy couldn't help staring at it as she drove into the circle. She was still staring at it, in fact, when she suddenly became aware of the car leaning to one side and the slapping sound coming from underneath the front end.

Oh, no . . . don't tell me . . .

Shifting into park, Lucy jumped out and gazed in dismay at the flat tire.

Great. Now what am I supposed to do?

She didn't know how to change a tire. She didn't have a clue where any gas stations were, or if any were even open at this hour. And a flat tire hardly qualified as a 911 emergency. Grabbing her cell phone, she dialed Irene's number and let it ring. And ring. And ring. When the answering machine finally came on, Lucy left a message. Then she clicked off in disgust.

She couldn't just wait here all night—God only knew when her aunt would get home. She'd left Matt's phone number on her dresser, so that was useless; she'd left the business card Dakota had given her, too. And even if she called Information for the Montanas' home number, Dakota and her dad wouldn't be back yet anyway.

Totally frustrated, Lucy looked over at the isolated house. She didn't have a choice, really—there was only one thing to do.

Shutting off the car, she slammed the door and locked it.

Then she took a deep breath, squared her shoulders, and marched determinedly up the steps to the front porch.

19

There was a black wreath on the door.

Lucy hadn't noticed it from the street, because it was hidden in shadows. But now she could see the black crepe and black ribbons, the dried black flowers and tiny black jewels, all woven together in an intricate, antique design.

She'd seen something like this once before. But it had been a picture in a book—a black wreath hung upon a door, an old-fashioned custom to show that someone in the house had died.

Lucy hesitated. The last thing she wanted to do was intrude on a family's grief. If someone in this house had indeed died recently, maybe she should go somewhere else.

She was still trying to make up her mind when the door swung open.

Startled, Lucy found herself confronted by a tall, bony woman with a sour face, pointed chin, and frizzy gray hair. A starched apron was tied over her shapeless brown dress, and she was drying her hands on a dish towel.

"What is it?" the woman snapped.

Lucy quickly recovered herself. "I'm sorry to bother you, but—"

"I saw you lurking out here—don't you know what time it is? Well, whatever it is you're selling, I don't want it."

"I'm not selling anything. I'm just having car trouble."

The woman eyed her suspiciously. "Look at you. You been in some kind of wreck?"

"I . . ." Lucy's hand went self-consciously to the bruises on her face. "I . . . tripped on the stairs."

The woman considered this. Then she craned her neck and squinted toward the street. "Is that your car?"

"I've got a flat tire—I was wondering if I could use your phone book."

"A flat tire, you say? I don't see any flat tire."

"Yes, it's right there on the passenger side.

There in front." Lucy felt the woman's sharp gaze rake over her, head to foot. "Please. I just need someone to change it."

"Well, *I* can't change it. There's nobody here who can change it."

"I meant, I need to call someone."

"Why don't you call your parents?"

"I tried, but nobody's home."

"That's the trouble with kids these days. Parents never around when they should be."

Keeping respectfully silent, Lucy endured several more minutes of scrutiny. Then, apparently satisfied she wasn't going to be mugged by a desperate teenage girl, the woman motioned Lucy inside.

Despite the well-worn exterior of the house, the hall was clean and shiny. Lucy could smell floor wax and lemon polish and the faint scent of lavender as she was ushered into a small, snug living room. And though the furniture looked antiquated, there wasn't a speck of dust anywhere.

It didn't seem like a house where someone had died, Lucy thought. No flower arrangements, no stacks of sympathy cards, no all-pervasive feelings of sorrow and emptiness and despair. Maybe the people who lived here just liked black wreaths.

"Phone book's over there." The woman jerked her chin toward the far wall. "Phone, too. And don't be leaving any smudges on that desk."

"I won't. Thank you."

"What are you doing out this late anyway? Can't be anything good, young person out this late."

"I was on my way home and got lost. I was just trying to find somewhere to turn around."

"Hmmm. Turn around or scope out the neighborhood?"

Lucy ignored the accusation. "I haven't lived here very long. And I'm really bad with directions."

She walked over and picked up the phone book. The woman stood in the doorway and watched.

"Do you know who I could call?" Lucy asked politely. "A gas station? A garage?"

"What do you think this is, New York City? You're not going to find anyone this time of night. Everything's closed."

Lucy's heart sank. She laid the telephone book on the desk.

"Oh. Well . . . thanks anyway."

"Thanks for what? You didn't call anybody. And your tire's not fixed."

Lucy sighed. "Thanks for . . . letting me in."

But as she reached the front door, the woman stopped her. "Where do you think you're going?"

"My cell phone's in the car. I left a message on my aunt's machine—she might be trying to reach me."

"People talk too loud on those cell phones, act like they're the only ones in the world who have something to say. Well, let me tell you . . . nobody cares about hearing their business."

I should introduce you to Mr. Montana, Lucy thought, but aloud she said, "Well . . . I only use it for emergencies."

"So in the meantime you're just going to sit out there in the cold? Catch pneumonia? Get your purse snatched? Or worse?"

Lucy was getting irritated. It had been a long day, an emotional night, and she wasn't in the mood for any more upsets.

"It's not like I have many options," she replied, more sarcastically than she'd meant to.

The woman's lips pinched tight. "Come into the kitchen. Take off your coat, and put it in that closet. And for heaven's sake, hang it up neat."

Surprised, Lucy did as she was told. When she entered the kitchen, she saw gleaming countertops, a well-scrubbed, though outdated, stove, and a table with a blue flowered cloth. Pots of ivy lined the windowsill over the sink, and a large gray cat peered at her from beneath one of the straight-backed chairs.

"You like pie?" The woman's back was turned away from Lucy, bent inside a pantry, taking out dishes.

"I love pie."

"Then sit down. You don't eat pie very often, I can tell. Home cooking either. You're puny."

Lucy sat. She could feel the cat rubbing against her legs, could hear its loud purr of contentment.

"One more thing wrong with kids today," the woman went on. "Never have a decent meal. Never sit down as a family. Too many divorces."

Since she didn't get the feeling that she was expected to answer, Lucy kept quiet. She leaned down and scratched the cat behind its ears.

"There were ten of us when I was growing up. Dinnertime was nonnegotiable. We all had chores to do. Made us learn responsibility. Made us appreciate what we had."

Lucy watched as a pie was sliced, transferred to a plate, and shoved into the microwave. Within seconds, the warm fragrance of apples and cinnamon and buttery crust filled the room. She heard her stomach rumble. She'd forgotten just how hungry she was.

"Kids today expect handouts. Something for nothing, and right when they want it." Indignantly, the woman set a plate and fork down in front of Lucy. "Use that napkin there. And don't make crumbs all over the table."

It was the best pie Lucy had ever tasted. Flaky and sweet, it melted in her mouth and warmed her all the way down.

"This is wonderful," Lucy sighed, feeling almost as contented as the cat. "Really, this was just so nice of you. I didn't want you to go to any trouble."

"If it was trouble, I wouldn't have done it."

The woman pulled out a chair. She sat down across the table, took a tissue from her apron pocket, and dabbed it over her brow. Lucy swallowed another bite of pie.

"So you haven't lived here very long." The woman had obviously been thinking about this. "*How* long?"

"Just a few weeks."

"You go to church?"

"I . . . really haven't decided on a particular church yet."

"You should go to church. Young people today—no morals. No values. That's what happens when you don't go to church." She leaned toward Lucy with a frown. "There's a new priest at All Souls. He's too young to be a *good* priest, but with Father Paul having problems, we're stuck with him."

Lucy stared at her. "You mean Father Matt?"

"And how can I call him Father? It's like calling my grandson Father."

"I've met Father Matt," Lucy told her. "He's one of the grief counselors at my school."

"And what would he know about counseling

people? He hasn't lived long enough to counsel anybody."

Giving a noncommittal shrug, Lucy casually checked her watch. Where *was* Irene, anyway? What if she'd been home for hours and just hadn't checked her answering machine? *How long will it take her to realize I'm gone? How long will it take her to notice the time and—*

"So you didn't have time to know Byron, I guess."

Lucy's head came up. The woman's eyes were narrowed on her like lasers. The last bite of pie stuck in her throat, and she struggled to choke it down.

"As if his grandmother hasn't been through enough already," the woman added, not giving Lucy a chance to reply. "Well, it's not my place to say anything, is it? I'm just helping out. You've heard what you've heard at school already, so you know how he died in that wreck. But he was a good kid, not like most. Took care of his grandmother, just the two of them. Oh, there was an older girl once—mad as a March hare. But she took off, and no one's heard from her since."

A strange feeling of dread began to creep over Lucy. A feeling of secrets and doom, of being in the wrong place at the worst possible time.

"That's him there," the woman said, pointing. As Lucy's eyes moved to the refrigerator, she noticed for the first time a small photograph stuck to the door with a magnet. "That's Byron. Sad. He was such a good-looking boy."

Oh my God . . .

Lucy's throat was closing. Closing up around that wedged bit of food, so that she couldn't swallow, couldn't breathe. Her chest was squeezing. Her hands were frozen on the tabletop.

"This . . ." She could barely get the words out. "This . . . is his house?"

"Didn't you know?"

The woman got up and walked to the refrigerator. Lucy couldn't move, not even when the photograph was thrust in front of her.

"Well, I guess you *wouldn't* know," the woman concluded, "since you haven't lived here that long."

"You're Mrs. Dempsey," Lucy mumbled, and those flinty eyes bored into her once again.

"Have we met?"

"No. Father Matt told me you were staying with Byron's grandmother."

"She's bedridden. Stroke. Been that way for a long time. Oh, the nurse comes, but Mrs. Wetherly appreciates *little* things the nurse can't make time for. Fresh flowers every so often. Nice music. Being read to. Company when she's not too tired."

Mrs. Dempsey returned the photo to its rightful place. Then she studied Lucy with a pensive frown.

"In fact, maybe you should go back and see her. Since you're from Byron's school. Just to say hello."

The kitchen walls gave a crazy lurch, rocking the chair with them. Lucy held on tighter to the edge of the table.

"I don't want to bother her," she whispered.

"You won't. Come with me."

There was no getting out of it. As Lucy took the long walk down the hall, she felt like a prisoner bound for the execution chamber. She could see an open door at the end of the corridor. A glow of light spilling over the threshold, slanting across throw rugs on the floor.

Please, please, let her be asleep . . . please just let me slip out again without her ever knowing . . .

Lucy wanted to turn, to run—but she had images of Mrs. Dempsey grabbing her by the neck and throttling her into submission.

"In here," Mrs. Dempsey said. She stopped just inside the doorway, and Lucy could see the old-fashioned bed, and the mounds of fluffy white covers, and the soft, stacked pillows trimmed in lace.

"Odelia," Mrs. Dempsey announced, "here's one of Byron's friends to say hello."

The frail figure lying there seemed pitifully lost among the bed linens. As Lucy gripped the edge of the footboard, she could see how small Byron's grandmother was, how pale and still, her face a mass of wrinkles, her long braid of silver hair draped across one shoulder of her cream-colored nightgown.

But to Lucy's distress, Mrs. Wetherly wasn't asleep. In fact, her huge dark eyes, every bit as dark as Byron's had been, were directed toward the end of the bed, resting calmly on Lucy's face.

"She can hear you," Mrs. Dempsey advised Lucy in an undertone. "She can understand you, and she can move her left arm a little. But she can't talk. So she uses those things there."

She indicated a small slate and piece of chalk on the nightstand. Lucy managed a stiff nod.

"Well, go on," Mrs. Dempsey insisted, nudging her. "You can't visit clear across the room. Tell her your name."

But Lucy's feet were rooted to the floor. She tried to open her mouth. Her tongue was like cotton; her lips wouldn't move.

"Well, tell her your name, for heaven's sake. You expect her to read your mind?" As Byron's grandmother made a weak gesture, Mrs. Dempsey pushed Lucy forward. "Give her the chalk, and hold the slate so she can reach it."

Lucy felt sick. She crossed the short distance to the bed, wondering desperately what to do. She couldn't tell the truth—she just couldn't. That Byron had died was devastating enough. But that *she* was still alive, standing here in his grandmother's bedroom—that was just too horrible for anyone to bear.

The old woman's eyes had never left her. Even as Lucy picked up the stub of chalk and placed it in the blue-veined hand, those faded eyes continued to watch her, showing no hint of emotion. She heard the doorbell ring and fought a moment of panic as Mrs. Dempsey marched from the room.

But still the words refused to come. Words of comfort, words of remorse—though they tore at Lucy's heart and welled up into tears, she just couldn't bring herself to speak them aloud.

And then, to her amazement, Mrs. Wetherly's hand began to move.

Slowly . . . painstakingly . . . the old woman's fingers clawed around the chalk . . . motioned at the slate. Lucy lowered it in front of her. Held it tightly as the gnarled hand began to write.

The letters were like a child's letters. Crooked and crude, but clearly readable as they printed across the blank surface of the slate.

Lucy stared at them in silence. Four clumsy letters that she recognized at once.

L U C Y.

20

"Oh God," Lucy whispered. "Oh God . . . how did you know?"

The old woman's eyes looked deep into hers. In the dark fixed stare Lucy saw a sorrow that was endless . . . and a compassion that was immeasurable.

The sheer power of it left her breathless.

Unconsciously she took a step back, but before she could look away, Lucy saw something else.

Something forming in the depths of Mrs. Wetherly's eyes . . . something gazing back at her . . . haunting and achingly familiar . . .

Byron's face.

Byron's face trapped there in the dark . . .

"No," Lucy mumbled, "no, it's not possible . . ."

Somehow she made it out of the room and

down the hall. She snatched her coat from the closet, not even bothering to put it on. Fumbling with the lock on the front door, she didn't hear Mrs. Dempsey calling from the kitchen, wasn't aware of the footsteps approaching, until hands suddenly grabbed her shoulders and turned her around.

"Lucy!" Matt exclaimed. "What are you doing here?"

Lucy's head was throbbing, her eyes blurry with unshed tears. She jerked away from Matt and resumed her struggle with the door.

"Mrs. Dempsey told me someone had a flat tire, but I didn't know it was you." Reaching out, Matt pried her hands from the doorknob and took them in his own. "Lucy, it's not a problem. I'll be glad to give you another ride home."

"I don't want a ride home!" Lucy's thoughts were spinning—she couldn't get the image of Byron's face out of her mind. *It wasn't real—I just thought it was. Their eyes are the same, that's all. Just the eyes are the same, just the eyes, that's all it was, the rest of it was just in my mind.* "I'm sure Irene's called by now. I just need my phone. I need to get my phone from the car."

"I'll get your phone—you stay in here where it's warm. What a coincidence I happened to stop by at the same time you did."

"I didn't stop by. I didn't even *plan* to stop by. I never should have come inside, I never should have stayed. I want to go. I need to go!"

"You mean . . ."

Matt finally seemed to be comprehending the situation. For an instant he looked disconcerted.

"You didn't even know whose house this was, did you?" he asked her at last. "You didn't have a clue it was Byron's grandmother."

Lucy turned back to the door. *She knew me—how could she possibly have known me?* Shaking her head, Lucy kept silent. She heard Matt sigh deeply behind her.

"Right," Matt mumbled under his breath. "What are the odds?"

And I saw Byron . . . Byron in her eyes . . .

"Save that tea for me, will you Mrs. Dempsey?" Matt shrugged into his jacket and ushered Lucy out the front door, leaving the woman to stare after them in bewilderment.

"Lucy, I can't imagine what a shock that must

have been for you. How'd you end up here anyway?"

"I don't know," she answered miserably. "I kept taking wrong turns and hitting dead ends. And then I was on this street, and I saw the porch light."

"Let me take a look at that tire."

Lucy watched impatiently as Matt knelt down by the Corvette. But after a thorough inspection, he shook his head

"It's split wide open; you'll have to get a new one." He stood and brushed off the knees of his jeans. "Okay, two options. I can put your spare on right now, or I can take you home."

"Please. I just want to go."

"Then I'll call a tow truck for you in the morning, and you can pick it up sometime tomorrow. Glen's Repair over on Hawthorne Street. It's the one Father Paul uses, and that antique car of his still runs like a dream. So I figure this Glen guy must be some kind of miracle worker."

Lucy took her backpack from the car and locked the doors. Then she followed Matt to his Jeep and got in.

"How come you're out this late?" Matt asked curiously as they wound their way out of the neighborhood. "Not that this is *late*, of course—but late for Pine Ridge."

Lucy stared at the dashboard. The heater was on, but hadn't had a chance to warm up. Unconsciously, she held her hands out toward the vents.

"I was studying with a friend. Her family has this old bookstore in Pine Corners."

"Dakota Montana, right? Yeah, I've been to that bookstore—it's pretty amazing. You could spend hours poking around and still not see everything."

"I saw Byron," Lucy said.

Her eyes widened slowly as she realized what she'd said. *Oh God . . . why did I do that?*

From the corner of her eye, she caught Matt's quick glance. "You . . . what?"

Should she pursue it? Go into detail? Hadn't she acted crazy enough around Matt for one night?

"I was looking out the window. And I thought I saw Byron," she mumbled at last.

"Oh. You *thought* you saw him."

Lucy shut her eyes. "I *did* see him."

An uncomfortable silence settled between them. Lucy opened her eyes again, and focused on her outstretched hands. When Matt finally spoke, his voice was gentle.

"Where? Where'd you see him?"

"Don't talk to me like that."

Matt was surprised. "Like what?"

"Like you'd talk to some three-year-old with imaginary friends. I'm not making it up. And I'm not crazy."

"Lucy—"

"No. I'm tired of people not believing me. I'm tired of people treating me like I belong in a mental institution. And you know, it's all such bullshit. Everybody says *talk* about it—get it *out* so you can move on with your life. But when I *do* talk about it, everyone says oh dear, she's *hallucinating*. It's the *head* injury, it's the *pain* medication."

"Lucy—"

"Out of all the houses I could have picked to ask for help tonight, why was it *that* house? And do you know what happened when Mrs. Dempsey made me go into that bedroom?

Byron's grandmother *knew* me! She wrote my name on her slate! How could she know me, she's never even seen me before!"

"Well, maybe—"

"No. Just listen to me. If you don't believe when I *tell* you things, then maybe you'll believe something you can *see*. Maybe you'll believe *this*."

Furiously, Lucy dug into her backpack. She found the notebook she'd wedged in there earlier, and yanked it out, spilling papers all over the front seat. As Matt kept one eye on her and the other on the street, she started flipping through the pages.

"So you think it's all just in my mind? Then what do you think about solid proof? What do you think about messages written in blood?"

Matt pulled over to the curb. He put the Jeep in park and gave Lucy his full and silent attention. As Lucy kept turning the pages of the notebook, her movements grew more frantic. She got to the end, and a look of confusion struck her face. Immediately she began flipping backward, then forward again, then back. Jerking up the notebook, she turned it sideways and shook it violently, trying to dislodge any loose papers that might be stuck inside. Confusion turned to disbelief. Disbelief turned to desperation.

"Lucy," Matt said quietly.

"No! It was *here*! Someone put it in my notebook, and it was *here*! I *saw* it! It can't be gone—there's no *way* it could be gone! I had it with me every minute, and then I locked the car!"

But then she remembered.

She remembered placing her backpack behind the counter at the bookstore. Going off with Dakota for a tour. Not checking the backpack again when they'd sat down to study. Not checking again after she'd gone to search for Byron and Dakota had gone in search of her. Just assuming the notebook was still there, exactly where she'd left it.

"Someone must have taken it," she murmured now. "Someone must have taken it at the bookstore. That's the only place it could have happened."

But maybe it had happened while she was inside the Wetherly house. Maybe someone had broken into the car, then locked it up again. Anyone could do that . . . an expert could do that. Someone who enjoyed playing mean, cruel tricks could do that or . . .

Someone who follows me. Someone who watches. Someone who hides in the shadows of a cave . . .

She looked beseechingly at Matt. "It said, 'very soon.'"

And she suddenly realized that Matt had ahold of her hands and was leaning toward her, his brow creased with worry, his eyes full of sadness and sympathy.

"What did, Lucy?" he asked her.

"The message. The warning. It was in my notebook when I opened it this morning. It said, 'Very soon, Lucy.' And it was the color of dried blood. In fact, I'm *sure* it was dried blood—it *looked* like dried blood . . ."

Her voice trailed away. She felt Matt draw her closer, and as all the strength drained out of her, Lucy pressed her head against his chest.

"I don't know how it got there, Matt," she whispered. "And I don't know how it disappeared."

She closed her eyes and kept very still. She

could feel the warmth of his jacket and the strong beat of his heart. She could feel the steady vibration of the car, and the rush of heat from the vents.

She could feel Matt smoothing back her hair.

She could feel his arms starting around her, and his sudden hesitation, and the way he shifted away from her then, ever so slightly.

"Lucy." His voice was low. "I want you to have this."

Lucy drew back. She watched Matt reach up and remove a chain from around his neck. He stared at it for a moment, then eased it carefully over her head.

"What are you doing?" she asked, surprised.

The chain was thin, but sturdy. It slid into place, its small, round medallion resting lightly upon the front of her coat.

"Someone gave me this a long time ago." Matt smiled faintly, as though remembering. "It's helped me through some pretty rough times. Maybe you could give it a try."

"Oh, Matt . . ."

Lucy didn't know what to say. Lifting the medallion, she held it up close, trying to see the design. In the dim interior of the Jeep, it appeared to be carved with some sort of pattern, but one that Lucy didn't recognize.

"It's an ancient holy symbol," Matt explained.

"It's beautiful. But, Matt, I can't keep it."

"Why not?"

"Because it's special to you. You can't just give it to me like this."

"But I just did. And now I hope it'll be special to *you*."

Then, before Lucy could protest, he switched his attention to the steering wheel.

"Better get you home," he said quickly.

And it wasn't till much later, when Lucy was lying awake in bed, that she realized she'd never even asked him what the symbol meant.

21

She dreamed she was back at the tomb.

Back in the old cemetery, standing outside the Wetherly mausoleum.

She was alone.

And someone was following her.

In the nightmare, Lucy looked back over her shoulder, into the pitch-black night, through the wind-lashed trees, beyond the pounding rain. Thunder shook the ground beneath her feet. Thunder loud enough to wake the dead.

She pressed her face against the wrought-iron gates of the family crypt. The gates were locked, but she wrapped her hands tightly around the tall spikes and began to pull. Lightning flashed overhead, throwing the graveyard in and out of shadow. And with every stab of lightning, she caught just a glimpse of the tomb's cold interior, the leaf-littered floor, and the catacombed walls.

Terror rose inside her. The terror of being stalked, the terror of imminent danger.

The rain fell harder.

The air reeked of death.

Without any warning, the gates swung open. Yet Lucy remained on the crumbling steps, powerless to move.

"Byron," she called, "Byron, please help me!"

And then a voice—*his* voice—faint and sad and empty, from somewhere she couldn't see . . .

"Keep away," he warned her. "There's no one in this place."

Lucy shot up in bed.

Her heart was racing, and her nightgown was damp with sweat.

As she tossed back her covers, the last bits and pieces of dreaming clutched at her mind before fading and vanishing altogether.

She was out of breath. She swung her feet to the floor and padded barefoot to the sliding glass doors, parting the curtains and gazing out at the darkness.

Snow flittered against a velvet backdrop of night.

The pane felt icy to her touch, yet her body pulsed with heat.

That ache again.

That deep, insistent ache that made her want to moan, that ache that couldn't be filled.

Slowly she drew her nightgown off over her head.

She pressed her naked body to the glass, savoring the smooth, shocking cold against her skin.

How she longed to be out in that darkness.

Out beyond the backyard wall . . . out beyond those trees shining silver beneath the moon . . .

For some weird, unknown reason, the longing to be outside was suddenly—almost painfully—overwhelming.

Lucy started to unlock the doors, then remembered the security system was on. If only she could step out to the balcony, feel the snowflakes on her cheeks, the wind through her hair. The room was getting warmer; the walls were closing in. She couldn't stand being here one more second. Grabbing her robe from the foot of the bed, she slipped it on and tiptoed through the silence of the house.

She paused to disarm the security system. Her breath was coming faster now, her heart fluttering in anticipation. As though she were bound for some forbidden rendezvous. As though the night were her secret lover.

Without a sound, Lucy crept out the back door.

The wind loosened the sash at her waist, blowing her robe open and easing it down off her shoulders. It whipped around her as she spread her arms wide and embraced the cold.

Stimulating . . . invigorating . . . it made her feel strangely alive.

As though sorrow had never touched her . . .

As though she *belonged* somewhere . . .

"Lucy? What in heaven's name are you doing?"

The voice came from behind her. Startled, Lucy hastily tied her robe together and turned to see Irene hovering in the kitchen doorway.

"Lucy," her aunt asked again, but more puzzled than angry, "*what* are you doing out here?"

"I . . ."

Lucy stared back in confused silence. Irene obviously expected some sort of answer from her, but the longer Lucy stared, the more she began to realize that she didn't actually *know* what she was doing out here. Out here in the cold and the snow, in the middle of the night.

"I . . . needed some air."

It was the only thing her brain could come up with on such short notice. She shivered violently and realized she had nothing on her feet.

"Come back inside." Irene's frown was colder than the temperature. "Honestly, Lucy, this makes me wonder if Dr. Fielding should increase your medication. Instead of acting so foolishly, why didn't you just adjust the thermostat?"

Lucy took the scolding in her stride.

She went back to her room, donned a pair of flannel pajamas, and piled more blankets on the bed.

And then she stood there in the darkness,

peering out through the sliding glass doors, hugging herself against the chill that lingered in her veins.

She stared off across the lawn and past the low stone wall, and she realized that something had changed.

Something about the night.

Something that made it different now . . . different in a way she couldn't quite understand.

Almost as though it had been alive before . . .

But now, it was only a dream.

22

"You haven't said three words since we sat down," Dakota chided gently. "And you haven't touched your lunch."

Startled from her reverie, Lucy gave her friend a guilty look. "Sorry. I just don't have much of an appetite, I guess."

"I guess, too," Dakota echoed. "Lucy, you have to start eating better—you need to keep up your strength." Then, when Lucy didn't respond, she added, "Are you still worried about your notebook? I'll ask my dad about it, but I'm sure he'd have seen it behind the counter if you left it."

She watched as Lucy picked up a napkin, folded it into fourths, then absentmindedly dropped it on the table.

"Is it your aunt?" Dakota tried again.

Lucy looked down at her plastic tray. "You know, it's a sad state of affairs when school cafeteria food looks better than what you get at your own house."

"You didn't answer my question."

"Okay," Lucy sighed. "She caught me by surprise. Even though I should know better by now."

"I can't believe it either. I mean, what kind of mother takes off like that when her daughter's still missing?"

"Dr. Fielding advised her to go. He said it would be therapeutic. He said she couldn't do anything here anyway, except worry and be constantly reminded that Angela's gone. And she can stay in touch with the private investigator anywhere."

"Still . . . I think it's sad. It's like she's already decided that Angela's not coming home."

"It's so dark here . . . I can't get back . . ."

Remembering the ghostly telephone call, Lucy's shoulders stiffened. "Maybe she *has* to decide that. Maybe it's the only way she can cope."

"Maybe." Dakota gave a reluctant nod. "But it

sort of makes you understand why Angela's run away so many times, doesn't it?"

But this is the last time. The thought loomed darkly in Lucy's mind, though she tried to push it away. *This is the last time Angela will ever leave . . .*

"Lucy, I'll be leaving for a while. On very important business."

Irene's announcement had come that morning while she was driving Lucy to school. An announcement that was so casual and matter of fact, that at first Lucy hadn't even realized its magnitude.

"We're experiencing some difficulties with one of our foreign-exchange programs. It's necessary that I go to Paris and help with the reorganization."

Lucy had waited, not exactly sure what was coming next. Irene had cast her a pensive sidelong glance.

"It's going to take at least two weeks. Perhaps more. And frankly, I'm not sure what to do with you."

That's when the reality of the situation had

begun to sink in. And though Lucy felt stunned and hurt, she'd managed to shrug it off with a forced smile.

"You don't have to worry about me, Aunt Irene. I'll be fine."

"There's really no one I can think of to leave you with," her aunt had gone on, as though she found this mildly annoying. "And Florence can't be here full-time; she has a family and other clients to take care of."

"You don't have to ask Florence. It's not like I need a babysitter or anything."

A slight frown had settled between Irene's brows. "If you were Angela, I'd have to nag you about being responsible. I'd have to warn you not to let strangers into the house and not to throw wild parties while I was gone."

Lucy hadn't answered. She hadn't known what to say.

"But you're not Angela," Irene had concluded.

A pause had settled between them. And to Lucy's astonishment, Irene's eyes had suddenly glimmered with tears.

"And it's not your fault, Lucy," she'd said softly. "What happened is not your fault. I do not want you blaming yourself for any of Angela's rash behavior."

For one split second, Lucy had almost leaned toward her aunt. Almost touched her. Almost given her a hug.

But then the tears had vanished, leaving Irene's eyes as cold and hard as before.

"She'll come home. Eventually." As the car pulled up in front of the school, Irene's tone had suddenly matched her eyes. "When he breaks her heart . . . when she runs out of money. She'll come home like all the times before."

"Aunt Irene—"

"Don't be late, Lucy."

Crestfallen, Lucy had gotten out of the car.

She'd stood there on the sidewalk, and she'd even waved good-bye.

But Irene had never looked back . . .

". . . till she gets back," Dakota was saying.

Lucy looked up from her lumpy macaroni and cheese. The noise in the cafeteria was deafening, and she hadn't realized till this very minute how much her head was beginning to ache.

"Till *who* gets back?" she asked.

Dakota stopped sucking on her orange. She ran one hand slowly through her hair, her eyes fixed calmly on Lucy's face. "We were talking about your aunt."

"Sorry. I guess I zoned out for a minute."

"Oh, that's good. I thought maybe it was me zoning." Dakota slid her tray to the edge of the table. "I was just saying that you could stay with me while your aunt's gone. My parents would be totally okay with it."

"I couldn't do that. It's really nice of you, and I appreciate it, but . . ."

"But what?"

"But I just couldn't, that's all."

After a second's hesitation, Dakota reached over and squeezed Lucy's hand. "I don't know everything you've been through, Lucy. And I know this is none of my business. But I don't think you should be alone right now. So promise me you'll at least think about staying over."

"Yes." Lucy forced a weak smile. "I promise."

"When's she leaving, anyway?"

"Next week sometime."

"Well, you'd definitely start *eating* at my house," Dakota informed her. "My mom and dad are both great cooks. And I bet you'd sleep, too."

"I sleep now."

But Dakota wasn't fooled. Releasing Lucy's hand, she leaned even closer, a wise sadness in her eyes. "Be honest with me, Lucy—when's the last time you *really* slept? A sleep without nightmares . . . a sleep without pain?"

And Lucy couldn't answer.

Because she truly couldn't remember . . .

She'd stayed awake till morning.

Still restless from her need to be outside, Lucy had paced her bedroom in the dark, and she'd stared out for hours through the sliding glass doors. She'd sat on the bed with her arms wrapped around her, trying to give herself comfort. And she'd rocked back and forth, back and forth, but it hadn't lulled her to sleep.

As if she hadn't had enough on her mind already.

After Matt brought her home, she'd had more than enough to think about, a whole new set of fears to consider. She'd felt numb and strangely distant, as though her emotions belonged to someone else. For a while she'd held the medallion Matt had given her, turning it over and over in her hands. Then she'd put it in the drawer of the nightstand and collapsed on her bed, shutting her eyes and trying desperately to shut out the rest of the world.

A world she no longer trusted or understood.

A world of questions without answers.

The message in her notebook . . . Byron's face at the bookstore window . . . a series of wrong turns leading her straight to the Wetherly house . . .

And Byron's grandmother . . . Byron's reflection in those sad, dark eyes . . .

How did she know my name?

Lucy had lain there, too exhausted to move, and praying for sleep. Deep, senseless, peaceful sleep. Kind sleep . . . sleep without dreams.

But of course she hadn't slept.

Not then.

Not while those questions and conjectures had continued to rush blackly through her mind, like bats swarming at dusk from their cave.

Byron must have mentioned her, she'd decided.

At some point, Byron must have mentioned Lucy's name to his grandmother—or described her, maybe—and that's how his grandmother had known.

Yet how could Lucy explain the rest of it? Like her tire going flat, so conveniently near Byron's house? And Byron's grandmother recognizing her from countless other blond-haired, blue-eyed girls who might have happened to knock on her door?

"*Mrs. Wetherly was propped up in bed, almost as if she'd been waiting for us. She didn't even look surprised. Just so sad . . . calm . . . resigned, almost.*"

Matt's words had come back to her then.

Matt's account of the night Byron died—when Matt and Father Paul and the sheriff and doctor had all gone to tell Byron's grandmother the news.

Could it be true?

Yielding reluctantly to her memories, Lucy had opened her eyes and stared hard at the ceiling. Byron had told her once that his grandmother had psychic powers, the ability to "know" things other people weren't privy to. Could it be that Mrs.

Wetherly had *expected* Lucy to show up there?

Could it be that she led *me there* deliberately?

The idea had been too chilling to contemplate.

So Lucy had gone into the bathroom and run a hot shower. She'd stood there under the steamy spray, but her mind had continued to fret.

Should I go back to Byron's house? Tell his grandmother how much he helped me, how much he meant to me?

Or should I stay away from there forever?

And even beneath the soothing flow of the water, Lucy had felt bruised and battered by indecision.

How much does Byron's grandmother know about me? How much did Byron tell her? Does she know about Katherine's horrible death? And how I found Katherine that night in the cemetery, and how Katherine changed me forever?

Lucy had leaned her head against the shower wall, picturing Byron's house again. The second-floor windows had been dark, she remembered. Windows where Katherine had stared out at an unsympathetic world . . . windows that had become Katherine's prison.

And suddenly her heart had ached for Katherine.

Ached and cried for Katherine.

Not only for the girl's heartless death, but for the life she'd been denied. Denied because of her powers. Denied because of her gift.

"A gift sometimes . . . but also a curse," Byron had called it.

And now it belonged to Lucy.

And as the shower washed away her tears, she'd wondered about her own life and the strange direction it had taken.

And she'd asked herself—as Dakota had asked her in the bookstore that night—just what *did* she believe in?

"Hope," said Dakota, and once again Lucy looked at her friend in total bewilderment.

"What?" Lucy asked.

"The candlelight vigil. As an expression of hope." Dakota was standing up now, closing her knapsack with a tolerant smile. "Lucy, I'll be glad to go over all this again when you're back on the planet."

"I'm sorry. I'm just so out of it today."

"Candlelight vigil," Dakota repeated patiently. "For Angela. Tomorrow night in front of the school."

"Whose idea was this?"

"Some of her friends on the cheerleading squad. At least that's what I heard."

"Does my aunt know about it?"

"I'm sure someone plans on telling her. Do you think she'll come?"

Lucy shrugged. "I've given up thinking what she might or might not do."

The two headed off to class. They were just rounding a corner near the office when Lucy spotted several of the cheerleaders standing together, handing out flyers.

"Those are the notices," Dakota mumbled. "For the vigil tomorrow night."

As they got nearer, Lucy's heart began to quicken. She recognized one of the girls as Wanda Carver, and she stopped uncertainly in the middle of the hall.

"What?" Dakota stopped, too, her expression puzzled. "What is it?"

"Nothing. I'm okay."

"You sure?"

Lucy nodded. But her heart was beating faster now, and she could see Wanda starting toward her, one hand extended, passing Lucy one of the printed announcements.

Lucy stood frozen. Wanda was looking at her strangely, as strangely as Dakota was, and Lucy couldn't move, couldn't move even though she wanted to, even though she wanted to turn and run and never touch that paper that Wanda was touching . . .

But Wanda thrust the flyer into her hand, and Lucy had to take it. Had to take it and pretend nothing was wrong, while the quick, sharp flashes of danger strobed darkly through her brain.

"Lucy? You did this last time—what's wrong?"

And she could hear Dakota's voice so close to her as she whirled around and started away, away from the curious stares and away from the feeling of tragedy . . .

She's going to die on Thursday.

"I have to go back," Lucy said.

Breaking from Dakota's grasp, she pushed her way through the packed corridor. Wanda didn't even see her coming, not till Lucy was right beside her and leaning in close to her ear.

"Be careful," Lucy whispered. "Be careful tomorrow. Please."

The girl jumped back, completely startled and completely annoyed. "Hey, what do you think you are doing?"

"You could get hurt. You could fall and get hurt. Just please be careful."

"Get away from me! Are you *crazy*?"

Lucy pulled back. Wanda and her friends were staring at her with undisguised contempt, and Lucy's cheeks flamed in embarrassment.

"Sorry," she mumbled. "I just . . . It's a mistake. Sorry."

Turning on her heel, she ran to catch up with Dakota. But her heart was still pounding.

And the images in her mind had gone hopelessly black.

23

She and Dakota had almost been late for class.

Which is a good thing, Lucy reminded herself wryly.

There'd been no time for Dakota to question Lucy's strange behavior, no time for Wanda Carver to mortify Lucy more than she already had.

Still, by the end of the day, Lucy couldn't help noticing more curious stares and secretive whispers aimed in her general direction.

Lucy Dennison. Certified Nut Case.

She wished she could just go straight home and hide, but she'd already had to beg a ride from Dakota. Angela's car was waiting at Glen's Repair, and after that, Irene had asked her to pick up some dry cleaning.

"We can do that first," Dakota offered, coaxing

her truck from the school parking lot. "It's right next to the soup kitchen where I volunteer."

Lucy was impressed. "Do you really? I've always wanted to do that. What's it like?"

"Interesting. And humbling. It definitely keeps me grounded."

"Do you feed a big crowd?"

"Not like a lot of places, thank goodness." Dakota raised an eyebrow. "Pine Ridge is pretty affluent. But we have our share of homeless. You get to know the regulars. And then there're the ones just passing through town."

"So when do you work?"

"Saturdays mostly. But around holidays or when it's really cold, I work during the week, too."

"Do you think I could help out sometime?"

Looking genuinely pleased, Dakota nodded. "We'd love to have you. Would you like to stop by now and see it for yourself?"

"That'd be great."

As Dakota continued to drive, Lucy lapsed into silence. Several minutes passed before she cast her friend a troubled look.

"Dakota, I need a job."

She'd halfway expected shock at this announcement. At the very least, reminders about her aunt being one of the richest people in Pine Ridge. Dakota, however, kept her eyes on the road and creased her brow in thought.

"Doing what?" she asked.

"I don't know. Something useful." Shifting in the seat, she gave her friend a hard stare. "The thing is, Irene keeps telling me to use her credit cards. I don't want to ask her for anything. But there's stuff I need. And I don't have any money of my own."

Dakota's voice was quiet. "I understand."

"So do you know of anything?"

"Well . . . shops around here always need part-time help around Christmas. But they usually snap up the college kids first." She paused, fingers tightening on the steering wheel. "My dad might know of something. And I'll ask around, too. There's bound to be someone out there who needs you."

"You mean, they're just waiting for me to come along and walk right through their door?" Lucy couldn't help teasing.

"That's exactly what I mean."

The smile faded from Lucy's face. "You're really serious."

"Of course I am. You should know that by now."

"So you *really* believe that somebody who needs *one* particular job done is waiting *just* for me—out of *all* the other people in the universe."

Dakota's glance was solemn. "Lucy," she said, "there are no coincidences."

Lucy frowned, a sliver of uneasiness shinnying up her spine. Dakota's eyes shifted back to the windshield and stayed there the rest of the way. When they finally pulled up in front of the dry cleaner's, Lucy grabbed Dakota's arm before the girl could get out of the truck.

"Aren't you going to ask me?" she demanded.

Dakota gazed back at her, those pale blue eyes calm on Lucy's face.

"Ask you what?" Dakota murmured.

"You know. About Wanda Carver. About those weird spells I have. About what happened today."

"Do you want me to?" Dakota countered softly.

"Well, don't you think I'm crazy like everybody else does?"

That hint of a smile drifted over Dakota's mouth. She rested her hand on Lucy's.

"You're not crazy. You're a person with many secrets. And secrets should never be told until their time. And when they're ready to be told, then you'll tell me."

Lucy didn't know whether to laugh or to cry.

"Come on," Dakota said, shoving open the door. "Let's go sign you up."

Lucy instantly felt at home.

As Dakota showed her around the soup kitchen and introduced her to the staff, Lucy knew she'd made the right decision about volunteering. She hadn't felt such a warm, welcoming atmosphere since moving to Pine Ridge.

Not since her mother had died.

"See?" Dakota looked almost smug as she guided Lucy through the oversized pantry. "These are wonderful people. You fit right in."

"Thanks for letting me join."

"No. Thank *you*." Taking Lucy's arm, Dakota

led her to the main dining area. "Come on. I'll show you how we do the serving line. Just think of it as your friendly neighborhood buffet."

The room was practically empty. Three elderly women in threadbare coats sat at a table in one corner, chuckling over some shared bit of gossip, their raggedy shopping bags beside them on the floor. They waved to Dakota as she passed them, then went on with their conversation. Behind the serving counter, Dakota pointed out the contents of shelves and explained portion sizes, while Lucy listened attentively. She scarcely even noticed when the front door opened and the disheveled figure slunk in.

"Okay, here's someone," Dakota murmured, glancing toward the approaching stranger. "Perfect time to practice."

"Now?" Lucy asked hesitantly.

"Of course, now. Here. Just do it like I showed you."

Nodding, Lucy picked up a ladle and waited for the man to take a bowl. Dakota walked to the end of the counter where a few pieces of chocolate cake still remained in their baking pan.

"Hi," Lucy smiled, as the man stopped in front of the huge soup kettle.

For a moment he paused there, head lowered.

And then he looked up at her.

Dear God . . .

Lucy's fingers dug into the ladle, the smile frozen on her lips. For one panicky second she wondered if she'd actually been able to keep her face expressionless, if she'd managed to keep the revulsion from showing in her eyes.

His cheeks were scarred, this man standing before her—scarred and festering with sores. Across his forehead and through the matted beard on his chin, Lucy could see pus oozing out beneath big, wet scabs. Long hair lay over his shoulders in greasy strands. His body was rail-thin, his weary shoulders slumped, and the odor emanating from his tattered clothes made the bile rise into Lucy's throat.

She hastily tried to collect herself.

But she couldn't look away from his eyes.

His eyes . . .

At first glance she'd guessed him to be

young—somewhere in his twenties, perhaps. And yet his eyes were old.

The eyes of a very old man.

Eyes of vast experience. Intelligence and cunning.

Tragedy . . . but survival.

And as Lucy peered into their rheumy depths, she felt an unnerving shiver pass through her.

"Hi," she heard herself mumble again.

Beneath his coarse mustache, she thought he might have smiled. Rotten teeth and foul breath.

His eyes flickered dimly . . . some emotion she couldn't read.

Lucy plunged the ladle into the pot. Her hand was trembling, and she glanced up to see the man still watching her.

His hand was trembling like her own.

Trembling as he held out his empty bowl, waiting for her to fill it.

A rush of pity went through her. Pity and an understanding of his soul.

On his face . . . in his eyes . . . through the quivering of his hand, Lucy recognized the depth of isolation. The aching loneliness and despair. The qualities that kept him distant and apart.

Before she even realized what she was doing, she'd reached across the counter, taken his bowl, and in its place, laid her hand in his.

"I'm so glad you came today," she said softly.

He gazed at her in silence.

A penetrating silence as he slowly squeezed her hand.

Lucy's breath caught in her throat. For the space of one heartbeat, the air seemed to swell and split around her, as though something in the very atmosphere had changed.

Her head grew light.

Her skin flushed warm.

And from some very distant place came the burning familiarity of a deep, insistent ache . . .

"Lucy?"

Startled, Lucy turned toward the sound of a voice.

Dakota was standing beside her, easing the ladle from Lucy's clamped fingers.

"I think you've stirred that soup long enough," Dakota teased. "Save some of your strength for next time."

Lucy's eyes quickly scanned the room. Except for the three women still talking in their corner, all the tables were empty.

"Where'd he go?" Lucy asked.

"Who?"

"The man who came in to eat."

"He left about fifteen minutes ago." Dakota gave her a funny look. "Didn't you notice?"

"I . . . I guess not."

"Now, that's what I call being involved in your work." As Lucy stared down at the counter, Dakota stepped back, studying her with a thoughtful frown. "But you're upset, aren't you? About that man."

Lucy didn't answer. Her hands felt cold now, her mind hazy—as though she'd just awakened from a dream.

"I know how you feel," Dakota said, trying to comfort her. "It was hard for me, too, at first. Seeing people like that, and wanting so much to help them. But we *are* helping. Just for the time they're here, we *are* making a difference in their lives."

"Who was he?" Lucy's voice was tight. "Do you know?"

“That’s odd, isn’t it? He must be one of those transients I was telling you about. I’ve never seen him around here before.”

With a sigh, Dakota gazed out the front window, out at the people and shadows mingling together in the dusk.

“You were so kind to him, Lucy. He’ll probably never forget you.”

24

Her touch still clung to him.

He could still feel the pressure of her hand in his . . . the softness of her skin . . . the length and slender shape of every finger.

Her warmth had flowed into him, a surge of emotions that had shocked each one of his senses into wonder.

Her concern and compassion . . . her undisguised pity . . .

And the sorrowful understanding in her eyes.

It had left him stunned and seriously shaken, a wound within the nether regions of his soul, for seldom in his lifetime had he ever known understanding.

Understanding made one vulnerable.

A lesson he'd learned well, and long ago.

So now he paced, gripped by a strange,

trembling restlessness, his skin too tight, his face transforming into another. He paced like an animal in a cage, stopping only long enough to gaze out through the darkness—the deep, deceptive darkness that was his only friend.

This was his domain, as it had always been, as it would always be.

This kingdom of the night, as black and impenetrable as his soul.

"Damn her."

How could his plan have gone so completely awry?

"*Damn her!*"

What had he expected? Another ruse to get close to her, to hide behind the essence of his nature and see himself reflected in her eyes.

And for a single moment, he had watched her hovering there on the brink of disgust and aversion, startled by his ugliness and trying not to show it, drowning in the poison of his stare.

But then, without warning, she'd changed.

He had not expected it—not even seen it coming—when suddenly he'd *felt* it. *Felt* it like warm, soothing waves; like gentle arms reaching out to take him in, into a place of comfort and acceptance. He felt it a thousand times stronger than *anything* he'd felt from her before.

He had been so fascinated, so dismayed, he'd simply stood frozen there in place and squeezed her hand.

It had been all he could do not to moan out loud.

Moan with the desire for her, the *need* for her, the wild and desperate hunger for her.

For he had felt *her* longing, as well.

Her ache as strong as his, as deep and unfulfilled, the frantic throbbing of her pulse, and their connection so strong, so overwhelming, it had sucked his breath away . . .

Distracted his instincts . . . driven him mad.

Since he'd left the soup kitchen, he'd thought of nothing else.

He had no choice but to go to her.

Force her if he had to, take her *now* if he had to—he would *not* wait for willingness or surrender or the right and perfect time.

But even as he crouched upon her balcony, where he'd spent so many nights before, he knew that he must hold himself in check. Remain anonymous and watchful. Infinitely patient. Disguised as whomever she needed him to be.

Like fine gray mist, he slipped inside her room.

Gazed upon her silently as she slept.

Damn her for making him feel!

For touching him like that . . . with her hand and with her heart!

For making him remember another life in another time, times of understanding . . . times of sharing love . . .

No, he would *not* feel—he would *not* remember!

He would feed.

And he would kill.

And he would survive.

For these were the only things that mattered to him now.

The only things he loved and understood.

25

Lucy still couldn't understand what had happened.

Everything had been so normal, everything had been going so well—spending the afternoon with Dakota, and meeting the people at the soup kitchen, and volunteering for something that really mattered.

And then that stranger had come in.

That pathetic young man with the festering sores and the hunger in his very old eyes.

She hadn't been able to stop herself.

She'd reached out her hand and she'd touched him, and slowly she'd begun to recognize something.

Something that had touched her before.

Impossible.

Absolutely impossible.

But now she was lying in bed and thinking back on the whole unsettling experience, trying to tell herself it was only one of those blackouts Dr. Fielding had warned her about, one of those memory lapses.

After all . . . hadn't she lost fifteen whole minutes?

Fifteen minutes unaccounted for, while the stranger had sat down at a table and eaten his meal and left again by the front door?

Of course it had been just memory loss.

How else could she ever explain it?

Yet a doubt still persisted in the back of her mind . . . a nagging doubt and a lingering nightmare . . .

A nightmare swift and needle-sharp—stabbing like fire, piercing hot through my skin, sinking deep through my flesh, clamping down and holding on, suspended there . . .

Lucy turned restlessly, unable to sleep.

Shadows pressed around the bed and shrouded her in black.

Suspended there on boiling waves of panic and burning pleasure . . .

The room seemed to be holding its breath as her fingertips stroked the darkness.

Burning pleasure . . . waves rushing over me . . . through me . . .

Once again Lucy pictured the stranger's face.

She pulled the covers over her head and hid beneath them till morning.

26

He had felt her fingertips caressing his cheek . . . gliding over his throat . . . down the front of his chest.

She hadn't even known what she'd done.

Hadn't even realized how close he'd been standing, only inches away from her bed.

But now it was one stroke past midnight.

He'd been watching the hands of the clock on her nightstand, the minutes creeping by like hours, the hours stretching out like the endless decades of his life.

Lucy's restlessness was nothing, compared to his own.

His growing frustration, his need to be filled.

There was only one thing that could satisfy him.

And he would be no gentleman tonight.

He ran through the woods and on through the town, his midnight senses keen and alert, the darkness flowing over him like wind.

It was in the park where he finally caught the girl's scent.

Not virginal blood, but deliciously seasoned all the same.

She was small and well built, athletic and strong, with very short hair, like a boy's. She had books under one arm and she smelled of sweet powder, strained peaches, and soft, fluffy blankets.

She had been babysitting.

And now she was on her way home.

He trailed her over a footbridge, then slunk out of sight behind the trees and the bushes, just one more shadow among many. He kept pace with her and wondered how long it would be until she sensed she was being followed.

Not so long, after all.

Like countless times before, he recognized that first dawning hint of awareness, that first wary glance back over the shoulder, that first startled quickening of the feet.

He always enjoyed that initial shock. That

primal instinct of approaching death, innate to every species.

For a while she walked faster, and so did he.

Then suddenly she stopped and turned to face him.

"Who's there?" she called in a quivering voice, trying so hard to be brave. "I know you're there; you're not scaring me."

And so he let her see him.

He watched her eyes go wide; he smelled her helpless terror. The thrill of the hunt surged through him—that heady anticipation of the kill, that stamina and speed no mortal could ever hope to match.

Just for fun, he gave her a head start.

She screamed, but no one heard.

And for one desperate minute of her tragically young life, he let her think she might actually get away.

But he had no patience for the chase tonight.

And he was upon her so quickly, she didn't even struggle.

Afterward he lay there on the cold, wet ground, feeling empty and disappointed . . . gorged but unfulfilled.

The dead girl's eyes stared up at him. There was no malice there, no accusation—but rather a look of blank and sad surprise.

He took her to the footbridge that spanned the concrete drainage ditch.

With one swift motion he broke her neck for good measure, then tossed her over the railing.

New power for every life . . .

A new century for every soul.

With a bitter smile, he went back into the night . . . as silently and stealthily as he had come.

27

"You can't do this, Matt," Lucy said. "There's got to be another way. You *can't* just put her in some nursing home."

Startled, Matt glanced up from his desk. Lucy was standing rigidly in the doorway of the office, looking close to tears.

"Do we have an appointment?" Hurriedly he pretended to search through his calendar. Lucy was not amused.

"Matt, this is serious. How could you do such a terrible thing?"

"Lucy, *I'm* not doing it. And who told *you* about it?"

"Dakota heard some people talking in the bookstore last night. Some of Byron's neighbors, I guess."

Matt leaned back in his chair. He steepled his fingers beneath his chin and slowly shook his head.

"Mrs. Dempsey can't stay forever, and we can't expect her to. It was always understood that the arrangement was temporary."

"Yes," Lucy reminded him. "Till you could find someone else. But you *haven't* found anyone else yet."

"And it doesn't look like we're going to. Look, I'm as sorry about it as you are, Lucy, but we don't have a choice. Even with the nurse and with neighbors being kind enough to drop in, Byron's grandmother can't be alone at night."

"Then I'll do it."

Lifting an eyebrow, Matt stared at her. "What do you mean, you'll do it?"

"My aunt's going on a trip to Paris. She'll be gone at least two weeks and—"

"The woman's compassion knows no bounds," he groaned. "Are you serious?"

"She told me yesterday. Some sort of exchange program at the university. And I really don't want to stay in that house by myself."

"Well, you *shouldn't*. I'm really sorry, Lucy—"

"The thing is," Lucy interrupted, not feeling up to sympathy at the moment, "do you think Byron's grandmother would even *want* me there?"

"Why wouldn't she?"

"You know why. Maybe she couldn't even stand to look at me. And I wouldn't blame her."

"She's not like that. She's very sweet. Even Mrs. Dempsey says so." Folding his arms behind his head, Matt leaned back even farther. "And if anyone can manage to stay sweet around Mrs. Dempsey, they qualify for sainthood in my opinion."

"Can you arrange it?" Lucy pleaded, but Matt hedged.

"Lucy . . . are you sure you want to do this for the right reasons?"

"I have good reasons."

"Yeah, but . . . maybe you're thinking more about how bad *you* feel, than about how bad *Mrs. Wetherly* feels." Pausing, he added, "It won't work as penance, you know."

Lucy's voice lowered. "But won't my being there help *both* of us?"

For a long moment Matt said nothing. Then finally he gave a deep sigh.

"And I suppose you want me to talk to your aunt about it, too?"

"Would you? If anyone can convince her, you can."

"Thanks. I think." Matt's smile was dubious. "There's the bell. You better get to class."

But Lucy didn't move. "Are you going to the vigil tonight?"

"Actually, I've been asked to say a few words. What about you?"

"I'm coming with Irene."

There was another lengthy hesitation before he spoke. "You think you're up to this?"

"Do I really have a choice?"

With a grim expression she turned to leave, then promptly faced him again.

"Matt?"

"Yes?"

"That medallion you gave me? You never told me anything about—"

"Bell." He pointed sternly toward the hallway. "Late. Go."

Lucy made it to homeroom just in time. Sliding into her seat, she rested one cheek on her pile of books and gazed out the window as the morning's announcements came over the intercom.

In the distance she could see a large group heading off toward the athletic field—coaches, cheerleaders, band members, even some football players, it looked like. And though they were too far away to distinguish each face individually, it was obvious they were all in high spirits—laughing, jostling, joking around.

Lucy's heart melted in relief.

Everyone was happy. Everything was fine. It was Thursday and no one had died . . .

"And no one's *going* to die. And whatever I saw in my mind was a *mistake*. And I'm *not* turning into Katherine."

But she realized she was whispering to herself, and that her hands were clamped tightly over her ears, trying to drown out *another* voice—a sad, empty voice whispering far back in the darkness of her mind . . .

Everything's not *fine, Lucy* . . .

And it's only morning.

The candlelight vigil was scheduled for seven-thirty.

As Lucy let herself into the house that afternoon, it was obvious Irene wasn't there yet. No messages on the answering machine. No notes beside the phone.

She hoped Irene remembered.

How would it look if Angela's own mother didn't attend the service?

Lucy wished she could miss it herself. She dreaded the emotional impact of the ceremony—it had been looming over her like a dark cloud all day. Now she just wanted to get it over with.

Peeling off her coat and gloves, she threw them over the bannister and went up to her room. She was dressed and ready by six o'clock. Dressed for the weather and feeling edgy because Irene still wasn't home.

Darkness had already fallen, and as lights began coming on throughout the house, Lucy went downstairs to turn on more.

By seven, she was really getting worried. Pacing around the kitchen, she nearly jumped out of her skin when the telephone rang. She hesitated, suddenly afraid to pick it up, then heard Irene's voice on the machine.

"Lucy, are you there? I'm running late. Just go on without me, and I'll meet you at the school."

Relieved, Lucy started back to her room to grab another sweater.

But the doorbell stopped her halfway.

She hurried down again, then looked nervously out through the peephole. Within the distorted angle of the lens, she could see a tall figure standing on the porch, his back to her, a clipboard dangling from one hand.

Cautiously, Lucy cracked open the front door.

"Special delivery," the man announced. But he didn't turn around, and Lucy stood there on the threshold, watching him in wary surprise.

"It's kind of late," she said. "What kind of delivery?"

"Are you Lucy Dennison?"

Hesitating, Lucy nodded. "Yes, that's me."

"Then sign here."

She saw him turn around. Saw his pale sharp features and his deep-set eyes as he fixed her with a steady gaze. Both his truck and his uniform were black, but neither of them were printed with a name.

"What is it?" Lucy's voice tightened. "Who's it from?"

His gaze lingered a moment longer. "Well," he said at last, "I imagine that's part of the surprise." He thrust a clipboard at her. It had a pen attached to it, and a sheet of paper that was blank. "Just sign your name. I have other appointments to keep."

Again Lucy hesitated. Then she quickly scribbled her name.

"But what delivery company are you with?" she persisted.

"I told you. A special one."

Before she could ask anything more, the man turned and walked off. Lucy watched him climb into his truck and drive away from the house.

Then she looked down at the box.

It was fairly large—and seemed to weigh a ton. When Lucy couldn't lift it, she finally managed to drag it into the hall, then locked the door and stood there, frowning down at the package.

Who would be sending her a special delivery?

And why?

She chewed anxiously on a fingernail. She

stood and tapped her foot, trying to decide what to do.

She didn't have time for packages right now; she had to get to the vigil. She had to meet Irene. She had to be brave and strong.

She glanced at her watch.

If she hurried, she'd still have time to open the box. It wouldn't take that long to drive over to the high school, and since this thing was a special delivery, then it must be something important.

Yet still she stood and stared at it.

Watching as if something might suddenly unwrap itself and jump out at her.

She was being silly—paranoid—but her curiosity was stronger.

Retrieving some scissors from the kitchen, she cut away the mailing tape and lifted the cardboard flaps on top.

It was wrapped very tight, very thickly.

Whatever it was, it had been well protected and packed with great care.

Lucy got a knife from the kitchen drawer. With painstaking caution, she began to work the heavy padding loose.

She was almost there.

She could feel something beneath the filling now . . . something hard and heavy and cold and smooth . . .

No, not quite smooth . . .

Mostly smooth, but with something carved into its surface.

Words? Numbers?

With one final tug, the packing material came away in her hands. Lucy leaned forward into the light and gazed down into the box.

Oh God . . . Oh God, no . . .

The headstone was gray, crowned with a gently rounded arch.

And its design was stark and simple, except for the large black letters engraved deeply across the front.

ANGELA FOSTER

RIP

28

She thought she might have screamed.

Stumbling backward, Lucy heard a distant, anguished cry, the strangled voice of someone she barely even recognized.

She groped for the wall, for something—*anything*—to hold on to. Yet her eyes remained fixed on the headstone and the name that would be on everyone's minds, on everyone's lips, in less than fifteen minutes.

Her knees gave way.

She crumpled on to the floor.

Burying her face in her hands, she tried to think what to do, but her mind wouldn't cooperate. *Call the police? Get out of the house? Go to someone for help?*

Matt would be at the vigil by now. Dakota,

too. Thank God, Irene hadn't come home tonight.

Irene . . .

Lucy's hands slid away from her eyes.

She had to hide the headstone from Irene. No matter what course of action she ultimately decided to take, she couldn't leave the headstone here for Irene to see. She'd have to put it somewhere else. She'd have to *hide* it somewhere else. At least for the time being.

The vigil was just about ready to start. She was already late, and everyone was sure to notice if she didn't show up. There was no way she'd ever lift that box. Maybe she could get Dakota or Matt to help her later, but for now she'd have to hide it somewhere close. Somewhere close enough to drag it.

Frantically she looked around the downstairs. She couldn't focus, couldn't concentrate. *Call the police—I* have *to call the police! This time I have something* real *to show them—this time they'll* have *to believe me!*

But she couldn't call them right now, she couldn't tell them about the deliveryman and the unmarked truck and this horrible, hideous headstone; she had to get to the service for Angela.

Another sick joke?

If it was, someone had gone to an awful lot of trouble and expense just to pull it off. They'd have had to be sure it was delivered here just in time. They'd have had to be sure Lucy was home to receive it.

Would kids at school go to all that effort?

And if they *had* done it, would they be at the vigil tonight, waiting to see her reaction?

But she didn't have time to go over that now. She had to get rid of the headstone.

She could feel her thoughts jumping back and forth, exploding like firecrackers. No matter where she hid the headstone, Irene would be sure to find it. And if Irene didn't, then Florence *certainly* would—the woman was fastidious about cleaning every nook and cranny of this house.

So I can't hide it in here. I'll have to put it outside.

Her watch read seven-thirty now. Irene would be at the vigil, wondering where she was—and Lucy had no idea what she'd tell her.

I'll think of something—I'll worry about that later.

With all the force she could muster, Lucy began dragging the box toward the front door. If she could just get it out on the porch, she might be able to tip it off into the shrubbery. At least the front of the house was landscaped with evergreens—if she worked it underneath some of the branches and piled dead leaves over it, no one was likely to spot it, even if they stood right there and rang the bell.

At least it's worth a try.

At least till Irene's away from the house, so I can report it to the police.

Or at least till I can come up with a better idea . . .

Later she wondered if fear and shock had given her superhuman strength—but for now, all Lucy cared about was wrestling that carton underneath the bushes. As it landed with a dull thud, she hastily camouflaged it, then hurried to the car and drove straight to Pine Ridge High.

She didn't even remember the ride over.

It was as if her mind had detached from the rest of her, and stayed behind with Angela's headstone. She didn't know how she was going to face Irene, knowing what she knew, knowing what she'd just hidden beside the porch. How would she ever be able to act normally? Act as if nothing were wrong?

"But everything's wrong," Lucy whispered.

The sound of her own voice startled her.

Slowly, she began to come back to herself, and she realized she was parked at the school. She could see a huge circle of glowing light on the front lawn of the campus—dozens of tiny, flickering candle flames, and the shadowy figures of those who held them.

Voices were singing softly. Some popular song she felt she should recognize, but couldn't.

Go on. You have to.

Yet still she sat there, watching from a distance. Thinking about the headstone. Wondering what it meant.

She hadn't wanted to admit that Angela might never come home again, even though at times she'd felt it so strongly.

And now . . .

It doesn't mean anything!

Lucy shook her head, fighting back angry

tears. Angela had run away, just like all those times before, and Angela would come home again, just like Irene had predicted.

Lucy wanted to believe that.

Even now . . . she still wanted *so much* to believe that.

Taking in a deep gulp of air, Lucy willed herself to get out of the car. She stood for a moment, trying to empty her mind of bad thoughts, trying to compose her features into some semblance of hope.

She started walking toward the light.

And even before she got there, she sensed that something was wrong.

At first it was the subtle shifting of the crowd . . . the murmurs of curiosity and confusion . . . the gradual fading of voices, one by one.

Uneasy glances and eyes going wide . . .

Then cries of shock and disbelief.

As Lucy approached the circle, the first one she spotted was Matt.

He looked stunned and speechless, and all around him people had frozen in place like statues.

Irene was standing rigidly beside him. Her expression seemed to be caught somewhere between sheer relief and sheer horror.

Above each fluttering candle flame, faces had turned to stiff and bloodless masks.

Lucy saw the police.

She saw Dakota breaking through the circle, pushing her way slowly over to where Lucy had stopped to stare.

She felt her own lips move, though no sound came out.

And she heard Dakota answer her directly, as if Lucy's silent question had been spoken all too clearly.

"It's Wanda Carver." Dakota's face was the color of ash. "They found her in the park tonight. Just about an hour ago."

The world began to shimmer.

The world and Dakota's face and the glowing circle of hope, all shimmering through the swell of Lucy's tears.

"She's dead," Lucy murmured.

Dakota nodded. "She fell off the footbridge over that old drainage ditch in the park. She broke her neck on the concrete."

"When . . . When did it happen?"

"They're saying it happened sometime early this morning." Dakota's gaze was calm and unwavering. "But then . . . you already knew that, didn't you?"

29

She hadn't been able to talk.

She hadn't been able to answer Dakota's quiet accusation, or to defend herself, or to think of anything else except getting out of there and getting away.

She'd turned and run.

Run to the car and driven off.

She'd driven with no idea of where to go or how to get there—simply driven all over town, up one street and down another, till she began to think that Irene might be wondering about her and that she'd probably better get back to the house.

It had actually surprised her to see Irene sitting up, waiting for her. The woman's face had been taut and bewildered, and she'd stared at Lucy for a long, long time, as though her niece were a total stranger.

"When they said they'd found a girl, I thought it was Angela." Irene had finally spoken, though her eyes had been fixed on a place far beyond Lucy. "And then it was someone else. And I was glad."

Irene's numb gaze had turned to Lucy then. And her voice had faltered.

"How cruel of me," she'd mumbled. "To be glad some other girl's dead."

Lucy had felt so helpless. She'd walked over to her aunt's chair, and she'd laid a hand on her aunt's stiff shoulder.

"Aunt Irene . . ."

"She'll be home," Irene had said softly. "It's just a matter of time, you'll see—and Angela will be home."

"Aunt Irene—"

"Go to bed now, Lucy."

But she couldn't stay in bed any longer.

Now Lucy got dressed and slipped quietly from the house. She backed the car down the driveway and headed for Pine Ridge Cemetery.

What little sleep she'd managed to get last night had been fraught with reality and tormented with the truth.

The truth she must finally face.

The truth she must finally accept.

It's real.

Lucy watched the cold, gray dawn creep slowly through the trees. A patina of frost coated the houses and lawns, and a lazy sun continued to slumber behind a thin layer of clouds.

The gift Katherine gave me . . . the powers Katherine gave me . . .

Real.

They're all real.

How could she have ignored it for so long? Been so unwilling to believe?

Because to believe in this gift means believing in other things, too. The dreams and the nightmares, the feelings and visions, the instincts I've never been able to trust before . . .

The existence of unbelievable things . . . unexplainable things . . .

Evil and unseen things.

She felt as if she'd betrayed herself.

And somehow . . . even worse . . . betrayed Byron.

Tears dampened her cheeks. Her heart ached with grief and regret.

When Byron was here, he'd shown her the truth. Shown her a destiny and purpose. Convinced her that her journey, no matter how dangerous or uncertain, was still necesssary and worthwhile.

She'd lost so much in the accident that night.

Byron.

Her faith . . .

Her self.

If only she could have them all back again.

If only she could speak to Byron one more time . . .

So that's why she'd decided to visit the cemetery this morning. To sit beside Byron's resting place and try to sort things out. She wanted to tell him everything, everything that had happened since he'd died. And she wanted to think that somehow he might really hear her . . . help her figure out what to do . . . help her make sense of things.

She wanted to believe that maybe—somehow—she wasn't really as alone as she felt.

But after entering the cemetery, Lucy began to have second thoughts. She hadn't expected it to look so spooky at this hour of the morning. Like wandering phantoms, tatters of soft white mist hovered among the graves, and an unnatural quiet smothered the sound of her footsteps as she made her way to the remote section of the burial grounds. The dead slept deep and undisturbed. Remembered and forgotten alike, they surrounded her on all sides, rotting peacefully to dust.

In the distance, the Wetherly mausoleum came darkly into view, silhouetted against the gloom. As Lucy got nearer, she could see the wrought-iron gates and stone angels that guarded it, and for one unsettling moment, she remembered her dream about Byron and his warning.

"Keep away . . . there's no one in this place."

An icy shudder worked its way up her spine. Hesitating, she dug her hands into her coat pockets and glanced back over her shoulder.

Come on, Lucy, get a grip.

It was easy to imagine eerie whispers and invisible watchers in a creepy place like this—what had she been thinking anyway, coming here so early?

Stop scaring yourself. Nobody here can hurt you.

Giving herself a stern mental shake, she walked over to the front of the tomb. To her surprise, the double gates weren't padlocked as she'd assumed they'd be—in fact, they were standing partway open, one of them creaking rustily as the breeze swung it back and forth.

Heart quickening, Lucy glanced around a second time.

If someone *were* here, they'd be impossible to see, she admitted to herself. Anyone could be hiding close by or far away.

Lucy suppressed another shiver.

Turning in a slow circle, she scanned the graves and headstones, the sepulchres and statues, the trees and shadows and mist. A taste of fear crept into her throat, and she tried to choke it down.

Cautiously, she turned back to the gates.

Taking one in each hand, she eased them open the rest of the way. Cracks had widened along the foundation, and leaves had sifted in over the broken, weathered stones of the floor.

Holding her breath, Lucy walked into the crypt.

She saw the muddy footprints and tufts of clotted hair; the dark, reddish-brown stains smeared along the walls . . .

But she didn't see the figure behind her.

Not till she turned and screamed and stumbled from his arms, trying wildly to fight her way free.

And then she stared up, shocked, into eyes as black and deep as midnight.

"Oh my God," she choked. "Who are you?"

The dark-haired young man gazed coolly back at her.

"Byron's brother," he answered. "Who the hell are *you*?"

Woodwrit, Inc. Editions

Title:	Lake Isle
Author:	Tobi Little Deer
Imprint:	TOBI Books
Publication Date:	February 2019
Hardback:	978-1-949596-01-4 $20.99 U.S./$26.99 Can.
Paperback:	978-1-949596-00-7 $14.99 U.S./$19.99 Can.
Ebook:	978-1-949596-02-1 $9.99 U.S./$10.99 Can.
Pages:	312
Category:	Young Adult Fiction
For Ages:	14 & up

THIS IS AN UNCORRECTED ADVANCE PROOF
FOR PRE-PUBLICATION REVIEW.

The design, artwork, trim size, page count, format, prices and publication date are subject to change without notice during the course of production.

PLEASE SEND COPIES OF REVIEWS AND ANY MENTION TO:

Brian Feinblum
MEDIA CONNECT
301 East 57th Street, 4th floor
New York, NY 10022
brian.feinblum@finnpartners.com
212-583-2718

LAKE ISLE

Also by Tobi Little Deer

Little Tramp

Tobi's New York City adventure

LAKE ISLE

by

Tobi Little Deer

TOBI Books
New York

This book LAKE ISLE is a work of fiction. All of the characters, names, places, business establishments or other organizations, and all events portrayed in this story are either products of the author's imagination or are used fictitiously. Any resemblance to actual persons, living or dead, is coincidental.

TOBI Books
An imprint of Woodwrit, Inc. Editions

 For information, address Woodwrit, Inc. Editions, 135 West 10th Street, ste. 11, New York, NY 10014.

ISBN: 978-1-949596-00-7

IN MEMORY OF

REX

GENTLE, PATIENT,

VALIANT GUARDIAN

AND

BUTCH AND ZEKE

SIDELINED, ACCEPTING,

FOREVER WAITING

AND

LUCY

DELICATE WITH ATTITUDE

REIGNING TO THE END

With grateful acknowledgement to
Anthony,
Marilyn, David,
Frank and Lue,
for their invaluable help.

CONTENTS

PROLOGUE

Can you imagine me, a Chihuahua accustomed to the plush comfort of a New York City apartment, lost alone at night in a Vermont forest? Or appreciate my alarm, each time black clouds racing across the sky obscured the summer moon, drawing a cover of impenetrable darkness over the mountain? Or my terror, as the white disc reappeared only to reveal towering shadows all around me that quivered alive with each breeze?

An owl hooted repeatedly in the distance, then again closer by, followed by a scuffle and frantic squeaks . . . cut off by silence . . . . Then faintly, far away, a whippoorwill called, waited, and called again. Each disembodied sound, amplified by the ponderous quiet, riveted my attention. I shivered as much from fear as from the cold night air.

When I heard heavy paws crunching on dry leaves just beyond the thicket where I hid, I stopped breathing. When the plodding paused, I lay motionless except for my trembling, totally alert to flee, totally still but for the deafening pounding of my heart. The footsteps resumed and moved slowly away, too lumbering to be the fox I suspected was out there somewhere. I'd no idea what to do, so I just shook and waited, and listened with all my might in the dark.

How I got there and what happened was so unexpected.

1. THE TRIP NORTH

My holiday with Ted began with one of my favorite things, a car ride—although I do prefer a shorter one than we took that day. After a beautiful springtime in New York City with trees blossoming along the avenues and Sunday walks in Central Park to admire the flowers, after early weekends at our house by the ocean, Ted went out one morning after breakfast to get the car.

He'd packed travel bags the day before and set them in our apartment hallway. I knew the routine. After he parked on the street close by, he brought the luggage downstairs while I waited. He carried me out last of all on his arm, out the door he locked behind us, as always. I got a short walk along the curbside on the way.

Ted set me on the towel he'd folded for me on the front passenger seat and attached my harness to the safety belt. He adjusted himself in the driver's seat with a click, while I made a few turns to get comfortable on my bed. We drove off, first with the frequent turns and stops and bumps I don't like up the avenues of New York City, and then onto straighter, smoother interstate highways, and I settled down. A sunny day warmed me through the tinted windows, comfortable with the air-conditioning set on mild, just right. Soothed by the sound of the engine and the motion of the car, I did what I always do, I fell asleep.

By noon we reached a rest area surrounded by distant, low, green mountains, with a wide river meandering lazily below us. Then I knew we were on our way to visit Ted's family at the top of Vermont, a trip we made several times each summer.

Late in the day, by the time I'd grown tired of riding, we exited the Interstate for smaller roads that had sharper curves and deeper bumps. Ted drove more slowly on them, but nevertheless the car swerved enough to make me light-headed. Passing through miles of woodland we finally reached the little town.

When Ted made a sharp right turn up a steep hill and the car leveled on a very straight street, I knew we'd arrived. We were on Pleasant Street that overlooked the lake called Isle. Ted made a right turn between two grand maple trees into his family's driveway and came to a stop in the yard, between the large, white, rambling house and the correspondingly tall, white, wood-shingled barn.

Ted unstrapped himself and stepped out of the car, then reached back in across the seat for me, as I did my eager dance, wagging my tail so hard I almost fell over. He lifted me out and set me on the ground by his feet, and I ran around him happily. No harness, no leash—this was North Country where dogs roamed free.

2. FAMILY

Ted turned to the elderly woman coming out of the barn who walked towards us with her arms spread wide open as she exclaimed as if it were a wonder, "Oh, oh, oh, you're finally here!"

"Hello, Mémère, how are you?" he greeted her. Ted is a short man, but he had to bend to hug his even shorter grandmother who wrapped her arms around him. Heavy-set, built solidly even in old age, her face dark-skinned and lined, her silken white hair drawn back tightly into a bun beneath her beaten white hat, her long cotton dress covered by a broad, bibbed apron that reached down to her barnyard boots, she was a rough jewel glistening elegantly, the country farmwoman forged by work. Her embrace, the light in her eyes, the laughter in her voice made evident how happy she was to see Ted. She looked down at me. "Hello Tobi. Aren't you glad to be here?"

I was jumping up against Ted's leg. He remarked, "You'd think he'd take advantage, but all he wants is me to pick him up when we're around people." He couldn't very well, because then he grabbed a suitcase from the car trunk in each hand.

Ted's family had come out of the house to greet us. As he headed with Mémère across the yard towards them, he remembered his grandfather Pépère who used to be sitting on the second-story back porch overlooking the barnyard when we arrived. I saw Ted turn his face upwards, and I remembered him, too. Holding his pipe in one hand, Pépère would wave back with the other from above the array of flowers, blue morning glories, that climbed from the ground to where he sat.

I ran ahead to Rex, the farm dog, who stood and stretched where he'd been lying in the late afternoon sun on a wooden transom at the side of the house. The big grey and white tomcat named Nanook who'd been sleeping between Rex's front paws, disturbed now when Rex stood up, was stretching too as if just beginning his day. Rex was a young dog, about my age. Average dog-size, average dog-shape, with an inch-long black and white coat, he wasn't any particular breed, just a standard dog. We touched noses.

Ted went to Mom first and gave her a big, wraparound hug, and she kissed his cheek. A small woman, her tight waist emphasized by the fullness of her skirt, she had combed her shoulder-length hair back and had on earrings for the occasion. He shook hands with Dad, a thin, gaunt man who said, "Good to see you, Teddy," and high-fived his younger brother Robert who stood to the side grinning, tall and strong. Ted's nephew Lucien, fair-haired like his father Robert, stepped forward to give Ted a weak, albeit willing hug, upstaged when his younger sister, small, brunette Marguerite, having waited her turn, ran up to Ted with an effusive hug and kiss. They all walked into the house together, all talking at the same time. I followed Ted inside, but Rex stopped at the door. A farm dog, he had his bed and dish in the entry mudroom; he never went into the main house. I certainly didn't hesitate; I stuck close by Ted amid all these people, and when they sat to visit in the living room, he lifted me to his lap as I expected he would.

With Marguerite helping, Mom began setting supper on the large rectangular table in the middle of the kitchen. She could share the conversation through the multi-paned glass doors open on her left to the living room. Matching doors led to a dining room on her right that was reserved for major holidays.

"How was your trip?" Dad asked Ted.

"It was gorgeous, all the way up," Ted answered him enthusiastically. "It's a long ride, but I never tire of looking across the Connecticut River valley from the heights of Interstate 91 on a sunny day." With a nod to me he added, "Tobi gets a little restless towards the end," tickling me behind my ears as I looked out at everyone. "He always knows when we come off the Interstate and 'head for the hills.' He knows we're getting close."

Ted turned to his brother. "You about ready to start haying?" he asked.

"In a couple more weeks," Robert answered. "Can we count on you?"

"Ted has his book to work on," Mom said to Robert. "We'd best not interfere with that."

"Yes, I'll devote forenoons to the book," Ted said to Mom, but he assured Robert, "I'll be glad to help in the afternoons when you truck in the bales. I've always liked haying time. I'll drive one of the trucks, but I'll leave tossing the bales with the hired men to you."

"Robert grew taller and broader than you," Mom offered. "He's more used to it."

Ted laughed, "I'll help for the iced lemonade that Mom has waiting for everyone after each load through. That alone is worth the work."

"I still do," Mom told him, "made with real lemons."

"And Mémère will be out there with her hand rake, embarrassing Dad," Robert teased his father. "Last year," he said to Ted, "he asked her not to rake near the street because, he told her, 'people will think I'm working my old mother.' She scolded him for the idea. He couldn't keep her out of the hayfield."

Dad agreed amused, "She never listens to me."

As if on cue Mémère, dressed neatly now, knocked on the kitchen door and came in. "Oh, you're just in time, Sa Mère," Mom said to her. Mom and Dad called her *Sa Mère*; everyone younger called her *Mémère*. She and Mom called Dad *Te'dore*. Mémère and Dad called Mom *Rose*. Lucien and Marguerite called Mom and Dad *Mémère* and *Pépère*. Sometimes the family called Ted *Teddy*, except Lucien and Marguerite who called him *Uncle Ted* and called their father Robert *Dad*. The family had so many names; it could be very confusing.

They gathered around the kitchen table for supper. Ted put me down on the floor, and gave me my portion beforehand. However, during the meal I found Lucien and Marguerite quite willing to slip me bits of roast chicken, especially the skin which Marguerite called "Gross!" From under the table I continued to do well from "the kids." I could get used to this.

"What are you writing now?" Robert asked Ted.

"Another translation. I have a deadline for it before my trip."

"You'll do fine up on Mémère's sun porch," Mom assured Ted.

"Yes, thank you, Mémère," Ted said gratefully to his grandmother. "It'll be inspiring to work with that view of the fields and lake! I'll open a window at either end to let the breezes through. I'm thinking I might even sleep there on the cot, like I used to do when I was a boy."

I busied myself with a piece of gristle that Marguerite held to me under the table. After supper Dad and Robert changed into their barn clothes in the mudroom and went to milk the cows. Ted stayed back and visited with Mom, gathering up the dishes for her to wash while Marguerite dried them. When he sat down again, I was back on his lap.

"That dog sure loves you," Mom said.

"And I love him," Ted told her.

Later Dad and Robert returned from their chores, changed in the mudroom, showered out there, and came in finished and fresh. We all went out to Mom and Dad's windowed sun porch at the front of the house, directly beneath Mémère's porch, whose twin it was. I lay on Ted's lap, and the family looked out on the lake view at the onset of twilight. When Mom brought out apple pie and my favorite, vanilla ice cream, Ted got my dish and gave me some.

"That dog has a good life," Robert remarked.

"So does Rex," Dad said. "Happy in the mudroom."

"It depends what a dog is used to," Ted countered. "In New York we don't have a mudroom, or a barn."

"Which is perfectly fine," Mom interposed. "He's a little dog, and he's so cute—aren't you, Tobi," she said to me. The tranquility of the porch was conducive to peacefulness at that hour, and Mom held her family to ending the day agreeably.

I perked up from my dish when I heard my name. I made short work of my ice cream and returned to Ted who took me back on his lap when he finished his. There, lulled by the dinner I'd had and the family's soft voices, it was not long before I started to doze off and on. I'd look up each time I heard the family's quiet laughter.

As twilight was descending into darkness I became more alert when very fast little black birds began to fly across the lawn between the maple trees.

"The bats are out," Lucien observed.

A full moon was ascending over the lake. Without turning on any other illumination, the family conversed in its pale light. Against that backdrop I heard a sound that reached into the back of my head and resonated down my spine. Faint in the distance, it was the howling of wolves. I shivered and stood up on Ted's lap in riveted attention.

Ted laughed. "Look at Tobi. He hears the Indians' dogs across the lake."

"The water carries the sound," Robert commented, "just like you can hear the trains, too, when they're traveling along the far shore."

Lucien spoke up, "Now if the ghost deer walked across the lawn, that would really set him off."

"The ghost deer?" Ted asked.

"Some people claim to have sighted an albino buck lately, completely white," Robert explained.

"Maybe pink elephants, too," Marguerite giggled.

What alarmed me more, though, was another sound that started up closer by, a strange high-pitched howling that was more a yapping bark. It repeated several times, then went silent.

"That's the fox on the hill behind the barn, a vixen; I've seen her up there with kits," Robert remarked. "The moon affects them, too."

"Maybe she's barking because she hears the Indian dogs," Mom suggested.

Lucien snickered, "She's howling because she wants Mémère's chickens."

"That's why the henhouse has to be closed up tight every night," Mémère told them. "You've got to remember to do it if ever I can't."

"Yes, if the door is shut tight, nothing can get in," Dad said. "I built it with a cement foundation, so the foxes and raccoons can't dig into it, either."

"If the fox comes off the hill, Rex'll be after her before she gets anywhere near it," Robert assured.

"Maybe she's howling because she's frustrated then, if she's got kits to feed. You've got to see it her way, too," Marguerite suggested.

Dad yawned, rose to his feet, said, "Time for bed," and walked into the house, where his bedroom he shared with Mom was off the kitchen on the first floor. Mémère took his cue, said "Good night," and went up the living room stairs to her comfortable three-bedroom apartment that encompassed half the second floor of the rambling farmhouse. In turn, Robert said "Good night" to everyone and "Let's go" to Lucien and Marguerite, and they followed him upstairs to their rooms in the other half.

Only Ted, with me, and Mom stayed on the porch for a while more. I kept listening for the Indian dogs, and from time to time I heard them.

"Can you howl like that, Tobi?" Ted laughed. He said to Mom, "I have friends who have a Chihuahua that howls if you howl to it. I've never wanted to get Tobi started on that."

I began to think that Ted and Mom were going to stay out there all night, and I got restless on Ted's lap. "Tobi figures it's bedtime," Ted said getting up. He said "Good night" to Mom, and he carried me upstairs to our room next to Robert's.

3. SETTLING IN — PRESENTIMENTS

The following morning Ted and I rose early, just as we did in New York. However, everyone else but Lucien and Margeurite were already up before us. Mom was cooking breakfast, and it smelled very good. Ted gave me chicken, then oatmeal in warm milk as usual; but Mom was frying eggs, and I got a piece that included yoke, one of my favorite things.

Afterwards, Ted carried me upstairs to Mémère's sun porch, and we settled in, Ted at his computer and me on his lap. That's how we always did it. It was a sunny day. The temperature was perfect, not so hot as New York City at this time of year. There were no air conditioners, just screens in the windows at either end of the porch, enabling a gentle, refreshing breeze to waft past us. When Ted paused, he'd look out straight ahead at—as I've heard him describe—the "picturesque farm fields, golden with ripening hay, rolling down to the birch-lined shore of the deep blue lake with its dark wooded island in the middle."

"It's so beautiful. I was so lucky to grow up here, Tobi," he'd say to me.

The view didn't mean much to me. When we'd take a break and stroll outside, I was much more interested in meeting up with gentle Rex. Sometimes Ted would sit with me for a while in a lawn chair out front, absorbed by his thoughts, gazing at the view.

There were birds everywhere, robins and black birds on the lawn, swallows doing their loops in the air overhead, an occasional woodpecker in one of the maples, crows cawing as they flew overhead and perched high in the trees at the edge of the woods behind the barn. I tried to approach the birds on the lawn at first, but they flew away much faster than New York City pigeons did.

The barnyard was a living space. Sometimes chickens would wander in from their yard on the far side of the barn. Rex kept them away from the lawns, so I helped him do that when I was out there with Ted. Rex never chased them, but just herded them on. Mémère had a couple of white geese, too, and they were nasty. If Rex wasn't watching, they slipped into the street to attack the occasional passers-by until, alerted by the ruckus, the faithful dog herded them back. On the far side of the driveway the lawn was separated from the barnyard by a very tall, thick row of lilac bushes, at the base of which was a tiny pond fed by an underground pipe from a tank in the barn through which water always flowed. Mémère's six pure white ducks would waddle from the chicken area and splash in it, churning it muddy. It wasn't big enough for them to swim much.

Sometimes Ted would carry me, or I'd follow him leash-free, to the next house on the street where he'd visit with Aunt Florence, or to the house beyond that, with Aunt Linette. His uncles Bernard and Félix insisted on giving us tours of their respective huge vegetable gardens. Mom had a very big garden, too, and Mémère a bit smaller one, that they worked to keep clear of weeds. Robert helped them do that; and so did Lucien and Marguerite less enthusiastically. Mom talked about how much they would have to "can," to preserve, for the winter.

When Ted's mind was refreshed by a walk, we'd return to his computer on the upstairs porch, and he'd write for another two hours, until Mom called from downstairs that it was time for lunch.

There were rainy days, too, when we stayed mostly on the porch. Ted would take his breaks resting on the cot, and I'd lie beside him. It felt very cozy, with the rain all around us just outside the windows, sometimes pounding on them, but usually falling gently, while we were inside watching it, warm and dry. Its dull, soft patter put us to sleep.

Sometimes there'd be a big storm. The wind would dash the rain against the windows, and sway the branches of the maples back and forth, so that those big trees looked like they were dancing. Lightning flashes and loud roars of thunder bore down upon us from overhead. I'd nestle my face under Ted's arm.

One such storm was particularly dramatic one evening, when Dad and Robert already had finished their chores and come in from the barn. It arose suddenly, roaring down the valley from Canada a few miles north. Over the lake—over us—it crashed into another storm coming west, up the Nulhegan River plain from New Hampshire. Mémère, who was fearful of thunderstorms, hurried down the living room stairs to join the family on the ground-floor sun porch where they had gathered to watch the outburst.

Thunder didn't bother me much in New York City, but that evening the claps were so loud that I trembled like Mémère at the roar and burrowed further into Ted's arms. As the family sat watching, talking softly in the growing darkness, the lightning flashes became more dramatic, as if someone were turning the lights on and off repeatedly, instant by instant. When the height of the storm's violence rolled over us, its breadth made it seem fixed in the sky above, crashing down continually, pummeling us, beating against the window panes mercilessly.

The family waited and watched and endured it, suddenly startled sometimes, fascinated by its raw power, until the length of the storm, having coursed from beginning to end like a long parade over the valley, slowly but noticeably subsided as it moved away, leaving in its wake outside the windows a drenched quiet. Then everyone said goodnight and went to bed. Ted opted to sleep on the cot on Mémère's upstairs porch. Somehow, high up like that and surrounded by the glass windows, I still felt exposed, and I crawled under the sheet and cuddled beside him. Being with him, beside him as we lay there and fell asleep, made me feel safe.

Another evening, one that ended a beautiful sunny day with an orange and pink sky, Ted took me on his arm and walked with Mémère to Aunt Florence's house next door. She was Mémère's oldest daughter and Dad's big sister. A while later Dad joined us on Aunt Florence's wide, open porch. They talked in subdued voices while they watched twilight diminish over the hills and lake. I sat quietly on Ted's lap.

Ted remarked as he often did, "It's so peaceful here, so beautiful. I took it so much for granted when I was growing up."

"Someday that beautiful view won't be there anymore," Mémère said.

Ted clarified, "I don't just mean the view. I mean everything here, the whole farm, our family, everything." Then he realized what Mémère had said. "Why won't it be there?" he asked.

Mémère told them, "Because someday somebody will see only cash value in that field, and will fill it with streets and houses, and the people who move in will plant trees and hedges. You won't see much of the lake anymore from here." Looking at Aunt Florence she added, "If someone builds a house across the street right in front of yours, you won't have any view at all."

Ted objected, "We own the property, Mémère. No one can very well do that," Then he looked anxiously at Dad for confirmation, "You wouldn't sell out from under Robert, would you?"

"Of course not," Dad reassured him. "Why would I do that when everything is just fine?"

"What if your father hadn't had Robert to help him when you went away?" Mémère asked Ted. "Robert has only one son. If Lucien, like you, doesn't want to farm . . . and I don't think he will . . ." She warned, "Everything changes; everything passes; nothing ever stays the same."

"It's getting expensive to own so much lakeshore," Dad admitted. "The taxes keep going up. Maybe we'll have to sell that off, but we can keep the fields."

"Well, I hope we're not going to see a row of houses along the lakeshore! How will we see the lake?" Aunt Florence scolded him.

"You don't think Lucien is going to want to farm?" Ted asked.

"You should know how it is," Mémère said to him. "You didn't want to. If your father hadn't had Robert to take your place, he'd have had to sell sooner or later. A farmer can work alone just so long. Somebody would buy it to put houses in the fields, and cut down the woodland for pulp, and log the maple orchard. There has to be a son to take over, or everything goes."

I felt Ted's hand on me tighten.

Mémère added, "It used to be if you sold a farm the new owner would keep it going. Now people buy to sell lots for houses around the lake. The open fields will disappear."

I wiggled out of Ted's grip. The three continued to talk in the twilight until it grew dark enough for the bats to appear, swooping between the maples. Then Mémère and Dad with Ted carrying me walked home.

The following day at lunch Ted suggested Robert take some time with him for a boat ride to the island. I did my best to keep up with Rex as we crossed the field down to the lakeshore where Robert kept a canoe among the birches. As soon as Robert with Ted pulled the craft to the water's edge, Rex jumped into it. I was quite apprehensive when Ted placed me in the bottom of the wobbly thing, and I plopped down flat when he and Robert pushed it into the water, jumped aboard and took up their paddles. That's where I stayed, behind Rex who sat looking forward, quite enjoying himself. I lay for the duration on my belly, my legs extended to brace myself against the rocking. All sense of underpinning was gone. Too low to see much except the sky, I endured until the canoe slid onto the beach. Ted and Robert jumped into the water and pulled it onto the shore with me in it. Rex already had leaped out and splashed to the sand where he stood looking back at us, wagging his tail happily.

Ted spread a blanket, then waded into the water for a swim with Robert. I lay on the blanket in the sunshine, relieved to be on stable ground, enjoying the cool breeze coming off the lake. Rex busied himself sniffing about the bushes, then jumped into the water, too. Robert and Rex had a game. Rex ran up to Robert; Robert picked Rex up in his arms and flung him into deeper water; then Rex swam back to Robert, who grabbed Rex again and flung him again into deeper water. They did it until Robert was out of breath, but Rex still was ready for more. Ted and Robert came back dripping and laughing, and Rex shook water over all of us. The two men toweled; they lay on the blanket to sun for a while, with me between them. Rex, covered with sand because he'd rolled while still wet, was kept off the blanket, so he went back to sniffing and running around the bushes. So much energy!

"Do you think about getting married again?" Ted asked Robert.

"I don't know," Robert said to him, "Things are good the way they are. The kids are happy with Mom and Dad. I'm not looking for complications. It's all fine here."

"I envy you for that," Ted told Robert, "I never thought at all about being a farmer, but I love this place." There was a long pause, then Ted said wistfully, "I wish I could stay here all summer."

"We travel different roads, you and I," Robert said to him, "I don't envy you."

"It's quite wonderful writing on the upstairs porch. I don't know why I never thought to work there before. I wish I didn't have to leave." Then Ted said, "I worry about Tobi. The last time I went on tour, I boarded him in New York, and he went on a hunger strike. When I came back I had this skinny dog looking at me completely bewildered with the most wounded expression in his eyes. I couldn't do that again. I hope he's happy on the farm. Dad's not too keen."

Robert laughed, "Dad claims people say a farmer with more than one dog isn't much of a farmer. Seriously, I don't think he minds much. Dad just has to be a little contrary. He doesn't like an animal in the house, though. It's okay when you're here, and Tobi's on your lap most of the time. When you're not here . . ." Robert hesitated, then concluded, "He'll be okay."

"You mean Dad or Tobi?"

"Both, I think."

When the sun got too hot, I moved to the edge of the woods close by and waited in the shade. Rex would reappear from time to time, then run back into the forest of tall evergreens. Ted and Robert went for another swim, and lay in the sun again for a while more talking quietly. Rex, dry now, settled down beside Robert, nestling against his side, while Robert buried his fingers in Rex's fur, stroking him slowly. Rex rested his head on Robert's leg. Rex was not possessive of Robert the way I am with Ted, but Rex clearly was Robert's dog, and Robert was his person.

After a lazy while like that, the two men got up, and Rex jumped to his feet. Ted called me, then carried me to the bottom of the canoe again as Rex leaped into it; and they paddled back, rolling and rocking rhythmically, nauseatingly, to the birch-lined lakeshore at the base of the farm field. Ted and Robert walked back up the hill along a path through the thick hay that was waving gently in the breeze, and I trotted along behind them with Rex. At the house, Mom served them apple pie at the kitchen table, and Ted slipped me some bits of the crust, which I love.

That's how the first part of the summer passed. I was always inseparable from Ted. Early morning we began with a jog up the street, past the cemeteries, all the way to the Head of the Pond Road and back. By then Dad and Robert would be in from their barn chores, and Mom had breakfast ready. It was eggs and pancakes and maple syrup and bacon, and Ted gave me some of all of it.

Ted and I would go up to Mémère's sunporch. After we took a short nap on the cot, he'd write all forenoon with me on his lap or by his side, with only one or two short breaks, until Mom called him down for lunch. Then back to the sunporch, another nap, and he continued at his computer for the first half of the afternoon. The latter half might be taken up with tasks or errands, and sometimes we took Mom somewhere in the car. More frequently Ted read on the lawn and I lay in the shade under his chair while the sun arced towards the mountaintop behind the farm. Often he'd go with Robert down to the lake for a swim before supper while I waited on the shore. It was an easy life. I was happy with Ted wherever we were.

4. VISITING MARIE-ANNE

One trip we made with Mom took up much of the day. Some time after breakfast we set out to visit Ted's sister Marie-Anne who lived with her husband Ross and their four sons on a farm beyond Lake Memphremagog on high ground close to Canada, an hour away.

Ted was driving, so it was a long ride on Mom's lap on twisting roads. It seemed that I'd just have settled down when I'd be thrust to the side.

"Could you hold him a little tighter?" Ted asked Mom.

"But I don't want to hurt him," she objected.

"You don't need to squeeze him. Just hold firmly."

She did, and it was better.

I could feel the air grow thinner and cooler that summer day as the car climbed a long incline to a plateau of open, rolling farmland beneath a low-hanging sky.

"I always enjoy coming here," Ted said, "It's such a beautiful part of the state."

"Yes, it is," Mom agreed, "but I'm sorry Marie-Anne moved so far from Lake Isle."

"This isn't far. New York is far. When she married Ross MacIntyre you could have worried they'd go back to Canada where he was from."

"Don't think I didn't. We would've had to cross the line every time. They could have settled in Lake Isle."

"What you should have been glad about was that she chose such an ambitious fellow," Ted pointed out. "With hiring himself out and his father's help, he already had the down payment for a farm when he asked her to marry him. That was pretty impressive. Dad, of course, focused on the fact Ross wasn't French-Canadian."

"Yes, they gave all four of their boys Scottish names, Bruce, Malcolm, Errol and Angus."

"There's some justice to that," Ted observed.

We left the paved highway for a bumpy approach road, and soon after turned into a driveway where a house and barn and outer buildings rose up in the car windows. When Ted stopped, I jumped to my feet, eager to get out.

Ted's sister Marie-Anne came out of the house with her third son Errol, a tall, lanky seventeen-year old. Her youngest son Angus, thirteen, came running up from the barn to give his grandmother—Mom—a hug and a kiss, telling her eagerly, "I'm so glad you've come to see us, Mémère." Ted hugged his sister, and we headed towards the house.

"Ross and Malcolm are in the field, and Bruce is repairing the knotter on the hay baler," Marie-Anne said, accounting for everyone. "They'll be coming in to join us in a half-hour for lunch. In the meantime we can visit on the porch . . ."

She was interrupted by her farm dog Troy, a tall mixed-breed headed right for me in a sudden, growling rush. Ted grabbed me up with a quick swoop and held me high above his head as Troy stopped right in front of him and barked like he wanted to climb up him to get at me.

Marie-Anne was as quick, shouting "Troy, stop!" as she grasped a handful of the nape of his neck, pulling him back. He stopped. After she released him, he paid no more attention to me. Needless to say, Ted had no intention of letting me roam freely the way I did with Rex on Dad's farm. What a difference in temperament! Troy was all aggression. I wondered how he behaved with the cows. Did he bite them fetching them? Chances are, judging by how quickly Marie-Anne subdued him, he instantly did what he was told. No hesitation or mind games like my response to requests. No gray areas with Troy; it was all black and white. He lay down docilely on the doormat in front of the porch steps, and accommodated us by moving out of the way when we came by.

Ted carried me on his arm onto the porch, where everyone sat in the line of wicker rocking chairs facing outward to the expansive view, and I sat on Ted's lap. Troy returned to the mat at the bottom of the steps, where he lay facing outward, too.

"It's so gorgeous here," Ted commented reflectively, looking across the fields towards Vermont's central peaks. "I never get enough of it."

"Yes, when Ross and I bought this farm, I traded the valley-view of Lake Isle for this high view. The broad sky seemed so close sometimes that I used to feel as if the clouds rolling over might sweep me off."

Errol and Angus sat with us looking out. "We're pretty used to it," Errol offered.

"Your grandmother tells me you're quite the basketball player," Ted said to engage his nephew.

"No wonder! You got so tall!" Mom exclaimed.

"Yes, Errol's the tallest of the four now, taller than Malcolm," Marie-Anne said as she brought out a tray of iced tea. "They made him center, first string, just a junior, and he scored the second-highest in the league," she added proudly. "Imagine what he'll do, one year to go, with most of the team intact."

Errol smiled, feigning embarrassment, enjoying the praise.

"How come you're not out in the fields today?" Ted asked him.

Blushing, Errol began, "I . . . Mom wanted . . ."

Marie-Anne rescued him assertively, "I needed some help this morning. This is a big house to keep up, and meals for six people. Why should Ross get all the help? It's good for them to know a woman's work. They take turns."

"That makes sense," Ted acknowledged. "So, one more year and you're out of high school," he continued with Errol. "You guys grew up so fast I have a hard time to keep track."

Marie-Anne related the sequence, "Errol will graduate high school next spring, same time as Bruce finishes college. Malcolm will have completed his second year of college . . ."

"You had your boys two years apart—until Angus," Mom observed, the family chronicler.

"He's the baby of the family," Errol said teasingly to his little brother whose shoulders were as broad as his own.

"I'm starting high school," Angus answered, rocking.

"He's the same age as Lucien; just three months separate them," Mom affirmed, again the chronicler in case Ted were not aware.

"I hope he'll rouse some interest there," Marie-Anne said wishfully.

"I plan to try out for J-V basketball," Angus offered.

Ted continued to engage his nephews. "Are the two of you going to study farming like Bruce and Malcolm?"

"I want to major in computer science and get a city job," Errol said matter-of-factly.

"I haven't decided on college," Angus answered.

Ross and Bruce and Malcolm walked up to the porch. Ross, rusty-haired, tall, well-built, always carried himself self-assuredly and with an air of conscious authority; but good-natured, he often made light with a twinkle in his eye. Bruce, black-haired, of average height and darker complexion, recalled his grandfather, Ted's Dad. Malcolm was Bruce's opposite, tall and sunny blond, claimed by Mom for her ancestry. Spindly tall, brown-haired Errol had his mother's coloring. Of the four, freckled-faced, rusty-haired Angus was the one who with his sturdy features most resembled his father.

Despite my low-throated growl when the newcomers reached forward, they shook Ted's hand, and each gave Mom a kiss on the cheek.

"Don't you growl at me," Ross said to me playfully, "or I'll sic a big dog on you."

"Troy almost got in his licks already," Marie-Anne told him.

"I'm hungry," Ross said. "Are you men hungry?" he said to Bruce and Malcolm.

"I've been thinking lasagna all morning," Malcolm said cheerily to his mother.

"It's ready," Marie-Anne said to everyone, "let's go in," and they filed into the house where they took places at the long dining room table. Ted set me on the floor beneath it, where I could smell the exciting aromas of beef, basil, tomato sauce and cheese rising from the dish that Marie-Anne placed before them.

"About to begin haying?" Ted asked Ross, then interrupted himself and asked Marie-Anne, "May I have a little dish for Tobi?" While Ross explained the effect of altitude on hay-timing, Ted proceeded to carve some lasagna into it, and placed it under the table for me.

It was quite wonderful. I love meat lasagna, and Ted gave me a good portion, filled the dish, so I was at it a while despite how fast I eat. Usually once finished I'd beg for more, but that's probably why Ted gave me so much. I just lay down beside the dish at the center of the circle of feet surrounding me, and I waited because I knew there'd be dessert, too. And dessert in the north country usually meant pie, and pie meant delicious pieces of crisp, mouth-watering pie crust.

Ted told Marie-Anne, "This is so good. I always look forward to it."

"It's one of the few recipes I didn't learn from Mom, but it's a family favorite anyway," Marie-Anne said smiling at her mother. "I taught the boys, and today Errol made it while I was making pies."

Errol blushed again while everyone complimented him.

Ted asked Bruce, "How does it feel to be just a year from graduation?"

"It feels good," Bruce smiled.

"I expect they'll both show me a good return on my investment," Ross said including Malcolm. "And the land is a good place to build contentment."

"He's building contentment with Yvette," Angus teased.

"Children should be seen and not heard, Pipsqueak," Bruce quipped back.

Ted spent much of his conversation quizzing his nephews one after the other. Living away as he did, he didn't get to see them often, which, despite their gestures of welcome, made him feel he didn't know them well enough. However, it was evident the way he conversed with his brother-in-law Ross that Ted was very comfortable with him.

As lunch drew to an end, Marie-Anne brought out a freshly baked strawberry-rhubarb pie, and Ted reached under the table to hand me pieces of its crusty border. With the large portion of lasagna I'd eaten and these crispy, fatty pieces of pastry, my stomach felt loaded, and I lay where I was and fell asleep.

Eventually I was awakened by the sliding of chairs and the movement of feet. Ted reached under for me and carried me on his arm to the wide front porch to which everyone had retired. The family continued to visit until a sliver of black appeared at the edge of the horizon.

"It looks like the 'possible storm' forecast is now a 'probability,'" Ted said. "We'd better get going before it hits."

Good-byes were given, with everyone hugging everyone, and we drove off, traveling ahead of the storm.

5. THE MUDROOM

The weeks passed among these hardy people. Dad and Robert did chores and worked the farm together, with some help from Ted and Lucien. Mom kept up the house, cleaning and cooking with lots of baking, Marguerite assisting her. Upstairs Mémère and the memory of Pépère sat in their rocking chairs, each at a window on opposite sides of the kitchen. Mémère made quilts and braided rugs there, but she spent as much time these sunny summer days outside seeing to the chickens and this and that around the barn. She and Mom devoted hours to their vegetable gardens, with the help of Robert and the kids.

Forenoons Ted and I mostly stayed on the upstairs front sun porch where he continued at his computer. I slept a lot; nothing new to that. All that mattered to me was to be with Ted all the time, on his lap, or in his arms. When we went outside he'd put me down, and I'd run around the lawn or sniff where Rex had been by the flower beds. I didn't pay much attention to Rex, and he didn't pay much attention to me. He was a wonderfully nice dog, but very placid. No adventure there—I thought.

When haying season began, the farm became a flurry of activity. The young men hired to help appeared every day. Afternoons Ted drove one of the hay trucks as he'd offered to do, and I stood on the seat beside him trying to keep my balance in the slowly swaying cab. Everyone except Mom was out in the field, Lucien and Marguerite atop the load, and Mémère following along behind with her hand rake.

It was turning out to be one of the nicest summers I'd ever had, until Ted went away. It isn't as if he never left me home. He'd say to me, "You stay here now. I have to go to the grocery store in town, and I'll be right back. Dogs can't go into grocery stores, and I don't want to leave you in the car with the sun beating down on it." He'd hand me to Lucien to hold while he got into the car and drove off. So, the day it happened, despite doing my dance on his leg to persuade him to take me with him as I always did, I wasn't too alarmed, even though some things did seem different about it.

I'd seen Ted pack suitcases and put them into the car. The family had come outside to say goodbye to him, and he knelt on one knee, stroked my head, and said softly, "Now you be a good boy." He picked me up, hugged me, and handed me to Lucien again. When he drove off and Lucien set me down, I went to lie at the corner of the lawn by the driveway to wait for him to return. I had no way of knowing when he'd be back, but I expected it'd probably be in an hour or two, as usual. So I waited.

I waited all day in the shade of the big maple tree. I waited while blackbirds and robins scampered about the lawn in the sun, and I paid them no attention. I waited while the sun slowly descended in the sky. I waited while Mom called me for my supper, and I didn't move. I waited when Dad and Robert crossed the barnyard to go do their chores, and I waited when they had finished and returned back across the yard and entered the house. I waited until it began to grow dark. I waited, until Lucien came out and said to me, "Come on, Tobi," and picked me up.

Lucien carried me into the house, and set me down on the kitchen floor.

Dad said, "Dogs don't belong in the house. Lucien, you make a bed for him out in the mudroom with Rex. That's where he'll stay. He'll be fine out there."

Lucien picked me up again, carried me out the door, and set me down in the mudroom. He brought out an old blanket he got from Mom and folded it into a bed next to Rex's. My food bowl was placed right beside Rex's, too. When Mom put my supper into it, I wasn't hungry, and Rex ate it. I didn't care.

Days passed. Instead of having my food prepared as Ted used to do, I was fed the same as Rex, the leftovers from the family's meal. Lucien would stand there to make sure Rex didn't eat mine, and Rex understood pretty fast to leave it alone. I left it alone, too; I wasn't hungry, no appetite at all. All I wanted was Ted. However, I never thought he wouldn't come back, even as time grew longer and days passed. He always came back. He hadn't left me among strangers, but with his family; I knew he'd be back. I waited, and waited, every day by the corner of the lawn. No one bothered me; they let me wait.

Days passed. Then late one afternoon when Rex was sunning on the transom with Nanook nestled between his forepaws, he slowly rose to his feet, careful not to disturb the cat too much. He walked down the lawn to where I was and set himself beside me, and waited there with me until Lucien called us for supper. Rex led and I went along with him to our dishes in the mudroom. During the days following, he spent time with me at the corner of the lawn, but I began more often to lie with him in the sun on the transom and wait there for Ted instead. Eventually I began to live farm life with Rex.

6. BECOMING SECOND FARM DOG

Rex spent much of every day sleeping with Nanook on the transom, but occasionally he'd get to his feet to take a stroll around the farm or its neighborhood. With nothing better to do, I began to accompany him. In the morning he went first to Aunt Florence's house, the closest to the farm, and then to the next house on the street, Aunt Linette's, and then beyond that, to Mrs. Greer's. I found that Rex had a dish at the back door of each one. He got everyone's food leftovers. When I began to show up with him, they put down an extra dish for me.

Some days Rex would head out for a longer walk. He'd cross the street in front of the farm and go down into the fields, making a big circuit along the property boundaries. The grasses towered over me as I followed him through the hay, so once we were on our way I trailed him pretty blindly. We always came out beneath the white birches on the lakeshore. Rex would step into the rippling little waves and lie in the shallow water to cool off. I stepped into it once to follow him, but jumped back from its cold. Rex was not a long-haired dog; his black and white coat was only an inch thick, but mine was shorter still; I probably felt the heat less than he.

We'd walk beneath the birches along the shore, and then Rex would lie down under one of them, facing out to the lake, and I'd lie close to him in the shade, both of us enjoying the breezes wafting off the water. In a while Rex would get up, and we'd slowly continue tracing the edge of the field, all the way back home.

I realized that in his seemingly pointless meandering during the day, Rex was watching over the farm. Even as he spent so much time apparently napping on the transom, he was alert to the whole barnyard from that vantage point, particularly the chicken area at the opposite end. Sometimes we'd walk up behind the barn, and Rex would check out the lower pasture. From there we'd circle down to the chicken coop, not too close to it. The hens would be ruffling their feathers in dusty beds they created in the dry dirt under the blackberry bushes, while Le Coq the rooster stood by, often harassing one or the other of them. Le Coq never took his eyes off Rex and me as we walked by, but Rex paid him no mind at all, a complacency I learned later not to share if Rex wasn't with me.

With time, as I began to grow familiar with the barnyard, I'd occasionally walk about by myself while Rex was still sunning on the transom. One day when I ventured close to the chicken coop, Le Coq came running out to meet me. Like Rex I paid him no attention and walked by nonchalantly. That nasty rooster let me pass; but then he silently ran up behind me and jumped on my back. Digging in his claws to hold fast and balancing with his wings, pecking my head when he could, Le Coq rode me while I ran screaming and swerving every way to dislodge him. I stumbled, fell, and got up with him still affixed to me. I tripped again and rolled to knock him off, but the plucky rooster was back on me in a flash. In almost the same instant he jumped off as quickly, though, when a ruckus of barking alerted him Rex was dashing across the barnyard. Clucking loudly then in his own panic with Rex on his tail, Le Coq beat a hasty retreat into the blackberry bushes.

I got to my feet shaken, but seeing Rex's example, how violently he chased that rooster, a bravado came over me. My hair bristled, and from where I stood I barked, too. With the blackberry thorns preventing Rex from reaching him, Le Coq was safe under the bushes. He looked back out at us, cocking his head this way and that, watching us unperturbedly. Rex and I walked back to the transom, where I lay while my friend licked the scratches on my back. I was very wary of going anywhere near the chicken coop after that.

I was chased another time, too, when Rex and I followed Lucien to the lower pasture behind the barn and I met Bruno, Lucien's little pot-bellied pet bull. I jumped back in surprise and barked at him when he came running up to us. He nuzzled Lucien to get his forehead rubbed, and Lucien's fingers played in the curly hair between his eyes. The bull was still small, much shorter than the cows. A purebred Canadian Jersey, his coat was almost entirely black, transitioning to dark brown on his nose and belly and legs. Rex stood watching placidly, but I kept barking, and that got Bruno's attention. Turning his head from Lucien he looked at me, and I saw mischief in his eyes. Suddenly he ran at me. I yelped and sprang away, my tail between my legs. This time Rex didn't interfere, and Lucien laughed, as Bruno chased me round and round.

Just as spontaneously, though, the young bull stopped, turned his back on me, and walked towards Lucien for more face rubbing. That looked like retreat to me, so I went after him and snapped at his heels. Bruno kicked high in the air and fled with me in close pursuit. Abruptly he turned with a jump and came after me again, but I scampered out of his way, and he was going so fast he ran right past me. The game excited me, and I barked more. Then Bruno switched again and walked casually back to Lucien. I knew that when I was in the lower pasture I didn't have to be afraid of Bruno. I just had to make sure he didn't run over me.

While Lucien had Bruno, Marguerite had a pony named Trigger, quite another adventure. He pastured with Dad's young cattle, "the heifers," on the seventeen acres Dad owned by the lake farther up the road, separate from his main property.

Trigger was energetic, all-horse, but only about sixty-percent size, typical reddish brown all over. Marguerite loved him. Biking up the road on her fishing trips, she'd stop by the gate to give him a wild apple, and she'd rub his forehead and stroke his neck much as Lucien did Bruno's. However, she didn't ride Trigger often, probably because doing so at the distance of the seventeen acres was quite a production. One day Dad told her, "If you don't use that pony, I'm going to sell it." That's when I met Trigger.

In the morning Marguerite's friend Christine arrived on her bicycle. Marguerite went into the barn and came out with a small bucket of grain and a coil of rope. Hanging them from her handlebar, she and Christine bicycled down the driveway. Rex recognized what the grain and rope meant, so he trotted after them—and I trotted after him. Nanook stretched and lay back in the sun alone.

Our little parade passed Aunt Florence's house and Uncle Félix's, passed the length of the new cemetery, passed the Cole farm, and came to Dad's seventeen acres. When Trigger saw us, he trotted up to the gate and extended his neck over it to see what Marguerite might have brought him. She let him taste the grain in the bucket. Then we entered the pasture. Rex stood back, and I, not knowing what to expect, stayed by him. Christine waited, too, while Marguerite, hiding the coiled rope behind her back with one hand, encouragingly held out the bucket of grain to Trigger again with the other. However, he'd been through this before, so he trotted a few steps away instead of approaching, and looked back at her coyly. Maybe it was just a game he was playing, because eventually he came for the grain, and Marguerite put the rope around his neck.

Trigger's gear was stored in Dad's cousin's barn across the road, and Marguerite saddled him up there. Rex and I ran around exploring inside the structure until Marguerite called us out, just in time to see the girls flip a coin that decided Christine would ride Trigger down to the farm and, when they finished with him that afternoon, Marguerite would ride him back to the seventeen acres.

"I'm glad it's you and not me," Christine said to Marguerite, as she stored her bicycle in the barn.

The walk back to the farm, with Christine riding Trigger, Marguerite on her bicycle, and Rex and me trailing, was uneventful, as Trigger was compliant and kept a steady pace. Marguerite and Christine spent the rest of the forenoon and much of the afternoon taking turns riding him around the barnyard and over the back pasture. Later, in the shade of the lilac bushes they removed his saddle and groomed him, and he seemed to enjoy the brushing very much.

When Marguerite put Trigger's saddle back on him, Rex knew what to expect, and he was ready. Marguerite checked to make sure the cinch was tight. Christine readied herself on Marguerite's bicycle, laughing to her, "I'm glad it's you riding him." Marguerite mounted Trigger, and he walked calmly enough down the driveway. However, at the street she held the reins loosely and grasped the horn of the western-style saddle tightly with both hands, and Trigger took off. He was headed back to his easy life on the seventeen acres, and he knew it; and he ran uncontrollably at full break-neck gallop all the way. All Marguerite could do was hold on. Christine had to pedal her bicycle hard to keep up.

Rex, sprinting behind Trigger, gave an exhilarating chase. I tried my best, but my excitement turned desperate as my legs just couldn't go fast enough. With Trigger and Rex drawing farther and farther ahead, I had to stop, gasping and coughing, before managing the rest of the way at a slower pace. When I finally arrived walking, panting, Marguerite already had the saddle off and was about to release Trigger into the pasture. He ran through the gate, jumped and hopped a few times like a bronco, herded the bewildered heifers for a few minutes to show off, then trotted back and extended his neck towards Marguerite to see if she had an apple for him, and she did. When both girls started back down the road to the farm on their bicycles, Rex held back to walk with me, and I was in no hurry. Trigger had exhausted me.

As the days passed I generally followed Rex's routine. Most of the time he'd lie around, on the transom, on the front lawn, or in the shade of the mudroom, leaving occasionally for his walk about the farm or to visit the neighbors. He wasn't bothered at all when the family left to go somewhere by car. However, when anyone left the farm on foot, he usually rose to accompany them, unless they said to him, "Stay home, Rex," in which case he'd sigh and lie back down. Almost always he'd go with them, and I'd go with him.

Such was the case when Mémère and Mom went to pick berries. Rex and I accompanied them into the pasture behind the barn and followed them to a grass-covered road through the lower woods below the maple orchard. It led to a little field where the remains of a "sugar house" stood, a small building falling apart which had once sheltered the apparatus for making maple syrup. At the far end of the clearing Mémère and Mom crossed a fence into an adjoining pasture which had been neglected for many years before Dad finally rented it and put cows back into it. So raspberry bushes had had time to grow thick below the woodland. We reached them quickly across the rough terrain, and Mémère and Mom busied themselves filling their buckets with the ripe fruit. Each planned to gather enough for several pies.

While they picked, Rex explored all the smells and information the bushes furnished him—what animals had been by—or he'd chase a mouse or some other furtive creature for a moment, just for something to do. Mostly, however, he lay close to Mémère and Mom, surveying the landscape or dosing off, and I'd lie beside him and do the same.

This day Rex's head suddenly jerked up, and he growled throatily. He was closer to Mémère; Mom was farther to the right. At the other end of the berry patch, some distance away, I saw the bushes move. Mémère heard Rex, and she looked up, scanning the direction in which Rex was watching. I stood on a stone, and I looked, too. The berry bushes moved again, and a big black face appeared above them. Like Rex I growled. The bear eating raspberries noticed us, as well, and disappeared into the woods.

When their buckets were full and we started for home, Mémère asked Mom, "Did you see the bear?"

"A bear?" Mom said surprised. "Why didn't you tell me?"

"It took off fast enough when we got here," Mémère reassured her. "With the dogs we had nothing to worry about. Bears don't stay around dogs."

"Well, next time you tell me," Mom insisted with some exasperation.

"If I had, you wouldn't have wanted to pick any more berries, would you?" Mémère offered practically.

The following day the aroma of raspberry pies baking wafted out from Mom's kitchen to the mudroom, and also down the back stairs from Mémère's kitchen; and I knew we were going to get pieces of crust with tastes of filling adhering to it in our leftovers.

There were other occasions when Rex did similar guard duty, and he turned it into fun whenever we entered the woods. Marguerite often went fishing all by herself for brook trout. She kept a pole behind the mudroom door, a long, thin sapling she'd cut into a pliable rod and tied a fish line to its tip. Marguerite would set a dirt-filled can of worms into her bicycle basket, and then a small, light, empty lard-bucket next to it. Balancing her fishing pole across the handle bars she'd head down the driveway and turn up the street, calling Rex to follow her. He'd trot along behind the bicycle, and I'd follow behind him.

Marguerite's destination was past Dad's seventeen acres where she said hello to Trigger when he was in sight. We crossed a series of brooks that flowed through culverts beneath the road. Marguerite fished them all. She'd park her bicycle in the brush a few feet away and drop her line into the water holes, basins in the brook where fish lurked under overhanging mossy banks. She made her way upstream slowly. Rex stayed with her, and I stayed with him. Guard duty didn't stop him from having a good time; so he'd be running around the area until he got tired, sniffing every bush, sniffing every hole in the ground beneath the trees. Finally, he'd find himself a nice bed of soft moss to lie upon to wait for Marguerite, then move to one bed after the other, in sunshine or in shade as suited him at the moment, as she advanced along the brook. She never ventured far from the road.

Marguerite caught only one or two fish in the several hours. She'd pull the fish out of the water, carefully remove the hook, and drop them splashing into the lard pail she'd filled with brook water. The captive fish swam as best they could in their new, confined space. Marguerite kept them alive that way.

When we returned to the farm, Marguerite took her bucket of one or two fish into the barn where there was a large concrete tank through which fresh water continually flowed. It remained from a time before cows had automatic water bowls at their stanchions and had to be released one by one to walk over to the tank to drink. After Marguerite poured her catch of fish into the tank, there they would live out the rest of their lives. Lucien fed them worms he dug up to relieve his boredom during the evening milking chores, and they'd grow fat.

Rex and I followed Mémère into the barn one afternoon, and I learned why, despite the fact that Marguerite kept adding fish to the tank and Lucien kept feeding them, their number remained a constant three or four. Mémère had a fish line, too, no pole needed; and she'd fish out one of the fat ones. Rex and I saw her do it. She'd take it to her kitchen, and she'd have it for supper. We'd find some of the tiny bones in her leftovers.

7. FETCHING THE COWS

Each early morning, in the first grey of dawn, Robert came out of the house alone. Rex always heard him stirring inside and was waiting ready.

"Okay, let's go, boy, let's get the cows," Robert would say to him.

They'd head out together then. Rex usually walked in front of Robert—and I'd follow them both—to the lower pasture in back of the barn. Once across it, we'd climb the very steep hill leading to the wooded mountain behind the farm. We walked in the cow paths, deep ruts carved over time by sharp hooves, that followed the contours of the hill gradually but steadily upwards.

Invariably, at the top just before entering the woods, Robert would stop to sit on a stone or a stump for a few moments to catch his breath and to watch the sunrise, sometimes a pale disc, as often a fiery orange ball bathing the sky in scarlet, materializing above the foothills of the New Hampshire White Mountains on the eastern horizon, the farthest point of the vista that extended into the distance beyond the lake.

From so high up, the farm beneath us looked like a small, scale model on a three-dimensional map, with its rambling white house, and its white barn big enough to shelter all the cows and store all their hay for the entire winter. To its left was the "old cemetery" that climbed the low hill, where Mémère went regularly to put flowers on her parents' graves. To the right of the farm were three houses, each with lawns and garages and wide rectangular gardens between them, Aunt Florence's, Uncle Félix's, and Mrs. Greer's. They all were on the same side of the street, the mountain side, whereas on the lake side there were only Dad's fields, affording a wide open view of golden hay, grey now in early dawn, undulating in the breezes down to the border of birches at the shore swaying, too, in a synchronized symphony of paper-white and deep green.

There were many openings among the birches that offered a view of the lake from the road, but at this height we could see right over the trees to its entire extension, anchored in the middle by its distinctive wooded island of tall, dark evergreens rising above a thin strip of tiny beach resembling a piece of beige lint on a painting. To the immediate left on the northeastern side of the lake a train might be snaking along, hardly visible, perceived mainly by its lonely whistle carrying across the water. Still more to the left, at the northern end of the lake, some of the town was visible where it extended from behind Pleasant Street hill, as a cluster of buildings nestled at lakeside and on the rise beneath the high hump of its mountain backdrop.

When Robert turned his gaze to the right, where the street curved past the "new cemetery" and disappeared into tree cover, he could see far across the open surface of the lake where cottages dotted the opposite wooded shore all the way to "the town beach," a long, natural ribbon of sand along the southern edge, replenished each year and maintained for the use of the public free of charge by its longtime owner Uncle Chris Alden, Dad's brother-in-law, Aunt Charlotte's husband. A road-construction contractor, he had the trucks and materials for the task.

From the top of the hill Robert always smiled when he viewed "the town beach" stretching into the corner of the expanse, because it aroused both happy memories and anticipation. Several times during the summer on a Sunday after church, Mom prepared a picnic basket, and the family spent the afternoon under a very tall, solitary fir tree there. Comfortable in the shade and enjoying breezes off the water, they could see all the way across the lake's length to the town settled beneath its mountain at the opposite end. Neither Mom nor Dad went into the water, but Robert did with Lucien and Marguerite, and they'd laugh and splash; and that's where he taught his son and daughter to swim. Afterwards he'd take a long, graceful swim parallel to the shore and back while Lucien and Marguerite toweled shivering. When he came out of the water, Mom opened the picnic basket, and set out lunch.

While Robert gazed out in his reverie, Rex lay quietly beside him, his head resting on Robert's foot or against his leg, as I liked to do beside Ted when we were together. Then Robert rose to his feet, and the three of us walked into the mountain woods which opened immediately into the grand cathedral-like canopy of the maple orchard. Few bushes could grow in the shade of the tall, straight trees whose leafy branches, reaching across to each other, filtered the sunlight. The wide spaces between the tree trunks that stood planted like majestic pillars allowed us to see far ahead and high above. The cow path led almost the length of the orchard plateau, parallel to the street far below, before it resumed its ascent in thicker woods up the mountainside, picking its way through rocky climbs and occasional swampy patches. Then the terrain leveled, the trees grew scarcer, and we entered a large clearing that long ago had been a field. Low bushes were growing here and there now, but it still offered open pasture. Early morning the cows usually were lying together in one corner, awake by the time we reached them.

Robert sent Rex to circle wide to get behind them, and I followed Rex. The cows began to rise to their feet when they saw us, and a couple of them, always the same two leaders, started willingly down the cow paths in the direction from which we'd come. The remainder followed, cumbersome, slow-moving, burdened by their fat bellies and milk-filled udders. Robert pointed at laggards, and Rex promptly ran over to them to get them moving. He knew to approach from behind, and a bark or two when he reached them did the job. Like a big, sluggish caravan we headed down the mountain, the cows following the leaders filing along their well-worn paths, Rex right behind them, then Robert, then me. I saw no need to get too close to the lumbering herd.

Robert and Rex went for the cows every early morning, rain or shine. I made the trek once in bad weather. Robert in boots and raincoat didn't stop at the top of the hill for the panorama, but proceeded immediately through the maple orchard where the canopy provided some relief from the rainfall, distilling it into farther-spaced drops. When we reached the clearing at the top of the mountain the cows were more scattered, sheltering from the downpours among the bushes and trees on the periphery. It was Rex's job to go into the wet foliage and fetch them out. I followed Rex at first and barked at a cow, but she only stared back at me without moving, and then annoyed she chased me out of the brush.

Seeing what happened, Robert called to me, "That's one way to do it, Tobi, but I'm afraid you'll get trampled. Come over here."

After that, shivering in the frigid dampness, I stayed by Robert who called out, encouraging Rex, pointing to individual, reluctant cows, and sending Rex back into the brush again and again until all the herd was accounted for and headed down the mountain. Wet and cold and completely useless in the rain, I opted not to follow Rex out into it again.

Every morning when we reached the farm, Dad was in the barn with the doors open and with everything ready for milking. The cows filed into their individual stanchions where each eagerly found a pile of grain waiting for her. The milking took place before family breakfast.

Cows are milked twice a day, so late afternoons it was Lucien's job to fetch them, and the process repeated itself. Only once in a while did Marguerite do it for him, if he had a good excuse. Lucien would come by where Rex and I and Nanook were sunning on the transom, and he'd say, "Okay, Rex, c'mon, let's go; we have to get the cows."

On Lucien's watch it was more like playtime. When he stopped at the top of the hill to catch his breath, Rex didn't lie by him as with Robert, but instead busied himself exploring around the old tree stumps and rock surfaces for whatever he might smell or scare up. Following his example, I nosed around some, too. While in the morning Rex walked quietly through the majestic maple orchard by Robert's side, in the afternoon with Lucien the thick bed of brown, fallen leaves that carpeted the ground crackled noisily as Rex and I chased real or imaginary red squirrels. That's the reason why Lucien never took Rex with him on his nature walks. With Rex running through the dry leaves, the birds that Lucien wanted to observe close-up to identify in his bird book would raise the alarm and stay out of range. The trip up the mountain with Lucien was time for fun, but Rex always tended to business when we came upon the cows, and on the way down the mountain with them.

Once they arrived at the farm at afternoon's end, the cows lay down and waited in the lower pasture while the family had supper. Rex and I had time for another short nap on the transom, and sometimes Nanook joined us there if the wooden boards still held heat. The evening cooled early, though, because the mountain behind the farm shaded it from the setting sun. We'd get our supper then, too, the leftovers from the family meal, always quite sufficient, so many more tastes than I got with Ted, especially pieces of pie crust and vanilla cake I especially liked.

When Dad and Robert came out of the house with Lucien to go into the barn, we usually followed them. There was nothing for us to do there except stay out of the way, and not scare the cows as they filed into the barn. Each cow knew her stall. Each put her head through her personal stanchion to reach the pile of grain waiting for her. Once the cows were in place with stanchions fixed, Dad and Robert plied the milking machines, to the sound of the chug-chug-chug of the electric pump. The cows were mostly very docile, but once in a while one would deliver a sound kick at either the apparatus or the man. Dad would slap the cow's rump hard when it happened. Robert would merely step back, then approach the cow once more, talking to her gently, and try again. Sometimes a cow would try to swat the man with her tail, as if to rid herself of an annoying fly. When that happened her tail was tied to her leg with a piece of baler twine until her milking was finished.

Mostly the milking was an uneventful chore, the transferring of machines from one compliant cow to the next, interspersed with moments of waiting, given to chat or quiet thought. The two cats, Nanook who sunned with Rex in the afternoon and Chinook, the beautiful three-colored more furtive female, waited patiently by their dish for Robert to fill it with fresh warm milk. Robert was the only person Chinook would allow to stroke her.

Lucien didn't seem to have a specific job, but helped with the milking machines when Robert beckoned him to do so. He always spent some time turning over the rich soil outside the side doors to collect a few large worms he called nightcrawlers. Then each time he unearthed one, he brought it into the barn and dropped it into the water tank where Marguerite earlier had deposited her fish. I could hear the water always flowing through, and there'd be the sound of a little splash.

"Look how fat this one is," he'd say to his father. "I can pat it." The brook trout in the tank grew so big from that nightly feeding and so tame from it, that Lucien could stroke their bulging sides.

Rex often lay on folded burlap grain bags that Robert set for him by the side of the granary, but sometimes he'd simply plop himself down in the middle of the barn floor amid all the activity. He never bothered the cats when they got their milk, and a yell from Dad taught me not to, either. I mostly waited on the burlap bed.

After each cow was milked, she was released from her stanchion, and she ambled out the big side door back into the lower pasture. The cows might remain there for the night, or they might decide as they usually did to go back up the mountain, so Robert would have to fetch them in the morning, when the procedure repeated itself.

When the barn chores were over, I'd follow Rex back outside. Sometimes he'd head for the lower pasture behind the barn just for a look around. One evening when we'd walked back there and were watching the cows slowly ascend their hoof-carved paths up the hill, I thought I saw something move, probably a chipmunk like I'd chase sometimes on the front lawn. Curious, I trotted towards it, which took me a little distance away from Rex. Suddenly, the chipmunk was no chipmunk, but much bigger; it sprang forward, quite dog-like with a pointed nose and bushy tail. That's the moment I found out what a fox is.

She lunged at me, but I leapt out of the way. She pivoted to reach me, and I leapt out of the way again, and then she jumped, turning in mid-air in an instant, and we were face to face. I gave a nasty growl and barked noisily into the fox's face which made her hesitate only a moment, but that's all I needed to turn and run back toward Rex with her in close pursuit. Rex, whom the fox had not noticed in her fixation on me, was dashing at us and rushed past me to attack. With Rex bearing down, the fox did a quick turn on her heels to flee; and Rex chased her all the way up the hill to the edge of the woods. I ran in the opposite direction to the side of the barn and waited there, my heart pounding, until Rex came back.

We returned to the barnyard together. Rex didn't seem to think much of the incident, but I walked with my head high and tail straight up; Rex was my friend, and he'd shown that fox! However, I always had a healthy respect for the dangers in the woods after that, and I never again strayed from Rex if we went beyond the barnyard.

Normally our walk to the back pasture after milking was not so adventuresome. Rex would look around, and I'd stay very close by him. Then, satisfied, he'd come back down to the house, and lie on the transom in the last light of twilight. I'd lie beside him. The house went quiet not long after, almost as soon as it got dark, and Rex and I moved to our beds in the mudroom to sleep.

Probably because he slept so much during the day, Rex every now and then didn't sleep very long at night. Sometimes when the Indians' dogs could be heard across the lake, sometimes when a fox barked on the back hill, Rex would slowly get up and walk out the door. I was used to regular sleeping hours with Ted, so I didn't follow him, not at first at least.

8. NIGHT JOURNEY

One night, perhaps when I, too, had slept most of the day and so was not tired, but more probably because it was a night of the full moon, and I felt restless like Rex, I followed him through the open mudroom door into the moonlit darkness. As we set out we heard the Indians' dogs howling in the far distance across the lake, and that's the direction in which we headed.

Rex didn't take to the street. Instead, he crossed the field down to the lakeshore which we followed in and out of the trees past the Cole farm, past Dad's outlying seventeen acres, past Uncle Chris' cottages at the base of the Granet farm and all the way to his sandy "town beach," and then beyond that. It was proving to be a much longer trek than I'd anticipated, but I didn't mind. The moonlight roused in me a sense of adventure reinforced by the reassuring safety of Rex's company. We walked easily along the narrow beach in front of cottages poking out of the trees on the southeastern shore, with Rex making lots of incursions into their yards and woods, all the way to where a small watercourse bordered by a railroad track poured into the lake. There we turned onto a path leading upstream along the channel. Where it washed through a culvert under the roadway we bounded over it, then followed a short distance more to where it flowed from a small pond. As Rex resolutely pursued the new shoreline, the Indian dogs' howling grew nearer. I became apprehensive, but when I hesitated, Rex paid me no attention; so I'd no choice but to persevere forward or remain by myself. He was headed right for them.

Rex cut through the woods. We came out onto a driveway that we followed until, up ahead on one side, we saw looming in the moonlight a huge pen towards the back of which a row of dog houses stood sentinel. The howling stopped as we approached. In the pale glow each large, square house had a dog standing or sitting or lying in front of it. The dogs all were awake and vigilant; they all were watching our progress towards them. I followed closer behind Rex as he walked up the center of the drive. I supposed it would be like encountering dogs on the sidewalks in New York City where on leash we'd make a fuss but couldn't reach each other. I expected the ruckus to begin at any moment, and braced myself for it. The pen was tall and high, after all; we'd be alright, able to stroll right up to it safely.

I held back when Rex veered from the middle of the way and headed instead straight for a big dog *outside* the enclosure, a huge Newfoundland in black silhouette out in front of the pen. Rex walked up to him, and they touched noses. After a moment, Rex lay on his back exposing his belly. The big dog nudged him. Rex got up, walked on and greeted other dogs through the fence in similar fashion without the submission gesture. When he reached a white female he lay down against the fence beside her.

Standing in the middle of the driveway I felt at a loss what to do. I had no inclination whatsoever to walk up to these big dogs who were quietly welcoming Rex. Apparently, surprisingly, it was as if he were an honorary member of the pack. That didn't mean they'd be welcoming me. With nothing else to do, I simply lay down where I was standing in the middle of the drive and waited.

After some quiet, bathed in the moon's grey glow the dogs began to stir. The Newfoundland was first. He lifted his face upwards and howled, long and alone. Then one and then another dog echoed in chorus, combining long, quavering howls with mournful yowls punctuated with baying and barks. Rex and the white female sat up and called out with them. It was not an uproar, but more an intermingling of solos, one, then another, and another, overlapping into a duet or trio. It was low, plaintive, reaching back, far, far, far into their ancient past, and deep into their nature. Like a flood of feeling it drew me in. I was carried into timeless moonlit wilderness, and I, too, became a wild thing. Still lying on the hard dirt driveway, I looked up at the great pale orb darkly illuminating the sky amid wisps of cloud. Its light raying down on us riveted me as never before, and forcefully pulled the depths of me toward it. My voice rose from the bottom of my chest with a strength that rattled my head, at first joining into the huskies' chorus, then soaring into a high-pitched solo. I caught my breath, then emitted a yapping piccolo, counterpointing the throaty, bass howls of the big dogs. Our songs looped, as if for forever in that moment, until they fell away in a cacophony of barks and whimpers. It was membership in a pack, as birds fly in a flock, fish swim in a school, where all together become as one in a higher identity, the many becoming of one mind in the ecstasy of moonlight.

The experience was new, so new. It was reminiscent of what I lived with Molly and her pups in Central Park when we were free and wild there the summer I was lost. Yet this call tonight was deeper still. There was no freedom now for these dogs as I'd enjoyed with Molly. They were caged. No, it was not a celebration; it was more a vestige of a former Eden, the repetition of an instinctive ritual honoring a wildness that harkened still within them, and with them I felt it, too. Rex and I were not chained; we were Lake Isle dogs wandering free off-leash; but we were no less tied to our human circumstances. Rex was the freest of all, able to come and go, visit the neighbors, chase woodchucks and squirrels for the fun of it, always with a sense of home and belonging. We loved our humans, and were loved back, I more intimately than Rex, I thought. We didn't want it otherwise; but rousing the wolf within sent a quivering sensation along my spine that scintillated in the pale light calling us forth.

Clouds began to pass in front of the moon, creating elongated periods of pitch blackness. The dogs settled down. Some went inside their houses; some lay in front. It grew quiet. When the moon reappeared, one or the other might make a token sound, but it was time for sleeping, and it was time for us to move on.

Rex and I went the way we'd come, back towards the channel that led from the Indians' small pond to the larger lake on which our farm was located. Rex had accomplished what he'd set out to do, visiting this pack that at some time in the past on a different occasion had first admitted him. It had become his custom in his wanderings to renew the tie from time to time on a moonlit night.

Rex knew his way back through the brush, following the water's edge until it became sandy beach again, past the dark cottages that stood like outposts in the occasional moonlight now as thick clouds paraded in front of the luminous disc. We walked and trotted along Uncle Chris' "town beach," and across Granet's field, then jumped the brook and continued through Dad's open seventeen acres to the swampy woodland at its corner. It was there that disaster struck.

In the darkness something was moving toward us with an unfamiliar rustling sound, bigger than me but smaller than Rex. In a moment of moonlight it had a round body and a small pointed face. It stopped when it saw us. When Rex continued to approach it growling, it drew itself into a ball in our path, its long hairs standing increasingly erect all around it, so that it grew bigger and bigger. Rex barked at it but stopped short of biting it. It began to run away, but it was slow, with its stiff hairs clinking against each other and the ground. Rex was at it again, jumping and barking, still without biting it. However, as Rex hovered, the creature swung its tail and caught him square in the face. Rex screamed and jumped away, his snout and face full of porcupine quills. While the creature escaped into the underbrush, Rex tried to remove the quills by rubbing his face frantically against the ground. He cried the more with pain because that drove them in deeper. He jumped to his feet spinning in a circle on himself shaking his head violently, stopping only for instants to paw his face and yelp all the more each time. He shook his head as hard as he could again and again, rubbed his face on the ground again, and jumped away again crying out! I watched completely bewildered. When he finally stopped as if he'd come to his senses, he stood with his head hanging down, whining so pitifully, so sad. I walked over to him, and I nosed his face to comfort him—he yelped. I jumped back poked by the needles, but I'd not touched the barbed ends; those were embedded in his nose, his cheeks and close to his eyes.

Rex lay down then by the side of the path. He rolled onto his side, and turned his head further still toward the sky so nothing pressed anywhere against his face. He lay like that for a few minutes as I stood by helplessly. I whined to him, but he didn't react. While I looked for an indication from him how we'd get out of this, he was doing what dogs do, descending into a state of quiet endurance. So I lay down, too, to wait. However, totally perplexed and too frightened to lie still, I got back to my feet and stood in place trembling, watching him for whatever we might do. He soon rolled back to his feet, and stood, too, facing me, his mouth contorted like a snarl with quills piercing through his lips into his gums. I walked towards him. Thoughtlessly my nature was to lick his hurts. He turned his face away from me when I came near. Then he started slowly up the path in the direction we'd been heading, towards the farm. He led the way, head hanging, and I followed, he in painful endurance and I in devastated confusion. We stayed close to the lakeshore, near the trees that bordered it, and crossed the fields that way, the same route we'd come. The slow, pitiful trek, not that far really, seemed interminable.

Once home we lay on our beds in the mudroom, well named that night because we both were muddied from our adventure in the swamp. I hardly slept because I could sense Rex's pain, and he whined from time to time confirming it. Mostly he was silent, as dogs are when we hurt. We'd gone out, encountered and participated in the mysticism of wild wolves, and then returned from this disaster very much dogs waiting for their humans to rescue them from a predicament.

The following morning when Robert came through the mudroom and saw Rex's plight, he said to Rex, "Stay here, boy, stay here," and he went to fetch the cows alone. When Dad came through a little later, he said to Rex, "You stupid dog. The first time wasn't enough?" That's how I learned that this had happened to Rex before and was why he wouldn't bite the animal; poor Rex didn't count on it swinging its tail. It also meant that Rex realized the ordeal in store for him that I found out about when it happened later.

When Robert and Dad returned to the mudroom after chores, Robert pleaded, "Let's take him to the vet, Dad. It would be so much less trouble that way, both for us and the dog."

Dad looked down at Rex with disgust, and Rex, with his face full of quills sticking out in all directions, looked back with very sorrowful eyes. Some of the three-inch quills had been pushed in so far with Rex's rubbing that they now stuck out less than an inch. He wasn't touching his face anymore, and just lay resigned.

"No, that's a waste of money," Dad answered, "when we can do it ourselves."

"I'll pay for it. I insist," Robert said.

"No," Dad told him, "You can insist all you want. This is the only way he'll learn." Then he added, "After breakfast." Rex who'd waited in pain since nighttime had to endure longer.

While Dad and Robert were at breakfast, we waited. When Lucien put food in our dishes, we waited. Until Dad and Robert and Lucien all came into the mudroom together, we waited.

Dad put a rope around Rex's neck and led him to the barn, empty now with the cows out in the pasture. I followed them. There, Dad brought Rex to a post at the edge of a stall. He wrapped the rope around the bottom and pulled it so that Rex's head was drawn down to its base. Rex struggled mightily, but his head was tied against the floor. Dad straddled Rex, and sitting on him held his body down, and with his hands held Rex's head all the tighter to the floor. Robert took a position behind Dad, holding Rex with his weight, too. It took the rope, the post, and the pressure of the two men to hold him, while Lucien trembling held pliers in front of Rex's face.

"Ok, pull them out," Dad said to Lucien, "and be quick about it. Grasp the quill good with the pliers, and yank it out."

And that's what they did. Rex screamed for every quill pulled, and there were lots of them. I hid by the granary where I watched from behind a pile of empty bags. It took forever and forever. Rex struggled violently. The two men together could barely hold him down as he writhed, while Dad with all his weight pushed Rex's head against the floor to hold it still, so Lucien with the quivering pliers could pull each quill out one by one. Blood oozed from each extraction; Dad's hands were red with it.

"Get the short ones . . . get that one near his eye . . . stop shaking and get it done; you're almost finished!" Dad yelled at Lucien impatiently as he held on with Robert to the thrashing, yowling, screaming Rex as well as he could.

Finally, after Dad said to Lucien, "That's the last one," all went quiet, except for Rex's crying. Yes, he was crying. Dogs can cry, and Rex was crying. Then Dad and Robert climbed off him. Lucien put down the pliers, and turned away, trembling and crying, too.

Robert went over to his son and put his arm around him. "You did a good job," he told him." Looking back at his father, Robert said in a voice not loud, not accusatory, just matter-of-fact, "This wasn't necessary; it could all have been avoided. The vet would have anesthetized Rex, and he wouldn't have felt a thing until it was over."

"It will be over if it happens again," Dad answered him. "I'm not going to have a dog around here that's not smart enough to stay away from porcupines."

And that was the end of it. The men left. Rex remained where he lay, rubbing his face with his paws. It was quiet, very quiet. I was about to step forward when the barn door opened again. It was Robert with a warm, wet towel to clean Rex's face.

"You've had a hard time of it, boy," he said consolingly as he applied the cloth. "That was pretty awful, I know."

Rex tried to pull his head away because the slightest pressure hurt his sore face, but Robert persisted, encouraging him quietly.

"I'm sorry, I'm sorry," he said, "but you know you got yourself into it. You have to let me clean you up. I'm being as gentle as I can."

It was evident Rex trusted Robert and appeared to understand, and let him wipe the blood away as Robert reassured him, "You'll be okay. It may take a little while, but you'll be okay."

When Robert finished, and Rex lay his head down on his paws again looking so sad, Robert sat on the floor by him stroking his head gently and speaking to him softly to keep him company for a while. "You're a good boy, such a good boy, Rex. What would we do without you? You protect the farm. You fetch the cows. You're my pal."

Robert talked to Rex soothingly, then continued stroking him for a while in silence, thinking. Then he said, "I hope you'll stay away from the porcupines, Rex. But if it happens again, I promise I'll take you to the vet. You're my dog. No matter what Dad says, I'll just take you! We'll never put you through this again, I promise you that, Rex."

I watched and waited. When Robert left, closing the barn door behind him, I walked over to Rex and began to lick his hurt. And I licked it, and licked it. And I just kept licking, until I fell asleep beside him. We stayed in the barn like that all morning, until Mémère came in to fish a trout out of the tank. When she finished, we followed her out into the sunlight. I led Rex to the transom where we lay, our bodies touching each other side by side in the warm sunshine. Rex, exhausted, rested quietly. Nanook eventually came across the yard, silently as cats do, and joined us. Nanook couldn't sleep on Rex's paws though, because that is where he was resting his sore face. By the end of the day, life returned to normal. Rex ate his food after supper, except that he didn't return to the barn with Dad and Robert when they went to do their chores there. And I stayed with him in the mudroom.

That was all I could do, one dog for another, just be there. Rex was calm now; it was over. I was still having nervous moments of trembling. When it got dark, we went to sleep on our beds in the mudroom. Rex didn't venture out during the night for a long time after that.

That's how time passed while I waited for Ted. Lots of small adventures, and a few big ones, and naps on the transom with Rex. It was a dog's life. I spent many hours lying on the lawn under the maple tree by the corner of the driveway, facing the street, waiting to see Ted's car. I still felt he'd return, but it was taking him a long time. Sometimes I'd chase away a blackbird if it got too close; then I'd continue my vigil. Sometimes Rex would join me and lie not far from me, and Nanook would eventually come and lie by him. It was as if the three of us all were waiting for Ted, day after day. However, day after day Ted didn't come back.

We dogs live at the good pleasure of humans. That is the bargain our ancestors made, enslavement, for food and acceptance. Those who didn't make the bargain, the wolves, are reviled and exterminated. Bondage of body and mind enables us to live in human circumstances, but subject to our masters' free and arbitrary choices in our regard. Ted had chosen, for some reason he couldn't convey, to leave me on the farm. He'd decided for me, and left it up to me to make the best of it. I had to do that while pining for him, of never feeling whole, of missing him, and waiting and waiting for him, even as I adjusted somewhat to that life.

9. A DETERMINING EVENT

Some weeks later, one morning after Dad had driven off in his pickup truck and Robert had come through the barnyard with the noisy tractor and crossed the street into the field below, and Rex and I and Nanook were all three of us drifting in and out of sleep on the transom in the warming sun, Mom came out of the house and called to Lucien. He looked up at her from the chair on the side lawn where he was reading.

"Hurry down into the field to see if your father's okay," she cried out to him. "Mrs. Cavanaugh just phoned that she saw him drive behind the hill twenty minutes ago but she hasn't seen him come back up; so run and make sure he's alright."

Lucien set down his book, and he hurried down the driveway.

"Run!" Mom shouted after him, and he did.

Seeing Lucien break into a run, Rex jumped to his feet and raced after him, and I sprang after Rex as Nanook leaped out of the way. It was exciting to chase Lucien as he sprinted through the field towards the lake. The hay was high, and I did my best to follow the track that he and Rex made through it. I caught up with them when they paused at the crest where the hill falls more steeply to the shore.

Lucien stood for a second looking at the tractor resting on its side at the bottom of the incline with Robert lying on the ground just above it—conflicted whether to turn on his heels to run immediately for help, or take time to reassure his father it would be coming. He raced down, tripped and rolled, picked himself up, and caught up with Rex who'd reached the bottom first. Standing over his father, he cried out "Dad! Dad!" to rouse him. Robert lay with his lower body twisted, his eyes closed, his chest barely moving. "I'll get help! I'll get help!" Lucien yelled into his father's unconsciousness. Then blubbering, sobbing, he turned on his tracks and ran back up the hill. Rex went to Robert and began to lick his face. I wasn't sure what to do, but Lucien was running fast, and so I chased after him.

As we topped the incline, and the farm buildings and the street were again in sight, a tremor ran up my back as I heard Rex begin to howl. Although reminiscent of the Indians' dogs calling across the lake, it was a longer, more mournful yowl that reached deep into me and stopped me in my tracks. I finished the way home slowly, fearfully, with my tail between my legs. Something very bad had happened.

Lucien disappeared into the house, and in moments both he and Mom and Marguerite hurried out. Mémère was crossing the barnyard, and Lucien called out to her, "My dad rolled over the tractor!"

"Is he alright?" Mémère asked him with alarm.

"He's hurt; he's unconscious," Mom exclaimed. "I've called the ambulance."

Lucien ran off as fast as he could down the field again. When Marguerite wanted to follow him, Mom held her back then collapsed into a lawn chair and began to cry. Marguerite sat and cried, too.

"I'll tell Florence and Félix!" Mémère said, and she hurried to alert them. In minutes Aunt Florence came across the lawn towards Mom, took her hand, and waited with her. Uncle Félix ran down into the field very fast for such a big man, while Aunt Linette stood at the edge of their lawn and gazed across, even though her view of the accident, like everyone else's, was obscured by the crest of the incline. The fear and excitement I sensed from everyone made me nervous, so I just stood still, watching them. When Mémère returned, I lay on the grass close by her chair.

Aunt Florence said to Mom, "I called Charlotte to call Chris. He's at his shed where he keeps his equipment. He'll know how to raise the tractor."

To the left of the hill, below by the lake, we saw the ambulance and other cars hurry past Mrs. Cavanaugh's house to the street's end where they all drove over the hayfield and disappeared behind the crest. Soon the ambulance reappeared, racing back across, its lights flashing and siren blaring, and disappeared quickly down Shore Street. Uncle Chris' backhoe was making its way towards the field.

"Somebody has to tell us where they're taking him!" Mom said to Aunt Florence.

"I see Félix coming. He'll know," Aunt Florence reassured her. "I'll get my car so we can follow."

Uncle Félix was panting now, out of breath, walking slowly, and Aunt Florence was back with her car by the time he reached Mom. He spoke to her, and Mom broke down crying again. Aunt Florence helped her into the car, Marguerite hurried into the back seat, and they drove off. Still catching his breath, Uncle Félix talked with Mémère who cried on his shoulder. He helped her up her back stairs, and then he walked sadly home where Aunt Linette waited for news.

It was very quiet, very, very quiet, with just me and Nanook. Then Rex came back, walking wearily up the driveway, head and tail down, as if exhausted from a long journey. I followed him to the transom where he flopped down on the warm boards, rested his head on his paws, and waited, looking so sorry. Nanook lay by his side, and then I did, too. I could feel how fast his heart was beating.

The sun was still high, close to noon, when Aunt Florence brought Mom and Marguerite and Lucien home. The three went into the house, with Mom speaking softly to Marguerite who was crying. Aunt Florence left, and soon after, Marie-Anne drove into the yard. She walked quickly inside.

I stayed beside Rex on the transom that day. Poor Rex. He'd been licking Robert's face to revive him, to let him know he loved him. Now he lay there with us, as if far away, bereft by the absence he'd sensed so suddenly. With purring and rubbing Nanook asked from time to time to lie on his front paws, but that is where Rex rested his head. He didn't look up until Dad drove his pickup truck into the yard in the late afternoon.

Mom and Marie-Anne came out the door, Mom saying, "I can't have him simply walk into it. I have to be the one to tell him."

Dad saw them approaching. It was unusual, so he asked irritably, "What's the matter?"

"I have some bad news," Mom told him in a quavering voice.

"What is it?"

Mom's lip quivered; she was trying not to cry so as to be able to speak. She said slowly, "We've lost . . . Robert."

"What do you mean 'We've lost Robert'?" Dad repeated after her quickly, his eyes wide with alarm when she buried her face in her hands weeping. He looked at Marie-Anne. "What's happened? What's going on?"

Marie-Anne spoke softly, consolingly, like a person whispers in church, trying with many words to soften the blow, "There was an accident this morning while he was mowing the hill, Dad. You never know, and the worst happened. The tractor rolled over . . ."

"He's hurt bad?" Dad interrupted her.

Mom sobbed through her hands, "He's passed away."

Dad reeled, slammed the flat of his hand against his truck and leaned on the vehicle with his back to the two women and began to cry convulsively. Neither Mom nor Dad moved to console the other. It was a duet of solitary grief. Marie-Anne made the few steps forward to him, put her arm over his shoulder and, when he turned, embraced him. He held on to her tightly, then slowly relaxed his weight in her arms and slid to the ground, sitting with his back against the truck wheel. Her painful task done,

Mom turned away with her overflow of grief and walked back to the house. Dad cried in short bursts but mostly stared into the distance in disbelief. Marie-Anne extended her hand to help him to his feet, then sat by him and put her arm around him again and waited until he was ready. After a while he let her lead him to the house, and I could hear the chorus of Lucien's and Marguerite's weeping when he entered.

I waited with Rex and Nanook on the transom. When Dad's and Mom's grieving voices in the house grew louder in a moment of recrimination, Rex got to his feet and walked to the front edge of the lawn where he plopped down facing the lake, as if waiting, the way I waited for Ted. I set myself as close beside him as I could.

In a while Lucien came outside. Whatever occurred, the cows always had to be milked. He called Rex and they headed for the back pasture to climb the mountain to fetch them. I followed along, too. It took us a long time to get to the top because Lucien kept stopping to cry, and Rex was in no hurry, either. We were a sorry parade entering the grandeur of the maple orchard as the late sun pierced the canopy in long, ethereal rays. We made it up and back. There was something calming in the normality of the cows slowly plodding down their carved paths to the back pasture. Not so burdened as Rex was, I walked through the scene with my head up, an evanescent moment fixed now in my memory. At the base of the hill the overwhelming sense of sorrow enveloping the farm penetrated me again, and I returned to the mudroom, like Rex head down, tail down, feeling troubled and anxious.

When Lucien and Dad came out after supper to do the chores, Rex and I followed them into the barn. They hardly spoke the whole time. Dad was very impatient with the cows if they swished their tails or did anything else he didn't like.

The following day more cars and trucks came up the driveway into the yard than I'd seen at one time there ever before. Everyone looked sad. I could smell the many flavors of food dishes they carried to the house. No one except Aunt Florence stayed long; she was there most of the day. She spent a lot of time upstairs with Mémère, as did Aunt Charlotte and Aunt Linette after they visited Mom and Dad. Marie-Anne drove off shortly after noon. Otherwise the family didn't leave the house, excepting only Lucien to fetch the cows morning and afternoon, and Dad with Lucien for milking. A few times Lucien came out of the barn, sat on the stone step in front of the door with his face buried in his hands; then he went back in.

That evening after chores, all four, Mom and Dad, Lucien and Marguerite, along with Mémère, all dressed in their Sunday best, went away in the car. When they returned a few hours later, Mémère said to Mom, "I've never seen so many people at a wake. Robert certainly was loved in the town."

Soon after, the house went dark. Rex and I lay on our beds in the mudroom. Rex was very, very quiet, as if he were far away, and we fell asleep, too.

The day after that my wish came true. Ted drove up the driveway. I ran across the barnyard to meet him. I jumped so high on his leg that I fell over. He picked me up, and I wiggled in his arms trying to lick his face, while he kissed my head and said to me repeatedly, "Oh, Tobi, it's so good to see you. I've missed you so much." I nestled against his chest, and he carried me into the house. I'd not been in there in a long time.

The family had not come out; Dad was sitting alongside the kitchen table his elbows resting on his knees, and Mom was standing by the stove. Lucien and Marguerite and Marie-Anne and Mémère were nowhere in sight at the moment. Ted set me down. He looked towards Dad who'd turned his head away to hide his face. Ted looked across at Mom, who gave him a sorrowful smile that she was glad to see him.

Going over to her, his voice faltering, he said, "I can't believe it; it's like a bad dream I'm waiting to wake up from." He put his arms around her, bending his head to touch his forehead to her shoulder. "Oh, Mom, my little brother?" he asked as if there were doubt.

"It's not a dream," she answered him consolingly. "Robert is in heaven, looking down on us from up there now, and it's a very happy place. He was considerate and kind to everyone and everything, so I know in my heart he went straight there and so he's happy. We're the ones left behind here to miss him every day until we join him."

With his arms around her still, Ted said, "I just stare and stare at the thought of having lost him. I think he can't be gone, this can't have happened, while my head realizes that it has."

"Yes, we can't turn back the clock," she said, holding him close. "We'll live on with just our memories now.

We're going to miss him like sunshine on a cloudy day." They held each other. Then she dropped her arms and gave Ted a nod towards his father.

He walked over to Dad who sat gazing downward, and he took his hand. "I'm so sorry," Ted offered.

"What will I do?" Dad asked him looking up.

Dad quickly stood up as his face contorted to cry. He turned, but Ted stopped him and put his arms around him. Choking back a sob before pulling away, Dad hurried into his bedroom just off the kitchen and closed the door. We could hear his sorrow wash over him there.

Ted turned to Mom, "Will he be okay?"

"Will any of us be okay?" she asked. "Our hearts are broken."

Going over to her and putting his arms around her again, he said softly, "I'm so sorry, Mom. How will you make it through this? I'm concerned for you."

"I don't know how, but I have to," she answered. "I have to for them all. I'll just have to take it one day at a time. I know 'there's no pain like the loss of a child,' and I'm going to have to endure it." They held each other.

Forcing a smile, Mom pulled away and pointing to the counter shelves said, "Look at all the food everyone brought, so I won't have to cook at this time. Have you eaten? There's plenty here."

"Where's Marie-Anne?" he asked her. "Her car is in the yard."

"She's upstairs with Marguerite, who's been staying in her bedroom most of the time. The kids are just overcome by it. As if it wasn't bad enough they lost their mother, now they've lost their father, too. He was so good with them; they loved him so much! They don't have words; Lucien mostly holds it in, and Marguerite cries and cries."

"Marguerite must be inconsolable! She was so close to her father."

"Fortunately she's always been special with Marie-Anne, too. Hiding alone might help a little while, but people need to talk, even if everything we say is inadequate. We have to try. So Marie-Anne and I have been spending a lot of time with each one. Except your father; there's nothing I can do there, because he won't let me."

"When do *you* cry, Mom?" Ted asked her.

"I certainly cried a lot the day it happened. Now I cry when I'm alone, washing dishes or ironing, when no one's around. Mostly deep inside, when I can hardly breathe."

"I'm here for you," Ted assured her.

"You go in and see your father now, just the two of you. He'll take comfort from you. I want to go back upstairs to sit with Marguerite when Marie-Anne has to leave. I'll tell her to look in on you before she goes. In a while you take Lucien for a walk, and I'll make supper. Everything's moved up an hour, so we can get to the wake on time. Leave Tobi outside for a bit; focus on your father."

Ted reached for me and carried me outdoors. He set me on the transom beside Rex who was lying there very sad too, and he said to me, "You stay here for now, Tobi. I'll be back," and then he returned into the house.

I whined to him as he disappeared. I wanted to be with him. Cuddling quietly on his lap the way I always used to do had been one of my cherished memories sustaining me. With that memory I could feel Ted's touch all the time he was away. With a sigh I buried my face in my paws, and stayed there.

It was late afternoon when Ted came out again. He picked me up and carried me to one of the heavy wooden chairs on the front lawn, where I curled up on his lap while he stroked me slowly and softly, as he stared down at the lake for a long time. I pushed my nose into the snug crevice between his arm and his body to feel his closeness. I was so happy, so content to be with him again. I always knew that he'd come back for me, even as I suffered the wait, and even as I feared sometimes he might not.

My peacefulness was interrupted when Lucien appeared, saying, "I'm ready, Uncle Ted." Ted set me down and walked with Lucien towards the back pasture. Rex rose to his feet and followed them, and I followed Rex. The four of us climbed the hill to where Lucien always stopped to catch his breath and look out at the view on his way to get the cows, as his father did, and as Ted said he'd also done before them when he was a boy.

As they sat gazing out, Ted broke the silence. "How are you doing, Lucien?" he asked his nephew.

Lucien didn't say anything, so Ted ventured again, "Lucien, are you ok?"

"I don't know," he mumbled. "My mind's a jumble. Everything's going to be different."

"Very different not having your dad," Ted acknowledged, "but you're still surrounded by a family who loves you. We're all here for you."

"It's as if I suddenly have to make a lot of decisions."

"Really? Like what?"

"What I'm going to do with my life."

"Yes, maybe," Ted replied. "But right now all you have to worry about is doing the best you can getting through high school. A lot of your questions are going to answer themselves by how you handle the next four years—and the four after that when hopefully you'll choose to go to college." Ted paused to let that sink in; then he said very seriously, "In all that regards your education, I'll stand in for your father and make sure you have every opportunity you merit. You do your part, you study hard and help your grandfather the best you can, and I'll do my part." Ted extended his hand, "Shake on it?"

Lucien looked at him for reassurance, and shook Ted's hand. As they did so, Ted said, "I intend to do the same for Marguerite." Then with a smile and a cuff to Lucien's shoulder, he said, "Ok, let's get up the mountain." The four of us continued along the path to fetch the cows, through the maple orchard, and on up to the clearing. Lucien admired Ted; he was glad of this opportunity to be with him. That Uncle Ted went with him to get the cows that day was the height of the unexpected!

Ted said to Lucien, "I remember how, when he was a little boy, your dad always wanted to fetch the cows with me. We'd climb the mountain just like this; I'd be holding his hand because he was so little. What favorite things do you remember?"

"I remember times when he took us ice-skating, and to the beach swimming.... I remember when he took us places like the Granby Zoo.... I remember when we'd lie on our backs on the lawn with him to watch the stars in the sky...."

"Think about those things a lot," Ted said to him, "so they'll stay in your mind. Keep him alive that way, because he loved you very much."

They conversed all the way up the mountain and back down again.

Ted left me in the mudroom every time he went back into the house. After supper when Dad and Lucien went to the barn for milking, Ted accompanied them to help, and Rex and I followed them, as usual. Mom had given Ted a set of his father's barn clothes to wear. Ted talked mostly with Dad, and they shared memories until Dad started crying again. After the chores were finished, Dad made an excuse to check something in the back pasture so as to take a walk in the twilight alone by himself, while Ted returned with Lucien to the house.

"Where's your father?" Mom asked Ted.

"Just taking a little walk in the back."

"I hope he doesn't take too long. We have to get ready for the wake. Lucien, you go change into your good clothes."

I sat by the kitchen door where I watched Ted. I wanted him to take me on his lap, so I scratched the screen and whined. It worked, and Ted took me inside.

"Has Marguerite come out of her room at all?" he asked Mom.

"I brought her up some supper. I'm letting her be. She's getting ready to go to the wake. It's hard for her to see him laid out like that."

"Mom, this afternoon while I was in with Dad, I sensed there's something else wrong besides grief. He couldn't have gotten so thin and drawn in just two days."

"Yes, that's weighing on him, too; it scares him losing Robert. He's been feeling weak lately. One day he was fine, the next he could hardly lift his arm. He has to stop in the middle of walking up stairs."

"Has he been to a doctor?"

"He just went. He's anemic; he's getting iron shots."

"Do they help?"

"Not much. He has better days and worse days. It came on so suddenly, but now I see the signs were there."

"The weakness?"

"Yes, he'd tell me he was feeling old, that it was getting harder to do things. I agreed, we are getting old."

Dad came in then, and I went back into the mudroom with Rex. A short while later everyone came out dressed in Sunday best. Mom and Dad and Lucien and Marguerite left in Dad's car, and Mémère came downstairs and left with Ted in his. Much later they drove back in. They entered the house quietly. However, I didn't stay with poor, sad Rex in the mudroom that night; Ted carried me to his room with him when he went to bed. And I showed him how happy I was by licking and licking him until he said, "Enough!"

In the morning after breakfast Ted set me down in the mudroom again, and I went outside with Rex. Soon Marie-Anne with Ross and Errol and Angus arrived, and Bruce and Malcolm right behind them in a second car, all dressed in their Sunday best. Not long afterwards Dad and Mom and Ted, with Lucien and Marguerite, came outside with them, dressed in best clothes, too. Mémère came down her back stairs and joined them. Ted bent down and tickled me behind my ear as he walked by me. They all got into their cars and drove down the driveway.

Rex walked slowly in the sunshine to the corner of the front lawn where the driveway meets the street, and lay in the shade under the big maple tree where I used to wait for Ted. When everyone was gone, I joined him there. I felt pretty good this morning, but it was obvious that Rex did not. I could feel his sadness. It was as if we'd traded places. He lay facing the lake, and so I set myself down beside him, close enough to feel his heartbeat, to comfort him.

In a while a parade of cars came up the street and drove by very slowly, all following a long black car that led them past us to the "new cemetery" located beside the lake, not far beyond Aunt Florence's and Uncle Félix's and Mrs. Greer's houses. Rex and I sat attentively on the corner of the lawn watching, our eyes following them all the way to where they stopped just before the bend in the road. We saw them file in among the monuments and stand together in the morning sunshine. When they returned to their cars, many of them drove back towards us, came up our driveway, and parked wherever they could in the yard. They went into the house with Dad and Mom and Ted, and with Marie-Anne and her family, where we could hear them speaking in muted voices.

Some time later as people were leaving, Ted and Dad and Ross came outside. Ted picked me up, and the three of them went to sit in the chairs on the front lawn. I nestled on Ted's lap as he stroked my head gently.

After a silence, Dad spoke first. "I've looked down on this view of the lake so many times. It always made me feel lucky to buy this farm. I don't know if I'll be able to look down there anymore, now that all I see is where I lost my boy."

Dad buried his face in his hands. Ted and Ross looked at each other, then at Dad, both at a loss until he raised his head.

Dad said, "I never used to mow the steep bottom, but he insisted on doing it, so it'd look nicer without the brush. 'See, Dad,' he said to me, when he showed me how he drove on the side of a hill, 'See how I lean out on the high side of the tractor. I balance it with my weight, and I'm in a position to jump off if I have to.' He thought he could counterbalance that heavy machinery! I said to him, 'I don't like it, taking chances like that. And I don't want you to wreck my tractor either if you roll it down the hill.' Can you imagine? I said I was worried about the tractor!

"He wanted it all to look nice after haying. He cut it every year after I started letting him mow. It did look better, not having brush growing up in front of the lake, so I didn't stop him. I didn't realize enough what a gamble it was . . . I should've . . . I should've."

Dad went quiet and took out his handkerchief to wipe his eyes. Ted and Ross didn't say anything for a while. Ted stroked me very gently, but automatically, like he was far away. He was watching Dad, and I could feel Ted's distress through his hands. I nestled closer in his lap to comfort him, as I had earlier beside Rex, who was lying now not far from us, not paying us any attention.

"Dad," Ross' voice broke the silence, "I've told Ted I have an idea now that you're alone."

Dad looked up at him, challengingly as if it might be something he didn't want to hear.

"You need someone here to help you, to do what Robert would have done, so I'll come with my boys and help you finish up the fall. Lucien's young, but you can get through the winter with him when it's just the barn chores."

"Lucien isn't interested in farming," Dad said to Ross, "no more than Ted here was; and I have to respect that. He'll leave, too, after high school," he said looking at Ted. "I can get by, but why bother? What reason? Four years, with neither his heart nor mine in it? No, I'll sell the place. I'll retire on the seventeen acres I have at the top of the lake." He gestured towards the hill below, "I won't have to see that in my view."

Ross took the opening. "I'll buy the farm from you when you're ready."

Dad looked up at him surprised.

"Give it some thought—when you're ready," Ross said to him. "I have four sons. They're your grandsons—even if they don't speak French."

That made Ted chuckle, "Well, they understand it when we speak it. That counts for something."

Ross continued, "They're all farmers. I could settle one of them here." He paused for a moment to let his idea sink in. "Bruce has one more year of agricultural college; Malcolm has three. I'll help you get through the spring with Errol; then when Bruce finishes, end of May, he can come here and work with you."

Dad looked at Ross. "Yes, they're my grandsons, and I love them all four. I'm proud the way you've raised them with Marie-Anne. They're stalwart boys." He gave an emerging smile to this Scotsman his daughter had brought into the family, who'd always been "different" to him. Having a second son had once saved him; now his farm's destiny could be restored with these competent grandsons. His face relaxed; Ross' purpose became his own.

I felt Ted's hand pause on my back; I felt his anticipation, and an uptick in his heart. I felt him watching his father, and I felt through Ted's hand the relief he felt when Dad said, "Yes, that's a good idea, Ross, and I'll be grateful for your help."

10. MEMERE

Although Ted left me outside much of the time, he took me upstairs with him to his room the following two nights. In the morning he carried me to the kitchen, gave me my breakfast, and then let me go out with Rex. He took me back into the kitchen each time he fed me, but our time together, with him holding me, was mostly outdoors. So there was nothing unusual the third morning when he set me down and walked back inside. I knew he'd be back for me shortly.

In a while Ted came out the door carrying his travel bags and put them into the car. That made me so happy. I jumped and danced as I followed him back and forth across the yard. When he finished, he sat on a lawn chair with me on his lap, and stroked me, talking to me softly, telling me how much he missed me, and what a perfect little dog I was. His slow, warm touch gently penetrated me and spread a quiet calmness in me; and I quivered occasionally, too, bathing in the familiar immediacy of our mutual love.

When Dad and Lucien came back to the house after chores, Ted set me down and followed them inside. I went to lie by Rex on the transom. I was so excited, so eager; I watched and listened with total attention for the moment Ted would appear again at the door. The sight of those bags being placed in the car signaled that we were about to be on our way, back to New York, back to our apartment and life together, back to my fleece bed under the bookcase.

Time crawled as I waited, but Ted finally came out, with the family behind him to see him off. He was carrying a last small travel bag. I hopped happily beside him as we crossed the yard to where the car was parked. I was so delighted, so raring to go. Ted got into the car and closed the door with the window down, leaving me standing on the ground waiting, as the family spoke their good-byes.

When he started up the motor I realized that he was leaving me. Desperately I ran up to the car and jumped against the door, and I barked, "Take me, take me, take me."

"You'd better pick Tobi up," Ted said to Lucien. "I don't want him to fall under the car." Lucien picked me up, and I struggled hard in his arms. He held me close to Ted who said to me in a commanding voice, "Now you be good, Tobi. You be happy here, and safe. I'll be back. You be good and wait for me; I'll be back."

As Ted reversed the car to turn it towards the driveway, he waved good-bye to Mémère who was watching him leave from up on her back porch, and she waved back.

Mom said to him, "Call us when you get home," and Dad, his lip quivering like he was about to cry again, said, "Be careful on the road."

As Ted drove down the driveway, I struggled out of Lucien's arms, fell hard to the ground, picked myself up, and ran after the car, barking as loudly as I could, "Take me, take me, take me."

Ted's car sped down the street, as from the end of the driveway I watched it disappear. My heart broke then and there. Standing by the corner of the lawn where I'd maintained my vigil for so long, I wept with yaps and howls and intervals of whining. Lucien said, "I've never heard him make sounds like that. It's almost as if he's crying." I was crying.

The family left me there. Even Rex didn't come close right away but respected my space. I cried because I understood for the first time that Ted wanted me to live on the farm, that I'd probably never get back to my bed under the bookcase. For some reason I wasn't part of Ted's life anymore in New York City. He'd put me here with people who liked me okay, but no one loved me, and I didn't love any of them, either.

I stayed there most of the day facing the street, lying with my head on my paws in a dull cloud of depression, beset with choking and sniffling and whining whenever the stinging rose again inside me.

It was at one such moment I sensed someone standing over me. I didn't care; I just cried. A big hand reached under my belly and lifted me up. It was Mémère. She carried me to a lawn chair and set me on her lap. I was apprehensive at first; but when she began stroking me softly and her voice was kind, I relaxed.

"Poor Tobi. You're heart is broken, I know... I know.... When Teddy left today, he felt so bad to leave you. Each time after he drives off, I wait and hope just like you. At my age there's always a chance I won't see him again." She sat there for a while holding me. Then she carried me upstairs to her home, where she took me onto her lap again in her chair by the window, rocking slowly.

When I was on the verge of falling asleep, her voice softly roused me.

"I live between the two cemeteries," she said. "One with the beginning of my life; one with the ending."

I looked up; she was staring out the window. I didn't know if she was speaking to me.

"My parents' graves that I can see from this window, buried beside my two drowned brothers . . . alongside my brother Polidor . . . what a sad day when he broke his neck playing in the haymow . . . .

"My sweet, darling daughter Henriette, nobody dies of appendicitis anymore. I can see your headstone from here everyday.

"How terribly sad funerals are when the young die! How sad, as the passing years leave them behind.

"Me, I'll be in the beautiful new cemetery that overlooks the lake, next to my husband, not far from Robert and his cousin Philbert who went before him. Eternal rest give us, Lord."

Mémère sighed. "It's a lot of grass to mow, Tobi. Who'll put the flowers when I'm gone?

"Who'll remember my mother grieving all night for Napoléon and Philippe on the lakeshore? Who'll remember that Polidor is an unlucky name?"

We stayed like that, Mémère gazing out the window, and I on her lap lulled in and out of sleep as she stroked me, until the cessation of her hand on me indicated she was dozing, too.

Some days later Rex and I accompanied Mémère when she pushed a lawn mower down the street to cut the grass on her parents' and brothers' gravesite, and then on Henriette's. We returned there again with her when she put pots of geraniums in front of the monuments, and each time when she went to pour water into them. She did it alone, except for us two dogs. We went with her when she walked to the new cemetery, too. She didn't push the lawn mower there, but she brought flowers she placed beside those left by other family members.

I'd been prohibited from going into the house by Dad, and I guess everyone respected that. I found out, everyone except the one person whom Dad never contradicted. When Mémère crossed the yard and was approaching her back stairs with me right behind her hoping she had a morsel wrapped in paper in her apron pocket for me, she frequently reached down and picked me up, and carried me up into her kitchen, where she sat in her rocking chair with me on her lap. It was very comforting. She didn't let me run around her rooms much, though; she always held me. I was "Teddy's dog," and "Teddy's Tobi." I could feel love in her big farmer fingers when she tickled me behind my ears; it was her love for Ted.

I'd be on Mémère's lap while she made things by the window. She was always working on something, either a long braid of rags she'd sew afterwards together to create a flat, "braided rug," or narrow rag strips she'd hook through a burlap bag for "a hooked rug;" or she'd be crocheting "an afghan," a throw for someone's sofa, or knitting a pair of mittens or socks for the winter with yarn she'd spun on her spinning wheel. These endeavors made my perch on her lap precarious at times, and I'd panic when I started sliding off. One day she sewed the rag braid into a very small rug, just big enough for me; and when it was finished, she set it on the floor to see that it lay flat, and then she put me down on it by her. I understood that it was my little rug, my place to stay when she had me visiting her and too much was going on in her lap.

The fact is the farm was an interesting place, far more than being locked in a cage in a dog-boarding facility in New York City would have been, as had happened to me once. On the farm I had lots of friends with whom to interact. There was Rex first of all, and his nap buddy Nanook. There were Lucien and Marguerite who sometimes held me on their laps. There was Mom who fed me when Lucien didn't. Mostly there was Mémère, who took me in more and more.

My time with Mémère developed into a routine. In the morning I'd wait for her to come down her back stairs on her way to feed the chickens. I'd follow her to the edge of the chicken yard, no farther for fear of Le Coq. When she finished, and returned with her bucket of eggs, I'd follow her to the mudroom door where she handed the eggs over to Mom. Then she'd pick me up again and carry me up her back stairs to her kitchen. I waited on the braided rug by her rocking chair while she made her breakfast, hoping she'd give me some. There usually was a piece of bacon she broke up for me, a little scrambled egg, and some cereal in milk. Then, after she'd washed her dishes, she'd take me on her lap in her rocking chair for a while more. Finally, she'd get up, saying to me, "We have work to do." She'd carry me back downstairs and set me by the transom with Rex if he was there. I'd cross the driveway to do my business in the longer grass by the lilac bushes where Rex mostly did his, and then I'd follow him to the neighbors to see what they'd set out for us. I wasn't very hungry any more though, so Rex basically ate it all.

Back at the farm Mémère would pick me up again when she crossed the yard and carry me to her apartment. Lucien often came up the interior stairs to her kitchen and sat in the chair facing her rocker; he'd ask questions about her family years ago, and they'd talk, with me on her lap. When she put me down, I was happy to stay on my little rug at the base of the window by her chair. I spent many days like that. It suited me better than pining on the lawn. I liked being indoors, being with people.

I spent my nights with Rex, though. When it was time for evening chores and Dad and Lucien went to the barn to milk the cows, Mémère went to see to her chickens at about the same time, and she'd set me down at the bottom of her back stairs. I'd hurry to the mudroom where I joined Rex to wait for the table scraps that were our supper. Then we both went into the barn and waited with the cats for our dish of warm milk. When Dad and Lucien were finished, Rex and I followed them to the mudroom. There, when the men had changed their clothes and had gone through the door to the kitchen, Rex and I settled on our beds and went to sleep—for a while.

11. CHASING DEER

Sometimes a dog would begin to bark up on the hill a few hours after darkness fell, not a lot of noise, but a few yaps from the edge of the woods, then a pause, and then a few more barks, as if the dog were calling out. Rex would get up from his bed, stretch, and go out into the night. When he disappeared into the darkness, the barking stopped. Glad for the quiet, I'd simply fall back asleep. I've always enjoyed my bedtime. Evenings in New York I'd sit on the sofa watching TV with Ted, but when I knew it was time for bed I'd look up at him as if to apologize for leaving him, and then I'd jump down and walk off to our bedroom, go into my house in the base of the bookcase and fall asleep for the night on my fleece. My bed in the mudroom was just a folded blanket on the floor, but I enjoyed my sleep there through the night nonetheless.

In the early morning just before daylight, Rex would return, his legs muddied, panting as if he'd had a good run; and he'd collapse on his bed and fall asleep, too, until Lucien came through the door and called him to follow him to get the cows. Those mornings Rex always seemed a little reluctant to have to go up the mountain. Instead of running ahead with his usual exuberance, he followed head down behind Lucien.

"It's not my fault if you're tired out," Lucien would say to him. "Let's go."

The dog barking at the edge of the woods and Rex's consequent nighttime venture occurred several times, usually when there was a moon that lit the barnyard all the way to the woodland. Somehow I sensed it was not a visit to the Indians' dogs. He had invited me to follow him that time, but he wasn't inviting me now. What was happening on the hill by the woods? Rex certainly never hesitated. While I ignored it at first, my curiosity grew.

I didn't need an invitation. I was becoming enough of a farm dog, and fearless enough, to find out what was going on. So one night at the height of summer I followed him out into the moonlit night and up the hill towards the woods where he greeted a dog from over the hill. Both ignored me so I held back, but when they trotted into the woods I trotted behind them. We followed the path through the maple orchard and crossed the fence above the little field with the sugar house. There Rex's companion gave a few barks again, and in a short time out of the silence one dog and then another appeared. When all four had greeted touching noses, and they decided to greet me, too, we followed Rex and the lead female who'd called us up the hill.

Our pack traveled quickly along the cow paths that traversed the mountain side, taking us ever higher. Sometimes the female led us off those paths and across brush and branches littered about an open, cut area in the woods; and that's when I had a hard time keeping up, trying as I might to navigate through the debris that the bigger dogs simply leaped over. That's when I first began to feel anxious. I mustn't fall behind, because if I lost the other dogs, I'd have no idea where I was. Finally we reached the edge of a high clearing dotted with a few evergreens, not Dad's clearing where we got the cows, but one some distance beyond it. The female hesitated, tested the wind, and led us past a farmer's cows bedded down for the night, to the far side where several deer were browsing. We approached them slowly. As she got closer the female lead dog crouched to a stalk, belly almost to the ground. The other dogs followed suit, so I did, too.

We were going for the deer, and I felt an ancient knowledge possess me. It was as if I knew how to do this, and that I had done it many times before. I waited with the others for the female dog's signal. The deer sensed something was about; they stopped eating and looked out anxiously into the moonlight towards the clearing from which we were advancing. Their nervousness mounted; they were ready to run.

The female dog, almost upon the deer, suddenly leaped out at them; and the other dogs and I leaped with her, with no barking. It all happened in one grand motion, our leap at the deer and their leap away from us. The fleeing deer dashed headlong through the spaces between the trees, with fantastic leaps leading us through thicker and thicker underbrush, while we dogs burrowed through, jumping, too, over logs and around piles of branches. It was heady, it was fun! We were doing what we knew so naturally how to do as a pack, the ultimate survival sport.

As the going got harder, and the deer led us through ever denser undergrowth at breakneck speed, zigging and zagging, moving targets that the lead dogs could never quite reach, I banged into obstacles I could barely see, fallen tree trunks, branches, bushes, and even fell into a hole. I caught my leg, and it hurt then with every footfall. The pack was getting farther ahead of me, and I began to desperately fear losing them. The exuberance of the chase gave way to panic. I was being left behind. I tried to run faster; so I crashed into things all the more. The taller dogs were capable of this course and used to it. I had neither the size nor the experience, and bruised and hurting, soon reached the end of my endurance.

Just when exhausted I had no choice but to give up, totally bewildered, in shock with fear, a light flashed on in the distance. There was a quick succession of gunshots, a dog screamed out, followed by deep silence. I trembled, looked around me to run away, but there was no away except the surrounding darkness. I could choose to be lost alone in the woods at night, or I could proceed carefully towards the light that invited like a beacon through the trees. I could hear men's voices. There were people there, and people meant protection.

At the flickering periphery of lantern light, I came upon the female dog lying on her side on the ground with her head stretched back, her mouth opened wide, laboring to breathe. The other dogs and the deer herd were gone. There was no sound except the occasional breeze in the branches and the soft speech of the two men who were cutting up a deer carcass. I hesitated, frightened now by the harm the female had come to. Swayed by caution, I lay down quietly in the shadows by her, and watched the men until they wound a rope around the deer's neck and dragged it away. Their light disappeared with them, a vanishing glow beyond the trees, and darkness filled the vacuum. The woodland shapes surrounding us were only barely discernible now by occasional, dim moonlight.

I continued to wait near the female. Twice she emitted a soft whine, more like a moan, not directed to me. I whined back to let her know I was there, but received no response. I was drawn to move closer to her to comfort and warm her, but my stronger instinct did not allow me to presume that intimacy with this leader I'd barely met. I waited. Maybe she would rise up out of her agony, and we could get out of this woods together. Eventually instead, with a final whine and a sigh, the sound of her breathing stopped. Troubled by her silence, I took the few steps and nudged her with my nose; there was nothing there.

I looked around me, trying to see through the darkness. Palpably, like something touching me, like the damp dew and the chilly night air, my solitude enveloped me. There was no help left. I was alone, totally on my own, with no recourse. I was almost blind in the blackness, and I didn't know where to go anyway. Totally overwhelmed, I stood in place whining.

When the moon appeared from behind a cloud, I was able to make out the terrain somewhat. I started to walk, stepping into the surrounding trees simply to make an effort, to head somewhere whatever the direction; but doing so immersed me in darkness again as the shadows obscured that bit of light. So I simply lay down where I was. I couldn't see what to do, so I did nothing. I would wait for daylight.

I dozed off. I don't know how long I'd been asleep when I jerked awake at the sound of slow, padded footsteps approaching. A large head, followed by a much larger black body, like a silhouette came out from behind the trees. The bear walked over to where the deer had lain, and it began to eat remnants that still littered the ground.

I barked at the bear. It's what I do reflexively when I sense an intruder. He looked at me, then resumed scavenging. I barked again, and that was a mistake. He lumbered at me. With the sound of his steps crashing on the leaves, pursuing me, I ran as fast as I could headlong into the brush. The steps stopped, but I didn't. I knew I'd better get some distance away so the bear couldn't find me. My eyesight close-up has never been good, so now in the darkness it was almost impossible. I walked into objects, tripped over things, managed to circle around other obstacles, until I'd no idea whatsoever in what direction I was going or from what direction I'd come.

A break in the canopy admitted some moonlight to the woodland floor. I felt moss beneath my feet and decided to lie upon it at the base of a tree and wait for dawn. My legs felt weak, and my body sore from all the scratching branches. I hurt where one had poked my face near my eye, so tears blurred my vision further. I didn't dare sleep. I waited for dawn, and endlessly dawn didn't come, but only measureless, dark, cold, night hours to endure. As I lay there the temperature dropped further, and dew coated me as it did everything else. Growing wetter and colder, I shook myself from time to time and tried to curl tighter on myself.

Occasional light pierced through a break in the tree canopy above me whenever the moon reappeared from behind the fast-moving clouds, but it couldn't penetrate the shadows that danced in the intermittent breezes as if they were alive, or between gusts stood motionless, eerily still. Somewhere in the dark an owl hooted, and then closer some moments later a sudden squeaking was cut short. In the distance a whippoorwill hardly broke the silence, calling faintly, and calling again, and again.

My heart stopped when I heard heavy footfalls on the dry leaves beneath trees that stood beyond a cluster of bushes. I feared it was the bear I'd fled, looking for me now. When the plodding crunching paused, I crouched motionless, but for my trembling, totally alert to flee, until the steps slowly resumed and continued away.

My sense of relief was short-lived. Soon I heard a lighter pitter-patter upon the leaves, the sounds of a nervous animal moving about, and I sensed the fox there somewhere. I'd no idea what to do, so I just shivered and waited, listening. The pitter-patter came closer. I held myself very still. Suddenly the fox leaped at me; but my reflexes have always been quick, too, and I jumped to the side just as fast, enough that he overshot me. He turned in an instant to grab me, but that moment gave me time to face him. It was do or die; so barking fiercely, I attacked him. I may be the size of a small rabbit, but I am a dog nevertheless. And I guess the fox was afraid of dogs, because he turned on himself and ran. I chased him a few yards, barking and snarling as viciously as I could for good measure, and he was gone.

I lay back on the moss trembling. That had been a very close call, and my body felt so tense it hurt. Slowly, ever so slowly, I calmed down as I continued to listen to the disembodied night sounds. I was very tired, but didn't dare fall asleep. I stayed alert, head up, looking about me into the dark, or when moonlight shone through, into the shadows. I could hear things, little animals scurrying about, but I couldn't see any of them. I listened and listened. My sharp ears had saved me from the fox; they were all I could count on to save me again.

The longest night of my life dragged on. I remained awake the whole time. I thought about my cozy little bed beneath the bookcase in New York, and my warm fleece in it. The moss was almost as soft, but it was soaked. Lying in the dew on it , I was drenched and shivering.

No more bears came by and no more foxes sniffed about during the ensuing hours. I must finally have dozed a bit, as my chin rested on my forelegs, because I opened my eyes to a new sound in the faintest light of dawn, just enough for me to see shadows moving now cautiously, quietly, hesitatingly, through the trees.

Like phantoms they appeared, progressing slowly, grazing on the few clumps of grasses they found, but mostly browsing on the leaves of low-hung branches and seedlings they preferred. Regularly each would raise its head to look about, so that of the half-dozen deer that finally came out of the mist, there was always one surveying the woods through which they moved.

There were two does, gentle, cautious, and then two yearlings with sprouting antlers. One of the does was followed closely by two fawns, one spotted with white, one natural tan. Last to appear was a tall pure-white buck, whose color stood out in the woodland. He looked carefully about, and his attention fixed for a moment in the direction where I lay. I remained perfectly still, so I'm not sure he saw me right then.

At our house on Long Island where the deer are tame and come walking down the boardwalk, I usually bark. If I surprise them they jump away a few feet then stare back at me interested. Once when I wasn't yet a year old, a doe standing in the grasses to the side of the walk approached me with curiosity. Carefully she and I touched noses, and that was my first deer-kiss.

Under my circumstances in the woods that morning, though, I didn't bark. My heart welcomed these familiar, regal creatures, and I stayed quiet as they approached. I could sense that they were much more fearful than those at the seashore, and could leap away in a moment. I didn't want that to happen. I felt no instinct to chase now; rather a calmness came over me in their gentle presence. The white buck approached closer, and he looked at me. I looked back and didn't stir. The does were moving on, and he turned to accompany them. I rose to my feet, hurting, and quietly followed them all. They traveled very slowly; so I'd lie down and wait, then resume at a distance behind them. I had no other means to know where to go; trailing them gave me my only direction through the woodland.

The deer continued their slow journey browsing until morning sunlight grew brighter through the trees, and all the dew had dissipated. Then one after the other they lay down in the undergrowth to rest. The white buck did, as well, but he remained vigilant. He looked in my direction occasionally as if to check whether I was approaching, because he knew I was following. I kept my distance; I didn't want the deer to run away and leave me lost alone again. They rested through the height of the day, then in mid-afternoon rose and continued their browsing, and I rose and continued to follow them. I grew used to their company that night and early day with them, and I guess they grew a bit used to me, because they stopped looking up so often in my direction to scan for me.

12. MAURICE AND ARTHUR

It was not long after they rested that the deer crossed another brook, one whose bed glistened with marble-like quartz rocks, and they came to a small clearing. They stopped and looked out into it, where a cow and a horse were grazing. Beyond, at the lower end of the field was a small two-storied house of weathered brown shingles with a steep, tarpaper roof. Closer to the woods' edge stood a large weather-worn grey barn. Between the two a driveway dropped off steeply from the edge of a tiny lawn and disappeared downwards into the woods. At that corner and just at the dip, a small apple tree afforded the front lawn its only shade. On the gable side of the house, however, a tall, broad crab apple tree towered higher than the point of the roof. It was flanked by a large vegetable garden where a small, slight man was working, moving about awkwardly.

The deer walked out into the clearing and began to nibble low bushes here and there in the company of the horse and the cow who were grazing on the grasses. The man in the garden looked up and out at them, but then continued his work. The deer appeared accustomed to the place, and they paid him no heed, either. Only the white buck held back by the edge of the trees, where he browsed on seedlings sprouting just inside the small green field.

I felt relieved to be out of the trackless woods and back in the realm of people again. I still didn't know where I was, but here was a house and a person; and that meant to me a place where I probably could get something to eat and be able to rest without having to worry about a fox jumping on me.

I started across the field towards the house and the man in the garden. The cow looked up at me as I passed by her, watched my progress across the field, then went back to grazing. When I reached the garden, I cautiously went up to the elderly man who was bent over hoeing there. I stood looking at him, but it was a moment before he saw me. When he did, he jumped, startled. Then he looked at me as if he were examining me, cocking his head without saying a word. His expression changed several times, from serious to smiling to serious. Then standing there, leaning on his hoe to steady himself, without taking his eyes off me, he called out, "Maurice! Maurice! *Viens vite!* [Come quickly!] Maurice, *viens vite!*"

A voice from around the house called back, "What's wrong?"

"There's an animal in the garden!" the one staring at me called out.

A second elderly man, but this one tall and broad-shouldered, came around the corner of the house, brandishing in his hand a scythe, ready to clobber me. I stood beyond his reach, and ran farther back each time he stepped toward me. The two men stared across the garden rows at me.

"What is it?" the first asked.

Maurice looked at me like he wasn't sure. Then he said, "Arthur, I think it's a dog." He went down on one knee and extended his hand to coax me towards him. An extended hand has always began a danger signal to me, so I barked at the man. "Yes, it barks. It's a dog."

"But it's smaller than a cat," Arthur objected.

"It's a dog." Maurice moved at me and waved his arm to chase me away. I ran to the edge of the garden where I stopped, because I really had no where to go—certainly not back into the woods. Maurice turned and disappeared around the house, returning to cutting hay with the scythe.

Arthur looked at me, and I looked back at him. Finally, he set down his hoe and went into the house. I waited. In a moment he came out with a dish of water which he set on the flat stone slab in front of the door. He went back in and came out with another dish with a big slice of bread in it, and he set it down beside the water. Careful not to alarm me further, he circled back to the garden and resumed his work, pretending not to pay any more attention to me.

I wasn't thirsty because I'd drunk in the brooks I crossed with the deer. However, I was hungry, and the pattern of two dishes, one with water and one with food was familiar to me. Keeping my eyes on Arthur, I circled in turn and made my way to the bread. It was a big, solid piece with a rough crust, but I pulled it out of the dish and, lying on the warm, sun-heated stone, I grasped it with my forepaws and gnawed at it, all the while keeping my eyes on Arthur toiling in his garden.

I found Arthur's way of walking unusual. It was not like other people moved, but with swinging movements. He always seemed out of balance, as if he were about to fall over forwards. Nevertheless, with the help of his hoe as a cane when he needed it, he navigated successfully, and the little piles of weeds he was creating as he moved down the rows grew bigger and more numerous.

It had been midafternoon when I came out of the woods with the deer, and it didn't seem long before the sun descended in the sky. Arthur went into a woodshed towards the rear of the house and came out with a small wagon which he left by the edge of the garden. When he approached me where I still lay by the doorway, I jumped out of the way, then waited and watched him pass into the house. I heard him pump water into the sink and the sounds of his washing his hands. Then I heard the clanking of dishes and pots and pans and smelled the aromas of food being prepared that wafted through the screen door.

Maurice eventually appeared from around the house. He carried his scythe into the woodshed, came back out without it, and walked over to the garden where he filled the waiting wagon with the piles of weeds that Arthur had created along the rows. Maurice hauled the load to the woods' edge where he dumped it into a shallow gully, and then returned the wagon to the woodshed.

I jumped aside when Maurice came towards me to enter the house, as I had for Arthur, and he paid me no attention, either. Through the door I could see him wash at the sink. While Arthur continued preparing supper, the odor of tobacco smoke filled the house.

Supper smelled good, and I waited outside for some. The stone slab at the doorway still retained warmth the afternoon sun had infused into it. I was comfortable. I felt good with that slice of bread in me, but I was hungry for more food, especially considering what I was smelling. Maurice and Arthur left me waiting out there, however, while they ate their supper at the table just inside the door. It began to grow dark around me. I could smell the kerosene when Maurice lit two lamps inside the house, one on the table, and one on the opposite window sill.

They were ignoring me. I was hungry, and with on-coming darkness tiny mosquitoes and moths began to bother me. I looked in at the light, and I scratched my front paw on the screen door to get their attention. They looked up, but still made no move towards me. So I went at it with both paws as long as I could before I had to drop back to the ground to regain my balance. My claws on the screen made a very insistent noise.

"He's going to make a hole in the screen," Maurice said alarmed, as he moved quickly from the far side of the table towards me.

Arthur who was closer to the door stood up in his way. Turning his head from side to side with an amused smile, he asked me, *"Tu veux entrer, Petit Chien?"* [*You want to come in, Little Dog?* which he pronounced *P'tsee Shee-en*]?"

Before Maurice could object, Arthur opened the door, and I scampered inside. I stood at Arthur's feet looking up at him, wagging my tail, with my best smile. He smiled back down at me with quiet laugh.

Maurice walked back to his rocking chair at the far end of the small kitchen. "What are you going to do with that dog in here?" he asked Arthur who was steadying himself against the countertop while he reached for two dishes from the cupboard over the sink.

"I'm going to give him some food." A moment later, with his dragging walk, he'd done just that. In the corner, just past the sink near the side wall, he set down the two dishes, one after the other. Into one he'd poured water from the pump at the sink. Into the other he'd scooped some of the chicken stew I'd been smelling through the screen door. I was so hungry, and it tasted so good, I wolfed it down.

Arthur sat in his chair by the door and watched me, looking amused. "He's hungry," he said, and he laughed his quiet laugh again.

When I finished I lay down on the floor by the two dishes, resting my head on my front paws and looking back up at Arthur. Lying down and waiting is always a good time filler.

"What're you going to do with him now?" Maurice asked Arthur.

"I don't know," Arthur said still looking amused at me.

"You can't leave him in here at night when we go to bed. He'll mess on the floor."

"I guess he would," Arthur agreed. He rose to his feet, came over to me, and reached down. Normally I wouldn't let a stranger pick me up. However, he'd just fed me, this was his house, and right now he was all I had. So in a moment I was in his arms. In his dragging walk he headed with me for the door, then thought better of it and sat down in his chair with me on his lap. I stood there with my face very close to his as he patted me, and I surprised him when I began to lick his face. Arthur laughed, and turned his face away much as Ted does. So I licked his chin and neck, and he laughed some more. He said to me, "You make me laugh," just as Ted does.

I lay on his lap then, and he stroked me. I appreciated the cool, fresh air coming in through the screen door, because the room was filling with tobacco smoke from Maurice's pipe. When Arthur reached over to the table and picked up his own pipe and began smoking, too, the air grew very thick with smoke. It made me sneeze, and that made Arthur laugh, too.

Maurice went into the other room and came out carrying a large flat board. On it he had a partially completed jig-saw puzzle, and he set it on the table and pulled a chair up to it. Still holding me Arthur turned his chair towards the table, too, and began to fit the pieces on the puzzle with Maurice. Either hardly spoke. Perched on Arthur's lap I had a good view of their work. The puzzle was becoming a pretty picture of a big dog standing in front of a brick house. The dog's face was done, and his shoulders, along with much of the background, but most of him was still a gap on the board.

I looked up at all the pictures decorating the walls around the room. They all were completed jig-saw puzzles glued to boards, hung randomly, colorful against the drab, yellowing newsprint that papered the house's interior.

Maurice drew the table lamp closer. The flame flickered in the slight breeze coming through the doorway, and I amused myself watching the dancing shadows it created on the walls. The two men worked patiently, puffing on their pipes. Each would scatter the piles of pieces a bit, look at them, pick up a piece, hold it to the lantern light, then attempt to fit it to the picture. They were well-practiced, because the body of the dog, piece by piece, slowly appeared.

In a while Maurice and Arthur stopped, leaned back in their chairs, puffing on their pipes, and talked quietly about their plans for tomorrow, which weren't much different from what they'd been doing today. Maurice would go into the woods to fell a tree for winter's firewood, and Arthur would continue in his vegetable garden. Then Maurice took up the puzzle board and carried it back into the other room. Arthur picked me up from his lap, made his way to the doorway with me, opened the screen door, set me outside, then closed both the screen door and the solid door behind it. I heard the latch drop in place.

13. FIRST NIGHT AND DAYS

I'd not expected to be put out for the night. It wouldn't do. It was very dark except for the points of light that filled the sky. I knew there were foxes and whatever else out here. I barked to Arthur as loud as I could not to leave me outside. I barked and I barked, but the door stayed shut. I saw light move from the window by the door to the window by the stairs, and then appear in the window on the second floor of the house. I barked and I barked, but no one came for me. The light went out. The house was dark like the night all around me.

I absolutely didn't want to spend another night outdoors on the mountain. So I did what I could; I stood by the door and barked and barked, and scratched on the door with all my might. A long time passed that way, barking and scratching. I wouldn't let up, I was too frightened of the woods at night, and of the fox out there. My barking was growing hoarse, and the claws on my front paws were getting sensitive from scratching, but I outlasted Arthur.

The glow of a flashlight moved about the upper window. Then the light traveled from window to window, from upstairs to downstairs, and then to the door that opened. Arthur came out. He picked me up gently and carried me across the little lawn, and then across the driveway to the barn. In the darkness he pulled open a wide sliding door, dropped me inside, slid the door shut, and I heard his footsteps going back to the house. This is not what I wanted, either, so I barked some more.

I barked and barked at the door, until exhausted I couldn't bark anymore. The inside of the barn was pitch black; there was no light at all with which to see about me, but that seemed to make my ears and nose more acute. There was the musty odor of old hay upon which I stood. There was the denser, stale smell of re-breathed air, and the smell of horse and the smell of cow, reminiscent of the aroma of milk during chores, and the stink of manure. I could hear the source, the heavy breathing of the horse and cow going back to sleep. The odors oppressed me until I lay down by the door and stuck my nose through the crack under it to breathe fresh outside air, as if I'd liberate at least that little part of me.

The dark interior of the barn was not still. Like syncopation against the measured breaths of the horse and cow, I could hear things moving about, tiny things, mice scampering in the straw upon the floor, and a continual sound of wings in the air, bats hunting through the eaves, and then a great silence after the hoot of an owl penetrated from outdoors. While I listened I thought I heard very softly a slithering upon the straw that stopped. All the scampering sounds stopped, too, until suddenly there was the noise of a quick struggle and a moment of panicked squeaking until the sound went muffled. I dreaded what this predator was that grasped a mouse.

At the far end of the barn I could hear the occasional clucks of sleeping chickens atop their roosts. The scampering upon the straw stopped a second time when I sensed a newcomer in the barn. It moved in quick spurts, almost erratically. In the darkness, I heard the animal climb the roost, followed by a burst of complaining from a disturbed chicken, followed in the next moment by a cacophony of chickens clucking, and then squawking as they ran and flew about their pen in the dark. Something was after them. The ruckus didn't stop until the barn door slid open and Maurice stood there shining a flashlight on the chickens and on the weasel that was in the midst of devouring one of them on the floor.

"I thought it was you, *P'tit Chien*, after the chickens," Maurice said as he picked up a hoe and went after the weasel who was much too fast for him. The weasel escaped out of the pen right past Maurice and out the open door. I ran out the open door, too, straight for the house. I'd had enough of the barn.

At the house door I scratched desperately on it and barked some more for Arthur to open it and take me in. That's what he did, but he didn't comfort me; he held me tight—until Maurice came from the barn and said to him, "It wasn't him after the chickens; it was a weasel. He didn't even bark at it; he was no help at all."

"He's no match for a weasel," Arthur objected. Now his grasp on me grew more tender, as I trembled violently in his arms. "No use putting him back in the barn. He's too frightened. I'll keep him inside with me tonight."

"We'll see what happens," was Maurice's comment.

That's what I wanted, and that's what Arthur did. He took me into the house, finally, and by the light of his flashlight carried me up the steep stairs that ascended from a corner of the kitchen.

The second floor consisted of a single room where the two men had their beds, a few bureaus, and an armoire beneath the roof rafters. To make me a bed in the corner close to his, Arthur pulled a towel from a clothes line that crossed the room and set it upon a little carpet he pushed into the corner. I went to it, lay down and curled up, and Arthur went back to bed. A while later, Maurice came up, too, blew out the lamp on the bed stand, and returned to bed. I was safe at last.

The last thing Maurice said before falling asleep was, "I thought it was *P'tit Chien* going after the chickens."

"I did, too," Arthur said. And we three drifted towards sleep.

"We should've left him in the barn," Maurice added as an afterthought, "he might warn us next time when a weasel or a fox or a raccoon tries to get in."

"He didn't this time," Arthur answered him.

I hadn't barked at the weasel, because by then I was too terrified, pressed and trembling against the inside of the barn door, and I'd already barked myself hoarse.

"*P'tit Chien* doesn't want to be in the barn," Arthur said. "He's a strange dog; he wants to be in the house."

With that the conversation ended. It was not long before Maurice's breathing became a low, gentle snore, in chorus soon with smaller erratic toots and whistles that Arthur emitted. I fell asleep immersed in my relief to have found this way station, safe from another night out in the woods.

At sunup I awoke to Maurice's stirring, followed then by Arthur's. Despite the morning light pouring through the windows, I dozed a bit longer, until Arthur began rattling dishes downstairs, which I figured probably meant food. The stairway was very steep, so I stood at the top and barked down to him to come get me. He stood at the bottom, looked up me, cocking his head much like I do, smiled his wide grin up at me, and tried to coax me down. I wagged my tail to show him that's what I wanted, too, but that he was going to have to help me. I don't do stairs.

"*Viens-t'en, descends, P'tit Chien.* [Come on, come on down]," Arthur said.

I looked back at him, wagging my tail. Finally he understood that the only way it was going to happen was for him to ascend the stairs, pick me up, and carry me down. With his poor balance, he held me on his arm with one hand and supported himself by grabbing the banister with the other, and swung his body and me down by loosing his grip on the banister to grab it again lower. I feared the whole way we were going to fall, and I'd have jumped right off his arm if he'd not held me tight. We made it, and he set me down on the floor. First he let me run outside to do my business, and then without my scratching the door let me back in. I looked up at him eagerly, wagging my tail enthusiastically, for some of whatever he was making to eat that smelled so good.

I got a breakfast worthy of Ted's. Arthur had cooked cereal, which he set out for himself and Maurice on the table. Maurice came in from the barn with a basket of eggs, as well as a pail of milk which Arthur poured into large glass jars. One jar went on the table; the other later would be carried to the brook and immersed in the cold, flowing water. I got cereal in milk, and egg that morning.

Maurice went outside right after breakfast. Arthur tidied the kitchen while I lay in a corner watching him. When he finished washing the dishes, he put on the broad straw hat I'd seen him wearing the previous day, and he headed out to his garden. I followed him outside into the bright morning. The stone slab at the door was warming already in the heat of the sunlight, and I lay upon it and watched him. The horse and cow were grazing outside the barn. There were no deer to be seen. It was very peaceful.

My gaze traced the woods that encircled us so close by, like a wall beyond which there was only danger. The woods were there, but I was here, basking in relief to have gotten through them and sensing gratefully my newfound safety. Lying on the warm slab, my head resting on my paws, watching Arthur in his garden, or dozing, I had little energy left to move on after so much terror. For the moment my weariness subdued any urgency I felt to find my way back to Dad's farm, to be there as I had been, waiting and ready when Ted returned.

When I thought about it, perhaps all I had to do was walk down the driveway to the dirt road at the bottom of the field and follow it through the black hole into which it disappeared into the woods. It was the only road, so it undoubtedly was the way out and led down the mountain. However, today I'd rest. Unready yet to proceed further into the unknown, I fell asleep on the warm stone slab.

When Arthur came out of the garden at noon, I followed him into the house. He cut thick slices from a loaf of bread, spread butter from a jar upon them, heated soup on the stove, and poured glasses of milk, with a dish for me. When Maurice came in, the three of us had lunch.

Maurice had been working at his gold mine. "The assayers say it's not worth the labor," he remarked, repeating what they both knew, along with their hope, "only an ounce of gold to two tons of rock—but if I dig deeper, there might be more."

"Oh, there will be," Arthur quipped to him with a wishful sigh, "there'll be more rock, much more rock, more quartz rock."

"You have to believe," Maurice told him. "You never know . . . ."

Arthur got up from the table, went to the sink, and held up a couple of giant carrots for Maurice to admire.

So went the day. After lunch, both men napped, Maurice on his bed upstairs, and Arthur on the worn leather sofa at the far end of the kitchen. I put my front paws on the sofa for him to pick me up, he did, and I nestled beside him. When the heat of the noon sun abated, both men rose and went back to their work.

"Now that the dew's dried I can cut hay," Maurice said to Arthur. He went to the woodshed and came out carrying his long-bladed scythe, holding it by its gracefully bent handle. I followed him around the corner of the house to the small field beyond, to see what he would do with it. With rhythmic swings he walked into the tall grass, and it fell before him in wide swaths.

Arthur returned to his garden. I went back to my warm slab until it was almost suppertime, when Arthur returned to his kitchen to cook while Maurice did the barn chores. There were wonderful smells again in the pots he stirred on the black stove. When Maurice came in, Arthur filled their dishes with hot stew, and gave me a dish of it, too, this time indoors in the kitchen instead of making me wait outside as the previous evening. Later, when Arthur had put the food away and washed dishes, Maurice took out the picture puzzle again, and the two men labored quietly upon it by lamplight until bedtime, when Arthur carried me upstairs with him and set me down on my little rug in the corner by his bed. Where I would sleep at night was finally settled.

The following day, in the afternoon when the hay he'd previously cut was dry, Maurice pulled it this way and that with a hand rake and stacked it in piles. Then he harnessed the horse to the wagon and led her to each haystack, where she waited while he worked mightily, pitching the hay over his head, ever higher onto the load. After that, he drove her back to the barn, all the way inside, and with his pitchfork tossed it into the haymow.

While Maurice hayed, Arthur was getting stores ready for winter, gathering vegetables from his garden and preparing them in the kitchen. With a rollicking fire in the stove, he immersed jars into boiling water, retrieved them and filled them with his freshly cut vegetables, added water, sealed the jars, and then immersed it all into the boiling water again. It was much the method Mom followed, but she did it on a larger scale. Arthur's boiler was not so big, so he could do fewer jars at a time. With his strange gait, back and forth from the sink to the stove, I feared he'd trip forward.

When Maurice entered the house at the end of the day, Arthur was quite beaming with the completed jars of canning he'd lined up on the table. Maurice put them in a carton and carried them down through a transom in the floor to a dirt cellar beneath the house, and the musty smell of earth filled the room.

14. THE ROAD INTO THE WOODS

As I recuperated those first days, my exhaustion and hurts ceased to be an excuse for not moving on. Nevertheless, days followed days, and one week became two. My comfort with Arthur on the little mountain farm made it easy to delay. There was another reason, however, holding me there.

Daytimes I mostly sunned on the stone slab in front of the doorway where I could watch Arthur in his garden. From there I'd look from time to time across the tiny lawn to the stony dirt driveway, and my eyes would follow it to the narrow road it joined below the hill at the woods' edge. It beckoned me to go looking for Dad's farm, to be there when Ted returned. I knew that he'd never find me otherwise.

Once or twice a day I'd walk over to the driveway, follow it the few steps to the white-apple tree where the lawn transformed into a small downward-sloping field. There I'd lie in the shade and stare for a while at the road below. Sometimes I'd continue down the steep, rutted track and reach the road itself, but I'd stop where it plunged into the surrounding woods. I froze each time. I stood there trembling, too conflicted, too afraid to go farther. The struggle pulled me apart, whether to go to Ted or to stay safely out of the woods. I'd whine, weeping for what I wanted against what I feared. Then each time I'd turn back. I'd walk sorrowfully up the driveway, back across the lawn, back to the stone slab, where I'd gaze down at the road off and on until I fell asleep once more.

When two weeks had passed that way, my fears of the woods were confirmed one night. It happened at bedtime, when Maurice had put the almost-finished picture puzzle away and Arthur had carried me upstairs, swinging himself up as he did with one hand on the banister while he held the flashlight in the other, balancing me on his arm. Maurice always ascended the stairs right behind us, perhaps to be able to catch him if he fell. Arthur set me on the floor, so I could go to my bed in the corner, while he lit the kerosene lamp on the end table by his bedside.

When the room filled with lamplight, I jumped back and barked with alarm. A huge, round, black face stared at us through the window, looking surprised by the light but held fixed by it as well. A bear had climbed into the crab apple tree outside and had reached a height even with us. I hopped up and down, growling and barking, but it didn't seem to worry the bear. Arthur just about jumped out of his skin when he turned and saw why I was barking. Maurice, too, was startled for a moment. Instead of hurrying down from the tree, the bear leaned forward towards us, on a swaying branch that looked too small for so much weight.

"It's going to fall into the window!" Arthur cried out.

Maurice rushed back down the stairs, while Arthur watched the bear mesmerized, as if he feared it might step into the room if he moved. The bear surveyed us intently.

Each stood motionless, but for the swaying, as if neither knew what to do next. Then the bear turned as best it could on the branch, and looked downwards as if judging the distance. Just then a gunshot rang out, and the bear roared, let go of the branch and dropped from view. We heard Maurice cry out. Then it was quiet.

Maurice returned into the house. We heard him put the gun away. He came back up the stairs visibly shaken.

"I fired a shot into the tree to scare it," he explained to Arthur, "and it dropped out of the tree and almost landed on top of me. It missed me by inches."

"Where is it now?" Arthur wanted to know.

"It ran off in the dark, into the woods. It's pitch black out there except for the stars."

That's one thing we never had to worry about in New York City, seeing bears in our windows. Maybe Rex would've been alright with it, but my heart was pounding. The woods were full of terrifying creatures. Arthur noticed me shaking; he picked me up, cradled me in his arms, and spoke to me softly. It was reassuring, and with the return of quiet I calmed. We three went to our beds, and the lamp was extinguished.

We awoke to another sunlit morning, the mountain air deliciously fresh. While Arthur was washing the few dishes after breakfast, Maurice set out for his goldmine. However, it wasn't long before he returned and said to Arthur, "Come see. The bear's dead. I was only trying to scare it, but I guess I killed it. I'm going to have to harness up the horse to drag it into the woods. There's a cub."

"A cub?" Arthur asked surprised.

Arthur followed Maurice out the door, and I followed Arthur. Maurice stopped in the shed and took out a length of rope, then he led us in the direction of the gold mine. Just a few steps into the woods, he motioned for us to stop. The bear lay extended on the ground. Her little cub was prodding her with his nose, whimpering and crying for her to wake up.

Maurice took a few steps forward, and he stopped when the cub seemed about to run away. The cub looked at his mother, and then looked around for an escape, and then back to his mother, two instincts cancelling each other out. Maurice approached slowly, cautiously, while Arthur watched expectantly. At the last moment the cub ran for a tree, but he chose one too small, so he couldn't climb high enough. Maurice coiled the rope into a lasso, and after two tosses got it over the cub's head and pulled him to the ground.

The cub yanked and rolled against the rope, while Maurice laughing held tight. Finally, when the cub lay exhausted, gasping for breath from the noose tightened around his neck, Maurice dragged him over the leaves, out of the woods, through the field towards the barn.

"What are you going to do with it?" Arthur asked him.

"I don't know. I'll think of something. It'll just die if we leave it out here," Maurice answered as he struggled with the cub who, when he made it to his feet, began to run in circles at the end of the rope, and then reverted back to digging his paws into the ground as he was pulled forward until he choked again.

Once at the barn Maurice tied him by the outside corner. He and Arthur and I looked at the little bear, the cub looked back at us, and we all four wondered what was going to happen next.

"Maybe I can sell him," Maurice suggested thoughtfully.

"Where?" Arthur asked him, more like an objection. "Who'd want a bear?"

"Maybe a zoo," Maurice said.

"There aren't any zoos around here. You'd have to go all the way to Granby, Québec. How're you going to get there? The horse can't take you that far."

Arthur turned and went to the house. Maurice stood looking at the bear cub, and I did, too. The cub, quiet for the moment, looked back. Arthur came out with a deep dish which he filled at the brook and set close to the cub.

"He's small. He needs to drink milk," Maurice said. We'll feed him cow's milk just like a calf until I figure out what to do with him."

Mornings and evenings I went into the barn while Maurice was milking the cow, to beg for a dish of warm milk like I got on Dad's farm. It took Maurice a while to figure out what I wanted, but my attentive stare eventually worked. This evening he also poured some of the milk into a large, long-necked beer bottle as I watched. Arthur came into the barn to help him, and held the little bear's chain while Maurice straddled the cub, pulled his head back, and forced the glass bottleneck down his throat. The panicked cub struggled so violently that the bottle flew out of Maurice's hand, sending milk flying all over him and the little bear. Undaunted, Maurice picked up the chain that Arthur had dropped, wrapped it around a post so that the bear was held tight, straddled him as before, drew his head back, and forced the bottleneck down his throat again. The cub fought hard, but Maurice held him fast, and the cub had to drink or drown. Afterwards we three went back to the house, while the cub bleated for his mother. In a while the little bear exhausted himself, and the night went quiet.

Arthur washed the milk out of Maurice's overalls in the sink and hung them up to dry on a line at the back of the kitchen. "If they're not dry in the morning, I'll lay them out in the sun," he told Maurice.

At sunrise, while there still was dew on the grass, I followed Maurice to the barn, and it all was repeated. The bear cub still put up a fight, but he was small and Maurice was big. After a few days, the cub looked forward to the milk, and Arthur began to mix in some cooked cereal to get him to eat. That took time, but it finally worked, too.

"What are we going to do with him?" Arthur occasionally would ask, and Maurice had no answer.

Arthur talked to the little bear when he brought him food; he'd stroke the bear cub, and the cub would lie on the ground enjoying it. But the little bear had no life tied to that pole, so Arthur began to take his chain and tie him in the shade of the crab apple tree by the garden while he worked, and put down a dish of fresh water for him there.

As for me, mine was a good existence; I slept a lot. The stone slab was my transom. When I moved into the shade of the crab apple tree, I was careful to remain beyond the length of the little bear's chain. Nevertheless, he began to lie as close to me as it allowed him.

At some point everyday I'd walk to the edge of the tiny lawn where the driveway descended down the hill, and I'd gaze at the road below where it passed into the woods. I thought of Ted—how he always came back for me—and, staring at the point where the road disappeared, I knew I had to pass through that black hole to get to him, to be at Dad's farm for him to gather me up. The road was the only way out. Life with Arthur and Maurice was good, but as good as it was I yearned to return to the city with Ted. I dreamed of my plush little house at the bottom of the bedroom bookcase in New York City, where I belonged. Lying at the corner of the lawn under the white-apple tree, my chin resting on my paws, staring at the road, I tried to summon the courage.

One afternoon I did. I walked to the driveway and down the hill and to the opening in the woods. I watched myself do it. Arthur in his garden wasn't paying attention to me; nor was Maurice, who was in the field above the house with the horse and wagon loading hay.

I reached the black hole and very tentatively walked into it. Once I did, it wasn't black anymore. The road descended ahead beneath the tree canopy and curved around a bend. My courage rose, and I began to trot on down. Almost immediately I heard a rustling of quills on the dry leaves between the trees. A huge porcupine meandered out of the woods and start walking up the ditch towards me. I barked at it, but undaunted it didn't stop. I barked again, jumping up and down. That's when it curled on itself into a ball with long quills all bristling out toward me, and I remembered how a porcupine had done that before striking Rex with its tail. I turned and ran from it back up the road all the way to the house. "That was a narrow escape," I thought, and I didn't leave the lawn for the rest of the day.

It took many more days for my yearning to overcome my fear. This time, just inside the tree canopy where the light changed and played in patterns on the ground, I jumped back when a small garter snake that I'd not seen until the last moment slithered quickly away from me across the road and disappeared into the leaf cover. That startled me, but I kept going until I saw what for a moment looked like a bear bounding into the road. It wasn't a bear at all. It was the Indians' dog, the huge Newfoundland, running about the woods. I turned on my tracks and ran back to the house as fast as I could, with him loping along behind me.

I dashed up to Arthur in the garden and jumped against his leg for him to pick me up. The Newfoundland stopped at the garden's edge, looked at Arthur for a moment, then began to trot around the premises, exploring the place. Arthur called out to Maurice. The big dog ran over to the barn and came upon the little bear, where he stopped short. He was curious, but deterred by the smell of the cub. Maurice came running up with his pitchfork, and the Newfoundland raced back to the house, where he set himself down on my stone slab in the doorway, as if he'd always lived there. I waited by Arthur.

Maurice ran towards the dog, pitchfork in hand, waving his arms, to scare the intruder away. The Newfoundland simply lay there and looked at him like a big cuddly puppy. Maurice nonplused stopped and stared back. I was disappointed that he didn't clear him off my slab, and I stayed in the garden so close by Arthur's feet that he kept pushing me away so as not to trip over me.

Clearly Maurice hesitated because, puppy face or not, he was uncertain of such a big dog. Maurice walked over to the garden instead to confer with Arthur.

"I can't feed a huge dog," Arthur protested. "He'll eat too much."

"That's the whole point," Maurice said to him. "Don't feed him, and he'll go away.

That's the way it stayed. The Newfoundland hung around into the next day. He mostly lay on the stone slab, lifting his head to smell eagerly the delicious odors coming through the screen door as Arthur prepared supper. No food for *Gros Chien* [Big Dog]. He was still there at dawn, and he looked up as enthusiastically when the aroma of breakfast sausage wafted out to him. But no food for him.

I followed Arthur out the door to the garden. As the day passed, however, I became less fearful and increasingly curious about *Gros Chien*. He began to seem harmless enough. He'd hardly moved. Finally I walked carefully back to the house towards him. Lying there with his head resting on his forepaws, he opened his eyes and watched me. I stopped, and then sat looking at him, and for good measure growled to warn him off. That didn't work, but his big sorrowful eyes reached me.

I wondered whether *Gros Chien* was lost like me. Was he a big, glorious, homeless dog, trying this place and that, to find where he could belong? More likely he was just running around like all the Lake Isle dogs did, out and about for a little adventure, and then when he was tired of it he'd go home. I lay on the grass in the sun facing him, my head resting on my forepaws like him, watching him, and after a while I fell asleep.

I sprang awake when I sensed *Gros Chien* stand up. The big dog walked to the driveway and followed it down the hill into the black hole into the woods from where he'd come. Without hesitation he'd disappeared into it. He'd gone, but somehow he had changed the place. It no longer felt so far away, and no longer an island of security for me. Anything could come out of the woods any time, a bear, a big dog, maybe even a fox. Something also tugged inside me for *Gros Chien*. He was no different from me, really, just a lot bigger. He'd decided now he wanted to get back home. I read that in his eyes, and when he left I felt very sad that I couldn't do it, too.

We dogs are made for family. We can't be lonely creatures without suffering. That's why Ted hadn't wanted to look into the cages of the dogs at the Animal Care shelter years before. Their sorrowful eyes broke his heart. Our wolf ancestors live in families called packs. Those of us who became dogs became part of new families, human ones. With our ability to sense feelings far better than humans will ever realize, we learned to communicate. A dog needs a human. Humans enjoy us, sometimes love us, but they don't need us like we need them. That's what we became when we opted to join humans; that's how we're wired, and that's why I was missing Ted so terribly. When humans talk of love, of broken hearts, of loneliness, of the joys of friendship, they don't realize how much they are talking about us. We live to please even when we're beaten. We're not made to be alone. It is the worst thing that can happen to us.

That's what I shared with *Gros Chien* that afternoon. That's what I knew when I looked into his eyes. We were both lonely for home. I didn't know how to get back to mine, and he, tired of his adventure wandering, thought of his, too. That's what he must have seen in my eyes, and maybe sharing that sadness was too much for him. Maybe that's why he left.

I made a third try to go down the road. It was early morning after breakfast. Maurice had come in after his barn chores, washed in the sink, put on a shirt that Arthur had taken from the clothes line the evening before, and changed into overalls that were not so dirty as his regular ones. Except for his muddy boots he looked pretty good. He returned to the barn, brought out the horse and backed her up to the wagon. Then I was surprised to see him go for the little bear, whose chain he attached to the back of the wagon. Maurice set out that way, sitting atop the wagon, driving the horse, and drawing the little bear behind, who resisted at first, then walked along docilely enough. I thought, "This is my chance," and joined the parade some distance behind the little bear. I'd follow down the road protected by Maurice, the horse and the bear.

It was not to be. When Maurice saw me following, he stopped the horse and got down from the wagon. He picked up some small stones from the roadbed and threw them at me, then chased me back up the road waving his arms, yelling "*Va-t'en, va-t'en* [Go away]" at me. I turned and ran back to the house with my tail between my legs. I didn't know why, but clearly he didn't want me to follow the wagon.

I spent a quiet day with Arthur who worked in his garden in the morning, at noonday gave me a bite of lunch when he ate, and in the afternoon washed clothing in the sink and hung it out on the clothesline. In the evening Maurice and the horse returned, without the little bear.

15. A PRETTY GOOD HOME

One evening after supper it grew dark early and the air smelled of oncoming rain. Maurice and Arthur, taking their cue from the vanishing twilight, went to bed early, and I, of course, with them. Except for a distant whip-poorwill, the night was quiet. Maurice began to snore. Arthur's breathing grew heavy, as well. On my bed in the corner I remained attentive at first, listening into the stillness; but then I drifted, too, as the warm, dense air wafting through the open window drew me into sleep.

At the sound of a loud explosion right over the roof, a deafening thunder clap, I sprang awake. There followed what seemed a long silence while the three of us lay in our beds expectantly alert. A soft pitter-patter of rain began upon the roof. We all were startled again by a second thunderclap, even louder than the first, followed by a blast of wind that rattled the windows as much as the thunder had. Suddenly a heavy rain began to drum upon the roof and blow through the open window. Arthur, nearest, hurried to close it. Each time the lightning flashes illuminated the room we could see the water gushing upon the panes, with all outside a blur.

Maurice and Arthur lay back in their beds, and I relaxed on mine. The house felt cozy as it protected us from the storm. The rain pattering on the roof, with wind howling in the trees and rattling the windows, became an ambient music punctuated with bombast. It kept the three of us very much awake for the duration.

"Every time a storm blows this hard, I'm thankful *Son Père* [Father] was a carpenter and built with so much skill," Maurice said in a grateful voice to Arthur.

"He was a barn builder," Arthur affirmed. "He knew how to frame a building solid."

"This house will outlast us."

Arthur reminisced, "He'd say to you, 'Maurice, take the horse into the woods and haul out the logs I need.' Then he'd measure the beams with his axe handle, and tell the assembled farmers how to raise the barn with our brothers."

"They'd say, 'Jacques, tell us what to do'—or 'Jack, tell us,' Maurice laughed, "and he'd show them. Everything he built he built well."

That night in the pelting rain and buffeting wind blasts, amid lightning flashes and pounding thunder, the little house, a memorial on the mountain to its builder, stood firm and kept us safe. It held fast, and surely would for many years to come.

The storm came and went during the night. In the morning sunshine shone through the windows, and there was a refreshing scent of after-rain in the air when I went outside. The white buck and the doe with her twin fawns were browsing at the corner of the meadow. Maurice came in from the barn after releasing the horse and cow to graze with the deer, who started at first, raised their tails, were about to run, then didn't. He looked back out through the screen door at the buck.

Maurice said to Arthur, "That's my buck the first day of hunting season."

"Why will you kill it?" Arthur asked surprised. "It's so beautiful. I like seeing it out there."

"If I don't, then somebody else will for sure. It might as well be me. Everyone will say, 'Maurice got the ghost deer.' The whole town will be talking about it after I ride through the village to report that deer on my wagon."

"It'll be a shame," Arthur said. "I'll miss it."

"Somebody's going to do it. It might as well be me," Maurice repeated for emphasis, and they talked about it no more, but Arthur looked very sad.

It was still too wet to work in the garden, so Arthur fetched his wheelbarrow from the shed and headed out to pick apples from beneath trees at the meadow's edge. The creaking wheelbarrow approaching them was too much for the deer, and they vanished like spirits into the woods. I lay on the cool, damp grass while Arthur picked the fruit from the ground, carefully selecting the good ones he put into the wheelbarrow, tossing away ones with rot or bugs.

When the wheelbarrow was half-full he pushed it across the meadow to the house, as I kept expecting him with his strange gait to fall forward onto his load. Then after emptying the wheelbarrow he pushed it back out to the apple trees twice, and I followed him back and forth each time. He deposited some of the apples in a bin in the shed. He brought the last load into the house where, in the afternoon, he peeled and cored the apples, then cooked them into sauce which he canned in jars. Later when they'd cooled, Maurice stored them in the cellar beneath the floor with the canning from the garden. When Arthur was busy about like that, I spent my day following him, and napping wherever he tarried.

Maurice was alright. Just very big, and very gruff. He never tried to pick me up until one evening in the kitchen after supper when he scooped me up as he walked past me and sat himself on the black leather sofa with me on his lap. I was so surprised I didn't resist. It probably wouldn't have been a good idea anyway. I sat there at first with my ears back and my head turned watching him as he stroked me. He didn't pay much attention to me while he did it, so finally I relaxed. After that Maurice picked me up from time to time, and we enjoyed a half-hour together before bedtime.

It was different with Arthur. We became pals. He was a gentle little man, the younger of the two. He picked me up often, in the morning after washing the breakfast dishes and during the day whenever he stopped to rest from his work, inside or outside the house. He'd set down his hoe to mark where on the row he'd left off in the garden and come out of the enclosure and sit in the shade under the tall crab apple tree by the house, his back resting against the tree trunk, his legs extended straight out on the grass. I'd walk over to him, and he'd take me on his lap. He'd stroke my back and talk to me. He made cooing sounds to me, and he'd tell me very softly about his garden and how big his carrots or cabbage were, how enjoyable the sunny summer day was, how beautiful the horse and the cow were as they grazed in the pasture, and that he wondered whether the deer would come out to join them at the end of the afternoon. He spoke to the birds twittering above his head, the goldfinches in their bobbing flight across the lawn, the swallows with their fast, arching dives in and out of the barn, the bobolink calling out its strange word from the meadow. Or sometimes he just sat silently there stroking me.

It was enough to make me begin to feel quite content. More and more I knew I'd found a new home, this tiny farm on the mountain top with these two elderly men. Less and less I experienced the need to return to Ted, as more and more I drew close to Arthur. Slowly and slowly he was becoming my very personal friend. I didn't forget Ted; as time passed I just felt less urgency to get back to him. Going down the road through the black hole in the woods became less an issue, so that I began to think of it only once in a while. I ate well, I slept well, I received such tenderness from Arthur, and it awakened love for him in me.

At night I slept on my little bed in the corner of the loft, while Arthur slept in his. Sometimes he talked softly in his sleep. At the far end, Maurice slept in his bed, sometimes snoring rhythmically, softly. I'd listen to a whippoorwill in the distance before I fell asleep, too.

Over the course of weeks Arthur harvested his garden, preparing his vegetables and canning them, and storing them in the cellar, just like the chipmunks scurrying across the lawn were filling their winter garners. With the horse Maurice dragged felled trees out of the woods, and he sawed and split them and stacked them in neat rows to dry for firewood through the winter. Maurice cut the hay that grew thick in the field across from the barn and stored it in the haymow for winter food for the horse and cow. Arthur cared for the chickens by the barn, always checking each time that the fence was secure. He gathered the eggs, candled them and cleaned them, and put them in boxes for Maurice to bring to town to sell to the grocery stores for credit against his weekly supplies.

Sometimes in the evening after supper, instead of working on the jigsaw puzzle, Maurice sat in his wide rocking chair in front of the sofa, while Arthur played the harpsichord that stood in a corner of the only other room downstairs, pressing one note at a time, softly, gently, recalling their mother he barely remembered as a boy. It put Maurice to sleep in his chair, and did the same to me. I liked the dim, flickering light of the kerosene lamps in the evening, although not so much their smell. It was always very quiet. Compared to the constant noise in the city, the bustle of cars and busses and the roar of construction everywhere, this quiet was all-enveloping, not just of our hearing, but also of our minds. There was never any hurry with Maurice and Arthur, only the slow pace of self-sufficient days, sunny days spent outside about the farm, or cozily indoors on dark, stormy days, and a succession of nights, pitch black beneath a sky of stars, or lit in grey beneath the moon as when I'd been lost in the woods, silent but for the evening sounds.

I never saw another bear. They were around. I could smell where one crossed the lawn nighttime, but we never heard or saw them. Once in a while we heard a ruckus at the barn when a fox or raccoon managed to get into the chicken pen. Maurice would be up and out the door in an instant. There'd be more ruckus, a gunshot or two in the night, and afterwards all quiet again. Most of the time the invaders got away. The morning after he killed a raccoon, he skinned the carcass and gathered the fat which Arthur used to make soap in pie tins. Everything served, everything had its purpose; there was no waste.

As the summer progressed we saw deer less frequently. They are not grazing animals, but prefer to browse on the edges of the woods. Arthur exclaimed with delight to Maurice when they appeared. Sometimes among them was the white buck and the doe with her twin fawns growing tall now, one tan and one "spotted like a Guernsey cow." The first thing Arthur did in the morning after he had dressed and carried me downstairs swinging his legs from step to step, was wash his face at the sink while looking out the window for the deer. A couple of weeks went by since we had seen them.

One morning as Arthur was getting up, he grasped the edge of his bed and then fell backwards onto it and lay there. I wondered why he was acting strangely, but I wanted to go downstairs, so I barked to him. Maurice, already down in the kitchen, came back up to see what the noise was about. He came over to Arthur and sat on the bed beside him, while I watched wagging my tail to convey my wishes. Maurice put his large hand gently on Arthur's forehead and said tenderly, "Arthur, Arthur."

Arthur answered weakly, "I'm very tired."

"When I finish in the barn, I'll bring you downstairs, and we'll have breakfast," Maurice told him.

As if it all was normal, the big man straightened his frail younger brother on the bed, drew a blanket over him, then turned to go down the stairs. Clearly what was happening was not unfamiliar to the two men. I stood at the top of the stairs and barked at Maurice as he descended. I needed to go downstairs, too. He turned, picked me up, carried me down, and let me out the door. Arthur didn't set out absorbent pads for me like Ted did in New York, so I could get pretty desperate by morning.

It was not long before Maurice returned to the house. After washing his hands in the sink, which did nothing to remove the barn smell that clung to his clothes, he went to the large sofa that stood at the far end of the kitchen between the stairs and the door to the harpsichord room. Maurice draped a blanket over it and rearranged the cushions. I watched him go up the stairs. He came back down carrying Arthur in his arms as if Arthur didn't weigh anything at all. He set him on the sofa, went back up to retrieve Arthur's pillow, then placed it as comfortably as he could under his brother's head.

Maurice said encouragingly to Arthur, "It will pass as it always does, this infirmity. You'll have your strength back in a few hours."

Arthur simply said, "*Merci* [Thank you]." He lay there on his side with a delicate hand resting by his head.

Maurice went about making breakfast, and, although I'd never seen him do it before, it smelled as good as ever. Oatmeal with milk, and eggs, all things I love. He brought some of each on a dish to Arthur and spoon-fed him slowly, but Arthur didn't want much. He lay back and closed his eyes. Maurice went to the table and ate a hearty breakfast. After he washed the dishes, he placed a bell on the arm of the sofa by Arthur's pillow and assured him he wouldn't be far away outside.

Arthur extended his arm out towards me and said, "Give me *P'tit Chien* here." Maurice picked me up and placed me on the sofa beside Arthur. I lay beside him while Maurice pulled the light blanket over both of us. Only my head was sticking out. And that's how we stayed all morning.

We mostly slept. I'd awaken each time Arthur moved fitfully. Then he'd grow quiet again, and we'd fall back asleep. By instinct I lay close against him, to heal him with my warmth, or at least comfort him. We felt the rise and fall of each other's breathing as I nestled against his abdomen, or if he lay on his back, against his side inside his arm. To his restlessness I imparted calm. I didn't fear his jerking movements; I'd grown used to them. While we shared the sofa that morning, he grew quieter.

When Maurice came in at noon and made a sandwich for him, Arthur sat up and ate a piece of it, and I got the rest. He lay back, and fell asleep again, but I could tell he was getting better. When I saw Maurice heading for the door, I jumped down off the sofa and followed him outside. It was a beautiful, sunny summer day, and the sun had warmed the slab in front of the door. I lay basking on it. With Arthur much recovered, Maurice harnessed the horse and disappeared with her into the woods. I knew they'd be back in a while with the horse pulling a log that Maurice would spend the rest of this day and the next sawing into short lengths with his cross-cut saw and then splitting into firewood which he stacked to dry.

Maurice and the horse would be gone for a while. Arthur had fallen back asleep; I could hear his light snoring. I lay there on the doorway slab pretty much alone, and I contemplated the outside of the house, the little lawn, the driveway, the barn and barnyard and the tiny chicken yard, the fenced garden surrounded by an edge of the hay meadow, and the horse and cow's pasture beyond that. It was all so small, just the right size for me.

16. THE ROAD TO BOISVERT

I lay with my chin resting on my front paws. It was quiet, nothing but the twitter of birds in the trees, the chirp of a red squirrel in the tall crab apple tree, or in the maple tree beyond it, and the scurry of the busy chipmunk back and forth across the lawn, tempting fate as a hawk flew high overhead. My eyes closed, and I dozed in and out. All was quiet except the sentiment in my heart. Nestled beside Arthur that morning I'd thought of Ted, and now I dreamed of him.

I dreamed I was sleeping not on the warm slab in front of Arthur's house, but on the grass at the corner of the lawn on the farm. I dreamed I was thinking that Ted wasn't ever going to take me back, it had been so long. I watched myself whimpering for him because I was so lonely. I dreamed he'd left me at the farm because that was supposed to be my new home, and I'd better get used to it. Then in my dream Ted came back because he loves me. I was again in my cat house at the bottom of the bookcase in New York City, home with Ted in our apartment.

I awoke to a flurry of wings on the grass in front of me. The hawk had dived for the chipmunk who escaped under the garden fence just in time. The bird, no bigger than I so no worry to me, stood on the grass for a moment cocking its head towards where its prey had disappeared. Then it flew away to circle high in the sky again, waiting for the silly chipmunk to begin scampering across the lawn as before. However, he was the scared chipmunk now, and he didn't reappear.

I found myself more aware of Ted than I'd been in a while. Life had its ease with Arthur and Maurice, and I'd drifted into complacency. Some days Ted had become a farther memory. But not now. My dream had rekindled my longing for Ted.

What of Arthur? Such a dilemma. When I lay beside him that morning on the sofa, nestled against the pulse of his heart and the measure of his breathing, awakened repeatedly by his characteristically erratic movements, I could feel his need very palpably; and it drew me to him to comfort him. However, my dream had awakened my own need, for my old happiness, for that deep-seated original love, for my home in the city, where everything within me had been in balance. Every day I stayed here with Arthur and Maurice was a day Ted might be returning to the farm to take me back with him; and if he didn't find me when he came for me, he'd leave once more without me. I felt the urgency, but after I looked around me again at the circle of woods, I closed my eyes in the warm sun.

There was a movement at the far end of the pasture, by the edge of the trees. It was the white buck with his family. While they browsed there at some distance, I must have fallen asleep again, because I awoke with a start. The deer had come onto the lawn and were standing right by me. The buck stood alert watching me, while the doe and her fawns nibbled at the rough hedge that bordered the lower corner. They'd been very quiet, but the buck snorted and that had awakened me. I stared at him, and he stared back. I'd never been so close to him before. He was so high, so big. He snorted again and walked slowly towards the driveway; the doe looked up and followed. In turn the fawns turned and trotted after the doe. It was a silent, ghostly procession in broad daylight.

The buck led his family down the driveway. He didn't even pause when he entered the black hole through which the road led into the woods below. The white buck had brought me here. Suddenly, without any forethought, I rose to my feet and in the quiet and aloneness of that afternoon I followed the buck and his family back out. The deer walked down the steep mountain road full of curves and ruts with me a little distance behind them, until the road came out of the woods again and crossed open hilly fields. There the deer left the road to browse by the edge of the woods.

I looked up at them. It was evident that I needed to proceed forward to find Dad's farm, where with Mémère I could wait for Ted to return to take me home.

The road continued to descend. The clearing at first was dotted with trees, which is where the deer had chosen to remain still somewhat hidden, but it soon opened into a broad hayfield that bordered one side, with a fenced pasture along the other. The road, straighter now, led ever downwards to where it passed between a house and a barn, and just past them ended abruptly there in a T-junction with another, wider dirt road. I had to choose whether to go left or right.

I looked to the left. The road extended some distance between fenced pasturelands on both sides and disappeared into more woods. I looked to the right, where the landscape was more expansive, with pastureland continuing below the road, and the farm's hayfields sloping above it. The terrain to the right extended farther, it was more open, and the road didn't disappear into any woods. In the distance I could see a small house by the roadside, and beyond it fields and clearings that held the woods at bay. That seemed the way to go. I should expect to find Dad's farm in the open land.

So I turned to the right and followed the road in that direction that late, sunny afternoon. I hoped I was on my way to the farm, but I couldn't stifle a gnawing apprehension about the choice I'd made at the junction, because I sensed the terrain slowly rising rather than dropping as it should towards the lake. With that uncertainty I sensed myself lost again.

I reached the house I'd seen in the distance. It sat like an island enclosed by the road and hayfield. At the far side of its modest, sloping lawn a very small stream trickled into a tiny pool, in the middle of which with its own little causeway was a duck coop. Perched above that on the pool's closest bank was a dog house, and a spotted Beagle sat watching me as I came closer.

I hesitated when I saw him. He ran towards me but stopped at the edge of the road, the boundary of his guard territory. I approached him, both of us on alert, and we cautiously touched noses. He was twice my size, so he wasn't much worried, and he began wagging his tail enthusiastically back and forth in welcome. He probably didn't get many visitors along that road, and had only the occasional passing car to break the monotony. Anyway, he seemed very glad to see me. We jumped playfully together to confirm our acquaintance. He invited me to run up the lawn with him to his dog house, and I did. Tired from my long walk, I lay down near him to rest.

The day was waning. I could have continued my journey, but doing so would have had me out on the road alone when darkness fell. The alternative was to stay the night in the more reassuring, safer company of this newfound friend. At twilight the lights went on in the house. Not long later a woman came out the door and walked towards us with a dish of food. I scooted around to the back of the dog house, so she didn't see me. She spoke to my friend. "How are you, Spotty? You're a good boy. Here's your supper." She set the dish down in front of him and went back into the house.

The food smelled very good, a combination of leftovers and some grainy pellets mixed together. The dish was wide, and I was hungry. Very cautiously, watching for Spotty's reaction, I approached; I slowly pushed my nose into it and began eating with him, and he didn't object. He was a very friendly dog.

Not long later, still early twilight, a car came up the road roiling the dust behind it, slowed and turned into the driveway where it stopped. A man dressed in blue denim railroad clothes got out. I moved to the back of the dog house again, but my curiosity had gotten the better of me, and I didn't do it quickly enough. He saw me and walked over. "Well, what have we here? You've got company, Spotty?" Looking closer at me as I drew back, he said, "Why, it's Tobi. You're a long way from home."

The woman came to the door of the house and called out, "Gilles, honey, are you coming in? Supper's on the table."

"There's an extra dog out here, Louise," he called back. "It looks like Ted's."

Louise came down the steps and crossed the driveway to where Gilles was standing in front of the dog house. With him she looked over its roof to where I was staring back expectantly; I'd heard Ted's name. "I don't think it is," she said thoughtfully, "because I know he's gone. He'd have taken his dog with him."

"We ought to check," Gilles suggested. "If it is, and it's this far from the farm, it's probably lost."

"I'll phone Aunt Rose. Come on in. Your food's getting cold." Cuffing him playfully she said, "That's why you call me when your train's coming in, isn't it, so it'll be ready when you get here? Did you have a good trip?" Louise put her arm in Gilles' arm and led him into the house.

That night Spotty slept on the ground in front of his dog house, and I slept close to him. The night sounds didn't bother Spotty; he dozed through most of them. But when some small animal tracked through the leaves beneath underbrush on the other side of the pool, Spotty went into protective mode. In the moonlight he walked down to the pool's edge and growled. The tracking through the leaves receded. I was glad that I'd decided to remain with him through the night. I'd not have wanted to be out on the road alone; I'd probably have been as fearful as I'd been the night I was lost in the woods.

I shared Spotty's breakfast in the morning, even though Louise came outside with two dishes of food and watched us both eat separately. As soon as she turned her back a moment, we switched to clean up each other's. Afterwards she tried to entice me to her. When she came closer I sensed her kindness and let her tickle me behind my ears, and then I rolled onto my back and let her tickle my belly. However, when she tried to pick me up, I wasn't ready for that, and I jumped out of her reach. Gilles came out just then, and she said to him, "What am I going to do if he won't let me pick him up?"

"Even if you could catch him, it's not a good idea to put a dog in a car who doesn't want to be there," Gilles advised her.

"No one can come for him until this evening. But what if he goes off into the woods with Spotty while we're in town? He might not come back.

"We can lock him in the garage," Gilles suggested. "I'll put Spotty in there with him so he won't panic."

"No, we don't need to do that. He won't let me pick him up, but he lets me pet him, so I could get a collar on him that way, and we can tie him up by the dog house."

That's what happened. Gilles took one of Spotty's old collars, bored a hole in the strap so it would buckle smaller, and I ended up leashed by the dog house.

I lay there with Spotty and took an after-breakfast nap with him in the warm morning sun. However, I'd not understood who'd be coming for me that evening; I'd not yet learned that *Aunt Rose* was another one of Mom's names. So when I awoke, I thought only to move on to find the farm. I struggled with the collar. Fortunately, I'm a deer head Chihuahua rather than an apple head, and the collar wasn't tight. With a few tries pushing against it with my front paws, I was able to squeeze out of it. After a nose-touching farewell to Spotty, I set out up the road, leaving him sitting by his dog house.

The next thing I knew there was a patter of paws behind me; Spotty caught up and trotted along beside me. He'd decided that it was a good day for a walk. However, Spotty didn't walk; he'd only run or trot, checking out pretty frenetically all the underbrush we passed. He nosed and smelled everything that had transpired during the night.

The road crossed two small hills bordered by rougher pastureland, but then ascended a long, gradual incline where hayfields bordered it again. We could see quite far in the distance as we passed several more small farms. I found the rise worrisome because I continued to sense that the road should be descending instead, to the lake basin Dad's farm bordered. Nonetheless, I was influenced to continue on by the ambivalence of my uncertainty and by Spotty's familiarity with where we were. He never stopped running from one side to the other, sniffing the underbrush, occasionally jumping over the ditch to investigate something just beyond. Whatever my doubts, it was a sunny, warm morning and I'd come so far, and I was enjoying Spotty's energetic company.

Eventually the road turned sharply to the left, while only a smaller, less-traveled path extended straight ahead. Spotty rounded the turn without hesitating, and I followed him. I didn't like the woods and dense bushes on each side now, but at least I wasn't alone in them. That sentiment was reinforced when some distance in front of us a black bear with her cub crossed the road. Like an afterthought, a second cub tumbled out of the underbrush. The bears quickly disappeared. I hesitated. Was it safe to continue forward? Spotty didn't stop at all, but trotted on. He seemed so sure of himself, and I followed.

It wasn't long before the terrain opened again into small fields and pastureland. Up ahead I could see a small, grey-shingled farmhouse opposite a dilapidated barn of weathered grey boards. Spotty and I slowed our pace then and became all attention, because there was a commotion going on in the vegetable garden by the barn. What looked at first like a horse with antlers was standing in the middle of the enclosure placidly munching greens, while at a safe distance by the roadside an old man and an old woman were yelling and waving things to scare it away. The moose continued tearing up their vegetables while keeping an eye on the couple, watching that they came no closer. He'd look around from time to time to check for his escape route should he need one. Undeterred by the woman waving a newspaper at him, or the man throwing stones that fell short, the moose snapped to attention when Spotty headed across the field barking at him, with me right behind running and barking, too. It suddenly became such sport.

When the carriages passed Ted and me during our Sunday walks in Central Park, I sometimes enjoyed barking at the horses, but they ignored me and just plodded on past us. This moose really woke up, turned, and trotted out of the garden, then crossed the field, continually looking back at us. It disappeared into the underbrush beyond, and that's how far we pursued him. Then with a few warning barks at him for good measure, we turned back towards the elderly couple.

The woman was supporting herself on the man's arm as they crossed the road to return to the house. She trembled as she walked, seemingly with an uncontrollable, consistent shaking that made her head bob and her voice uneven. When they saw us returning to them they spoke to Spotty by name, and somehow they knew the name that Maurice and Arthur called me, because I could hear them saying, "*p'tit chien* [little dog]."

By now it was afternoon, and although Spotty and I had crossed a couple of culverts where brooks flowed under the road and we drank, I was hungry again. I hoped that these people might offer us some food, as Spotty led me following them back to their house.

That's what happened. When the couple went inside, we waited on the grass by the front steps. Soon the woman came out with a dish of food, and then her husband added milk to it, which he'd carried out separately so that she wouldn't spill it. It wasn't much, just a lunch, and we ate it quickly while they sat in their chairs on their open porch watching us. The man sat back and smoked his pipe, and the woman began shucking a bucket of peas she had at hand. Eventually, with little conversation, they both fell asleep in their chairs in the warm sun; and Spotty and I, resting, dozed off with them.

Suddenly, with a bang, the door of a shed close to the elderly farmers' house opened. Spotty raised his head with alarm, and I sprang to my feet. A man came out, unkempt in a shabby black suit, an open-collared white shirt really quite grimy grey, and a straw farm hat. In one hand he carried a walking cane carved from a sapling. The other held a rope tied around the neck of a shaggy, long-legged creature, a coydog—a hybrid born of a tryst one moonlit night between a farmer's dog and a passing coyote. Although more dog-like in form and stature, her grey-black coat, grey face mask and bushy, downward-sloping tail evoked her coyote ancestry. Spotty growled, and I was about to bark but not sure; and the coydog, surprised to see Spotty and me, reacted with a hiss, then leaped at us.

17. HARDWOOD AND THE COYDOG

The man yanked the coydog back, holding the rope fast. He walked over to the elderly couple on the porch and called out to the woman, "Madame Boisvert! Madame Boisvert! *Je m'en vais!* [I'm on my way!]"

She scolded him, "Why didn't you come out when I called you to drive the moose from the garden?"

"What moose?" he replied, and did a full body turn with a broad gesture of his arm, "I don't see a moose." He repeated, "I'm on my way."

"Come have some breakfast first. I'll give you a bag of food to take with you. Where are the shirts I washed?"

"I don't like to carry stuff. I like to walk free, unencumbered," he objected.

"You'll carry enough to get you through supper."

The man tied the coydog to a porch post. Monsieur Boisvert pretended to be asleep in his chair, keeping one eye open. As the man followed Madame Boisvert inside she said, "*Mon cher Hadrien* [my dear Hadrien], you look like a clown."

"Everybody thinks I'm pretty funny," he replied. "They call me Hardwood," making a clown-gesture.

"The English folk giving us English names!" she said impatiently. "For your beautiful French name Hadrien Boisvert! First it was 'Had Greenwood,' then 'Had Wood.' And now 'Hardwood'?"

A while later both reappeared. Madame Boisvert went to the shed and came out with two shirts, and Hardwood stuffed them into the small knapsack he now was wearing. He untied the coydog who looked at him hopefully to no avail. Spotty and I could smell the fried chicken in the bag, too.

Madame Boisvert watched Hardwood cross the road and head across the field along a lightly trodden path. "We're always glad to see you," she called to him. Her husband had opened his eyes, but he didn't stir from his chair on the porch and spoke not a word as he watched the man disappear. Then he said to his wife, "They say he lives in the coal shed in the railroad yard."

"I know," she replied, "it makes me heartsick."

Spotty jumped to his feet, walked to the road, looked back at me as if to see if I were coming with him, and began to trot in the direction from which we'd come. The Boisvert farm was at the border of Spotty's roaming, and he was heading back home, with a few detours. He had more fun in mind. He began crisscrossing the road, energetically sniffing the bordering brush; he was such a busy little dog. Suddenly he jumped over the ditch and rushed into the field. He'd scared up a rabbit, and it fled in rapid, long leaps with Spotty baying in close pursuit. I watched them trace a wide circle, and I didn't know what to do; so I barked excitedly, too. Spotty stopped to look back at me as if he'd just remembered I was with him, and the rabbit got away. Spotty came across the field towards me, and I went to meet him. We touched noses, and then he headed off again. I was more inclined to take the road, but was enticed to follow Spotty when he kept stopping and looking back to see if I were coming. He had fun in mind.

Past a little woods the land opened up again into a broad clearing covered with low blueberry bushes, what was left of abandoned farmland. Spotty chased another rabbit, and after that one another one. He was having such a good time. I could see Hardwood and the coydog walking across the clearing in the distance, somewhat parallel to the way we were generally heading. Each run, each wide circle, would eventually bring Spotty back to me, and we'd progress a little more; but we weren't getting anywhere very fast with all Spotty's fun. I quickly grew tired of it and wanted to move on, but I didn't know where to head without him. His and the rabbits' circles had turned me around enough to lose my sense of direction.

I stuck with Spotty because I was lost. He'd scared up a rabbit that was running the widest, farthest circle yet. In fact, the two were headed towards Hardwood and the coydog who'd reached the edge of another tract of trees. Spotty was getting so far away from me that I trotted after him for fear of losing him. I got just close enough to see what happened next. Hardwood dropped the leash, and the coydog intercepted Spotty's approaching rabbit. She was fast on her long legs. She cut Spotty off and pounced on the rabbit right in front of him. She shook it in her mouth to kill it, dropped it and ran hissing to chase Spotty away. Squealing in terror of this fierce adversary three times his size, Spotty disappeared into the woods with the coydog in hot pursuit, away from where I stood. It all happened so fast.

I whined bewildered, aware of my plight. Having driven Spotty off, the coydog came back, tore up and devoured the rabbit. She had learned, undoubtedly out of wretched necessity, to hunt and bring down her own food. Hardwood sat resting on a little knoll watching her while she ate. Blocked from trying to pursue Spotty, I had to wait. Afterwards the coydog, her face and chest streaked with the rabbit's blood, walked back to Hardwood; he picked up her rope, and they continued on their way.

Spotty was gone and wouldn't be doubling back I knew. I figured he wasn't chasing any more rabbits that day, but was running as fast as he could to his safe home with Louise and Gilles with his doghouse alongside. How I longed for my safe home in New York City—or even the safety of the farm at that moment!

With no idea where I was, I'd no choice but to track after Hardwood and the coydog at a distance or be left alone again in the wilderness. Hesitating repeatedly, peering from behind bushes, running to catch up when I lost sight of them, I followed as far behind as I could in hope they wouldn't see me, fearful that if they did, Hardwood would drop the rope again.

They led me through a woods, over another overgrown farmland and into more woods that finally opened onto a cultivated field where deer were browsing along the edge. Hardwood dropped the leash, and the coydog ran after them. Panicked, white tails up, the deer disappeared into the trees. Having cleared them out simply for the sake of doing so, the coydog returned to Hardwood who picked up the rope leash, and the two continued on.

They followed a footpath through swampland until a pond appeared on the right. It had a tiny island that was no more than a speck of bushes atop the water's surface. The path traced the wooded shore until we reached the pond's outflow, then veered to access a nearby road bridging the channel. Past the culvert, we came to a railroad track extending in either direction. Somehow the place seemed familiar to me. The road continued up a short, steep hill to a highway where automobiles were speeding by, but Hardwood turned left with the coydog to follow the track.

I'd stayed far back all the way, hoping they wouldn't see me. I didn't know if they knew I was following, since they paid me no attention—at least until they reached the railroad track. They'd already taken the path along the rails and seemed far enough ahead when I stepped out to trail them. The coydog was aware immediately and pulled to a stop. Hardwood looked back when he felt her resistance, and he saw me. I froze, and we watched each other. Then with hardly a motion he dropped the rope leash, probably to give the coydog another meal, and she barreled down the tracks towards me.

I turned on my heels and ran with all my might the way we'd come. The coydog was almost upon me when I reached the edge of the pond. Running as fast as I could, looking back fearfully, I tripped and rolled into the water. It was deep, and I rose to the surface gasping and coughing and blowing water out of my nose. The coydog stood on the bank staring at me with piercing focus while I paddled in place looking back at her. I guess she decided I wasn't worth the effort of jumping in and swimming after me, because she turned and trotted away.

I tried to climb back onto the shore, but the clay was too steep and too slippery for me to gain a foothold; so I had to paddle forward to find a place to climb up. I'd hardly gone a few feet, however, when the surge of current flowing into the channel grabbed at me. I tried to swim away from it, but I was engulfed and swept along, immersed again by its force. Fortunately it snagged me in the branches of a half-submerged tree fallen across the waterway. Lodged against the trunk, and thanks to its rough bark giving me footing, I succeeded in climbing up onto it.

I stood there dripping, with the current rushing around and beneath me. I carefully made my way along the top of the log to the shore a few feet away. Once on land I shook the water off me and lay there to recover. After I got my breath, I stood up and shook again to dry myself the best I could. I had to move on because the sun was getting low, and with my wetting I was feeling a chill.

18. MRS. BYRD

Swimming the channel, almost drowning in it, as I had done, had accomplished one thing; I was now on its opposite side. Rather than follow the railroad track with its sharp cinders going I knew not where, I opted to walk along the more inviting shore. When the underbrush gave way to an open stand of white birches, I could see ahead a small house on an embankment overlooking the pond. I headed for it. I was feeling hungry again, too, and not so cold now for walking quickly. It wasn't long before the birches dotted a mowed lawn that led up to the house. I approached carefully, hoping to find someone who might put out leftovers for me.

It was very quiet, except for the sound of wild ducks splashing by the shore and an occasional crow calling from the tree canopy. As I rounded a corner to the front of the house, I recognized a small Jeep parked there that I'd seen many afternoons in Aunt Florence's driveway next door to Dad's farm. It belonged to her friend, Mrs. Byrd, who often came by to visit her on Aunt Florence's wide porch.

In the instant of hope that gave me, I almost walked into a big pile of sleeping fur, that huge mass of shaggy, mingled copper-brown and black long hair, *Gros Chien*, the Newfoundland whom I'd met once when I came around the lake with Rex to visit the Indian dogs, and had encountered again when he'd wandered all the way to

Maurice and Arthur's mountain farm. He stirred and looked up, and I froze.

We stared at each other for a moment; he seemed just as surprised as I was. He gave a throaty growl, and I jumped back. He rose to his feet and stepped forward. I knew he could crush me with one paw, break my back with one bite. I looked quickly for someplace to scoot into where he couldn't reach me. The best I could do was run under a thorn bush where I cowered and growled back at him while he circled me slowly. Then he lay down next to the bush, his huge head resting on his front paws, and he closed his eyes.

We both waited—until I thought he was sleeping. I crawled out, my belly close to the ground, to dash away; but in an instant, quickly for such a big dog, he jumped to his feet and stood towering again over me. I did the only thing I could—rolled onto my back and exposed my belly, the instinctive act of submission I knew and always tried to avoid; but terror now was stronger than pride.

The Newfoundland dropped his chest to the ground with head high and back legs erect, the age-old invitation to play. And when I didn't move he crawled forward and began licking me, welcoming me like an old friend. His size still made me very wary. We were acquaintances, yes, but my caution had never given him the opportunity to come that close to me. I rolled off my back to a normal lying position, and we looked at each other. Then the Newfoundland wagged his tale again, and I wagged mine; and from that moment forward we were friends, great friends.

The days were getting shorter, and the evenings cooler. I was still damp from my dunking in the pond, so I began to shiver as I waited to see what the Newfoundland was going to do next. The door of the house opened, and Mrs. Byrd came out. Dressed in faded blue overalls she was a little woman, round-faced, with her greying hair drawn back into two short braids that stuck out below her ears on each side. I jumped to my feet, but my trembling only became more intense as my chill combined with my nervousness. She saw me right away. She stopped, surprised, and said to the Newfoundland, "Well, what have you brought home here?"

Mrs. Byrd recognized me, and she asked, "How did you get so far from home, Tobi Little Deer?" She liked my full name because it sounded Indian. She dropped to her knees and sat back on the ground, coaxing me to her. "Have you gone wandering?" She reached for me slowly, as far as she could. Somehow my instinct to run did not take over; rather I welcomed the gentle touch of her finger behind my ear. I was tired, and cold, and hungry, and I needed help. I could sense the goodness of this woman. She stroked my head and my neck, then reached under my belly and tickled me gently there, so I turned over on my back again on the ground. Then she got up, went into the house, and came out with a towel in her hand. It scared me and I jumped away, but she coaxed me back; and while continuing to tickle behind my ears with one hand, she toweled me dry with the other. I gave myself to it; it felt like the rubbing Ted gave me after my baths in New York. It felt very familiar, very reassuring that way.

Afterwards Mrs. Byrd proceeded to what she'd come outside to do, and walked over to her Jeep. She called the Newfoundland, "Come on, Captain, into the Jeep!" and that's when I learned his name. He followed her and hopped into the rear of it. Mrs. Byrd looked back and asked me, "Do you want to come, Tobi?" She walked towards me then, still with the towel in her hand, but somehow I was not ready, and I jumped back. "Ok," she said to me, "We'll see you later."

Mrs. Byrd drove down the driveway with Captain aboard, and I was left standing there. However, I didn't want to remain alone, either, so I followed them when I heard the Jeep stop up ahead. They'd not gone far, hardly more than around the bend where, when I got there, I saw on one side the large chain-link enclosure I recognized from the night I'd visited it with Rex. Inside was the row of large, individual doghouses that had looked so eerie in the dark, but clearly now each one housed an Alaskan husky. The dogs were gathered at the fence, and they barked a ruckus with Captain as Mrs. Byrd hauled from the Jeep a bag she dragged into the pen. She was greeted eagerly by all her dogs, each vying to welcome her the best.

Mrs. Byrd took time with each one, rubbing each roughly as they loved it, especially around the neck. It was a love fest, and none was neglected, and all were reassured. Also Captain had followed her into the pen and was affirming his solidarity with the pack, too. Then taking the bag, Mrs. Byrd poured and filled each dish in front of each doghouse. There were no water dishes because a clear stream flowed through the enclosure off to one side, and the dogs could slake their thirst whenever they wished. The pen encompassed a wide area, so large that it disappeared into the towering evergreen trees that provided the huskies shade when they wanted it, and another wide open area where they could sun and play; but the pack, so reminiscent of their ancestors the wolves, were not trusted, as a pack, to roam free.

While the dogs ate, Mrs. Byrd and Captain left the pen, got into the Jeep, and I followed them back to Mrs. Byrd's house. There she poured food from the bag into Captain's dish in front of his doghouse, set beneath a tree, facing into the yard.

"What about you, Tobi? Are you finished running back and forth?" Mrs. Byrd asked me.

She fetched a little dish for me and poured a bit of the bag's contents into it and set it in front of me. I smelled it cautiously. I realized it was supposed to be food the way she'd set it into a dish, but it was nothing I recognized or found appealing. So I turned away from it and stared up at her, instead, trying to convey my request for real food. She went inside and returned with a piece of cooked hamburger, which she could not very well put into my dish because Captain had already come up and was eating the contents. Instead, with the hamburger in her hand Mrs. Byrd coaxed me into the house, where she put it into another dish she set down for me. I scarfed it down I was so hungry, and then I stared up at her, looking at her intensely, my way of asking for more. She gave me more.

When I finished she reached down and tickled me behind my ear again, reassuring me, making friends. She slowly reached her hand under my belly and picked me up. I let her carry me to her chair by the window overlooking the pond, and she said, "We're going to have to get you home," and ever so gently rocked me to sleep.

It was some days before Mrs. Byrd proposed to do that, until she had to drive into town for groceries. By then I'd gotten used to the Jeep, a small, square vehicle with a canvas roof and no back seats but only a space where Captain could lie on a blanket behind the driver and passenger seats. I was used to the passenger seat up front; it was where Ted always set me. That's how we rode to Mrs. Byrd's horse farm across the highway, and I ran about with Captain as she did her chores. Sometimes the boy Brady was there to help her. We rode, too, to a far side of the pond where Mrs. Byrd cast a line and pulled out fish that she tossed into a basket. It fascinated me to look over the edge and watch them thrash until they went quiet, their gills palpitating.

Mrs. Byrd's fishing hole was at the end of a continuation of her driveway that extended from her house to part way around her pond. There the woods by the shore extended into a glen where the ground was low and moss-covered, supporting a stand of alder, beech and birch trees that created a low canopy. These were interspersed with evergreens—pine, fir, spruce and cedar—which, where they grew thicker, particularly along a wrapping northeastern slope, protected the area like a surrounding wall. A scent of pine pitch and cedar was everywhere, interfused with a musty scent of damp moss. Birds chirped and called out above in the trees amid the alarm chatter of red squirrels, but their isolated, echoing sounds contributed only to a sense of deep quiet in that woods. Mrs. Byrd felt it too, because she called the place her "enchanted glen." However, I didn't feel threatened at all by the woods because Mrs. Byrd and Captain were with me. Like me, Captain seemed to feel reverence in the place and didn't run about. When Mrs. Byrd had caught supper we got back into the Jeep and returned to the house, where she made quick work of preparing the fish.

Twice a day we drove to the huskies' pen, and we played with them before they were fed. Mrs. Byrd stroked and rubbed them; Captain held court with them, sniffing and licking with them; and I was introduced, too. It had been harrowing the day Mrs. Byrd set me down inside and the dogs rushed over. With a quick command she slowed them down, and they approached me more gently, sniffing, introducing themselves and learning about me under Mrs. Byrd's watchful eye. If one nuzzled me too hard, she reprimanded him. Calmness ensued, and I was accepted.

One particularly made me feel welcome, Snow, the white female who had nosed with Rex through the fence and then had lain down beside him, side by side, with the fence between. She was a very intelligent dog, ranking very high in the pack, but not Captain's consort. Perhaps because he was a different breed, twice as big as the big huskies even, and because he could come and go freely outside the pen, and because it turned out he was the lead dog, he stood alone. I shadowed Captain even though I had no reason to fear. I ranked well by my association with Captain and Mrs. Byrd.

Mrs. Byrd fed me in the house, and shared with me whatever she was making for herself, human food like I was used to having. None of those grain pellets the other dogs ate. She also worried about my shivering, and so didn't put me outside to sleep; she made a bed of towels for me in a corner of the main room by the window, near her rocker where she took me on her lap when she wasn't occupied. "I could get very used to you, Tobi Little Deer," she told me. She was always doing something, either outside with her dogs and horses, or inside cooking wonderful smells and sewing feathers and beads.

19. GIVEN AWAY

A few days had passed when Mrs. Byrd took me in the Jeep without Captain and we drove to town, just the two of us. She left me in the Jeep to wait while she went into the grocery store and then again in front of the hardware store. Then she drove through the village, up a steep hill, and along a street I recognized, past Dad's farm and into Aunt Florence's driveway next door. Carrying me on her arm, Mrs. Byrd greeted Aunt Florence, Dad and Mémère who were sitting in a line of rocking chairs on Aunt Florence's porch.

"Look what I have," Mrs. Byrd said to them, "Ted's dog. He wound up at my house."

"That dog was gone for a long time," Dad said. "I didn't think we'd see it again."

"Ted wouldn't have been very happy if that had happened," Mémère remarked.

Mrs. Byrd sat in a wicker rocker with me on her lap. "He showed up four days ago, out of nowhere. I recognized him and called Florence and said I'd bring him my next trip into town."

"He disappeared two months ago," Mémère said to Mrs. Byrd. "He was upset when Ted left him behind, and I think he went looking for him."

"Short-haired and small as he is, I made a bed for him in the house because nights are getting cold," Mrs. Byrd told them. "I was pretty sure he'd be well-trained, and he is. It's obvious that Ted takes good care of him; I saw how much they meant to each other this summer."

"It'll be better if we don't say anything to Ted," Mémère suggested. "He won't be happy we lost his dog."

I decided that I wanted to transfer to Mémère's lap. Standing up on Mrs. Byrd's knees as she continued to hold me, I looked across to Mémère and wagged my tail. Her eyes were turned to Dad, but I kept my gaze glued to her for the moment she'd look in my direction. I always spoke most effectively that way, and sometimes got what I wanted if I stared intently enough.

Mrs. Byrd gave me a squeeze, "I'm going to miss this Tobi Little Deer."

"Why don't you keep him then," Dad suggested.

There was surprise on the three women's faces.

"What are you saying?" Mémère objected.

I wagged eagerly for her attention, but she was focused on Dad.

"Look," he explained to her, "Ted left the dog here because he can't keep a dog now. It'll probably wander off again, and could freeze in the winter if it does. But if Heather takes it," he turned to Mrs. Byrd, "because you don't mind having it in the house, it'll be happy to be living the way it was raised."

Mémère mumbled her displeasure without objecting further, because there was a certain logic to Dad's argument, given the circumstance he continued to create.

Aunt Florence looked at her friend Mrs. Byrd. "Do you want to keep him?"

Mémère's eyes still had not connected with mine.

"I'd certainly be happy to, but what will Ted think of the idea?" Mrs. Byrd asked.

"He'll be glad Tobi found a good home, that Tobi's happy," Dad reassured her.

Mrs. Byrd held me tight, and stood up with me. She said to Dad pointedly with a polite smile, "I'm surprised anyone would feel they can't give him one. I'll keep Tobi Little Deer safe."

"You know what they say about a farmer with more than one dog . . . ," Dad grinned.

Giving her friend a hug with me between, Mrs. Byrd said, "Florence, I'm on my way. I planned a short visit today, just to bring Tobi Little Deer. Please let Ted know I have his dog, and he can get in touch when he wants him. And if it ever turned out he didn't, I'd be glad to keep him. . . . You're still coming tomorrow?"

Mrs. Byrd went over to Mémère and gave her a kiss on the cheek, telling her, "I hope you'll come to visit me and Tobi Little Deer," and looking at Dad, she said to him with a smile, "We won't let him freeze, will we." Then down the steps she went with me, put me in the Jeep, backed out of the driveway, and waved to Aunt Florence as we left. This was not what I'd expected.

I stood on the passenger seat of the Jeep with my paws on the window sill as we drove away. The farm and Aunt Florence's house with the three people in wicker rockers on the porch, and then Uncle Félix's house passed by my view. I'd been so happy to see Mémère. I'd made it home to the farm to wait for Ted. However, here I was leaving it again, being taken away. I whined; I jumped in circles on the seat, then watched the farm recede through the back of the Jeep. After we made the small curve by the cemetery, I couldn't see it anymore.

By the time we drove down Mrs. Byrd's driveway I was distraught, and just lay on the seat whimpering. She parked, walked around to the passenger side, opened the door, very gently lifted me into her arms, and carried me into the house. She took me to her chair by the front window, and stroking me slowly, spoke to me tenderly, soothingly.

"Don't be worried, Tobi Little Deer. When Ted returns, Florence and her mother will tell him where to find you. He'll come, and you'll see him again. Don't worry, Tobi Little Deer; don't be worried. You'll be fine here with me; you'll be safe here."

She held me a lot the first few days. She became concerned because I had no appetite and let the food she gave me stand untouched most of the time. She enticed me with morsels that smelled very good, and eventually I got hungrier and I had to eat. Eventually, too, day by day, I grew more accustomed to my new circumstance, perhaps increasingly resigned, perhaps most of all comforted by new routines that imposed themselves, as days passed.

Mrs. Byrd doted on me. She loved me from the beginning. First thing, she set a more permanent bed for me in the corner of the main room by her chair near the window. There she'd easily reach down and pick me up, so that on her lap we both could see out across her pond. From my bed I could watch, too, as she worked about.

Mrs. Byrd had a food dish and a water dish for me in a corner of the kitchen, and having recognized already that I didn't care for dog food, she shared her human food with me as I was used to having. Not just leftovers; she really shared, like Ted did.

Mrs. Byrd's work table with her sewing machine was near a second window in the main room, at the end opposite the fireplace. I managed to get her to take me up onto her lap there even while she worked. She started sewing me a jacket the first thing.

"It's getting cold outside, Tobi Little Deer," she said to me.

When she finished the jacket and was trying it on me, she said, "You'll wear this one now, Tobi Little Deer, in the fall temperatures." Then she began constructing a second, heavier one that fitted over the first, and that she beaded on the outside. I felt very fat when she tried it all on me. "Now you're ready for winter," she said.

For the moment, when we went outside midday and the sun was high, I was glad running around with Captain that I didn't need to wear anything. But evenings I was equally glad to have the first coat; it was light enough that it didn't hamper me but kept me from shivering. Within a few weeks, however, as the leaves began falling and covered the ground in a crunchy blanket of gold, I wore my coat every time I went outside.

With his long, thick fur Captain didn't need any clothing as I did; he ran about on frosty mornings and dewy evenings like he didn't feel the temperature dropping, and I believe it didn't bother him at all. He loved it.

Captain and I had fun playing hide and seek among the trees. The leaves went flying in the air each time we jumped up among them when we found each other. Because Captain was such a huge dog, I was always careful that he didn't step on me. However, he was surprisingly agile, too, and I never ever got hurt playing with him.

Captain's house was under a tree near Mrs. Byrd's home, just to the side, in view of the front door. He was her sentinel, her security, and the big, gentle dog knew it. He had a deep, throaty bark; and when anyone drove into the yard I'm sure he could be heard across the pond. However, as loud as he was standing there, he was wagging his tail and actually was welcoming instead of threatening. Nevertheless, strangers who drove down the driveway were not eager to get out of their vehicles until Mrs. Byrd came out and Captain quieted. He slept mostly on the ground beneath a favorite alder tree, and didn't use his house at all that fall.

The temperature continued to drop as the season progressed, and it got cozier and cozier inside Mrs. Byrd's house. I spent a lot of time on her lap as she beaded and glued feathers and sewed clothes. Mornings and evenings we visited the huskies' pen and greeted the dogs who were so glad to see us. Captain romped and played with them inside the pen. Afterwards Mrs. Byrd and I always drove in her Jeep up the long driveway and across the highway to the horse barn. I rode on the passenger seat beside her just as I had done with Ted, while Captain often stayed back at the house, hanging out about the huskies' pen or walking the perimeter around the house and yard.

It always was warm in the horse barn, and I lay on some straw in the corner while Mrs. Byrd pitched hay to the horses. Most days Brady was there, so she didn't have much to do but to talk to them. Whenever the temperature was warm enough, even if there were a few inches of snow, Brady let them run outside. The horses relished the opportunity as their breath steamed in the brisk air.

Afterwards we sometimes drove into town where Mrs. Byrd parked in the grocery store parking lot, then the post office parking lot, then on the street for the hardware store to do her errands. I lay wrapped in a blanket on the Jeep seat while she went inside, so I stayed reasonably warm. Often we drove then to Aunt Florence's house where Mrs. Byrd carried me inside and I sat on her lap while they visited.

The two women spent longer time together when Aunt Florence came to Mrs. Byrd's house on the pond. Dressed in woodsmen's clothing and boots, they'd set out hiking together and be gone for hours. Now that the temperatures were dropping Mrs. Byrd left me back inside the warm house, and I'd fall asleep.

Whenever a car came cautiously down the driveway while Mrs. Byrd was away, Captain always made a big fuss. The car would wait a few minutes then leave because the driver didn't want to deal with Captain. Once I heard the louder, deeper sound of a truck drive right past the house and continue on down the extension towards Mrs. Byrd's fishing hole and her "enchanted glen." A while later it passed the house again with the sound going in the opposite direction.

When Mrs. Byrd returned with Aunt Florence and was coming in through the door, she was talking about it. "The tire tracks in the snow don't even stop at the house. Somebody drove through, went right by, and kept going down along the pond. I think I know what they're up to."

First thing when Mrs. Byrd came home she'd let me run outside. I didn't take long, then was back indoors, focused on the food Mrs. Byrd was beginning to set out.

The two women sat in the rocking chairs in front of one of the big windows facing out over the pond. As they ate their lunch, they shared bits of it with me if I stared at them long enough; and they sipped hot chocolate with marshmallow, which I didn't get. That same day the truck had come through, they watched a string of deer tracing the shoreline on the far side making their way over the light covering of fresh snow.

Mrs. Byrd remarked, "I'm always impressed by the numbers I see making their way to the deer yard this time of year . . . ."

"Look at it, it's the white buck! He's almost invisible against the snow," Aunt Florence called to her attention.

"This is my first time ever seeing him," Mrs. Byrd said appreciatively, and the women watched the deer's progress.

"People said they saw him on the hill in back of my house a few times. I never did," Aunt Florence told her. "Others said he'd been sighted in the high clearings, including old Maurice, but we figured he was making it up to keep the story going. This is quite a long way from that mountain."

"When the cold starts to grab hold they'll migrate pretty far to the lowlands to find their winter deer yards, places like my 'enchanted glen' over there, deep and quiet and sheltered from the wind. But I wonder sometimes, too," Mrs. Byrd mused, "whether they've learned that the onset of the cold is a sign hunting season is about to begin, and that in this particular valley they're safe."

"That no one disturbs them there? All your land is posted, isn't it?" Aunt Florence asked.

"That's right," Mrs. Byrd affirmed. "All around the pond, all the way to the highway, and the horse farm across the highway, all a big refuge. No shooting allowed anywhere on my land, for the safety of my animals. There are people out there ready to shoot anything that moves."

"That's very true," Aunt Florence agreed, repeating to Mrs. Byrd how during hunting season two years back Dad had found a young cow shot, "same color as a deer, but certainly doesn't look like one," in a stand of cedar trees on the hill behind the barn. "He was furious. A cow is a big loss! But public opinion makes farmers reluctant to post. All my family hunts. You remember my daughter Leone got a buck that year. Her picture was in the Boston Post."

20. HUNTERS, DOGSLEDDING, AND SNOWMOBILES

It was about a week later, after a big snow storm and Mrs. Byrd had plowed out her driveway, a mild day when I was outside in my jacket nosing around with Captain, that I heard the sound of the truck approaching again. It was a pickup, that drove up and right past the house as before without stopping and kept going along the pond. Captain barked at it, and I did, too; and Mrs. Byrd hurried out of the house a moment later, jumped into her Jeep and went after it, with Captain and me running behind. Captain had no trouble, but I wasn't so fast.

We barked all the way. When I caught up, there were two men dressed in orange standing by the pickup with rifles, and Mrs. Byrd was standing by her Jeep she'd driven right into the path that entered her "enchanted glen." She hushed us.

"This land is posted," she was saying to the men. "No hunting allowed. People in this area respect that when they see it. You'll please leave."

"We don't mean any harm, Ma'am," one of the men said to her. "We just want to get into the valley from this side, to hunt on the other side beyond the postings."

"The whole valley is posted, and the rises around it. It's my land; no hunting. I have animals, and I can't have shooting.

"We won't shoot your animals, Ma'am, but we know there's deer in there. We scouted them."

I could feel the tension in Mrs. Byrd, and the hunter looked quite frightening, so I stood there in the snow trembling not just from the cold. I looked at Captain whose eyes went back and forth between Mrs. Byrd and the hunter, checking with her, and repeatedly giving a low, throaty growl as he watched the man who kept his gun pointed casually at him.

Mrs. Byrd stood adamantly blocking the way. "If there are, they're protected, too, on my land. I'm asking you to leave, right now, please. If you won't, I'll report you; you'll lose your license to hunt anywhere in the state."

The second hunter holding back said to this friend, "Let's go."

"No, I want you to be reasonable, lady," the first continued to Mrs. Byrd, and he took a few steps towards her. He stopped short, however, when Captain leaped in place barking loudly, blocking his way, and I barked, too. We made a wonderful ruckus. I was jumping up and down, and snarling. And the dogs back at the pen heard us, and in the distance they started up, too.

"Let's get out of here," the man by the truck said. "If there were deer in a mile and a half of here, they're scared away now anyway."

Mrs. Byrd said, "Observe the signs and stay off posted land, if you don't want to run into my dogs."

"Have it your way, lady," the first hunter said.

He turned back to the truck, and both men got in

with their rifles and drove off. Mrs. Byrd picked me up, put me in the Jeep, and with Captain running behind, we drove back to the house.

Thankfully, there weren't anymore confrontations. For several weeks we often heard gunshots echo across the distant hills, but no more hunters came near the pond. Eventually the sounds of guns ceased, and I could sense Mrs. Byrd more relaxed as I sat on her lap by the window. When she gazed out, she wasn't scanning the pond shore anymore, but just resting her eyes from her sewing or reading. She'd sigh and say as we watched the snow falling outside, "Oh, so beautiful," and snow fell often.

Whiteness covered everything, the ground, the tree branches, the dock, the pond iced over, all the way to the beavers' lodge by the far shore. The deer grew less furtive during the following weeks, and early mornings we'd see them more frequently, evanescent creatures, appear by the pond's edge before sunshine dissipated the mists, sometimes the white buck among them, venturing out from their deer yard so diligently protected by Mrs. Byrd.

On Mrs. Byrd's lap I could see through the window, just over the sill, and I'd look out at Captain who'd station himself in front of the house watching across the frozen pond, too. During a snowstorm he'd sit out there like it wasn't happening, and soon he'd be covered in white. He could have stayed in his house under the tree if he'd wanted to, but the snow didn't seem to bother him a bit. He looked so funny, coated like a big, scruffy polar bear. It was not long before the snow brought with it a new adventure, one I'd never have imagined.

Every morning first thing, Mrs. Byrd, Captain and I went to the huskies' pen to give them their breakfast. We got a big welcome, and the dogs chased each other back and forth in their happiness to see us. As Mrs. Byrd doled the food from a bag into their dishes, they trembled eagerly with little anticipatory whines and wagged their tails excitedly. As soon as each dog received his portion, he scarfed it down. Captain often ate with the huskies, but Mrs. Byrd and I returned to her kitchen for our breakfast.

One beautiful morning when the sun was reflecting blindingly off the snow that the latest storm had deposited, Mrs. Byrd dressed to be outdoors for a while. She had on her plaid logger pants; her coat bulged from an extra heavy sweater, and, with double mittens on her hands, she wore boots that laced up to just below her knees. As always since the temperatures had dropped, she had me in my double coat that wrapped so snuggly around me that I waddled when I walked. We returned to the huskies' pen, and got the typical big welcome again when we went in.

This time Mrs. Byrd went over to a shed to which I'd never paid much attention before, and she opened the door wide. With my curiosity piqued, I was right on her heels. The other dogs didn't seem to notice much at first. The shed housed a long sled that Mrs. Byrd pulled outside. Once she had it in place, she lifted leather harnesses from hooks on the wall and set them by it. Then taking these one at a time, she called whichever husky's name was on the harness she had in hand. The dogs were growing excited; whatever was about to happen, they apparently loved to do. Each of the them came forward in turn to be harnessed. I found it all so interesting that I had a hard time staying out of the way.

Mrs. Byrd attached Captain's harness to the tow line that led back to the sled. She said, "Line out!" and he pulled it taut so that each of the other dogs' tug lines and neck lines could be attached to it. The six huskies stood two-by-two, one on each side of the line behind Captain, jumping in place, barking and howling, eager to start. Mrs. Byrd buried me in a blanket on the sled, so that only my head stuck out; then she cried out, "Mush!" and the dogs and sled flew forward. With a yelp I hurled myself off as fast as I could, and landed rolling in the snow. Mrs. Byrd yelled, "Whoa!" and the dogs stopped. They whined and barked, eager to run on.

Mrs. Byrd picked me up and held me close. "Tobi Little Deer," she said gently, "what am I going to do with you?" As I trembled, she knew what to do, and she got my leash and harness out of the Jeep, put it on me over my jacket and fastened me to the sled, then wrapped me again in the blanket. After that she mushed the huskies, but slowly this time, very slowly down the driveway, while she spoke encouragingly in a praising voice to me with, "Good dog, good dog, Tobi Little Deer, learning to ride the sled," and words like that.

Of course I jumped out of the blanket again, but I could go no farther. So I didn't have much choice but to stand there on the sled in the cold protected only by my jacket. Mrs. Byrd mushed the dogs to go faster, and they were glad to do it. I trembled in the wind and tried to burrow back into the blanket. Mrs. Byrd stopped, rewrapped me in it, and we were on our way. The driveway reached the end of the woods and opened onto the wide open fields that lined each side of the highway where the horse barn was. Mrs. Byrd had the dogs pick up the pace, and we flew over the open, flat terrain. I began to enjoy the wind in my face, and the excitement of the dogs was contagious. It was like running with the pack.

Being a pack, hierarchy was natural to the huskies, but more than that, the dogs were a team. Captain was the "lead dog." Snow and Frost were "swing dogs" right behind him, who drew the sled into curves with him in response to Mrs. Byrd's "Gee" or "Haw" to turn right or left. Next were the two youngest dogs, Rusty and Belle, followed by the biggest dogs, the "wheel dogs" closest to the sled, Rufus and Duke, whose job it was to use their power to pull the sled out and around close corners or trees. The huskies were work dogs, and pulling that sled was their fulfillment. Mrs. Byrd loved them and hugged each one before harnessing, and again when she removed each harness. She would become as exuberant as they did on the runs, and she'd call out, "Mush Captain, mush, mush, Snow, Frost, mush, Rusty, Belle, mush, Rufus, mush, Duke, mush, mush, mush!"

I soon learned to love the excitement of the sled. Mrs. Byrd set me in the middle of it each time, calling me her "dog in basket," wrapping me there in a blanket with only my head sticking out. If the wind was too cold, I pulled even further back into it, like a turtle into his shell. Cars on the highway would pull off to the side to stop and watch our progress over the fields. We must have been quite a thrilling sight. And wasn't I the little prince, riding while everyone else worked! It was quite wonderful, and I always looked forward to it.

We followed a well-practiced routine. First were the huskies, then breakfast, then the horses, and then often back to the huskies and the dogsled, but not just to dash for fun over the snow-covered fields; we had places to go.

The driveway extended past the house, around the left shore of the pond and ended by a path into the deer yard, where a month before Mrs. Byrd had confronted the hunters. Now when Mrs. Byrd drove her sled to the end of the road there, she didn't turn into the valley which would have disturbed the wintering deer, but proceeded on a trail that continued forward close to the shore around the pond. At the farthest point it headed straight into the woods and soon came out on Lakeshore Drive which circled the lake. We crossed the road at the edge of Uncle Chris Alden's beach, where the frozen lake extended like a wide, white field in front of us. The winter winds kept it swept of deep snow, and the dog team could run easily over what small drifts remained.

Out onto the lake the team usually picked up speed, especially if the wind was behind us. The expanse looked so wide, the houses on the opposite shore so far away. Mrs. Byrd didn't let the team run as fast as they wanted, but maintained them at a steady pace, so they wouldn't tire themselves out. The island in the middle of the lake, quite far-off, grew closer and closer as we progressed.

We were not alone on the lake. There were a few snowmobiles zooming along in the distance, going this way and that, seeming more interested in revving their engines than getting anywhere in particular; and Mrs. Byrd kept an eye on them. When any began to approach, she waved them off, and they usually understood.

Once we reached the village at the far end of the lake, Mrs. Byrd drove the team onto shore and then down mostly back paths and alleyways. A coating of packed snow covered the main streets, because the townspeople didn't spread salt that would corrode their vehicles; however, the streets were sanded, which made them impassible for the sled. Mrs. Byrd had worked out what was accessible, including the sidewalks if few people were on them. Otherwise, she parked the team and walked the short distances for her errands to the Post Office, the hardware store, or the clothing store, for whatever supplies she needed. I remained nestled in the blanket and fell asleep while she did.

Our main destination was the grocery store, and fortunately we could get all the way to it by approaching it from the back. There was a pipe by a corner of the store to which Mrs. Byrd could tether Captain, and tying him anchored the entire team with the sled. She was not long inside, and soon reappeared out the back door with a clerk carrying large brown bags which he set in the sled basket next to me.

Mrs. Byrd always chose one of the warmer days for this trip, but also a cloudy day so that the bright sun reflecting on the white surface of the lake wouldn't blind us. When we got home, she unloaded the sled at her front door, then drove to the pen and once inside it released the dogs, hugging and talking to each one she unharnessed. "Thank you, Snow; thank you, Frost," she said. "You were so good today, Rusty. What a wonderful dog you are, Belle. Oh, my strong Rufus. My powerful Duke." And they loved her in return with licks and affectionate whines. They knew they'd done well; they felt affirmed in her love and reinforced as a pack. Then Mrs. Byrd and Captain and I walked back to the house.

Often Mrs. Byrd and her dog team were not the only ones riding across her fields along the highway, any more than on the lake. We'd sometimes hear approaching in the distance the roar of snowmobiles that would burst out upon us. Mrs. Byrd would slow and often stop the dogs, because they became disoriented when the loud machines came too close. Invariably, the snowmobile strangers—"flatlanders" Brady called them—would stop and want to take pictures of the dog team and sometimes even of themselves with the sled. Mrs. Byrd accommodated them; they'd move on, and then so would we.

21. COMPANY

When Mrs. Byrd's son Daniel visited with his family at Christmas time, she pondered with him whether in addition to her no-hunting signs she also should post no-trespassing ones. "Dan, those machines are so loud," she said, "they scare everything away for miles. It's intrusive, and there's such an invasion of them! I'd do it if it weren't perceived as such an offensive thing in this part of the country." She described as well to him and his wife Grace her encounter with the hunters by the deer yard; Dan's face looked worried when she did.

Mrs. Byrd's grandchildren Oliver and Amelia loved riding the dogsled; we were out everyday. They also wanted to play with me, but I wasn't used to children's energy. I crawled behind the sofa in the front room and fell asleep. When Mrs. Byrd saw that, she put down a pillow for me there and declared, "This is Tobi Little Deer's private space. There's to be no bothering him when he's back there." It worked.

My hideaway reminded me of my little house at the bottom of the bookcase in New York. I'd been too distracted lately with the horses and dogs and hours sitting contentedly on Mrs. Byrd's lap to think much about Ted or the city, but the memory came back to me during these unquiet days. I couldn't sleep nights now in Mrs. Byrd's bedroom, either, because her husband Forrest had arrived at the same time as Daniel and his family. So my new bed between the back of the sofa and the wall became my new house. During my naps there, I often dreamed I was living the quiet, contented life I'd had with Ted. I'd awake thinking I was in New York City, before realizing seconds later it was a dream. Then I'd try to fall asleep again to return to it.

During the family's holiday visit I spent more time outdoors with Captain. Mrs. Byrd let me out at my normal times, but she didn't always open the door for me to hurry back inside so quickly. So when I tired of running around sniffing with Captain and began to feel chilled despite my jacket, I'd go into Captain's house under the tree. He'd lie down blocking the doorway and look in at me, his big body keeping the wind out. When Mrs. Byrd called me back in, I'd usually go behind the sofa.

One day when I was slipping in and out of sleep enjoying a quiet time—Dan and Grace and Oliver had gone outside snowshoeing and Amelia was taking her nap—there was only the sound of Mr. and Mrs. Byrd talking in the front room.

"Heather, have you been thinking about what we should do concerning the state's offer to buy land?" Mr. Byrd asked.

"Is it still all the way to the pond's edge and all that shoreline over there?" Mrs. Byrd asked in a regretful voice.

"Yes, it hasn't changed, and I don't believe they'll take any less. Their camp ground plan for the state park still extends right through the woods, from here to the lakeshore on the other side."

"Where would we find a place like this again?" Mrs. Byrd reasoned.

"We could keep the house with a couple of acres around it," he suggested. "We'd still have the horse farm intact. The driveway would be the same, and we'd be overlooking the pond just like now—except for the view of a few campsites and camper trailers."

"Forrest, how much choice do we have?" Mrs. Byrd asked him.

"It depends how much they want it," Mr. Byrd shrugged. "They possibly could declare eminent domain."

"Nothing perfect ever stays that way," Mrs. Byrd observed pensively. "We've been so content here. I thought when we bought the entire pond it would be ours for all time, for our family, quiet, private, just us and unspoiled nature. Once again the Indians are to give up their land."

"The state's buying half of Chris Alden's beach. They're going to push the road back from the shore, haul in more sand and build a beach house. And he'll be closing off what he has left."

"It won't look the same. What a shame."

"The town's delighted, though."

"They won't be when that entire beach Chris opens to them for free is reduced to half the size, filled with out-of-towners, and they find out they have to pay to use it."

"What do you want to do?"

"I'd like to hold them off as long as we can, Forrest."

There was only quiet for a moment. I stepped out from behind the sofa and stretched—I'd had a good nap. Mr. and Mrs. Byrd were standing in front of the window holding hands looking outside. Then Mr. Byrd turned to Mrs. Byrd, and the big man hugged the little woman tightly, enveloping her in his arms.

"I always look forward so to your coming home," she told him softly.

"I do, too," he said.

When Amelia awoke, Mrs. Byrd fetched her from the bedroom and offered her a cookie and a glass of milk in the kitchen. I got a piece of cookie, too. Not long later, Dan and Grace and Oliver returned, stamped the snow off their boots and came into the kitchen, where Mrs. Byrd had set out the tray of cookies with a pot of hot chocolate.

So the week went. One evening Mrs. Byrd asked Dan to try on the clothes she'd been making for him for the spring powwow in Canada. He came out of the bedroom wearing a fringed leather shirt and leggings, with a square apron in front and one in back, all of it heavily decorated with Mrs. Byrd's beading. On his head he wore a crown of tall, white, black-tipped feathers that trailed all the way down his back.

"I love it," Dan said appreciatively to his mother.

"You won't have any trouble living up to your powwow name Dancing Bird in those," his father commented.

Mr. Byrd took up a flat drum, beat it with a stick and started singing. Dan began to dance around the front room, his feet stepping up and down in his soft, brown leather, beaded moccasins. Mrs. Byrd began clapping her hands; then she got up and joined Dan's circular dancing. Oliver began dancing, too, imitating his father. Amelia clapped her hands and rocked in place from one foot to the other. Soon everyone except Grace was dancing to Mr. Byrd's drumbeat. Dan turned, twisted and hopped to make the feathers sway.

Grace said to him, "Isn't that a Plains Indian headdress?"

"It doesn't matter," he replied. "We all wear them now."

"I like it when we're Indians," Oliver said. "Oh-oh-oh-oh," he sang like his grandfather.

"Well, you can like it a quarter of the time, because you're not but a quarter Indian," Grace reminded him. "Your granny Byrd is a very proper English woman. So you'd better like that, too."

Mrs. Byrd gave Grace a look. Mr. Byrd continued drumming, and Dan and Oliver and Mrs. Byrd danced on. When they stopped, Mrs. Byrd collapsed in a chair, and Dan retired to the bedroom to change back into his clothes. Oliver followed him, then came back out wearing the huge headdress, dancing and chanting like his father had. Grace laughed, and Mrs. Byrd told him, "You'd better take it off, Oliver; I'm afraid you'll step on the feathers. I promise I'll make you one your size. I'll have it for you when you come back next time."

My ears were grateful that the drumming lasted only one evening. I can't complain really. Dan and his family were outdoors much of the time. There was a lot of dog-sledding and snowshoeing, and cross-country skiing, and admiring the horses that were let outside for a while in a corral by the barn on warm days. The family, these three generations home together for a short week, treasured their idyllic holiday reunion, because it wouldn't be long before they'd be setting off again, leaving Mrs. Byrd alone by herself with me.

By the pond one evening, looking into a red sunset spreading in the sky as a whippoorwill was beginning its nighttime call and a loon could be heard intermittently out across the water, Dan said to Grace, "This is where my roots are. This is where my soul is refreshed, where I encounter my ancestors who lived in these northeastern woodlands, alongside ponds like this, looking up at similar skies. Whenever I come back I feel connected, and I hope Oliver and Amelia will someday, too."

I begged for some of the hot chocolate that smelled so good when we came back in. "Dogs aren't supposed to have chocolate," Mrs. Byrd said to me; so she substituted a little warm milk, which was fine.

The day came when Dan and Grace drove away, up the driveway with Oliver and Amelia waving through the car's rear window. Mr. Byrd left the following day. After waving good-bye to him with me in her arms and Captain by her side, Mrs. Byrd returned alone into the house with me; and everything became just as it had been before. She looked sad, though, and she took me onto her lap by the front room window.

"I'll be fine, Tobi Little Deer," she said to me. "It's hard the day they leave and the first day afterwards, but past that I'm okay."

Aunt Florence came often to visit Mrs. Byrd. Sometimes the two women sat by the window looking out at the pond and talked over a pot of tea. When they did I always was on Mrs. Byrd's lap. Often, however, dressed in warm parkas, they'd go snowshoeing. I watched them strap their boots to the wide frames netted with shellacked leather strips that distributed their weight over the snow, so they could walk easily on the surface without sinking down through it.

"It's six feet deep in the valleys," Aunt Florence remarked as she tested her boot bindings by walking on the snow at the edge of the driveway. "You step off your snowshoe, you're in it up to your hip."

Mrs. Byrd agreed, adding, "This is the way I love to travel the winter woods. On snowshoes. We can walk through them silently; we can hear the birdsongs, see the rabbits scamper on their paths, observe all the life out there, participating as we pass. I can't imagine missing all that, roaring through on machines that scare everything off for a mile ahead of them."

With their snowshoes attached properly, Mrs. Byrd picked me up and put me back into the house, where I waited, napping, until they returned some hours later.

Mrs. Byrd continued to visit Aunt Florence at her home next to Dad's farm, as well. Sometimes she drove there in her Jeep with me on the seat beside her. Other times, however, we reached Aunt Florence's when we were crossing the lake by dogsled. Mrs. Byrd would mush to the shore where Robert had kept his canoe. As the dog team pulled us across Dad's fields and the farm drew closer, I felt a tightness grow in my chest. Maybe we were returning me to the farm where I'd find Ted waiting for me. I became so sure of it I stood out of the blanket with my eyes searching for sign of him. Invariably we passed on by and stopped instead in Aunt Florence's driveway, where Mrs. Byrd staked the dogs and carried me inside.

Sometimes Mémère would be at Aunt Florence's when we arrived there, and she always was glad to see me. She'd take me onto her lap and stroke me the entire time of our visit. I looked forward to seeing her.

Our visits to Aunt Florence by dogsled were not very long ones. The winter days were short, and Mrs. Byrd had to get us across the lake and through the woods before darkness obscured the paths. Once home the joyfulness of the dogs with Mrs. Byrd unharnessing them and hugging them, talking to them and thanking them, was always the same delight. We were a happy pack, and I was the little prince in it. I should have been content. There was a lot of love.

That winter, my first in the north, I marveled how clean the white snow stayed, how crisp and fresh the air was, how the pond and woodland glistened so brightly on a sunny day, or how cozy I felt nestled on Mrs. Byrd's lap watching a snowstorm at the window. In New York City the snow was beautiful for only a few hours before it mixed with salt everywhere and turned to black slush, and Ted had to put boots on me so it wouldn't burn my feet. I didn't miss the boots, but I continued to think of Ted, even if slowly less and ever more faintly.

22. THE GRIEF OF LOSSES

We continued to encounter snowmobiles whenever Mrs. Byrd exercised the team in her fields up by the horse barn. We frequently heard their distant roar in the woods beyond the pond. To avoid them, Mrs. Byrd no longer dogsledded on the snow-covered back roads or logging trails that once had been so available. However, we were most exposed when we crossed the lake to go to the village. Snowmobiles dashing across the ice were growing more numerous, to the extent that some days there rested upon the lake a mantle of blue haze from their exhausts.

The noise of the machines made the huskies nervous whenever they approached. When Mrs. Byrd waved them off, the snowmobilers usually understood and kept their distance. Some cut their motors completely to take photos of our sled driving by, and Mrs. Byrd would slow down for them. If they waved or walked forward, she'd greet them.

One day in the latter part of winter we set out once again across the lake to get our groceries. We were more than halfway, still on the open lake just before passing the island, when a snowmobile came up quickly from behind and drove right alongside us. The man on the machine shouted laughing to Mrs. Byrd, "I'll race you;" and the woman sitting on the seat behind him, holding onto him tightly, yelled, "Hurray!"

Mrs. Byrd cried out "Whoa!" to stop the dogs who were beginning to run in disarray, and she dragged her foot to brake them. But the snowmobiler gunned his machine just then, and her command, barely audible to me, was lost in the engine's roar. The spooked dogs dashed forward instead. The snowmobiler raced alongside for a moment, but came too close, and, perhaps inadvertently as he pulled ahead, cut them off. The dogs jumped away, trying to escape over the rigging but tripping on it and each other, turning the sled so quickly that it rolled over onto its side and skidded into them in a pile. I flew off onto the ice, as Mrs. Byrd did, sliding in the thin snow cover until I stopped with the breath knocked out of me. I struggled to my feet, and hurting and bewildered beheld the chaos in front of me. The dogs caught in a heap were barking and screaming in a panic to escape. Mrs. Byrd crawled over to them and talked to them by name while she labored to undo the tangle of lines to free them. One, Rufus, lay still with the weight of the sled upon him.

The snowmobiler, seeing what he'd caused, sped away, but another snowmobile pursued him. Two other snowmobiles approached, cut their motors, and the men ran over to assist Mrs. Byrd. They were afraid of the dogs, so there wasn't much they could do until she undid the tangle by herself. Once freed, the dogs sat around on the ice licking their hurts, staying close by Mrs. Byrd who in a moment of relief began to cry. She controlled herself, and the men helped her to right the sled. They lifted Rufus onto it. One of the men offered to tow the sled to the village, but Mrs. Byrd replied that it would be better if she harnessed the dogs to it again and let them pull it the rest of the way. "I can handle them better that way. We'll all get there together with some semblance of order."

One of men told her, "I'll go ahead to make sure the ambulance and the vet are waiting at the shore by the time you get there."

"I'll stay with you," the other said to Mrs. Byrd, "just far enough away, parallel." And that's what he did, an escort, to make sure we made it to the village.

Rufus lay quiet, taking up most of the space in the sled basket. I trotted alongside Mrs. Byrd, and bedraggled as we were, we reached the town at a walk.

The veterinarian and his son were waiting on the shore. They laid Rufus in the back of their SUV. Then they checked all the dogs. They lifted onto the back seat of their vehicle both Frost and Belle who were limping badly, and they drove off with them. Mrs. Byrd turned the sled back out onto the surface of the lake with only four dogs to pull it, and we made our slow way home.

Mrs. Byrd was very concerned for her dogs after the accident occurred on the lake. She visited the pen several times each day to care for the three who remained, talking to them and hugging them. Soon we were able to fetch Frost and Belle, who were exuberant to see us. Mrs. Byrd lifted them into the back of the Jeep, where they rode quietly, unaccustomed as they were to it. Each still walked with a limp, Frost more so; but they were much improved, and managed to jump for joy when they re-entered the pen to the greeting of their friends. I expected to go with Mrs. Byrd to bring Rufus home, too, but we never did.

Mrs. Byrd didn't take the sled out of the shed again, but she spent more time with the huskies, as if they were all she was thinking about. She gave them very long hugs, sometimes rubbing her face against their furry necks while she talked to them. When her husband Forrest returned to visit at Easter time, she told him she thought it best she give them up.

"I don't have a full team any longer, and there's no use replacing Rufus, or wondering about Belle and Frost. I'm so hampered lately where I can go with them that the enjoyment has gone out of it. I feel bad for the dogs, because they should be somewhere they can freely and joyfully work, which is not the case around here anymore. Lake Isle is becoming more and more a snowmobile resort, and justifiably people are glad about the business it brings; but it's speed and power and noise now over nature."

"I'll see about it," Mr. Byrd told her.

"No, I will," she answered him. "I want to personally put the time into it to make sure I find the right home for them where they'll be happy and safe."

One morning after breakfast when Mrs. Byrd had set me outdoors, Captain sprang to his feet at the sound of a truck approaching down the driveway. He waited with deep-throated growls, but it stopped out of sight around the curve where the pen was, and the huskies began to raise a ruckus. With me behind him Captain trotted forward to investigate. We rounded the curve on full alert, and then we barked as loudly as we could at the two men we discovered standing by the pen looking through the fence at the dogs. When they saw us approach, they got back into their truck. It would have been a standoff, but Mrs. Byrd came up the driveway right behind us; she shushed us and then the huskies. With a degree of quiet re-established, the men got out again and greeted her.

One of them went around to the back of the truck where he pulled out a ramp. Mrs. Byrd walked up it, went inside, and through the windows we could see her looking about. When she came out she held a harness in her hand, and she entered the pen with it. She knelt by Snow first, gave her a big hug and then harnessed her, much as she would have done if we were about to go sledding. She gave Snow another hug, telling her, "You'll be happy with longer winters and more space to sled. I'll miss you so, my beautiful." She led Snow out of the gate and up the ramp into the truck. One of the men followed. Captain stood by wagging his tail anxiously, not sure what to do next. He whined softly as Snow disappeared into the truck. I stood near him watching, too, sharing his concern by barking at the man who reappeared with Mrs. Byrd. She shushed us again.

Mrs. Byrd did the same for each one of the dogs. "Rusty, you have so much energy, always so eager, always so ready. I'll miss that enthusiasm. I'll miss you," and then she slowly, silently guided him up the ramp. Rusty looked back at us, but he trusted Mrs. Byrd.

"Belle, thankfully your leg is better. My sweet dog, I'll miss those eyes, your admirable gaze. Gentle, gentle Belle, how I'll remember your beautiful face, and your happy welcome every day!" A long hug, and she led her up the ramp. Belle scooted in.

She gave Frost an especially big hug. "Frost, my patient Frost, I worry because you won't be able to work if you don't get over that limp. I'd keep you back, but you'd pine for your friends; better to go with them. You'll be cared for. I promise I've made sure." I watched him limp up the ramp behind her. When he hesitated at the door, a light tug pulled him through it.

Mrs. Byrd looked tired, more and more as she led off each dog. Most of the huskies, like Snow, remained quiet in the truck, but Frost barked for her after Mrs. Byrd came out.

We could sense the finality as she approached the last. "Duke, my big, wonderful Duke." He stood almost as tall as Captain, and she buried her face in his fur and began to weep, even as she tried to stifle her little cries. "How can I let such a magnificent dog go?" she said through tears to the man standing by, and again to Duke, "How can I let such a big, gentle soul as you go, let such strength, such integrity, go? You enfold the whole pack in your heart." Duke licked Mrs. Byrd's tears. She held tightly to her last sled dog for the longest time, then slowly led him up the ramp. He followed docilely as the others had. When she exited the truck for the last time, after a look back Mrs. Byrd said to the man at the base of the ramp, "It's the end of an era, for me at least. Hopefully it isn't for them."

The men boarded the truck, and with a parting goodbye and a wave to Mrs. Byrd they drove off. We were left standing there, Mrs. Byrd and Captain and me. The pen looked eerily empty. Mrs. Byrd turned and slowly walked back to the house, and we followed her. She remained indoors all the rest of the day, pensive, stopping whatever she was doing from time to time to go over to the window to gaze out over the pond. Outside Captain lay silently by the side of his doghouse, and when I was outside I lay near him, quietly, our chins resting upon our paws. What we'd witnessed didn't feel right, at all.

The next morning another truck came down the driveway, a large flatbed, from which a crew of workmen descended. Off and on Captain and I watched them dismantle the pen. They loaded it, and hauled it away in late afternoon. Afterwards, Captain and I approached where it had stood in the open area uncharacteristically bare now. Only the doghouses remained, stark, empty, abandoned. Captain whined, and I echoing him murmured softly. If we'd had any incomprehension when the huskies were led into the truck the previous day, there was no doubt now. Our friends were not coming back.

The third day when two workmen broke apart the doghouses and began sawing them into lengths of firewood with a small chainsaw, we didn't linger to watch, but turned away from the aggravating noise. Although mitigated somewhat by the density of the trees, it pursued us back to the house. Thankfully it didn't last long.

There were no more trucks and no more workmen the fourth day. When Mrs. Byrd put me outdoors after breakfast, I couldn't find Captain. I circled the house twice looking for him. Back in the driveway I barked a couple of times to call him. A single bark answered me, and it told me immediately where he was. I walked around the curve to find him lying in the middle of the wide area where the pen had been, empty now but for the stack of wood by the fir trees. Sprawled on his belly, with his legs spread out, and his head, too, resting on the ground, it seemed as if Captain was covering as much of the bare surface as he could. Only his eyes moved, looking sorrowfully up at me. I lay down, too, only a few feet from him, with my head on the chill earth, missing the huskies as he did—until staying still too long in the cold I began to shiver violently, and I returned to the house and scratched on the door, where Mrs. Byrd took me inside.

For some days afterward, we seldom saw Captain. He lay continually where the pen had been, mourning quietly, sadly motionless, grieving for his departed pack. I missed his company, as I missed with him, too, the comradeship of the huskies. An anguished tranquility rested over the place, and we three moved slowly through it. Mrs. Byrd often sat in her chair looking fixedly out the window. There were only quiet sounds the night of the full moon; the mysticism had departed, until Captain raised his face and howled towards the orb long and alone a cry of heartache.

There was a void, too, each morning in our routine. Instead of stopping at the pen to greet and feed the huskies, they were a memory as we drove right past the barren spot on our way to the horse barn. Sometimes Captain still lay there keeping his lonely vigil, hardly looking up, his chin resting on his forepaws, and Mrs. Byrd parked the Jeep and walked over to console him. He'd jump to his feet wagging his tail and look at the surrounding woods and bark a couple of times as if he expected the huskies to reappear, trying to convey to Mrs. Byrd that he wanted her to do something about it and get them back.

Only slowly the sorrowfulness healed with passing time, while ducks landed on the pond and flew off it, while raccoons ambled along the shore, while beavers created a wake crossing to their lodge in the distance. Only slowly Captain returned to us.

I could sense the weather changing. The days were not cut so short by twilight at the end of the afternoon. The sun shone warmer, and snowmelt dripped steadily from tree branches. Mrs. Byrd tapped the sugar maples in the vicinity of her house to make syrup like Mémère did.

Daniel visited with his family, and Mrs. Byrd had a feather headdress waiting for Oliver much like his father's, but smaller. When they drove away, I welcomed the quiet, with just Mrs. Byrd and Captain and me and the horses.

Then another visitor arrived one afternoon, a big surprise. I snapped to alert when Captain started making a ruckus outside, and I barked loudly as I always did when I heard a knock at the door.

Mrs. Byrd opened it and said, "Well, hello, Ted. What a nice surprise. Tobi Little Deer will be delighted."

"I've come to see both of you," Ted replied. "It's always a pleasure to visit you, Mrs. Byrd."

Mrs. Byrd offered Ted tea. He stood in the kitchen doorway while she prepared it, and I jumped against his leg for him to pick me up. He reached down and gently lifted me into his arms. His touch sparked alive in me a tactile memory that I'd begun to forget.

"Your Aunt Florence told me you'd be coming for your grandmother's funeral. You have my sincerest condolences," Mrs. Byrd told Ted.

"Mémère's life was a good one. She and my grandfather raised a large, devoted family on three successive, successful farms. My dad was her baby, her youngest, and he enabled her and Pépère to live out a happy retirement in the environment she loved, with her family all around her up and down the street."

"How is your father taking it?" Mrs. Byrd asked him.

"Not very well at all. It's apparent he was dependent on her emotionally. It's as if on top of losing Robert so recently this is too much for him."

"That's what your Aunt Florence has told me, too," Mrs. Byrd acknowledged.

"He's not as tough as he puts on," Ted concluded. "He's in a daze, like something of him is gone. He's very depressed. Just quiet and depressed."

"So much in so short a time," Mrs. Byrd said to Ted.

Mrs. Byrd set out tea and cookies in front of the window overlooking the pond. I nestled on Ted's lap as the two sat looking out.

"This is such a special place," Ted said to Mrs. Byrd.

"It has always been magical to me," Mrs. Byrd agreed.

The sensation of Ted's touch, the memory of which had begun to dim, coursed through me in instant recall. Like an overpowering infusion flooding through me, it reestablished my bond with him in an instant. I whined and buried my face in the crevice where his elbow touched his side. In my urge to meld with him, I pushed my face deep under his arm into the warmth of his soft flannel shirt and I snuggled there quite still.

It was the sensation I grieved for those months ago when I cried at the edge of the lawn. Finally now, he'd come for me. I nestled against him, enveloped in my sense of him, completely content, and I licked his hand to let him know so.

"Tell me, please," Ted asked Mrs. Byrd, "how you found Tobi. What had happened to him?"

"I didn't find him; he found me. He was outside the house here one day with Captain, and I took him in. Your Aunt Florence confirmed he was your little dog who'd wandered off. I brought him back to your family, but your father suggested he'd be better off with me. It revolved around where he could spend the winter in the house."

"My dad can't get his mind around the idea of pets. For him, animals exist for purposes. He's not unkind; he doesn't own a gun, and he won't slaughter an animal, but he doesn't have pets. The cows give milk, the chickens eggs, the dog fetches the cows and protects the barnyard, and the cats keep the barn free of mice. They're not pets."

"That's what I felt that day, when he suggested I keep Tobi Little Deer," Mrs. Byrd said.

"Keep?" Ted asked surprised. "Tobi wasn't his to give," he objected quietly.

"That was clear to everyone there, but we realized that Tobi Little Deer would be safer with me in the meantime. Your grandmother voiced fear he'd wander off again looking for you. Your Aunt Florence and I agreed he'd be better off with me until you came back."

"I raised him as a puppy, so I'm very attached to him," Ted explained.

"That's why he's so attached to you. Chihuahuas, especially, are one-person dogs," Mrs. Byrd affirmed.

"Even though that's the case . . ." Ted paused then set out to clarify his situation. "Unfortunately I'm committed to a lot of travelling for a while yet, and I can't be leaving him alone in New York all the time. Which is why I thought of the farm. That he'd be safe and content there, but apparently neither is the case. I can't take him back right now, but I don't want to give him up, either."

Mrs. Byrd sighed.

"I plan to stop all this traveling by mid-summer, because I don't like living out of a suitcase, and, of course, I miss Tobi." Rubbing me behind the ear, he looked intently at Mrs. Byrd—what he needed, one does not ask lightly. "Right now, however, he's better off with you, and I'd be very grateful if you'd be willing to keep him for me until then."

Mrs. Byrd looked down towards her hands resting on her lap. She hesitated. "I've grown very attached to Tobi Little Deer, too," she said. "And the problem is I grow more attached every day. The longer he stays, the harder it will be to say good-bye when the time comes." When she remained silent for a moment, Ted's hand on me tensed. "But I want what's best for Tobi Little Deer, too," she continued. "Yes, until you're ready to come for him."

I felt Ted relax. "I'll gladly reimburse any expenses," he said, but she assured him not to worry in that regard.

Mrs. Byrd poured Ted another cup of tea and offered him more cookies, and I snuggled on his lap and fell asleep while she reminisced how Ted and his friends when they were young used to visit her and Dan summer afternoons to dive and swim off the dock. "The young people still come to play off this dock; now they're the children of the ones who used to."

I dozed off in my contentment, but I jerked awake when, thanking Mrs. Byrd for her kindness, Ted rose to his feet with me in his arms. Then he handed me over to her. It wasn't what I wanted, what I'd yearned for, or in what for the past hour I'd immersed myself. I leapt out of her hands all the way to the floor and banged my chin. My head reeling, I looked through my tears of pain and jumped on Ted's leg for him to pick me up again. Ted reached down, took me up and handed me over again to Mrs. Byrd who held me tightly this time as she whispered into my ear, loud enough for Ted to hear, "I love you, too, Tobi Little Deer." I struggled and struggled; she had all she could do to hold me.

"I'd better hurry up," Ted said. "This is getting too difficult for all of us." And he said to me in a sterner voice, "Tobi, stop it, you be good! Be good, Tobi!"

I wasn't interested in being good! I knew what was happening *again*!

Outside Ted got into his car, started it up quickly, turned it in the yard, and drove away up the driveway, away from Mrs. Byrd and me.

I jumped out of Mrs. Byrd's arms to chase the car, barking as loudly as I could for Ted to stop for me, as it disappeared. When I ran around the bend, he was gone. I stood barking for him to come back until my throat hurt. Then, totally discouraged, I lay down by the side of the road, near where the pen had been; and out of sight of Mrs. Byrd I cried.

In a while I sensed Mrs. Byrd standing over me. She reached down and picked me up. "You're breaking my heart, Tobi Little Deer," she said, and she carried me back to the house.

I scooted into my hideaway behind the couch, and I stayed there, and I didn't come out for a long, long time. Mrs. Byrd put my food dish and water by the edge of the couch. She emptied the dish when I didn't touch it, and she put food in it again when it was meal time. I lay in dull shock with my head buried in my blanket.

When Mrs. Byrd finally reached in and pulled me out, she carried me to her chair by the window, holding me tight. "Tobi Little Deer, you're breaking my heart, too," she said to me again. We sat there like that for a long time, I on her lap, curled up in her open hands that embraced the length of my back. I felt her warmth, her love, but I couldn't relax, not yet. When she put me down, I scooted back behind the couch. So she waited, and I did, too.

23. BUILDING FENCE

Spring came with its warming breezes amid longer, sunny days and frequent showers. Tender, light green shoots pushed up through the soil, and new buds grew out on bushes and tree branches, quickly covering them with flowers everywhere. A few robins appeared, followed soon by thc tiny birds, brown or brightly colored, chirping and flitting about, joining the chickadees and noisy jays who'd stayed the winter. In the mornings the cawing of crows in the highest trees became more insistent, as the intermittent cries of loons echoed over the water.

Daytime, the distant, muted quacking of geese and ducks drew our eyes to the sky where far overhead they flew across in waves of undulating V's. Evenings, those fly-bys abandoned their formations and descended noisily onto the pond, disturbing the white egret wading along the edges pursuing her patient quest, who flew gracefully then into the pink sky over the woodland to the lake beyond. Soon the urgency of nest building began everywhere, and swallows swooped over the fields by the horse barn gathering materials. With warmer days the horses could spend more time outdoors. There were two new foals with their mothers among them, running about on spindly legs.

New growth was springing up where the pen once stood, so our friends Snow and Frost, and Rufus and the rest of the pack would live on only in our memories as we looked at the colorful blooms of wildflowers and weeds.

Ted lived on in my memory, too, slowly, very slowly less painfully. As time healed me, I appreciated Mrs. Byrd more and more. She took perfect care of me, fed me delicious food, held me often on her lap, stroked me and spoke to me lovingly. She kept me with her all the time, taking me with her everywhere she went, while Captain often stayed back to watch the house. I basked in her warmth when she touched me, much as I remembered the huskies had, and reminiscent of the sensation I got in Ted's arms. From time to time she'd say to me, "I'm going to miss you, Tobi Little Deer," sitting there with me, looking out the window. I could grow quite content like that.

Springtime brought the happiness of things to do. Mrs. Byrd took me to the horse barn almost every day, and often Captain jumped aboard, too, when he stood by the Jeep wagging his tail to go. After her regular chores were finished, she'd do spring work the rest of the day. Meanwhile, Captain and I had the run of the place, with all its interesting distractions.

It took a while for the sun and the warmer days to melt all the snow off the fields, and even more time in the woods. Mrs. Byrd didn't let the horses run about their pasture immediately, however. She confined them to a smaller corral by the barn while the melt and rain showers encouraged a tentative blanket of new grass to cover the pasture and take hold. Meanwhile she walked the horse fence perimeter with Captain and me running about, and she painted a white X on some of the posts. Later, with both of us following close by, she brought Brady out into the field to show him where she wanted to extend the pasture.

"The foals will grow fast," she said. "The Morgans will need more room." *Morgans* was Mrs. Byrd's name for the horses.

Captain and I had a good time on these walks, sniffing at all sorts of things, running from one point to the other. "Watch Captain," Mrs. Byrd told Brady. "See if he discovers any groundhog holes. A horse can snap a leg in a hidden one. So watch for them carefully."

I was fascinated by the foals in the corral when we returned to the barn. They were jumping and skipping and chasing each other which seemed like a lot of fun. Watching them was exciting. Once I ran under the fence to join in, but when I reached them I wasn't sure what to do. I stopped, and they stopped. They looked at me, more curious than surprised. I barked to invite them to play with me; they both jumped back a step or two. Then when one and then the other trotted towards me, I ran out of their way. I quickly turned, faced them and barked again; and they ran, and I ran after them. Instead, they separated and headed for their mothers who already were walking towards me with the three other towering Morgans, five in all and two foals. I scooted out of the corral as fast as I could. The horses looked at me over the fence snorting, and one pawed the ground. I never tried that again. I'd expected they'd play like Bruno, the young bull on Dad's farm who understood the game of chase-me-and-then-I'll-chase-you; these horses didn't get it.

A few mornings later when Captain and I arrived with Mrs. Byrd in her Jeep at the horse barn, Brady already was there dragging a bale of hay to the horses' corral. I ran up to him. As he tickled me behind my ears, a wind gust grabbed his hat. Mrs. Byrd, approaching, exclaimed, "Oh, my!" Most of his curly blond hair was gone.

She laughed, "Well, don't you look the Mohawk!"

"That's what they call it," he said, a bit embarrassed by her reaction.

His head was shaved bare, except for a short hedgerow from his forehead to a point at the back of his neck.

"It makes you look severe," she told him.

"It makes me look Indian," he told her. "Everyone's getting them, now they've seen mine. It's cool for summer."

"It represents bravery and manhood, you know."

"I'm brave," he told her with a self-assured smile.

"You'd better get your hat back on, or you'll get sunburned," she advised him.

Mrs. Byrd and Brady spent that day removing all the X-marked posts from the fence and stacking them behind the barn. Captain and I took up time running about sniffing by the edge of the woods. I was learning to interpret these wild scents, too, this and that and everything just like Captain was doing, and as Rex had done at a time I was less enthusiastic about it. When we tired we lay in the sun and simply watched all the activity around us, the fence-building, the horses milling about, swallows swooping over the fields, the bobbing flight of goldfinches, a woodpecker knocking his way up the tree by the barn.

Mrs. Byrd and Brady completed removing the posts the following forenoon. Then, right after lunch Mrs. Byrd hitched her Jeep to a machine that had been standing in the yard, and she towed it into the pasture. Captain and I trotted after her as usual, and we watched inquisitively while Mrs. Byrd showed Brady how to use it.

"This fencepost digger is going to save us a lot of work," she said, "but you have to watch out using it. You have to be careful of the recoil."

Captain and I dashed off then and busied ourselves around the woods' edge again. I even scared up a rabbit, my first, and chased it like Spotty would have done, but only the distance of a few feet before it got away. That made me quite proud, and I strutted back to Captain with my ears and tail straight up, just like I did in New York after jumping at a bigger dog on the sidewalk. Suddenly Captain's head jerked to attention, and he was off. I followed him at a run to the workplace where Mrs. Byrd was lying on the ground.

"Are you okay? Are you okay?" Brady was asking her. He'd fallen to his knees and was looking into her face.

At first Mrs. Byrd did not answer him at all. I could see his relief when she opened her eyes. He was pressing her forehead with a handkerchief he'd pulled out of his pocket. "Don't move," he told her, "I'll call for help." He gripped his phone with his other hand.

"No," Mrs. Byrd said to him weakly, and she raised herself on one elbow. "Just give me a minute to clear my head." She took the handkerchief from Brady and held it to her forehead herself. "Do I have a gash?" she asked him.

"A little one."

"I guess you could say I just showed you what not to do," she said. "Help me to get to the Jeep, and take me to town, please."

Brady reached beneath Mrs. Byrd's shoulders and assisted her to her feet. With him supporting her, her arm over his shoulder, she walked unsteadily to the vehicle.

"Just one moment of inattention is all it takes," she said. "I looked to see what the dogs were chasing."

"We don't need the fencepost digger," Brady told her, helping her into the passenger side. "I'll dig the holes with a shovel."

"Nonsense, that would take forever," Mrs. Byrd objected.

Brady jumped into the driver's seat, drove quickly out of the yard and up the highway. Captain and I stood watching the Jeep speeding away until it disappeared around a curve in the distance.

Captain lay down in the driveway to wait. I sensed he felt unsure. We were used to being left alone at the house often enough, but we'd never been left at the horse barn. Getting home would mean crossing the highway. I lay down on the grass by the side and waited for what Captain might do—and he simply waited.

We stayed most of the day like that, getting up only once in a while to slake our thirst at the runoff by the water pump. Then back to the driveway, watching the road for the Jeep to reappear. We both realized that something had gone very wrong; I could feel Captain's apprehension, which affected me, too.

The brightness of the day had passed into the pink light of evening before Brady arrived driving the Jeep with a companion who sported a similar haircut. He put the horses in the barn, and closed and secured the doors. He took Captain and me into the Jeep and drove us down to Mrs. Byrd's house by the pond, with his friend following, driving Brady's car. After he parked the Jeep by the door and let us out, Brady looked to filling Captain's food dish with pellets. With that done, he turned to leave. When Captain followed him to the car, Brady said, "You stay here, Captain, stay! I'll be back in the morning," and then drove off with his friend. Captain and I stood watching them depart.

We lay for a while right where we'd been standing in the yard. Then I followed Captain to the top of the embankment overlooking the pond, where we lay and waited a while more. It grew darker, and a whippoorwill began to call. Ducks settled on the water. We heard the occasional splash of a fish snatching an insect from the surface. Despite the night sounds, with a soft wind rising up and rustling through the trees, it felt very, very quiet. It was new to me this calmness I felt in the woods there with Captain, that reached far back to my wolf ancestors who listened to these same sounds at night protected by the pack. I began to shiver in the night air. I doubt Captain could feel the cold, but he got up, rounded the house and walked into his doghouse. I followed him, and I slept snuggly that night buried in his coat between his paws.

24. ALONG THE TRACKS

A robin's solitary chirping announced the dawn, and then another responded, followed by first light which expanded in a symphony of birdsong. I was so comfortable in Captain's fur that I continued to doze there, only half-awake, until the slap of a beaver's tail on the pond woke him. I wouldn't have stirred if he'd not stood up.

I followed Captain around the house to the top of the embankment to look out as we had the evening before. It seemed as if the denizens of the woodland knew the house was deserted of people. Two beavers swimming by, closer to our shore than usual, were creating a long wake behind them that shimmered in the early light. When one spotted us, he slapped his tail again hard, and both disappeared. On shore a raccoon and her family that had been scurrying around the dock vanished into the brush when they saw us. A white egret that flew in fished for a while, wading on her long legs in the shallows to the right. Crows landed to the left of the dock, and pecked through the grasses, while their lookout in a tree above called out when Captain or I moved. The sun rose slowly. It was going to be a clear, bright day, as the air warmed while a few voluminous white clouds crossed slowly overhead.

Captain stretched. He looked out over the water for a few moments more, as if he were committing his contemplation to memory, then went off into the trees to the side. When he returned, I followed him back around the house and lay down with him by the edge of the driveway.

We waited there expectantly all through the morning and into the forenoon, until the sun had risen high in the sky. I got so hungry. I'd not eaten any of the pellets the evening before because I was unaccustomed to them. If there'd been any left that morning, however, or if Brady had appeared with more, I'd have devoured them. Brady didn't come.

Eventually Captain rose slowly to his feet, stretched, stood for a moment, turned and started up the driveway. He walked away without looking back. Not sure, I hesitated. However, I figured that by now Captain was thinking of food, too, so I caught up with him as he entered the woods. I followed him through the trees along the same route I'd taken to arrive from the railroad crossing the previous fall. When he reached the tracks, Captain turned onto the well-worn path along the edge of the ties in the direction Hardwood had taken. The rails stretched before us, two straight lines that curved in parallel some distance ahead. Captain walked casually, unhurriedly, while I trotted behind him to keep up with his longer strides. Soon, the lake appeared close by on our left. We came to a cove where camper vehicles were lined up along the edge of a small beach. Then the rail track led through a cut in a hill that opened out onto houses on both sides.

Captain veered off to the left onto a short street that took us to the lake. There was no beach here, only homes close together with small green lawns that reached right to the edge of the water. Just beyond what looked more like a wide channel than open water was the island, amazingly and beautifully close. Past it, the lake extended broadly across, and I barely could see Dad's farm in the distance on the opposite shore. It was a long, long way off. Captain knew where he was going. He approached a house that stood close to the water with small white birch trees dotting its lawn. A man was busying himself in the yard.

"Well, hello, Captain," the man greeted the big dog who stood staring at him. When I followed cautiously, he said, "Look what we have here! Little guy hanging out with big guy! Who's your friend, Captain?" He walked to the front of the house facing the lake, and we followed him.

A woman stood at the water's edge looking across at the view with the high sun still enough at her back for the colors to be perfect. When she turned, she was surprised to see me. "Joe, doesn't that look like your cousin Ted's dog?" she asked the man.

"Could be, but I don't think Ted's here now. It's probably a dog from the campground. "

"Would you get the leftovers I saved for Captain?" she asked him. And that's when I found out that, like Rex, Captain made the rounds to the neighbors, too, even if the neighbors were a lot farther from his home.

"Ok, I'll do that for you. I'm not doing anything right now," Joe quipped. He went into the house and came out with a dish of food. Captain, wagging his tail, was right there with him, and buried his face in the dish as soon as it was set in front of him. I looked up eagerly, wagging my tail, too.

"Maddie, you got any more for the Chihuahua?" Joe asked the woman, "Captain's hogging the whole thing, and I don't think it's a good idea to interfere."

"Why'd you give it all to him?" she asked.

Maddie went inside and returned with a second, small dish that contained a variety of foods, mostly pieces of cold hot dog and a few slices of meat that were spicy for me, but I was hungry. Apparently she wasn't afraid to interfere, because she stood between me and Captain so I could eat.

Afterwards we lay on the grass close by Maddie and Joe's chairs, enjoying the noonday sun as they were. In a while, Captain rose to his feet, turned away and walked back out onto the road, headed for other houses and probably more breakfasts he expected. I watched him for a moment; I looked at Maddie and Joe who were not paying any attention to either of us, and then I followed him. In all Captain visited two more homes that had leftovers for us. One put it all in one dish, so I didn't get anything there, but the other gave me my own dish and stood by me, so that's where I ate my fill.

Just as Rex used to do when I followed him about, Captain seemed in no hurry to get anywhere in particular after his round of begging, and he began to spend considerable time just nosing around. I dallied with him a bit, but then I became impatient to be on my way to reach the farm I could see across the lake. It meant continuing to follow along the shore the wide half-circle to get there, and the train tracks leading to the town headed in that direction.

The embankment on which the tracks lay bridged an inlet separating the houses where we stood from the town beyond, with lake water washing through the culverts beneath. Captain, busy sniffing near the edge, didn't seem inclined to continue on. He'd gotten what he came for; he'd no need to go farther. So I started out across alone. I was about two-thirds of the way along when I heard a train whistle behind me, reminiscent of the sound I'd heard across the lake on the farm, but now closer and getting louder, getting very much louder fast. I looked back and saw that a train was coming through the cut in the hill on the far side of the houses. There was water on each side of me now, so I had no choice but to run as fast as I could straight forward.

The noise overtook me rapidly; the distant purr of the engine became a roar punctuated with intermittent whistle blasts. Terror-stricken, I ran as fast as I could with every fiber of strength I could call up, checking back over my shoulder, as it sped and towered over me. I cried out as the huge wheels raced past me no more than my body-length away, and the whoosh of wind picked me off my feet and rolled me down the sharp cinder embankment into the water in an engulfing splash. I came up gasping and coughing.

The train had passed, the caboose diminishing as it drew away into the town. I barked, I cried, I whined as I swam to the embankment but couldn't find a foothold to lift myself out of the water. After several panicked, failed attempts I finally succeeded and, perilously slipping and sliding, climbed the rough cinder slope back to the top.

Standing by the rails again, I shook off the chilling water as best I could, and with my legs weak beneath me, I looked back. Captain was watching me from what was now the far side of the inlet. Fearful suddenly of being left alone, I barked and whined to him to come to me, because there was no way I dared cross that broad expanse again. Captain turned away, and I watched him walk back up the tracks until he disappeared in the direction from where we'd come. I'd no choice but to continue on to the town.

As soon as the causeway reached land I hurried off it. I was afraid another train might come, and I wanted to get as far from the tracks as I could. I crossed to the edge of the lake and then followed the shoreline, with the water and my distant view of the farm to my left and the multiplying train tracks to my right, and the town straight ahead. The shore transformed from cinders to a thin strip of sandy beach that widened in front of the town, where it was bordered by a narrow lawn with a few picnic tables. Two women sat at one, chatting while their little children splashed in the shallow water. They paid me no attention, and I continued cautiously by.

The beach gave way to an asphalt-paved, open area extending to a gas station. Crossing that I came upon an assortment of farm machines packed closely together right up to the water's edge. I worked my way through them as well as I could. Then I was stopped. I found myself standing atop a wall that channeled a small river flowing past, the outflow from the lake. I had to find a place to cross if I was to continue my journey along the lakeshore.

25. THE BLACKSMITH'S YARD

As I turned back to find a path through the machines along the river wall, I came face to face with a dog watching me, not much bigger than I am. He was a Jack Russell type, but black and white like Rex. Coming upon him so suddenly startled me, particularly with escape blocked by the river. I immediately went into defensive mode, but he instead wagged his tail vigorously when our eyes met, and dropped into play-crouch before we even touched noses. This was an exceptionally friendly dog, simply glad to encounter someone close to his size, I guessed. I abandoned my usual wariness. It was friends at first sight.

The dog initiated a game of chase. He jumped up and down and ran from me, inviting me to pursue him. When I did, he turned suddenly and ran after me instead, and I ran away. Then I turned quickly after him; and so it was, back and forth, chasing each other, playing hide and seek in and around the machinery until our hearts were pounding. When we stopped, approached and touched noses again, we both wagged our tails happily.

We were so taken up with our encounter that neither of us noticed two big work horses being led toward us up the driveway. Suddenly hearing their footfalls, I swung around to face them. Horses always excited me when I saw them pulling carriages in New York City Central Park. It was great fun to jump at the end of my leash and bark at them, even though they never paid me any attention and just plodded on.

Walking quickly behind a man holding ropes to their halters, the horses were almost upon me when I did what I always do, jumped up and down and barked loudly. I really surprised them, because the farther one quickly shied away and tripped over a plow by the side, and the closer one reared on her hind legs whinnying in alarm. The man tried to control them both, but the rearing horse pulled the rope from his hands, turned back, and ran down the driveway towards the street where cars were passing in both directions.

A stocky, grizzled man in a leather apron who'd been standing in the wide doorway of the adjacent building watching their approach snatched the rope of the remaining horse and cried out in a remarkably raspy voice, "Grab that horse before it gets to the street!" The horse got there first, running into the slow-moving traffic to the sound of screeching brakes. I ducked back among the machinery.

Dodging the veering cars the fellow caught up with his horse who'd stopped on the far side, and he brought her back through the halted traffic. "That dog there all of a sudden came out of nowhere and spooked it, Achille," he said pointing to my friend, the little black and white dog still standing by the driveway.

Achille shaking his leather apron at the dog looked down at him. "What got into you, Pitou [*Pee-too*]?" he scolded him. "You never barked at horses before!" He couldn't see me hiding behind the machinery, so Pitou took the blame for what I'd done.

Achille apologized, "I'm sorry, I don't understand it. He's never done that before," he repeated incredulously as he led the man with his horses through the wide door into his blacksmith shop.

My curiosity got the better of me. Horses always interested and excited me. I came out of hiding and followed Pitou to the doorway where we both watched. Achille led one of the horses into a metal collapsible stall that he pressed against the animal until it was immobilized, unable to move forward or backward or from side to side. Achille grasped then one of the horse's hooves by its fetlock feathering hair, straddled it through the slit in his apron, and with the bottom of the hoof facing up at him, began to carve and file it vigorously. Pieces of hoof flew off, emitting a peculiar smell that reached all the way to the doorway. Then Achille picked up a curved piece of iron and—bang, bang, bang, bang—nailed it to the bottom of the horse's hoof. Finished, he moved to another hoof and began doing the same again. Pitou and I turned our attention back to playing by the river's edge in and around the machinery.

Suddenly there was a crashing sound and a yell from Achille. It was the skittish horse's turn in the restraining stall now, and she was trying to rear and break the structure. Achille just stood by with the other man watching. "Let her get over it," Achille said to him. They both waited for the horse to stop, then Achille went up to her, facing her from the front. He spoke calmly, and the horse quieted. Then he went back, took up the horse's hoof again and straddled it. The horse kicked that foot, more of a push actually, that sent Achille off it. He came back, talking softly to horse, and he tightened the stall against her body. Another strap secured the horse's foot to the structure, so the horse couldn't move at all; and Achille proceeded to shoe her.

With the excitement over, Pitou and I played and rested some more outside, but mostly just explored, sniffing around the machinery parked there. There were all sorts of interesting smells, new ones for me, of small animals that lived by the river and came out only at night, and even of raccoons and beavers. Later he led me up the driveway and into the building through the front door, through a showroom to an office where he had a bed and a dish of water. I drank thankfully, and we both lay on his bed to rest. I liked Pitou a lot. While we were napping, Achille came through to his office. That's the first time he saw me. "Well, who's this?" he said to us. "You've got a friend, Pitou?"

It felt good to have found such a pleasant stop on my journey and such an enjoyable friend. I wouldn't have minded staying there for a while, maybe even a few days, it was that good.

As daylight turned to twilight, Achille closed the shop's blinds, picked up Pitou and said to me, "C'mon." I followed them out the front door, which Achille locked. Then he looked at me, said, "Ok, you go home now. You can come back tomorrow," and he carried Pitou up the side stairs to his apartment where they lived.

I stood at the bottom for a little while staring up, thinking maybe I'd like to go up there, too. That probably was where Pitou got his dinner, and I'd have liked some; but no one came back for me. As I looked around to decide what to do, at the end of what had been a gorgeous sunny day, I was startled by a sudden clap of thunder. It grew very dark very quickly. Heavy raindrops began to fall, only a few at first, then more. I looked for shelter, and crawled under one of the low, flat machines between the driveway and the river. I lay there on the grass to wait out the storm. I stayed dry, but I had to remain there all night. Although lightning and thunder came and went, the pelting rain didn't stop at all until early dawn.

26. WANDERING THE TOWN

The respite from the rain was a short one. Another heavy storm came through, more violent than anything before it. There was a flash of bright light, a lightning strike so close that its earsplitting thunder was instantaneous, accompanied by the cracking sound of splintering wood. Cracking, cracking, cracking, and the whoosh and crash of a tree right on top of the machine under which I lay. I was so scared that I ran out as fast as I could and fled down the driveway. I ran deeper into the town, in terror first, then to find shelter from the rain. I stood for a while under a narrow awning, but the water bounced off the sidewalk at me, hardly better than no protection at all. I ran on toward the town square, where on the corner I came to the clothing store. Mrs. Byrd used to park her Jeep in front of it and go inside to buy her woolen red-plaid Vermont-made winter clothes, and she'd come out with a tiny cup of ice cream from the soda fountain for me. I ran up the store steps to its canopied landing, and waited there for the storm to subside.

The rain finally stopped. The clouds dissipated, and the sun began to radiate brightly in the freshness of the recent shower. I'd not eaten since the previous forenoon with Captain, and my belly hurt as my stomach churned empty; so I set out in search of food. I wanted to find houses where, like Rex and Captain did so adeptly, and

Spotty, too, I might persuade someone to offer me their leftovers. However, the town center was not that sort of place. The buildings all stood adjoining each other, only contiguous shops and stores. I looked across the square at the town green with its monument; behind it was the railroad station. To the left I recognized the grocery store that stood solitary in its broad lot where Mrs. Byrd always parked.

I remembered my friend Agnes in New York City used to find plenty of food outside the grocery stores. I checked the street. There was little traffic, but the few cars driving through the town were going quite fast, so I crossed carefully. I circled to the back of the store. There were no garbage bags to open the way my pit bull friend, Molly, back in New York had once shown me how to do. There was only a high dumpster sitting on clean-swept asphalt. I could smell food odors wafting from it. Then I saw one thing on the ground that had fallen to the side. I smelled it tentatively, then made short work of the transparent wrapping which had protected a solid loaf of unsliced bread from the rain. It was too big for me to bite, and the crust too hard, but I gnawed on its pointed ends like a bone. The bread softened as my chewing moistened it. It assuaged my hunger, but I wasn't inclined to fill up on stale bread. I wanted some real food, like other dogs got when they went roaming. I scanned the streets that converged there.

I looked across again towards the monument green. Behind the railroad station a wide expanse of tracks cut through the town, rounding the base of a cliff too steep to climb. I decided to follow the street that bordered the tracks, because it had individual houses lining one side. People were beginning to appear, and I stopped and stared hopefully at each person I met.

Not far along I came to a fork. I'd begun to sense that this street by the tracks was taking me out of town again, but the one that bore to the right, crossing them, led up a hill lined with more houses. As often happened the decision was made for me when children behind me yelled, "Look at the little dog, catch him!" and pounded towards me. I escaped across the tracks.

Trotting up the rise as the morning freshness advanced into a sun-filled day, I found myself drawn by an enjoyable sense of adventure. I knew instinctively that the lake had to be downhill, but there were houses in this upward direction, and my hunger, curiosity, and freedom led me on. I was getting used to being out on my own, being a tramp again of sorts. My circumstance recalled the independence I'd felt back in New York City when I'd joined up with the pit bull Molly and raised her pups with her in Central Park two years earlier. I felt some of that hankering for a feral life.

The fact that dogs went about freely without leashes in this town had most of us halfway there. Two leashes remained, however, shelter and food. Dogs like Rex and Spotty and Captain knew where their homes were and returned from their occasional wanderings to where food was set out for them. It was rather a nice way to live, when you think about it, this cocktail of freedom, food and shelter. What more could a dog want?

My ascent ended abruptly at a cross street. Always this choice, right or left, without knowing which to take. But I was exploring, and right looked interesting. I'd not gone far when it led between two big buildings, one a church on the high side, and on a lower terrace a large, square, multi-storied house where women dressed in black were sitting in a row of rocking chairs on an open porch. I paused at the stairway that led down to them. Maybe they'd offer me some food. That's how Rex did it, and Captain, too; they'd just visit people's back yards and look up at them with pleading eyes. So I gazed hopefully.

When nothing happened, I suspected that I was too far from them. I hesitated because there were many steps down, and more up to the porch. I am farsighted; my near vision is not good, so I trip on stairs easily. Then one of the women pointed to me, and they all looked up. I was sure that meant food. So I carefully began to descend one step at a time. I quickly misjudged and rolled forward head first, only stopping my fall by twisting my body violently. I lay across the width of a step until I dared to budge. Then fearfully I crawled the short distance back up to the top. There, I looked again at the women who'd been watching alarmed, but no one had moved. They hadn't understood what I wanted. I gave myself a good shake and walked on.

As I wandered forward, looking for any opportunity, my energy began to wane for lack of food. I sensed that I should be heading back downhill, but once again I turned onto a street that resumed a gradual ascent instead, because its houses spaced with lawns looked promising—

until I encountered dogs sleeping on those lawns or running out from back yards to chase me when I ventured to approach. One after the other drove me farther and farther up the tree-canopied pavement until the houses grew scarcer, the trees more numerous, and the street transformed into a dirt road heading out of town.

While I wondered what to do, a car drove by and parked just ahead of me. Two people got out, and I recognized Joe and Maddie from my morning with Captain. Joe took a knapsack and strapped it to his back; and the two of them started walking up a trail that led into the woods. They'd fed me the day before, and I could smell food in that knapsack; so I followed them. Each time they stopped I'd look at them with entreating eyes.

Joe and Maddie didn't stop often, however, only a few times to rest. I stared hopefully, but no one opened the knapsack. They did recognize me, though.

"I think it's that same little dog that came begging with Captain yesterday," Joe said.

"How'd it end up here, unless it's really lost?" Maddie questioned. "Could it be Ted's dog? Do you think he left it at the farm?"

"If he did, it should know its way home. I think Ted's dog had some black around the face, though, not so much tan."

They continued up the mountain path with me following. All I had was my little acquaintance with Joe and Maddie, who were kind, and who'd fed me before and might again. So I followed what security I felt with them, up the footpath through the woods.

After some steady climbing, along with increasing rest stops, we reached a very small opening in the trees at the top of the mountain. I followed them onto a wide, conveniently flat rock where they sat down; and I sat, too, just a little distance from them.

Joe set the knapsack on the stone. Maddie opened it and took out a tablecloth she spread by them. I could smell ham. I'd not eaten anything since the stale bread that morning, and with all the exercise I'd grown hungrier than ever. I edged a little closer to them and the food, and I waited.

Joe warned, "Watch the dog."

"I am," Maddie reassured him.

They sat for a while then gazing out at the vista with their arms around each other's shoulders.

"I love this view so," Maddie said to Joe, resting her head on him, "the way the town nestles at the mountain's base. Can you see our house by the lakeside? The lake's contours look like they're drawn on a map. The distance makes it two-dimensional. "

"Yes, from here the basin looks so flat. You wouldn't think that way down there Lake Isle is one of the highest elevated towns in the state. "

"You were right this morning. The weather's perfect; the view is clear. We can see all the way to the White Mountains."

I crossed the rock on which they sat and gazed down, too; and I saw the lake far away.

"Do you think it might be Ted's dog?" Maddie asked again.

"Ted was staying at the farm for quite a while earlier in the summer, but I know he's gone now. It has to belong to one of the campers," Joe reckoned.

"Maybe we should take it and drop it off at the campground so it can get home," she suggested.

Maddie set out sandwiches, and Joe poured cups of a sweet, yellow drink. I edged close enough to be within reach, and it paid off. Each of them broke of bits of meat from their sandwiches as they ate and hand-fed them to me with pieces of cheese. Joe took an ice cube from his drink and set it on the rock by me. Licking it was good; it quenched my thirst and cooled me at the same time.

Joe and Maddie talked for a while afterwards as they continued to look out at the view. Then they lay back where there was soft moss on the rock, Joe laying his head on Maddie like a pillow, and they napped in the sun for a while. I nodded asleep, too.

When I heard them stir, I jumped up. I watched Maddie put everything into the knapsack. Joe shouldered it, and they headed back down the footpath with me following them.

"Maybe we should take him," Joe said to Maddie when we reached the car.

"It's up to you," Maddie answered.

Joe came towards me to pick me up, but I wasn't ready for that. Every time he advanced I backed away.

"Well, that answers that," Joe said. They got into their car and drove off.

I watched the car disappear in the direction I knew I had to go anyway, and I couldn't help but give a whine. I wished I'd had the courage to go with them. I hadn't been thinking, only reacting. My innate distrust of strangers had overwhelmed better judgement.

With all my wandering that day I'd maintained a sense of where I was, confirmed by the sight of the lake from the mountain top. I knew that I had to get back through the town to reach Dad's farm. However, I was blocked by the gauntlet of dogs that had chased me up the street, and that realization made me quiver fearfully now. The car that could have gotten me beyond them was gone.

I ran down the street as fast as I could at full gallop to get by those dogs before they discovered me. It worked. They each spotted me when I was already past—except the last one, alerted by the loud barking of the others. He stood ahead waiting for me.

I'd no choice but to dash up a street to the right to avoid that dog, as tall as Captain but less bulky, built to run well. I leapt forward with all the strength in my heart, my short legs trying to make up with speed for the difference compared to his strides; but there was no way I could outrun him, and he bore down on me.

I made straight for two women who were sitting in lawn chairs in front of the nearest house, and I scooted under one of the chairs. I cowered there looking out, my heart banging in my chest. My pursuer stopped short and sat on his haunches at the edge of the lawn panting, waiting. Of course I startled the women, but the one under whom I lay looked down at me and said, "Oh, you poor little thing," while the other got to her feet and walked towards the dog, swishing her newspaper, saying to him,

"Go home, Topsy, go home." Topsy turned and walked back up the sidewalk. As soon as he was out of sight, I dashed out from under the chair, across the lawn and down the street as fast as I could. I could hear the amused women laughing in surprise behind me.

27. SUNDAY CHURCH

I was on a street now which paralleled the base of the mountain. With Topsy somewhere behind me, I'd no choice but to proceed forward, hoping that another cross street would lead back down into the town center. However, when I came to one I was thinking about food again, so I chose instead to continue up a short, steep hill where I could see at the top a row of rather large houses looking out over the town. On the front lawn of the first, an elegant, ornate Victorian, an elderly woman in a broad straw hat was irrigating her flower beds with a watering can.

"Well, aren't you the cutest little dog," she said when she saw me.

I hoped she'd offer me something to eat. Those bits of ham up on the mountain had not taken me very far. I looked at her and wagged my tail. I stared with my most hopeful eyes. She only watched me; no food yet. So I turned up the appeal. I walked up the embankment at the edge of her lawn and approached her to within a few feet. I wagged my tail some more and gave an entreating whine.

"You're such a pretty dog," she said. Then she called out, loud enough to startle me, "Clarence, Clarence, come here, Clarence, come here, and see this pretty little dog."

An elderly man came around the corner of the house, carrying a garden rake. Like the woman he wore a broad straw hat.

"Look, here's another one like Ted's dog," the woman said.

"Yes, fancy little dogs with pointed ears," Clarence agreed. "It resembles Ted's." Not much interested he turned to go back to his tasks.

"He's certainly very friendly," the woman said, "he walked right up to me."

"Well, don't feed it, Olivia, or we'll be stuck with it," Clarence warned her as he disappeared.

"Yes, he may be hungry," Olivia said to herself after him.

She put down her watering can and went into the house, while I waited hopefully. She came out with a dish of beef stew and set it down in front of me. She'd even warmed it for me. I devoured it—as Clarence came back.

"I thought I told you not to feed it," he said. Olivia ignored him as if she didn't hear. Clarence grumbled "... every dog in the neighborhood" and "then they dirty the lawn ... " and he disappeared again.

After my best dinner of the day, I lay down there on the front lawn and watched Olivia continue watering her flower beds, and I dozed a bit. When Olivia finished, she walked around the house to the back where Clarence had gone, and I followed her. Like everyone in Lake Isle it seemed, they had a big garden; but this one was spectacularly beautiful, full of flowers, tall ones, small ones, every sort. The flowers were Olivia's focus, while Clarence was puttering about his vegetables. I lay then on the back lawn at the edge of the garden and watched. I felt in no hurry; I'd already put in quite a day.

Clarence suggested to Olivia, "I'd call the farm to see if that's Ted's dog."

She said, "I can't imagine it is. Ted's gone. But I'll call."

Olivia was cutting some of the flowers at the base of their stems and placing them carefully in a basket. She took them into the house. Clarence carried his tools into the garage. I began to doze off again where I lay.

When I awoke neither Olivia nor Clarence were anywhere to be seen. The sun was getting lower in the sky; it was late afternoon. I stood up, stretched, and decided to continue on my way. I walked back down the steep hill and down the cross street at the base. It leveled off and widened into a parking lot in front of the church I'd passed earlier.

Off to one side little children were playing with tiny trucks in the sand at the edge of the pavement. They looked up at me. I gave them a wide berth. A boy jumped up, and another followed. As they ran for me, I retreated in the direction from which I'd just come. I saw Olivia coming down the hill with her basket of flowers. The little boys stopped; she said hello to them, and they did to her. I was safe from the children with her, and I followed her along. The boys trailed behind watching me and asked Olivia if they could pat her little dog.

"Not today," Olivia told them, noting my wariness. "I don't think he's much interested in being patted right now, boys."

I stayed close by her, and followed her up the steps of the church. I was right behind her into the entry, but she was careful not to let me through the inner door. I lay by a stairway and waited while I could still hear the boys outside. Then I heard voices approaching up the steps. Conversing, two of the women dressed in black I'd seen earlier in the day came into the vestibule. When they opened the inner door, they didn't see me enter the church with them. They continued forward. I stood back for a panoramic gaze at the cavernous interior.

The whole building was a very long room, very broad and incredibly high. It was filled with innumerable rows of benches. In the far distance a railing separated a wide, red-carpeted area where steps led up to a shiny, stone table covered with a white cloth, on which six tall candlesticks stood in a row, with a big golden box in the middle. There were statues of people in long dresses everywhere, and one of a man in almost no clothes hanging by this hands.

I saw Olivia get up from the bench where she sat with her basket of flowers, and come forward to the black-dressed women. "Good afternoon, Sisters. I have more cuttings from my garden for the altar."

"Thank you, Olivia," the older nun said, accepting the basket, and to the younger one, "Won't these irises stand pretty between the altar candlesticks, Sister Claire."

"As beautiful as the gladioli Olivia brought us last week, Sister Jeanne," she answered.

Handing Sister Claire the basket of flowers, Sister Jeanne asked her to "put them into one of the tall vases with water to keep them fresh," and turning to Olivia she exclaimed, "You grow such beautiful flowers!"

"*A la plus grande gloire de Dieu!*" Olivia answered.

I stood watching Olivia and the Sisters walk towards the front of the church. Sister Claire crossed the carpeted area and disappeared through a side door, emerging moments later with Olivia's empty basket which she returned to her.

I wandered over to one of the side aisles. My sniffing didn't turn up anything but a stale, very old mouse smell. When Olivia walked towards the back of the church, I went round to follow her out; but I dawdled too much getting there, and she left, closing the door behind her. I lay down nearby to wait for the Sisters to leave, so I could exit with them. They were busy in the carpeted area that was bathed in brightness now from the lights they'd turned on. The array of gold fleur-de-lis painted against a matte maroon background glistened on the walls. The two nuns came and went in and out of the open doors on each side of the red-carpeted area, talking softly to each other all the while; and their muted voices echoed quietly through the cavernous space. They replaced the white table cloths and put tall glass vases of Olivia's irises between the tall candlesticks.

I waited, maybe dozed a bit, and then I realized that I didn't hear them anymore. They'd left through a different door, probably one behind the red-carpeted area. It was very quiet in the church now. I waited alone for a long time for someone to come, but no one did. Light shining through the colored windows turned to tinted twilight, then dark grey. Almost nighttime, while I still could see a bit, I noticed a structure in the back corner not far from the vestibule door where I'd been waiting. It looked like a closet, with a door in the middle, and a curtain hanging on each side. I crawled under one of the curtains into a narrow enclosed space. There was a small flat cushion on the floor, and I lay upon it. It felt better there, like bedding down in a den.

When I awoke during the night, I looked out from under the curtain. The church was illumined eerily by bands of moonlight entering through the colored windows. It was very still, except when here and there I heard the building creak. I was glad I'd found my den; I pulled my head back under the curtain and went back to sleep.

In the morning a clanking awakened me, and I looked out to see the large, main doors not far from me in the back of the church opening wide. I was halfway from under the closet curtain, ready to run outside through them, when the gnarled little man who'd finished opening them turned to walk in my direction. So I pulled back and waited until he was out of the way. When he passed through the smaller door to the vestibule by which I'd entered the previous day, I stepped out and headed for the open doors. I'd not gotten more than a few steps, however, when a deafening clangor from above reverberated right through me. Beyond the partially open door to the vestibule I could see the little man pulling with all his body weight on a huge rope that swung back up and almost carried him with it. He let go of it, and when it came back to him, he pulled it again, then released it to swing back up, and then pulled it again. With each heavy pull an unbelievably loud bell rang overhead, pounding my body and paining my ears. I ran terrified back under the curtain to hide in the darkness of my closet, where I crouched fearfully into the farthest corner. The wooden sides magnified the tremors of the pealing as if I were inside a drum.

When the bell finally went silent, I waited some minutes in the ominous quiet, wanting to be sure the earsplitting sound was over and past and not about to resume on top of me. Then I cautiously looked out again from under the curtain, to make a run to escape through the inviting doors. But people, crowds and crowds of people were coming in through them now, and I could hear many more laughing and greeting each other outside waiting to enter. As soon as they passed through the doors they stopped talking, except occasionally in a whisper. So many people gathering so silently felt threatening somehow. I decided for the moment to stay hidden.

While the church filled with people, I waited. The carpeted area up front became brightly, blindingly, illumined. Soon boys wearing long black dresses with white blouses filed from the side doors into the brightness—the same doors into which the Sisters had disappeared the day before. Then a man in colored robes came out flanked by two more boys. He stopped, looked out at all the people and said, "Welcome everyone, and welcome all our summer visitors, to Our Lady of Lake Isle church today." Then he walked up to the shiny stone table. I can't see so well up close, which is why I trip on stairs and don't jump up on furniture; but I can see really well far off. Ted always says I can spot a dog at the end of the block. This time what I saw made me so happy. Lucien was one of the boys walking beside the man.

So instead of going out the open doors as I'd intended, I trotted down the main aisle to meet up with Lucien. Suddenly all the silent people who'd stood in unison when the man and boys appeared, started whispering almost out loud, "There's a dog in the church, there's a dog in the church," and someone whispered, "Did you ever see a dog like that?" while other people in the balcony overhead began to sing.

Men stepped out from the benches on both sides with their arms wide apart to catch me. I'm quick, and I ran right through their legs, right through the low railing, and onto the carpeted space where Lucien was seated now. I ran up to him and wagged a vigorous hello with my best smile. I was so glad to see him.

Lucien, however, just sat there stupefied. His face turned red, and he stared at me bug-eyed without moving. Right away all the other boys came running to catch me. I slipped through them so fast as they were jumping for me that I heard a couple of them clunk heads and cry out. I didn't know what Lucien's problem was, but I had to get out of there or get squashed.

I could see the wide doors in the back were still open. I ran for them through the gauntlet again, zigzagging past all the people stepping out from the benches with hands reaching for me and the ushers chasing me. I scooted out the doors, and heard them closed behind me.

28. A DEEP HOLE

I kept running. I ran down the terrace to the street below. It led to another street past another church, and then past a third church, then over an overpass across the railroad tracks, and finally to the lake that spread out clearly now before me. Only when I reached the lakeshore did I stop, panting hard, gasping for breath. I hid in a box that lay open on its side on the little sandy beach, and waited for . . . I don't know what. I'd never had so many people chase me all at once. And what was wrong with Lucien?

I hid in the box for a long time. The open end faced out towards the lake whose tiny waves, mere ripples, monotonously rolled in and out a few inches on the sand. The box was like a little dog house, much the same size as my house at the base of the bookcase in our bedroom in New York City. "*Our* bedroom," Ted's and mine, in "*our* apartment," I'd thought. Life there was so easy. I missed it so much. I yearned for that secure peace even as the memory of it grew dimmer and more distant. I still believed Ted would come back to get me, maybe. Or was this my life now? A horrible chasm inexplicably authored by Ted separated me helplessly from everything I'd known and enjoyed with him. I thought of Ted that day for a long time in that box, as the sun rose higher in the sky and then descended, from one side of the lake to the other.

It was only when the enlarged orange disk was close to touching the mountain tops to my right that I was aroused from my grief again by hunger. I hadn't eaten all day. I thought of the grocery store dumpster on the other side of the town square, and I stepped out of the box and out of my sorrowful thoughts to find it.

There was little traffic, so it was easy to cross Main Street to the monument green in the town center and then to the train station behind it. I followed the sidewalk to the grocery store at the far end of the circle. It felt better to be up and out again, walking, doing something, than just waiting and waiting to catch up with myself as I'd done in the box most of the day.

When I reached the dumpster I went around it twice, but nothing had dropped from it to the ground. I hesitated then. I decided to explore any alleys I might find between the buildings on the adjacent streets. An hour later I found myself standing in deepening twilight across from Achille Lambert's store, but it was closed, and my friend Pitou was not in the window or anywhere to be seen. So I walked down the driveway where I'd scared the horses. Past all the machinery spread about, I reached the lakeshore again. All I was thinking of then was food; I was famished. No more sad thoughts, only a gnawing hunger. With no options left, I realized that if I followed the shore back the way I'd come, I'd find Joe and Maddie's house past the railroad yards. I felt confident they'd feed me. That's what I did. I didn't even think about the causeway.

By the time I reached the edge of town where the lakeshore presses against the cinder embankments of the railroad tracks, twilight had passed. There was no moon to light my path, just the darkness of a black sky full of flickering stars. The only means to find my direction was to follow the tracks, but I suddenly realized that there were many of them. Which to follow? I chose randomly the rails nearest me at the outer edge. When they joined into others, I followed them. The going was difficult. My poor near-vision compounded the darkness, so I tripped over the ties and lost my way in treacherous footing at the railroad switches. I trekked on.

I was almost upon them when I saw two figures barely discernible in the darkness, like dim silhouettes waiting for me. At first I welcomed the sight, but almost as quickly stopped to scrutinize them. It was Hardwood, I knew, when I heard the coydog hiss. Was she on leash? No, because while he stood there, she began to walk towards me, and then broke into a run. I jumped across the tracks I was following, and then across more tracks to get away from her. I could hear her behind me as I ran with all my might headlong into the darkness. I looked back as I sensed her almost on top of me, and suddenly there was no more ground beneath my feet and I was twisting in midair. I hit the bottom with an impact that went through me.

Dazed, lying where I landed with the breath knocked out of me, I couldn't move at first. Then I only managed to roll off my hurting shoulder, which left me on my back facing up, and I made out the coydog looking down at me from the edge above, a black silhouette against the dark star-filled sky. Hardwood appeared beside her, looking, too, down into the blackness where I lay.

The two disappeared while I stayed motionless, still gasping and in pain. It took me some time to regain my senses, and as I did I trembled all the more with terror. I staggered to my feet as best I could and then stood shaking in place, my mind in shock, not able to think at all. When my eyes adjusted a little to the utter blackness and my ears to the total quiet, ever so slowly my panic ebbed enough for me to try to help myself. I licked my painful shoulder as well as I could reach it. While still trying to perceive through the fog in my head, I limped to investigate where I was and what to do. I immediately bumped into a wall. It took me a long time, in stops and starts, to feel my way around its perimeter. The hole I was in was a very big semi-circle. Its perfectly round side was bordered by a small track I tripped over. Its straight side was some sort of massive machinery. There was no way out. So, more miserable now than ever, I curled up by the wall, and beset with shoulder pain, hunger pains, and still trembling, I somehow fell into a fitful sleep.

The side walls were very high, too high for me to see anywhere but up as dawn approached and then as it grew lighter. I limped the perimeter of the hole again once it came into sight, even though from where I'd lay it obviously was the semi-circle I'd imagined it to be in the dark. I began to hear noises, people coming and going above, but no one appeared. Then there was the loud blast of a factory whistle so close that it frightened me completely, and I began leaping futilely against the sides of the hole. My terror increased when the machine that was the straight border of the hole began to roar, and that edge started to turn slowly. It stopped, and a locomotive engine moved onto it. Then it turned some more, not far, and the engine moved off it. With all the noise and the moving parts of my huge hole, I went berserk, jumping, leaping against the sides, barking and screaming. I've never been so scared in my whole life.

I saw the heads of men appear over the top of the sides. They said things like, "There's a dog down there" or "I think it's a dog." Someone said, "Get a ladder," and that's what they did.

A man came down the ladder and walked over to me where I was cringing now by the side. I normally would not let a stranger touch me, but I was so desperate for rescue at this point that anybody was welcome. He cautiously reached for me and picked me up, then carried me up the ladder with him. Several other men crowded around to look at me.

"Funny-looking dog," one said. "You ever see a dog like that?"

"Awfully small, probably just a puppy," another suggested.

One asked my rescuer, "What you think, Jack?"

"I think if it shakes any harder, it's going to fall off my arm," he laughed. "It's scared out of its wits." I was still feeling spasms of terror, but Jack's arm was strong and reassuring, that of a good person.

"What're you going to do with it?" one man asked.

"I don't know," Jack answered, "You want it?"

No one wanted me. Jack said, "We can't let it run around here. It'll just get in trouble again, get run over or something. I'll just hitch it to my bench, and after work I'll take it home for now, see if someone wants it." That's what he did.

He carried me into a building that surrounded much of the wide hole into which I'd fallen. Tied to Jack's machinist bench in the roundhouse was almost as frightening as the night had been. Looking out the huge doorway I could see that the hole was really a full circle with a bridge extending from one side to the other that cut it in half. The men drove engines onto that bridge they called the turntable, and then the bridge would turn in the hole to point the engine at one of the roundhouse doors. They drove the engine into the building and started climbing up and down on it, and clanging and banging things on it, with sparks flying, and take wheels off and put wheels on. This was happening to several engines at the same place, so it was very noisy. My ears hurt. There wasn't much I could do, however, tied to Jack's bench. I was so unhappy. There was all the noise, and I'd not eaten since yesterday, so my stomach ached. I lay by the bench hiding my face beneath my paws. How could Ted have left me like this?

At noon the loud whistle blew again, and all the men stopped working and took out their lunchboxes. Jack sat by me, and while he laughed and talked with other men sitting by him, he picked out some of the bologna from his sandwiches and gave it to me by hand. It wasn't much, just enough to stop my stomach from grinding. Later the whistle blew again, and all the men went back to clanging and banging on the engines. The roundhouse was a very busy place. Nobody except me seemed unhappy, though.

The men talked and joked and laughed as they worked steadily. Finally, towards the end of the afternoon, the whistle blew again. It seemed right over us, so very loud.

"The four o'clock whistle," one man said as he took out his pocket watch to synchronize it. "The signal for every wife to start supper." The other men laughed.

Jack untied my rope from his bench and led me out among the parade of men leaving the railroad yard. When we reached his pickup truck, he got into the driver's seat and set me beside him on the passenger's seat, and we drove off. I was so low on the seat that I couldn't see anything. I wouldn't have known where we were, anyway. We didn't go far. I sensed the truck climb a couple of hills then level out, and then we stopped. Jack took me out of the truck, removed the cord from my neck, and set me on the ground.

I looked about. It was a little farm, with small fields on each side of the long driveway dividing them, and woods seemingly all around. We'd parked in front of a low, broad house. Before Jack entered through the sun porch and left me standing outside, he called out, "Jody!" A boy came out; he was curious when he saw me. However, Jack was thinking about something else. He called Jody's attention to a single animal standing in the middle of the hayfield grazing contentedly.

"That pesky little bull has come through the fence again," he said to Jody, pointing to the animal. "Get him out of there and take him home."

I followed Jody into a small barn adjoining the house in the rear. The boy got a rope and headed for the field with me behind him. As we approached closer, I realized it was Bruno, Lucien's pet bull. He looked up at us, munching Jack's grass sticking out the sides of his mouth, and, docile as he was, made no effort to escape when Jody tossed the lasso over his head. Then he followed placidly as Jody led him out of the field and down the driveway away from Jack's house. At the edge of the field the dirt road dipped down a steep hill alongside a cemetery that was instantly familiar to me. Beyond it I could see Dad's farm. And that's where we went with Bruno, Jody in the lead, and I following behind. A nice little parade.

29. TRANSITIONS AND UNRAVELING

Lucien was mowing the front lawn, and I ran over to him. Absolutely thrilled, I jumped up and down against his leg. "Tobi!" he said surprised. "Where'd you come from?" he asked, as he stooped to tickle me behind the ears. I licked his hands enthusiastically, hopping and twirling all at the same time, I was so excited. I was back at the farm! I was back where Ted would find me!

Then Lucien saw Jody coming along with Bruno, and he turned serious and walked over to meet him, while I was still jumping up and down against his leg and running in little circles around him, I was so happy. He greeted his friend Jody, took the rope holding Bruno, and asked, "Was he in your pasture? I hope it wasn't the hayfield again."

"It was the hayfield," Jody told him. "My dad says to tell your granddad. The bull's out there almost everyday, grazing and trampling. We won't have any hay if he keeps it up."

"I don't know what to do . . . Pépère's going to be awfully mad if I tell him again."

"You've got to, Lucien. My dad says the time comes when you have to pen up a bull, or tie him to a post or keep him in the barn. My dad says that if we end up short of hay, he's going to have to ask your granddad to pay for it."

I stood in front of Lucien wagging my tail eagerly, but he wasn't paying me any more attention. Jody noticed my excitement, though. "It your dog?" he asked.

"It's my uncle's, from New York City. It wanders off and just showed up again."

"Yeh, because it was following me," Jody said. "My dad brought it home just now from the roundhouse. It was down in the turntable. Lucky it didn't get crushed."

"It gets around," Lucien said.

The two boys led Bruno through the barnyard, and I ran looking for Rex, first to the transom, then to the barn and over by the chickens. I didn't see him, so I joined Lucien and Jody bringing Bruno to the pasture behind the barn. I stayed with them as they walked the fence line between their farms to see where Bruno had gone through.

"There's no holes in the fence," Jody concluded. "It just goes through anywhere it feels like it."

With his rope wound over his shoulder, Jody crossed over to head for home. Looking back he said, "Lucien, you've got to tell your granddad. Or my dad will end up coming over and telling him himself."

I followed Lucien who walked unhappily back to the farmyard, as I kept knocking my nose against his leg and jumping to express my enthusiasm. At the house he called out, "Look who's back."

Mom came to the door and looked at me through the screen. I was hungry, and stared up at her with my best, most intent smile and wagged my tail. She said to me, "Well, why don't you stay a while." Then she turned back inside and finished getting supper ready. Quite wonderful smells wafted out into the mudroom where I waited.

While I lay by the door, Marguerite came hurrying out to see me when Lucien told her I was back, and she picked me up and hugged me and danced with me while I licked her face. Dad came through and didn't say a word.

While the family was at supper, I wondered where Rex was. I went outside, went to the transom again where he always lay with Nanook. The cat was alone in the late day sun. Rex's scent there was very, very faint, telling me that he'd not been there in a long while. I walked to the back of the house, went behind the barn, then as close to the chicken yard as I dared without arousing Le Coq. When I heard Mom calling me, "Tobi, Tobi, here Tobi," I ran back to the mudroom and gulped down my supper and licked up the warm milk Mom had poured on it. Then I lay on my little bed in the corner that Marguerite had set out for me while I ate. There was no bed for Rex.

I dosed in a rush of contentment. Ted would find me. Maybe he was back; maybe he was just gone for the evening, and he'd grab me up and hug me when he returned. Dad and Lucien came into the room, put on their barn clothes, and went out. I had no inclination to follow them. I fell asleep, and woke only when they returned.

"I'm not going to talk about it anymore!" Dad was saying to Lucien. "He keeps going through the fences and ending up in the neighbors' fields, and the neighbors are not happy about it. You can't blame them."

"But you gave him to me for 4-H," Lucien protested feebly.

"Yes, and we always knew he'd grow up. It won't be long we'll have to lock him up in the barn because he'll be getting ugly, and dangerous, and could hurt somebody unaware crossing the pasture."

"Bruno won't ever get ugly; he's a real Ferdinand," Lucien objected. "He trusts me," he protested wearily. "If we sell him, he'll be slaughtered. That's what they do."

"Of course, that's what they do!" Dad said to him impatiently. "That's what we raise them for. What do you expect to do with a bull, keep it forever?"

"But Bruno! I love Bruno. I can't..."

Dad interrupted emphatically, "Farm animals aren't for loving! I didn't give you a bull calf for a pet! I gave it to you to learn how to raise it so it would be good to sell. That's what farming is all about. It's not about pets. It's about growing food! I shouldn't even have to have this discussion!"

Lucien, his back to the mudroom wall, looked down at the floor and went silent. He wasn't defiant; he was ashamed. "I'm sorry, Pépère," he said.

Dad felt sorry, too. "I'll tell you what, you know that red English bicycle you asked for? You let me sell the bull, and I'll buy you that with the money. How's that? It solves everything."

Lucien knew he didn't have much choice, and the bicycle was a very attractive consolation prize.

After they went into the house I fell asleep again enjoying a deep sense of relief and contentment. I slept there all night, by myself in my corner of the mudroom, until I heard stirrings in the house at dawn. Dad and Lucien came through again to suit up for chores, Lucien to get the cows and Dad to prepare the barn.

I walked out to the front lawn. The morning light augured a bright, sunny day. Looking down at the lake I watched the steamy mist rising from its surface as the sun climbed in the distance above the eastern mountains. A heavy dew lay upon the grass, and the air was still cool. I focused my gaze up then down the street to see if perhaps I could spot Ted's car returning, and then I lay on the wet grass at the corner of the lawn to wait. I went back to the mudroom when Mom called me for my breakfast. Afterwards I walked over to the transom and sunned lazily for a while, paying little attention to Nanook who joined me.

I'd not been there long when a big, square-bodied truck came up the driveway and stopped in front of the barn. A short, very heavy man got out, walked to the rear and with a winch lowered the top of the tall tailgate all the way to the ground, making it a ramp up to the truck bed. He went into the barn, and soon came out leading Bruno at the end of a rope halter, followed by Dad. The man was strong, and he pulled the resisting Bruno up the ramp into the truck, with Dad's help pushing from behind. After that the man winched the gate back up, locked it, gave Dad money and drove off. That's the last I ever saw of the little bull who led me home. His final foray into the neighbor's hayfield had sealed his fate earlier than might have been.

Lucien was nowhere to be seen when Bruno was on his way. He came out of the house around noon with Dad, and they went off in Dad's pickup truck. When they returned, they unloaded a shiny red bicycle. Lucien rode it happily around the barnyard to show it off, and Mom came out with Marguerite to admire it. I stood beside them watching Lucien go around in circles.

"I didn't get any bike when Dad sold Trigger," Marguerite said as much to herself as to Mom. "He didn't even tell me he was going to sell him. I came home one day and Trigger was gone. That's the deal I got."

"Shhh, don't say anything—not right now," Mom advised her. "Don't spoil it for your brother."

"Well, when?" Marguerite asked.

"I don't know, but I'll speak for you when the time is right."

"His first bike was new, and this one is new. And my bike is second-hand."

"Pépère bought both Lucien's bikes. Your father bought yours. With all the medical bills for your mother, your father did what he could."

After a short pause Marguerite said to Mom, "No, Mémère, it's ok. I treasure my bike."

"Let's get back to our baking," Mom suggested, and they went into the house.

Every morning afterwards I continued to lie at the corner of the lawn for a while to watch for Ted, except rainy days when I waited in the mudroom. Slowly I got used to some things. I stopped wondering where Rex was; he became a memory. I didn't let Nanook near me when he tried to sun with me on the transom. I stayed away from the barn; it held no interest for me. I built an expectant relationship with Mom each day because she is the person who fed me. Sometimes I stayed by her when she worked in her garden.

The farm usually made for an interesting day. I could wander about outdoors, and sniff things, and watch the birds flying up and down from the lawn to the fields. I might have gotten more and more used to it; it was not a bad life. Still, I went to the corner of the lawn at the end of the driveway and waited every morning, and then again towards the end of the afternoon. I missed my friend Ted, and I waited patiently for him return to the farm. At first I was pretty sure he would.

No one else bothered much with me. Not Lucien nor Marguerite, and certainly not Dad. I was just "the dog." I lived on the farm in a dog's place, the way Rex had. They'd not doted on Rex nor pampered him the way I was used to getting from Ted. Neither, however, did they treat me like they did Rex. When Lucien went for the cows, he didn't call me to go with him. He could see I didn't want to go, and he knew I wouldn't be any good at it anyway. When Marguerite took her bike to go to the brooks fishing, she didn't call me to go with her. They let me be, because a Chihuahua didn't fit on the farm the way a bigger dog like Rex did. They took care of me because I was there; it was what they'd agreed to do for Ted. It wasn't a bad life, but more and more I'd still go to the corner of the lawn, lie there with my chin on my paws, and grow very sad.

When another month passed and then another, and Ted didn't come back while I waited expectantly at first, then more and more disappointedly, I descended into quiet. I'd made such an effort for such a long time to get back to the farm to be there when he came. Now the unfulfilled anticipation disheartened me. I hardly left my bed in the mudroom. I'd drift down close to sleep where my feelings dulled, countering my grief. I was a Chihuahua; I didn't want to be a farm dog. I wanted the life I remembered with Ted. As I gave up, I declined more. I stopped being hungry; I'd pick at my food when I bothered to check it out, ate a little only when my stomach hurt for it. That made me skinny, and I had a harder time to keep my footing walking. If Rex still had been there, I might not have felt so alone. Without Mémère around, there was no one to console me.

From my corner of the lawn I saw Mrs. Byrd's Jeep drive into Aunt Florence's driveway from time to time. However, she didn't come to find me, and I didn't go looking for her.

Aunt Florence told Dad, "Ted said to her he wants the dog back eventually, and she's afraid she'll be too attached, that it's better to leave things the way they've turned out now that he's found his way home."

I wanted to stay where I was, too, where I could be with Ted when he came back. However, having achieved that, having made it back to the farm, and waiting endlessly now all the time he didn't return, I sank slowly into my sense of loss with the confirming realization that when he did, he'd probably leave me again. I was surrounded by people and a cat. The people looked shaking their heads.

"I don't know what to do to make him eat," Mom said.

"Why don't you take him out for a walk, Lucien," Dad suggested.

"He doesn't want to walk," Lucien answered. "He just wants to be unhappy."

Lucien was right. I preferred they leave me be.

I was not the only one headed down, though. Dad was losing strength. Sometimes when he was going out through the mudroom to the barn to do the milking with Lucien, he'd exhaust himself just changing into his barn clothes. He'd grasp the window sill to brace himself, and tell Lucien to go get started alone. It was as if he first had to summon the power to walk across the yard. Sometimes, he'd begin chores, then have to come back to the house, leaving Lucien to complete them.

When Ross and Errol came to help with the spring work, fertilizing the fields, repairing fence, they ended up having to do it all. Lucien could have helped fixing fence, but he didn't offer; and although Errol suggested it, Ross didn't ask.

"He's got enough to help your grandfather with the milking," Ross said. "He's not used to getting up so early in the morning as he has to do now before school."

"I do it," Errol objected. "I get up."

"Yes, you do. And you have a future you can depend on because you learned to do it. Be glad of that."

One evening when Dad had come back early from the barn, leaving Lucien to finish up, he tripped while he was taking off his overalls in the mudroom and landed sitting on the floor, his back against the wall, right next to my blanket, as I dashed out of the way. He sat there dazed for a moment, looking up towards the ceiling; then he buried his face in his hands.

I watched him resting exhausted like that. Then I sensed his fear, and his helplessness, and his hopelessness. It is in my nature to comfort. I moved over beside him and lay the length of my body against his thigh. A few minutes passed, and then Dad rested his hand on my back. Perhaps he wanted to draw more of my warmth. Perhaps he felt my pain, as well. That's when I gained acceptance.

It didn't get me entry into the house, but Dad began to spend more time resting in one of the lawn chairs those warming, sunny days, and sometimes he'd reach under me and lift me onto his lap. He'd cup his hands around me as if warming them, or sometimes stroke my back slowly; and we'd sit like that, with Nanook the cat purring and rubbing against his leg. Who'd ever have thought?

In the meantime Bruce finished his agricultural course at the university and came to live on the farm. He was less deferential towards Dad, whom he called Pépère, than Robert had been. Perhaps it was because Dad was weaker and could do less, and Lucien was little help; perhaps it was because Bruce's dad Ross clearly was in charge now and had confidence in him. Ross absent, Bruce very much took over. He moved into what had been Mémère's apartment upstairs, his fiancée Yvette often with him. Marie-Anne, and Mom whom Bruce called Mémère, saw to it that the apartment was "well-furnished for a starter," Marie-Anne's words as they walked by me one day.

Of Marie-Anne's four sons, Bruce, with black hair and less Celtic complexion, resembled Dad's family more than did the other three who looked Scotsmen through and through—although Mom claimed blond Malcolm for her side of the family. The four, even young Angus, stood sturdy and strong from school athletics and steady farm work. Dad, however, had always been partial to Bruce, the oldest; and now after chores in the evening the bond grew between them.

Invariably Dad would ask Bruce to sit with him in the chairs on the front lawn while sunset turned to dusk, and he'd ask Bruce about his plans for the next day, for the week, even for the whole summer. If Dad took me on his lap, I could feel peacefulness come through his hands resting on me while he listened to Bruce's ideas for the farm. When the light had all but disappeared, at about the time the bats flying overhead between the trees started making me nervous, Mom would call from the front porch for them to come in for cake or pie. Bruce would get up, help Dad to his feet, and call back to her, "We're coming, Mémère." I'd follow them as far as the mudroom. There I'd lie on my blanket and wait, because in a while Bruce would come out with pieces of pie crust for me that I love.

Everything got better after Bruce arrived. When he and Dad were sitting together, if I wasn't on Dad's lap, Bruce would pick me up. His touch spoke his love for animals, like I'd felt from Poor Boy years before. Having him around felt safe. However, I still longed to be home with Ted in New York. There still were many days when sadness overtook me and I ignored my food.

30. WHERE'S REX?

One afternoon Marie-Anne came for Dad, and they drove off together, with Mom in the yard waving good-bye. When Marie-Anne returned later, she was alone. Days later she drove into the yard again, this time for Mom who carried a small suitcase when she got into the car, and they left together, too.

While Mom was away Marguerite fed me, and Bruce looked after me, picking me up, taking me onto his lap. It was at that time he also brought a new puppy to the farm, a yellow Labrador retriever and golden retriever mix he called Bucky, that he bedded down in the mudroom with me. Bucky followed Bruce everywhere he could, but he didn't make it into the house. Like me, like Rex, he stayed outside. I kept my distance from the floppy, hoppy puppy. Only months old, he already was three times my size, and he had far too much energy. Rex would've been great with him, I know. I figured Bucky was meant to be Rex's replacement. I sure wasn't. Lucien didn't ever take me to get the cows, because if I barked at a cow she just stood there and looked at me.

One day when I was lying at the corner of the lawn feeling depressed again, Marie-Anne drove up the driveway, and she had Mom and Dad with her. I was glad to see them, though. When Dad stepped out of the car, he walked with more energy.

"It feels good to be home," he said to Mom.

"You did the right thing going to Montreal," Marie-Anne told him.

Bruce came out of the barn and across the yard to greet them. "You're looking good, Pépère," he said. "I'm so glad. I was worried you'd miss the wedding."

Marie-Anne told him about "a new drug" and "remission" and her "hope that the local doctors can maintain that level of care."

Bruce's puppy came running up, and Dad asked him, "What's this?"

"We need a work dog to protect the perimeter and get the cows. Now we've got one," Bruce said as he picked up Bucky and gave him a hug, and Bucky jumped around in his arms and licked Bruce's face joyfully.

"Well, it's going to take a while for that puppy to be able to do that," Dad's commented, but he added, "You're right, though, we needed a dog."

From that day on Bucky might seem to have put me in the back seat on the farm, but he didn't really. I always was in the back seat on the farm. Bucky didn't get all the attention during the following days, either, because there was a new excitement. I kept hearing the word "wedding."

One afternoon soon after, as I lay on my blanket in the corner of the mudroom descending into myself again, I heard a car come up the driveway. I heard the motor stop and the car door open and close, and I heard Lucien say, "Hi, Uncle Ted, you been around the world again?"

I heard Ted's voice, "No, Lucien, just around the country."

"I want to travel, too, when I get out of high school," Lucien said.

"Traveling gets tiresome. Take my word for it," Ted answered him. "I hope you're planning to go to college when you finish high school."

"Can't I do both?"

I heard the car trunk close, and the two approaching across the yard.

"You all set for the wedding?" Ted asked Lucien.

"It's going to be grand," Lucien said enthusiastically. "I figured you'd be coming for it."

Ted walked into the mudroom a suitcase in each hand. Mom and Marguerite were waiting at the kitchen screen door to greet him, opening it wide for him, everyone saying hello at the same time.

Ted saw me. He put the suitcases down and knelt on one knee to reach for me. I looked up at him, my ears back. I'd anticipated this moment for so long, so very long, but now confusion came over me. Suddenly I was not sure of myself or him.

"What's wrong, Tobi?" he asked me. "You're so thin!" he said.

I looked up at him, and I began to tremble. Cowering I searched his face, trying to wag my tail as humans try to smile when they are unsure, but it only beat a thud on the floor. His was my world, and my devotion to him fixed. His leaving me, breaking my heart, rose up as incomprehensible rejection. What had I done wrong?

"My goodness, Tobi," Ted said, "you're acting like you think I'm going to hit you."

"He missed you," Marguerite said. "He'd cry."

"Oh my poor Tobi," Ted said, "I thought you'd be just fine on this beautiful farm. With Rex and freedom and so many things here to interest you, what more could a little dog want?"

Ears back, my eyes conveyed, "I've only wanted you."

I uttered a small whine. Ted stroked my head while everyone watched.

"He'll be okay," Dad said.

Gently, so gently, Ted reached under me and picked me up. He held me close to him tenderly . "Oh, Tobi," he said, and he carried me into the house.

Lucien took Ted's suitcases upstairs and returned quickly not to miss any conversation.

Mom told Ted, "I'm always glad you phone me on your way in, so I can plan supper. It's almost ready." She turned to Marguerite. "It's time to set the table," she said, while she checked the kettles on the stove. Everyone gathered on the front porch.

When Ted sat down he held me on his lap, and doing so, his touch dissipated my apprehensions like the sun dispels the morning mists. The vision of loss disappeared, the uncertainty of trust became inconsequential, because the bond of my love overcame everything else when I was with him. I nestled contentedly, aware then only of the present moment, pushing my nose beneath his arm and closing my eyes to sense only the familiar warmth of his body.

Stroking me, Ted looked out towards the lake appreciatively. He said, "Nowhere is more beautiful than this."

"Then why'd you go away?" Lucien asked. I'd have asked him the same thing.

"Lucien, when I was your age growing up, I loved it here. The farm, the animals, the birds hopping on the lawn, the cows in the fields, this beautiful acreage on the lake!" Ted said with a gesture. "I was very happy growing up here, but these mountains surrounding our valley beckoned me to cross them. I knew there was a big world beyond Lake Isle, and I wanted to experience it. That's what I did, Lucien. I gave up this beautiful place to experience the big world out there."

"Right here is big enough for me," Bruce said to him as he walked onto the porch and extended his hand to shake Ted's. "How are you, Uncle Ted?" Seeing me on Ted's lap, he looked at Dad and laughed, "I see Tobi gets house rights when Uncle Ted's here."

Mom appeared in the doorway and announced that supper was set. Everyone filed into the kitchen and sat at the table in the middle of the room. Ted put me down on the floor and gave me my dish, with meat from the table and a few vegetables. Dad didn't mention the mudroom. When I finished, I went under the table by Ted's chair. Everyone in the family was talking happily, glad to have Ted back, so I didn't get much more attention. I nudged Ted's leg a couple of times, but he didn't slip me any tidbits, so I lay down there and waited for him to finish.

The next morning I awoke beside Ted. While he got up and washed and dressed, I remained in the covers drifting in and out of sleep, reluctant to part from the warmth he'd left behind. Then he took me and carried me down to the kitchen where I could smell breakfast. Mom said, "Bruce and your father and Lucien are still doing chores. They'll be in soon. Can I pour you some coffee?"

Ted carried me outside, trying not to spill his cup as he set me down on the gravel in the yard. While I went to do my business, he walked about enjoying the brisk morning air warmed by the sun rising in the blue sky. Then he picked me up again and carried me back to the kitchen and set me down.

Ted asked Mom, "Where's Rex? Last evening when I didn't see him I figured he was off wandering. But he's still not home this morning. And his bed and dish are missing from the mudroom."

Mom hesitated a moment before answering, then she said, "I'm afraid we don't have Rex anymore."

"What do you mean *we don't have Rex anymore*? Did he have an accident?"

"In a way. He got his face full of porcupine quills again. Your father called your Uncle Félix to take him into the woods."

Ted understood, "He had him shoot Rex?"

Mom answered quietly, "I guess so."

"Because Dad was too cheap to take Rex to the vet to get the quills pulled out!" Ted shouted so angrily that I hurried under the table.

Mom cautioned him, "You go easy on your father. You know how sick he is."

Ted sat down at the table, looking steadily at his mother, as if he were bewildered by the need to yell and to grieve at the same time. We could hear Dad and Lucien come into the mudroom. Not long later they walked into the kitchen, and Ted was waiting for them. Ted looked right past Dad to Lucien.

"Did you know he was going to have Rex shot?" he asked his nephew accusingly.

Lucien looked back frightened. He said, "I told him I'd help pull the quills."

"Well, that was very generous of you!" Ted said. Then he looked straight at Dad and asked him point blank, "Why did you have Rex killed?"

"I don't have to explain. I was tired of pulling quills out of his face. He never learned."

"It didn't occur to you that that patient, loyal, courageous dog was trying to do his job, guarding the perimeter of the farm? That he counted porcupines with foxes and raccoons!"

Lucien volunteered, "It made me cry when I saw the rifle, and the rope go around his neck...." He didn't finish when Dad gave him an angry look.

"Breakfast is ready. It'll get cold," Mom interjected, and everyone sat down.

But Ted wouldn't stop. "Dad, I always respected the fact that you were the only man I knew who didn't own a gun. But what's the difference? You have somebody else do the dirty work! If you'd taken him to the vet to take care of the quills, like Robert and I both urged you to do in the past, instead of that horrible thing we used to do with a screaming dog, sure, I can see not wanting to repeat that. The vet would've put him to sleep to pull them out."

"The vet costs money," Dad said to him dismissively.

"You get the vet all the time, in fact 'house calls,' for your cows!"

"You don't understand anything," Dad said.

"I understand you shot Robert's dog! I understand that. Think about that!"

Dad looked away; then he got up and walked out to the porch, and closed the door.

"Are you satisfied?" Mom said to Ted.

"Yes, I am," he answered her.

"Well, I'm not!" Mom told him. "You crossed the line, especially under the circumstances. Go out there and apologize to him, or there'll be a day you'll wish you had."

Ted sat silently, not speaking, not eating, willing his anger to subside.

Mom waited, too. "Lucien, would you like some eggs?" she asked.

Ted got up and went to Dad. I followed him to the porch, where he stood near his father who was staring out a window with tears on his cheeks.

"Mom says I crossed the line, and I guess I did. I apologize."

"It's ok," Dad said, still looking away. "I'm used to that from you. You're always so sure of yourself, ready for the world."

"You've always been good to me," Ted said. "You never said no, never stood in the way, always made possible whatever you could. I recognize that. I'm sorry."

Dad paused, then still gazing out the window said, "When your Mémère died this spring, your aunts divided up her things as fast as they could, for memories and keepsakes. But me, I didn't go back upstairs until the apartment was empty. That's how it was for me when Robert died. Every time I saw Rex, I was reminded what I'd lost. So when Rex got the quills, I let him go, so I wouldn't be reminded anymore."

"But," Ted objected compassionately, "Rex wasn't a thing, a picture or a tablecloth. He was a life, a person."

Dad continued his thought, "I was sorry afterwards. And I still am. If I had Rex around, something of Robert would be, too. Something I could be holding onto for him. I hope Robert can see I regret it."

Ted got up, leaned over and hugged his father, which I'd never seen the two of them do, and he said, "Dad, truly from the bottom of my heart, I'm sorry."

31. WEDDING DAYS, MOVING DAYS

Ted and I spent his days back much as we had the previous summer before he went away. He was happy to be working at his computer on the upstairs sun porch. "I'm on top of the world here," he'd say when he looked out over the fields and down to the lake. The birds flying by the windows between the maple trees out front broke the monotony. If I wasn't watching them, I spent most of my time sleeping on a flat cushion on his lap while he wrote, just as we did at home in the city. When he took breaks and walked outside, I was right with him.

Everyone else was very busy getting ready for Bruce and Yvette's wedding. Marie-Anne was downstairs with Mom everyday. Malcolm, who often came to the farm to help Bruce and who shared with his brother the upstairs apartment when he did, was there ready to stand in for him on the farm during the marriage trip. Mom and Dad and Ted talked often about "the new house," and Ted took me with him when he went to look at it poised on the central hill of the seventeen acres.

The day came at the farm when Ted and I watched from the upstairs porch as Bruce and Malcolm and Lucien set tables near the house on the front lawn. Then, after a truck delivered a load of folding chairs, they set those in place, too. Marie-Anne supervised it all, directing that this should be placed here and that there.

The following morning beckoned a bright, sunny day. After chores and breakfast everyone in their Sunday clothes drove away down the driveway. They all returned before noon, with Bruce and Yvette together in Bruce's car driven by Malcolm. Ross MacIntyre in his car had Marie-Anne beside him and Errol and Angus in the back. It was unusual that they parked on the grass on the other side of the driveway, in front of the lilac bushes and ducks' pond. Then it seemed a parade was arriving, as car after car came up the driveway and parked either in the barnyard or on the grass by the little pond as the family had.

Everyone in their Sunday best, aunts and uncles, cousins and friends, walked across the driveway to the front lawn talking and laughing happily. So many people showing up at once was exciting, and I barked as each car arrived. Yvette was wearing a long, white dress and veil, and she and Bruce spent time standing with their families in front of a photographer. Then Marie-Anne directed that tables in the sunshine be moved into the shade under the broad maple trees, and the women brought out dishes of food they set upon them.

I held back, staying close to Ted as he walked about, but Bucky wanted to be everyone's friend. Mom told Ted it would be better if "the dogs" were not around while people were eating, so he carried us to the barn where he made a grain bag bed on the floor for us and left us there. I didn't mind because all the people milling around and sitting about talking loudly agitated me. However, I'd begun to anticipate some of that food. Ted returned soon with a sampler of dishes being served.

He'd chosen things I like. There was roast chicken and roast beef, as well as pasta casserole, baked beans, sweet potato, and my favorite vegetable, broccoli, cut up for me. With my stomach full, I curled onto the grain bag and took a nap, while Bucky stood by the door, wagging his tail, waiting to go back out.

The sound of the barn door's metal latch opening woke me. It was Ted coming for us. Bucky scooted out the minute he had the chance. Ted carried me back to the reception. The dishes had been cleared, and the party was winding down with Ross and Malcolm still pouring drinks and Marguerite refilling coffee cups. There was wedding cake and ice cream left over, and Ted gave me some.

Uncle Félix with his fiddle and Mom at her keyboard were concluding a sing-along. Then Gilles led *"Alouette"* and *"Frère Jacques"* on his piano accordion, after which, with everyone talking and laughing, I became in Ted's arms a topic for each group he entertained. "What a cute dog," and "We can see you love your dog," and "Do lots of people in New York have little dogs like that?" and the usual "It's smaller than a cat; can it catch mice?" ensued.

I spotted Aunt Olivia, Mémère's younger sister, with her husband Uncle Clarence, standing close to Mom who was putting away her music at the keyboard. Aunt Olivia was dressed very stylishly, dated only by the feathered hat she was wearing. I recognized her right away; she was the lady in the garden on the hill whom I had followed into church.

"I didn't realize he was your dog when he was wandering around my neighborhood," Aunt Olivia said to

Ted, and she laughed, "and ended up in church on Sunday, mind you. You remember it, Lucien; you were at the altar. People are still having a good laugh about it."

Lucien blushed crimson, at the same time giving her a bug-eyed look. The family hadn't told Ted what had happened to me, and Aunt Olivia was "letting the cat out of the bag."

Marguerite said teasingly, "Lucien was too embarrassed to catch him."

Ted looked questioningly, "Tobi went lost again? And showed up in church?"

"He was all over the place," Dad said, like it was of no importance.

"We didn't hear anything for a while, and that was worrisome," Mom explained, "because people who saw him didn't realize you'd left your dog behind. Sooner or later someone would mention that there was a dog wandering around who looked like Tobi. Or if they called to inquire, by the time we'd find out, he'd already moved on."

"Who saw him?" Ted asked. "How far did he go? How often did he wander off?" He was not pleased at all.

"All the time," Marguerite said.

Mom listed my appearances for Ted. It seemed I was visiting all the cousins. "Louise and Gilles saw him with their Beagle. Joe and Maddie saw him on the other side of the lake running around with Mrs. Byrd's dog, and after that they saw him again when they were hiking up Breaux Mountain. Then Aunt Olivia and Uncle Clarence . . . "

"Breaux Mountain!" Ted exclaimed.

When Mom gave him a look he suppressed his concern while company was present, but later he cornered Lucien. He learned that Aunt Florence went looking for me after Mrs. Byrd was hospitalized, but I'd disappeared again. Laughing about it now, Lucien described how I showed up in church, "right in the sanctuary!" I ended up at Jack Callahan's, and I came home with Bruno. He didn't know details.

The photographer was busy taking wedding pictures again, but on the lighter side. Malcolm had run into the house and returned with barn overalls which he and Bruce donned over their clothes, contrasting with their starched white shirts and black bow ties. Bruce sat in a chair placed beneath the corner maple tree, holding a 30's-style flat straw hat, with Yvette standing just behind him to his side with her hand placed on his shoulder, imitating the old tintypes. Then other members of the family joined them in the pose. Finally, while Yvette took her turn in the chair with the men standing around her, someone got the idea that I should be on her lap for the picture. There's a memorable photo of Yvette holding me while I am eying a jump to the ground. I ran to Ted with my tail between my legs and leaped against his leg for him to pick me up. When he did, that's where I stayed for the remainder of the event.

At the end of the reception when Malcolm was supposed to bring up Bruce's car for the newlyweds to depart, he drove down the driveway instead with the farm tractor decked out in white ribbons and a "Just Married" sign, dragging a cluster of tin cans. His gunning the engine and the clatter of cans and the volley of everyone's laughter startled me, but safely in Ted's arms I could be heroic, and I barked loudly at it.

Malcolm leaped off, and joyfully Bruce jumped up into the seat, with Yvette climbing on and standing behind him on the machine's rear bar. They waved goodbye to everyone as the photographer took more pictures. Then Bruce drove the tractor down the street, both of them waving back all the way amid the clanging of cans to Uncle Félix's house where Bruce's car was waiting ready.

"This is the happiest wedding I've ever seen," Aunt Olivia said to Ted.

While Bruce and Yvette were away on their honeymoon, the farm was a flurry of activity. Dad's truck was backed up to the mudroom door, and Ross and Ted, and Malcolm, Errol and Angus, and Lucien, too, under Marie-Anne's and Mom's directions, moved all of Mom's and Dad's and Lucien's and Marguerite's belongings out of the farmhouse and onto the truck, then off the truck and into the new house atop the hill on the seventeen acres. The transfer had been well prepared, so it took only two days.

On the second day, when everything had been transported, Ted brought me to the seventeen acres. A gracefully curved driveway landscaped by nature extended like a land bridge from the height of the town road to the hill on which the new house stood. On the front lawn three flowering crab apple trees had been planted, and there Uncle Félix had built a multi-apartment bird house he'd set on a tall pole rising from the center of a circular flower bed. Dwarf apple trees dotted the steep sides of the hill.

Marie-Anne and Mom and Marguerite were busily putting it all back together in the new house when Ted carried me through. He offered his suggestions liberally to Marie-Anne who was the organizing force. They clashed over how the living room, more a family room with adjoining kitchen, should be set up to take best advantage of the lake view through the large windows on that side. Both were just a bit less assertive in the three bedrooms, where Mom and Lucien and Marguerite were trying to determine their own spaces. Then, leaving the fray, Ted joined Dad on the windowed back porch that had been built purposely reminiscent of the front porches on the farm. Ted took me onto his lap, and the two men engaged in quiet conversation, gazing out at the new vista together.

The back of the house with its porch felt more like the front because that is where the land sloped gradually down to the lake, affording a broad view across the field, expanding with the property lines on each side down to the white birches at the water's edge and beyond, over the tops of the trees to the cottages embedded in the woods on the opposite shore, and over them onward across the miles of plateau emblazoned by spectacular sunrises, all the way to the distant foothills of the White Mountains where the Connecticut River sourced.

Sitting there Ted said to his father, "You should be very happy here."

"Yes, for what time I have left. It's not easy."

"Oh, Dad . . ." Ted scolded him.

Dad said to him, "I'm glad things worked out as they have. The farm is still in the family. That must make your

Mémère happy. It would've passed on to Robert, but she was afraid after him it'd be a dead end with Lucien; and she was right, just as it would've been with you if we hadn't had Robert. Funny, I didn't care that much for Ross MacIntyre when your sister was going out with him, because he wasn't one of our people."

"And you and Mom are secure now with what Ross is paying you for it," Ted reminded Dad.

"Yes, it's worked out well."

Back at the farm the following days Marie-Anne and her sons readied the vacated house for Bruce and Yvette. There was papering and painting, with colors she and Yvette had negotiated. Because time was short she was a taskmaster, and she had Errol and Angus cleaning until their fingertips turned puffy white. Malcolm was doing all of Bruce's work, and Ross worked alone for the week on his own farm, while also coming by each evening for dinner to check on everyone's progress.

Ted and I moved into the upstairs apartment, where Mémère had lived, for the rest of his visit. We remained on the sidelines on the upper porch where Ted continued to work at his laptop computer. It was as if the whole intervening year had never happened—as if we'd just arrived from New York a few weeks previously and soon would be going back. However, my expectations seldom worked out at Lake Isle.

When Bruce returned, Malcolm who had been living with us in the upstairs apartment remained to help over the summer until he'd have to return to college in the fall. Marie-Anne and Ross used the apartment, too, when they came. During that month Ted spent less time on the upstairs porch and more at the new house with Dad who was growing weaker again. Mostly the two would sit with me in the chairs on the back lawn, looking down at the lake. Dad did most of the talking, reminiscing, as Ted listened attentively.

"... You were only three years old. I said to your mother, 'Where's Teddy?' And she looked at me surprised, and she said to me, 'I thought he was with you.' Everywhere we asked, no one had seen you, and pretty soon the whole town was searching. I thought of where I'd been working in the woods, and that's where I found you. You'd gone looking for me, but I wasn't there that day, and you were coming back down the path crying, just three years old. We were so scared."

"That really happened?" Ted said surprised. "I've always had the memory, but I thought it was a recurring dream, of being a very little boy, walking down a path with the woods high up on each side, and I'm frightened and crying, and it ends when I see you coming up the path towards me. I never realized it really happened; I always thought it was a dream."

32. RIDES AND REMINISCENCE

Sometimes Ted would take Dad for a car ride, Dad in the passenger seat with me on his lap. We had become solid friends. One time we made a day of it and drove all the way to Pinkham Notch in the White Mountains while Ted and Dad talked. More often though, we took shorter hour-long drives up the road that passed the new house. It extended in a wide circle past old farms, many abandoned now, growing to brush, in the back territory beyond the southern end of the lake, eventually connecting to a highway that led back into town.

Sometimes on that road we drove up a hill to the farm where Dad had grown up, from which the view extended over the treetops far to the lake. Or we stopped at the farm below that one which Mémère and Pépere also had owned and where Ted remembered as a little boy visiting them before they retired to Dad's farm. Both farms belonged now to Ted's cousins. Farther along Dad would point to clearings covered with wild blueberry bushes that had been farmland. He'd say, "I used to play baseball in that field."

It was on one of those rides one evening that, passing the Boisvert farm Ted suggested they stop. As we approached, lights were popping up in several ground-floor windows as Monsieur and Madame Boisvert were lighting their kerosene lamps against the oncoming dusk. The old couple, isolated as they were on that back road and happy to have company, came to the door together to greet us. When Madame Boisvert saw Ted carrying me, she exclaimed, "*C'est le p'tit chien* [It's the little dog]!"

Ted and Dad had sat down, and Madame Boisvert was offering them tea, shaking badly as she did when she served it, when Ted asked her how she recognized me. She described how Spotty and I had chased the moose out of their garden. Other than the fact she had fed us afterwards, she had no other details for Ted. Spotty and I had appeared, and not long later had both disappeared; that was all. Ted seemed glad to know a little more where I'd been on my wanderings, and he turned to reminiscing with Madame Boisvert how he used to come around on his bicycle to visit the elderly couple when he was a boy to sell them garden seeds.

For me at least, the most significant ride I took with Ted and Dad occurred one afternoon on a bright, sunny day when Ted suggested they visit Dad's uncles. At the top of the driveway, as we usually did on these rides with Dad, we turned left to follow the gradually ascending road into the back country where Dad's memories lay. Some distance along, Ted turned onto an intersecting perpendicular road on the right that appeared more like a driveway between a house and barn, a layout that struck me with *déjà-vu,* and then led up the long hill between two fields. The Benoit's lived there now, but years before it had been the Williams.

Ted said to Dad as we drove through, "I still remember coming to the wake for the Williams boy. His mother greeted you and Mom at the door of that house, and you had me with you. She brought us to where the boy was laid out in the living room. I remember her describing how he'd been riding a harnessed horse back to the barn, when he spotted a bird's nest or something, stopped the horse under the tree, and stood on the horse's back to look at it. The horse took off, and the boy fell, his foot caught in the harness, and he was dragged to his death." Ted said, "I've never forgotten it, as young as I was. When I remember the face of that woman telling that story, it breaks my heart. Later their barn burned to the ground—or was it before?—and all the farmers came from everywhere around to help them build a new one. It's one of my very oldest memories."

"They had a lot of bad luck, those people," Dad said. "Some people do. It never seems to stop."

The road ascended gradually to the edge of a woods. Then beneath the tree canopy it continued climbing, over rutted bumps, around steep curves, rocking the car, scraping its underside, leading steadily up the mountain. I stood nervously on Dad's lap as he held me tightly so that I wouldn't fall off. "I'm glad this is a rental car fully insured," Ted remarked. Finally we topped the last hill, and we found ourselves in front of the house I knew so well!

Maurice came out the door with a big, welcoming smile, followed by Arthur very happy to have company. Ted greeted them, "*Bonjour, mon oncle Maurice. Bonjour, mon oncle Arthur. Comment ça va* [How are you]*?*" as he walked towards them. They were Pépère's brothers, Dad's uncles, who lived in the house built by their father

Jacques, Ted's great-grandfather, a carpenter and barn-builder, who when he came south from Canada after his wife died, carved the little farm out of the woodland atop the mountain as a place to raise his five children. When Pépère passed away into memory, Maurice, estranged from his brother, and Arthur too frail, had not come off the mountain.

Ted was carrying me. Arthur's eyes lit up, and he exclaimed, "*C'est mon p'tit chien* [It's my little dog]*!*"

Ted certainly was surprised. He asked Arthur what he meant, and then found himself explaining as gently as he could his prior claim. "*C'est mon petit chien, mon oncle, depuis des années* [mine, for years]." We all went into the house. Ted, of course, wanted to know right away how they knew me. While Arthur brewed tea and cut thick slices from a large loaf of bread he'd made, he told Ted how I'd appeared one day by the garden and then weeks later disappeared. Meanwhile, I let Ted know I wanted him to set me down, and tail wagging I ran over to Arthur for some bread, too, the way he always gave it to me. He put a piece into a dish and poured milk over it for me.

"*P'tit Chien* showed up here with *le chevreuil blanc* [the white deer]," Arthur related. "We let him sleep in the barn, but he wasn't happy there; so we let him sleep in the house. One day he was gone. It made me very sad to lose him. I thought you were bringing him back to me today when I saw him with you. My heart leapt for joy," he said to Ted.

Arthur pointed to his garden, then proudly exhibited a bunch of foot-long carrots he'd been washing in the sink.

Maurice sat in his chair, puffing on his pipe, talking with Dad, who addressed him always as, "*Mon oncle* [Uncle]."

When we left, the two men stood in front of their house waving good-bye, seemingly savoring every last moment of our company, until our car disappeared into the black hole in the woods. I think of them fondly, especially Arthur, even as they begin to fade in my memory now.

33. THE SEVENTEEN ACRES

One morning, instead of carrying me to the upstairs front porch, Ted began packing his travel bags again. As he went back and forth in our bedroom, taking clothing from the bureau drawers to place in the open bags he'd set on the bed, gathering his toiletries from the bathroom, sliding his computer into its slot in his knapsack, the same one he took to the Long Island shore, I stuck by him like glue, so much so that a couple of times he almost tripped over me. I kept my eyes on him, looking at him anxiously, making it as clear as I could that wherever he was going I expected to go with him. His bags packed, Ted said goodbye to Malcolm who'd just walked into the apartment. He carried his bags to the car and me with them; he set me on the passenger seat where I always rode; and we drove off together, down the driveway and up the road, about a mile, to where Dad and Mom and Lucien and Marguerite lived now in the new house on the seventeen acres.

Lucien already had left that morning for his summer job in town. Marguerite was setting the table. Ted put me on the floor as Mom began to serve breakfast, and I wagged my tail and looked up at Ted eagerly at the smell of oatmeal and eggs. Dad sat off to the side in his own soft chair with his breakfast on a tray because he was too weak now to sit at the kitchen table. Mom put down a dish of cereal with milk for me—the eggs would follow—and Ted pulled up a chair where Mom invited him to do so and had breakfast.

Looking across from where he was sitting, Ted asked Dad concernedly, "How are you feeling this morning?"

"He had a bad night," Mom answered him. "His temperature went sky high, and I had to rub him with alcohol all night to get it down. And while I'm doing that, he's scolding me the whole time."

"For goodness sake!" Ted said to Dad.

Dad didn't say anything. He ate his breakfast quietly. When he was finished, he asked Ted to help him to his chair on the porch. Ted did, slowly, carefully, and then he wrapped a light blanket around Dad and set me on his lap.

Looking up Dad said, "When you have your health you have everything."

"I'll remember that," Ted assured him. "It's easy to forget when we start worrying about other things." He placed his hands on Dad's shoulders, gave him a long hand-hug, then went into the kitchen to say good-bye to Mom. "Anytime you need me, or if anything happens, phone me right away."

I heard Ted go out the kitchen door. I heard the car door close and the engine start up. I flew off Dad's lap, hit the floor running, and raced through the open porch door and around the corner of the house just in time to see Ted drive away—again!

I stood there, stunned, whining my disappointment—there was nothing else to do. A void spread within me. I'd been so sure he was taking me this time, this person whose life I lived to share. All the signs had been there that he would, most of all our bond renewed these weeks every time he held me. Touch had restored my confidence. I'd returned to a very stable place. Suddenly, again, that space was empty, and yearning flooded into it, this time without fear or hope. This time, finally, recurrence left me no doubt whatsoever there'd be no going home.

I walked slowly up the driveway away from the house, my head down, my tail between my legs, and I lay down with my chin on my forepaws by the corner where the driveway reached the road. I lay there empty, a vacuum in an encompassing void. I had nothing left, for myself or for anyone else that day. Consciousness ebbed away, and I fell asleep an old, old dog. There I remained into early evening, through dusk, into the blackness of a cloud-filled, starless night.

Dew collected on me and eventually penetrated me with chill. I rose to my feet, I stretched, and I walked slowly back down the driveway to the house. There was no light in the windows; they'd all gone to bed. They weren't worried about me, these country people. Dogs live outdoors, take care of themselves, eat the food scraps, get the cows and are grateful for it. I set myself down on the wooden step in front of the door, wrapped my body in myself for warmth as well as I could, and shivering I fell back asleep. Several times I woke when I heard noises in the dark, but I didn't bother with them and only dropped back into numbing sleep. When blackness turned to grey, I slowly got up, walked around the house to the back lawn, and lay there facing across the lake, watching the sun rise slowly in a fiery ball, welcoming its warmth. It was morning, and this was my first day in my new home. Such a sad homecoming.

Lucien left on his bicycle to go to his summer job in town. Mom put a dish of food out for me with a dish of water by the shed. A little while later Marguerite helped Dad to his chair on the porch. Once he was settled he called me, "Tobi, come here, Tobi, come here."

I wanted to pine alone. I ignored him.

"Tobi, come here, Tobi," he called me again.

I ignored him.

"Marguerite, would you bring me Tobi," he called to her.

Marguerite came out, picked me up, carried me to the porch, and set me on Dad's lap. He and I sat there together, his hands cupping me for a long time as the sun rose higher in the sky, and I fell asleep. Finally, he set me down and walked back into the house. I'd not had any breakfast yet. I was getting hungry, so I went down from the porch to my dishes by the shed where it was waiting for me.

The day grew warm. I lay in the house's shadow and appreciated the breezes that blew gently over the hill. It was such a beautiful place; I could see so far in the distance. I watched a chipmunk busy in bushes to the left of the lawn. I watched the swallows fly in acrobatic curves overhead. I became aware of a groundhog farther along the bushes eyeing me, until he thought better and disappeared. Later I took a walk, first to the front lawn where I got too close to Uncle Félix's tenement birdhouse, and the swallows dive-bombed me. I ran down the hillside to escape them, and then I walked over to the brook, licked up a little water, lingered there along its bank under the trees awhile, then turned back to the house. I lay again on the lawn looking down on the lake and dozed off.

The second day I felt a little less sad. The third still less obsessed, and so it went. Slowly, gradually, resignation set in as I lay on that back lawn during the following days, and with acceptance peace settled over me there.

Life at the new house was easy. There was just me and all the little wild things around to watch. Mom kept me fed. I spent a lot of time on Dad's lap when he sat on the porch mornings and sometimes in the late afternoon. It was a good life, a country dog's life, and I got quite used to it.

Marie-Anne visited often. She was the person who watched over things. Anything needed, she took care of it. She'd sit in the kitchen with Mom. Bruce and Malcolm came by often, too, together and individually; they'd sit with Dad and tell him how their work was progressing on the farm. They came mostly evenings when the day was over. Dad would have me on his lap, and often he'd be stroking me gently while he listened to them and asked them questions, and told them how he'd have done something differently. Mom brought them slices of pie or cake, and they'd say, "Thank you, Mémère." Yvette often came with them and talked with Mom. There was a peacefulness in the new house I'd not felt among that family on the farm.

"Dad had to get sick to calm down," Marie-Anne remarked to Ted one day when he was back.

"Who'd have thought?" Ted agreed. "I think Tobi makes a difference, too," he added. "I was planning to take him back to New York, but Dad said he wouldn't mind if Tobi stayed until fall. His way of asking me to leave him."

Ted came often to spend as much time as he could with Dad. When he did, Lucien gave up his bedroom and slept on the sofa in the living room. Almost every day Ted took Dad and me for a ride, again and again up the road into the backcountry where Dad had grown up. After Dad went to bed early in the evening, Mom and Ted would talk in the kitchen, and Ted held me on his lap. I loved his touch, it was always special; but with resignation came indifference when he arrived and when he left.

When Ted got in his car and I didn't make a fuss, he praised me. "You're being such a good dog, Tobi. It makes me happy when you're good like that." He didn't question at all why.

The last half of summer passed quietly for me on the hill over the lake with Dad and Mom and Marguerite and Lucien. As afternoons shortened and evenings edged towards uncomfortably cooler air, fall drew closer. It was at that time, one dew-covered morning while Ted was back in New York, an ambulance drove into our yard. I barked at it and growled at the two men who entered the house, but I was quiet when they came out afterwards rolling a stretcher with Dad lying upon it. Lifting him into the vehicle, one stayed with him in the back; the other closed the doors. That was the last time I ever saw Dad. I watched them leave, until the ambulance disappeared from view on the road. Marie-Anne drove down the driveway soon after, then drove away with Mom.

When Marie-Anne and Mom returned that evening, Ted arrived with them. He held me on his lap while he and Marie-Anne and Mom sat in the living room talking softly as if they didn't want to waken someone. With them Marguerite sat quietly, and didn't say much. When Lucien got home he didn't speak much, either.

A day came when everyone in the house, dressed in their Sunday best, drove away and were gone all forenoon. I remained alone atop the hill, with the chipmunk and the ground hog and the swallows and sparrows and goldfinches. Early afternoon when they returned, all Marie-Anne's family was with them. She quickly made lunch for everyone, and at the end of it Ted slipped me some pieces of pie crust. Mom didn't talk very much, but everyone focused on her. Ross and her four grandsons each gave her a hug when they left, and Marie-Anne hugged her, too, and said she'd be back the next day.

Ted stayed through the week. He set up a lawn-mowing schedule with Lucien, and had a rack built behind the shed for Robert's canoe. On one afternoon he went blackberry picking with Mom in a gully below the house. I lay under a bush in the shade close by them.

Ted said to her, "How about we get you a little dog like Tobi for company?"

"I don't think so," Mom answered him. "I'm okay with my canary."

"Are you sure?" Ted objected. "A dog will bark if anyone or anything comes around."

"Yes, I'm sure, but thank you for thinking of it. The nights are getting cooler, and they're going to be too cold for a small dog outside. If we get snowed in, how do I let him go out when he has to? What I'd worry about most, as I do with Tobi, I'm afraid I'll trip over him."

The evenings and nights were indeed getting cold as the leaves in the trees changed color. This was the second time I'd seen that happen. The smaller maples on the lawn turned bright red, the sugar maples intense orange, and the birches bordering the lake became sentinels of yellow and white. Mom had begun letting me sleep on the living room carpet at night.

34. DEPARTURE

A few days later, right after breakfast, I saw Ted pack his travel bags again. While he moved about the bedroom, taking his clothing from closet hangers and folding it into his open bag on the bed, getting his toiletries out of the bathroom cabinet, sliding his computer into its slot in his green knapsack, the same one he used weekends at the shore, I lay close by watching him. I wasn't much bothered; I'd gotten used to his coming and going. That he left each time without me was just how it was. Home was the seventeen acres, and it was a beautiful, peaceful home.

Ted took his bags to the car, and I followed him outside. He folded a towel on the passenger seat. I followed him back inside the house where he gave Mom a hug, reassured her to call him "for anything, anything at all," and said good-bye to Marguerite who gave him a kiss on the cheek. "Tell Lucien to keep these lawns up," he said to Mom, as he was back out the door, holding it for me to follow him. Ted set me on the passenger seat, put my harness on me and attached it to the seat belt, walked around the car to the driver's side, got in, rolled down his window.

He was taking me! He was doing it! I realized I was on my way home. I jumped up and down and in circles in the little space I had, which tangled me up, and wagging my tail, I gave Ted my biggest smile.

"Oh, Tobi!" he said, and untangled me.

Ted waved to Mom and to Marguerite who were standing at the top of the steps now as they called out wishing us a good trip. I stood on the passenger seat looking out the rear window as we drove up the driveway, much as I had done in Mrs. Byrd's Jeep, but much happier this time. Ted steered with one hand, still waving with the other, which Mom and Marguerite could see along with my face as they waved back.

I settled on my towel bed as I was accustomed, and got ready to fall asleep. There wasn't much else to do, because down on the seat I was so far below the windows that I couldn't see much, just the treetops rushing past when I looked up.

There were long expanses of driving punctuated with stops at rest areas, where I ran outside each time on the grass above the Connecticut River valley extending below us. We drove the length of Vermont, the width of Massachusetts, and a long time through Connecticut, until I felt an old excitement course through me entering the city of New York. I could smell it and hear it. I was suddenly aware of being back. Through the car windows high above me I could see the endless array of tall buildings rushing past for almost an hour as we drove deeper and deeper into it. When we finally stopped in front of our building, Ted unloaded his bags while I waited on the front seat. Last of all, he walked me a bit in our familiar Greenwich Village, then brought me up to our apartment, where he left me inside while he went to return the car.

I stood there alone. First I went into every room. Everything was just as it always had been, just as we left it.

Before going back out, Ted had set down a dish of water in the kitchen for me. I took a few licks of it, and it was refreshing. Then I went into my little house at the bottom of the bookcase and curled up on my fleece until Ted returned.

I felt a quiet contentment. Everything I treasured was restored as if I'd never lost it. I felt glad, yes, peaceful, yes, reassured of my home, and of Ted. For dogs, our love is an incredibly deep bond, characterized first and foremost by faithfulness, and by a dependence which humans have created in us. Our love is trust, and I had no more thought to question or doubt or distrust. I was back home safe with Ted. That was all that mattered to me.

EPILOGUE

Returning to the city that day was not the end of Lake Isle for us. Ted and I have continued to make the long drive north every month except in deepest winter to look in on Mom who is alone now much of the time. In early summer we spend a month, sometimes two, writing on her front porch, then weeks more in the fall during the foliage. It's our second home. When I'm there with Ted, I watch the chipmunk and the ground hog and dodge the swallows, and nap on the back lawn and gaze over the lake. Marie-Anne comes by often, but we always visit her and Ross on their farm, too, and Bruce and Yvette on theirs where my friend, the farm dog Bucky and I sit, yes, on the front porch with them. Ted loves that view from the farm. Then we come back to New York City together every time.

BE MY FRIEND

Let's stay in touch. I'll be very happy to share my photo albums with you, and let you know what new adventures I might be having.

My email address is:

tobilittledeer@gmail.com

My personal website is:

http://tobilittledeer.com

My Facebook page is:

https://www.facebook.com/tobilittledeer

On Twitter:

https://twitter.com/tobilittledeer

On Instagram:

http://instagram.com/tobilittledeer

And on tumblr:

http://tobilittledeer.tumblr.com